W9-AVL-225

*Praise for Tranquility Denied*

# Tranquility
# Denied

## A. C. FRIEDEN

For other titles and author news, visit:

**www.acfrieden.com**

Avendia Publishing Inc.
444 North Michigan Avenue, 12th Floor
Chicago, Illinois 60611 USA

ISBN-10: 0974793418
ISBN-13: 9780974793412

Cover art by A.C. Frieden
(based on a photograph by Andre Frieden and K. Bierman)

Author photo (back cover) by Warren Johnson

Published in the United States of America
B-II/0804

*to my father*
*1922 - 2006*

ICELAND

Reykjavik

NORWEGIAN
SEA

Faroe Islands
(Den.)

NORTH ATLANTIC

Shetland Islands
(UK)

NORWAY

Bergen

Oslo

NORTH SEA

Skagerrak

Edinburgh

DENMARK

Dublin

Hamburg

IRELAND

UNITED
KINGDOM

Amsterdam

NETH.

London

Portsmouth

BELGIUM

Brussels

English Channel

FRANCE

LUX.

Paris

A. C. Frieden

# Acknowledgements

This novel would not have been possible had I not been immersed in the richness of two spectacular cities: New Orleans, Louisiana and Moscow, Russia. In their own ways, they offer a cocktail of mystery, danger, beauty, melancholy and sagacity, with few rivals elsewhere on the planet. While they are also bastions of mischief, fueled by mystical influences, political turmoil, grossly uneven wealth distribution and a visceral approach to human behavior, they continue to intrigue us. Through tragedy and triumph, New Orleans and Moscow have changed the course of history. They've nourished some of the world's greatest minds and inspired countless artists. These great cities, and their people, will remain in the spotlight of civilization. For these reasons, they are the ideal settings for this novel.

I am thankful for the high-spirited camaraderie I experienced with the citizens of New Orleans and Moscow. It was a privilege to hear their stories and peek into their lives during my humble journeys through their streets, abodes, classrooms, parks, museums and, of course, taverns.

Many thanks to Patricia (Pinianski) Rosemoor for her astute mentoring, and to her talented fiction writing group. And to Julia Borcherts for her masterful editing and patience. I am grateful as well as for the advice and support from my close friends and circle of readers, including Michelle Chapman, Philippe Ravanas, David Kouidri and

George Sanders. And many thanks to Irina Khan, to Embassy Attaché Florian Gubler, and to Duma Parliamentarian Vladislav Tretiak for helping to make my Moscow book launch a success, and to Beverli Dvorkin and Oliver Ernst for making the U.S. launch equally superb. Thanks also to Rob Heiser for directing and editing a video trailer of the novel, and to Mitch Brown and Philippe Ravanas for looking so convincing in uniform.

Also to my friends Martin von Walterskirchen, Karena Bierman and Patrick Wagner for sharing their fascinating recollections of Russia, and to Suhaib Ghazi for his friendship and creative input. Huge thanks as well to my friends in the intelligence community, both in the U.S. and abroad. I appreciate their willingness to share their phenomenal accounts from the trenches. And much appreciation to Francis Gary Powers, Jr., for his encouragement and advice as I pursue my literary endeavors.

My gratitude to Mike Carbo, a fine New Orleans lawyer, law professor, mentor and friend. His insight on the inner workings of Louisiana's judicial system reassured me that amid the often unfair outcomes, there remains a modicum of hope for the future.

A special thanks to Stephanie Veit for the strength and support she gave me during the challenging months of finishiing and launching this novel. And finally, to an extraordinary woman who never ceases to motivate me: my mother, Dulcinea Frieden.

A. C. Frieden

# Prologue

*Russia*
*August 19, 1991*

THE ELEVATOR GROUND NOISILY AS IT DECELERATED, bouncing a few times before it stopped on the third floor. The door opened and a wall of cool, damp air instantly thrust onto the short, stocky woman, an envelope clenched tightly in her hand. She crowed her neck forward and peered down the poorly illuminated corridor, a place she had never before visited.

The thunder crackled outside and tumbled down to her end of the hallway, followed by the more docile sound of rain. She took a deep breath before taking her next step. The floor appeared abandoned, and for a moment she wished her colleagues had just pulled a joke on her. But she knew better.

*Doctor Vadenko*, the name echoed in her head. *He must be here, somewhere*. She had heard strange things about the *Zapretnaya Zona*, the forbidden area. It had been the topic of wild rumor since she had arrived here from nursing school. It was the dominion of a handful of weird doctors and a couple of reclusive nurses, both of whom had left, so she had heard.

*I'm here to deliver this and that's all*, she told herself as if to feel reassured that her visit would be brief. She stepped out of the elevator. Strangely, the air didn't have the usual odor of ammonia-based disinfectants that permeated the rest of the building.

The blue tile floor was cracked and faded, exposing the aged concrete below that made a gritty sound with every step she took. She followed the single row of yard-long incandescent lights that ran the length of the hall-way. Some bulbs were lit but filthy, others were extin-guished.

The skin on her exposed calves and arms shivered, and the warmth in her chest was quickly dissipating. The temperature had dropped by several degrees in the thir-ty paces since she had left the elevator. It was even cold-er than the outside air the last time she had gone out for a smoke. She rounded the corner to another corridor, just as desolate as the previous one. Each room she passed was vacant, the wide open doors revealing dilapidated rooms with warped, mattressless bed frames and torn curtains. The windows were so dirty that the trees out-side appeared like giant ghosts, the lightning turning the branches into dark silhouettes that looked like arms scraping the glass as if they were trying to claw their way in.

"Office nineteen," she whispered, glancing at the doors and walls in search of the room.

She rounded the next corner and stopped. The hall-way ended at a wide metal door a few feet away. It looked like it weighed more than a car. She was puzzled, having never seen such a large door anywhere else in the building. Its riveted surface reminded her of an armored door she'd seen in an air raid shelter during her training. A double-wide steel chain ran from the door's large, oblong handle to a steel hook bolted to the adjacent wall. The ends of the chain were secured by an oversized pad-lock. That wasn't all. Two bulky latches secured the bot-tom edge of the door to the floor.

A brief low-pitched noise stole the nurse's attention. She looked over her shoulder and spotted another closed door a few feet behind her. She glanced at a plate on the doorframe. "Here we are," she announced with a bit of relief, noticing the number nineteen. She turned, straightened her skirt and hat, cleared her throat and knocked.

Only the faint, steady sound of rain came from the other side.

As she waited, her curiosity again drew her to the armored door. She took a few steps and examined it more carefully. Parts of the chains were rusted. She touched the top one and felt a layer of dust coat her fingers. She then tugged at a metal viewing slot at the top center of the door. With her strong hand, she slid it open, revealing a small window built into the door. She stood on her tiptoes to have a glimpse of what lay on the other side, only to find the glass frosted with dirt. She only saw that the hallway continued, and that it was brighter on the other side. Why it was sealed off from the rest of the floor didn't make any sense.

Another sound came through the door of office number nineteen, taking her away from the armored door. She approached and knocked. "Comrade Vadenko, are you there?"

Again, there was no answer. Only a strange murmur drowned by the rain crept through the door. She leaned her head against it, trying to make sense of the bizarre noise. She closed her eyes, listened intently and quickly gathered what it was: someone crying—a man.

"Is everything all right?" she asked hesitantly.

"Dammit, who is it?" The male voice was as deep as it was unfriendly.

"Katia, from radiology," the nurse answered apprehensively, now asking herself why she—and not someone else—had been so unlucky as to be given this chore.

The man didn't respond.

She waited, rubbing her arms to warm herself. It was cold enough that she saw the white vapor of her breaths exit her lips.

"Can't this wait?" the man groaned, his cavernous monotone voice sending shivers down her spine.

*It sure can*, she thought. *I could slip this letter under your door and never have to see your face.* But an odd sense of duty, coupled with her instinctive curiosity, tugged at her to persist. "I have a letter for you. I've been told it's important." She began to smell something burning. It was coming from the doctor's office.

"Nothing is important anymore . . . Nothing!" the man said. "But come in if you must."

Katia turned the knob and cracked open the door. The edge of a wooden desk came into view. She pushed the door further, glanced straight ahead and jumped back. "Doctor!"

The man was slouched behind his desk with a gun in his hands, the barrel pointed at the wall to his left. The window behind him was wide open, and the large raindrops battered the sill. His eyes were closed, his cheeks moist with tears.

Katia glanced at a metal garbage can with small flames and smoke rising from it. It appeared that papers and file folders were burning. She then turned her attention back to the armed doctor in front her. "What . . . what are you doing?" she asked, her eyes never leaving the weapon. The faint smell of liquor seeped into her lungs.

The doctor opened his eyes. They were red with dark gray bags under them. He speared her with an angry yet hollow gaze, but said nothing.

"You should put that down," she suggested, her heart now racing. "Please!"

"Why?" he barked, his face turning stone-cold. His gaze descended to the black revolver in his hands. "It's all over anyway. I can't take this wretched existence, condemned to be the guardian of what lies behind that steel door. For two years! Two years where nobody gives a damn about my career, my life, my dreams. Even my trusted allies have abandoned me. Even Comrade Karmachov, that swine, that wretched swine. I can't do this one more day, not one more hour!" His shoulders sank as he shook his head, his eyes staring more intently at his gun.

"I came only to—" Katia said before interrupting herself with a more important thought. "Maybe I should call someone to come help you."

"No one can help me, unless—" Doctor Vadenko stopped speaking as his eyes fixated on the envelope in her hand. His sulky gaze intensified. "It's from the Ministry, isn't it?" he asked, though his pitiful look told her he already knew. He turned his head away.

"What is it, Doctor?" she asked.

"So, you came to deliver the bad news," he said with a long breath behind his words.

"I don't understand?"

"It doesn't matter anymore. Haven't you heard, you stupid woman?" he asked loudly as if she ought to know.

Katia's feet were frozen to the floor. *Is it loaded?* she asked herself, hoping it wasn't, wishing it was all one huge joke. But it wasn't. Her heart continued to race. *Of course it is loaded; of course he can use it.*

The doctor slammed his gun onto the top of the desk. "Didn't you hear me? Don't you know what's going on?"

Her hands began shaking. Her legs too. "What are you saying?" she asked, almost shouting.

"It's the . . ." he began, but paused, appearing lost in his own imploding thoughts. "It was on the radio, minutes ago. Our country is falling apart. *Everything* is falling apart!"

"I don't—"

"You idiot. Moscow! There's a state of emergency, MVD troops are surrounding the Parliament, Yeltsin is calling it a coup and our Ministry has shut down." He heaved a yard of air before clumsily scraping the gun in an ark along the surface of the desk. "Hold that envelope up in the air."

She did as she was told, her hands trembling.

"Higher!"

"Can I just give it to you?"

"No, I know what it says," he uttered with disgust. "Those bastards. But now it is not only me who is doomed. We are *all* finished."

He suddenly reminded her of her husband: drunk, despairing of life and occasionally bellicose—but not nearly as dangerous as a deranged, plastered scientist holding a firearm. She wanted to listen, to understand the troubling news. Hell, she wanted to tear open the envelope to know what on earth this insane man meant. But she couldn't as long as his weapon was so close, so imminently able to terminate her existence with a simple gesture. "Please put that down and let me call for help."

Her suggestion angered him. "Shut up. What do you know? You're just a peasant girl in a uniform. You probably think working in this place is just fine. Where mediocrity reigns and where your stupidity blinds you from ambition. You can rot here if you wish. I will *not*."

If Katia had her way, she would have knocked his teeth out. "You should be glad to be here. Safe, away from Moscow. Away from the chaos."

"Then you will die here." He cocked his head back and wiped his tears with his sleeve. He then tightened his hold on the gun's grip, slid his index finger around the trigger and aimed the weapon up.

Katia took a step back without even thinking.

He swung the barrel over the desk, a pinging sound resonating as it tapped an empty vodka bottle that lay over his papers. The bottle rolled off the edge of the desk and shattered on the floor. Bits of glass sprayed over her feet, and pungent vapors of alcohol quickly came her way. She stared at the doctor's vacant expression and gauged his every movement by the millimeter.

Perhaps with deliberately exaggerated flair, he pointed the revolver at his temple. His eyes narrowed and then shut as he strained his face. "Save yourself, woman, while you still can—"

Katia had to do something, anything to stop this lunacy. She lunged at him, her body clumsily flying over the desk, her arms stretched forward. "*Nyet!*"

A loud bang ricocheted through the thunder and rain.

# 1

*November, 1996*

JONATHAN SPRINTED DOWN THE STAIRS, HIS MIND FIGHTING off the anxiety that had fermented through the long night, and all because of his latest case—that dreaded case—unlike any he'd ever handled before.

The radio echoed across the entire first floor. "It's twenty to eight and let's go to Scott for the traffic report and the latest on the overturned semi on the eastbound ramp of the Crescent City Bridge . . ."

"Linda, please change the station," Jonathan said testily as he scurried into the kitchen with folders under one arm, struggling to put on his jacket with the other. "I need not be reminded how late I am. Judge Breaux—the nasty dinosaur—will have me for breakfast."

Linda returned a peaceful gaze, her beautiful eyes wide open. "Don't be fussy. You'll win the trial, and the old fart will retire knowing how brilliant you are."

"He'll retire with my head mounted on his wall."

The traffic reporter's voice pierced the airwaves accompanied by the palpitating sounds of his helicopter. "Folks, traffic's awful, backed up all the way to Metairie."

"You hear that?" Jonathan said as he downed his lukewarm coffee. "The last time I was late for this judge, he pushed back my settlement conference three months. So, please turn that off."

"Would you rather listen to Nick banging his spoon on the Gerber jar? Today's flavor is banana."

"Bananas?" Jonathan asked. "How appropriate for a day that's starting off this bad. And why does your brother always drop him off here when I'm so busy? I'm starting to wonder if the kid still has parents."

"Now, be nice," Linda said, gently tapping Jonathan's shoulder. "And don't forget that lucky pen of yours," she added with a grin.

Jonathan checked his pocket and cocked his head back. "Yep, got it." He was unashamed of this instrument of legal mystique. The pen had inked the complaint in his first major lawsuit, one that catapulted him to the top tier of New Orleans' admiralty lawyers. And ever since, his superstition demanded that it sign all his pleadings.

Linda smiled and turned off the radio, its last sounds eclipsed by Nick's screams from his highchair.

"You should watch me in court one day," said Jonathan, reminding himself of his twenty major trial wins—an impressive record for a man just turned thirty-seven.

"You don't need to brag, my dear," Linda said almost rolling her eyes. "I love you, whether you sway a jury or not."

Her words comforted him, but the edginess he'd carried for nights upon nights wasn't going away. Not as long as the Victory Lines case wasn't resolved. That *damn* lawsuit. Unlike its name, it had nothing to do with winning. Jonathan saw only defeat from the moment he joined the plaintiff's team.

The phone rang. Jonathan darted to the wall, clumsily grabbing the handset with his already full hand.

"It's Gary." His voice crackled from a poor signal.

"I know, I know! I'm late," Jonathan said, barely able to hear himself speak over Nick's tantrum. "I don't need reminders. Besides, it doesn't matter. We're getting killed in this case. On time or not, our client is screwed either way. I'll be—" He suddenly interrupted himself as a horrible thought bolted through him. "Gary?"

"Yes, this is Gary Moore. I . . . I just called to ask you to bring those new charts from last week."

Jonathan's chest just about dropped to his testicles. It wasn't Gary Green, his law partner; it was the other Gary—his *client*. President and chief executive ogre of Victory Lines, Ltd., a company on the verge of collapse, but which represented the second largest source of revenue for Jonathan's firm that year. An uncomfortable silence lingered. He couldn't think of a thing to say. An apology would have been meaningless and an explanation even worse. "I gotta run. See you in court."

The embarrassment sunk in quickly. Jonathan was always careful. Everything about his practice was prudent. He hadn't earned a partner position in a prestigious local admiralty firm by being cavalier, and he needed his measured advocacy to do what he really wanted one day: to resurrect his profession. The city's practices had taken a beating in recent years as a result of the downturn in brown-water traffic and the increased reach of East Coast and Texas maritime law firms. A passionately proud citizen of the South's busiest port city, Jonathan was eager to reverse the trend. This is what got him up every morning. It was what drove him to accept risky cases, like the Victory Lines litigation.

Jonathan landed a peck on Nick's forehead, embraced Linda, and darted out the back door.

Huge branches draped St. Charles Avenue like vast umbrellas, shielding the traffic below from the bright morning sun. Dew lined the road, but it was slowly dissipating. A streetcar idled along the grassy median.

Everything seemed peaceful. But Jonathan's commutes rarely were. One house along the way had the effect of a roadblock, powerful enough to divert him to other streets, depending on his mood. It was the house of countless bittersweet memories: parents whose candid smiles at each other reassured Jonathan and his brother, Matt, that life was good; laughs with a brother whom he protected and cherished. A brother who was now forever gone, as were his parents.

He reeled in from the past the galvanizing images of that grand old house. A double-galleried Greek Revival home, all white, with lacy, cast iron balconies, it stood in its splendor on St. Charles, just west of Napoleon Avenue. Its chaste facade, radiating from the morning rays, edged into view. Jonathan simply stared, embellishing the thoughts that his mind haphazardly gathered: young Matt playing ball in the yard; the festive tables of friends gathered at crawfish boils; his father teaching Jonathan to master a crossbow. That enchanting house.

*         *         *

JONATHAN'S lead foot made no difference this morning. Panting loudly after a mad dash from the parking garage off Lafayette Square, he raced across Camp Street and up the steps of the Federal Courthouse. He scurried through security, took the elevator to the fourth floor and sprinted to the courtroom. He quickly straightened his tie and walked in as discreetly as possible, complete with a bow of deference to the judge that was more akin to prostrating to the Pope. Under the stolid gaze of the dinosaur, Jonathan made his way to the plaintiff's table feeling not much larger than an ant.

Judge Breaux shook his head but said nothing.

Jonathan took a seat next to his colleague and lead counsel, Gary Green, and waited to be scolded. After all, Gary—who possessed all the colorful traits of a sagacious Cajun—was the firm's sixty-five-year-old managing partner and thus was entitled to say anything he damned well pleased.

"Nah hear me, Johnny boy," Gary began, his pungent coffee breath hitting Jonathan like a blunt instrument. "If for once you were early, I would hand you ma wife."

She was well-endowed, vivacious and half his age, with a self-proclaimed addiction to aphrodisiacs. The insult, Jonathan mused, was either in being called

Johnny—which he detested—or the chance of catching a nasty bug from a woman who used to twirl around a brass pole in a fine establishment off Bourbon Street.

His other co-counsel at the table, Allen Cledeau, appeared unfazed by Jonathan's tardiness. But he was always less everything. Less energetic, less colorful—a bit like lunar rock. But he possessed one notable skill: an extreme attention to detail, not unlike a watchmaker's.

Gary leaned into Jonathan. "We're waiting for their witness, Captain Tucker." He then nodding in the direction of defense counsel, Bernard Peyton. "Look at him, that scoundrel. He's avoiding the judge."

Jonathan didn't know the guy, but he could tell a lot by a man's suit: fitted by a blind tailor; purchased in a discount store; and worn by a short lawyer with the physique of a baboon.

"Did I ever tell you he was once one of our own?" whispered Gary.

"What do you mean?"

"He practiced here years ago, until he was seduced by a Texas firm for twice the pay. So he dumped his wife and handicapped son and moved to Houston. And now he's got the balls to show his face around here again."

"You don't say." Jonathan gave Peyton the evil eye, then turned his gaze to the judge.

Senior United States District Judge George P. Breaux was not the kind of man one should keep waiting. His black robe, inflated by his broad shoulders and barrel chest, amplified his harsh stature. He checked his watch and adjusted his mic before letting his deep voice send a cavernous echo across the courtroom. "Well, Mr.

Peyton, is your witness on Central Time?"

Peyton stood up. "I apologize, Your Honor."

The judge was unimpressed. "It may not matter to be late when you're at sea, counselor, but it is in my courtroom," the judge said and then turned his viperous eyes at Jonathan. "Isn't that right, Mr. Brooks?"

"Of course, Your Honor," Jonathan replied in his native N'awlins accent, a melody that could swoon anyone with nostalgia for the Old South. Anyone but the judge.

"I apologize," Peyton said again. "Our witness must be stuck in traffic—something you don't have at sea."

Peyton's jest might as well have been in another language. Judge Breaux kept a stern gaze, his lips as straight as a hyphen.

"If you were pretty little ladies, I wouldn't mind waiting. But you're not." He pulled his chair back and got up. "I'll be in my chambers," the court heard him say as he stormed out through a side door.

His impatience was understandable. Though the trial was in its eighth day, the first had been almost five weeks ago. The proceedings were interrupted so often, it was a miracle the jury still remembered where to sit. First, key witnesses were not available. This was followed by a death in the judge's family, and then the bailiff's epileptic seizure during opening arguments, a juror's drunk-driving arrest on her way to court and a power blackout hitting all of Orleans Parish.

"Another full house," Jonathan said lightheartedly to Gary as he glanced at the back of the courtroom, finding an audience of only five people, aside from their clients.

Gary chuckled. "Insomniacs looking for a cure."

The slow pace frustrated Gary, but he'd been uncharacteristically patient through it all. Perhaps because the trial was his baby from the start, since he was the most senior admiralty lawyer in town. There was nothing new to him about a shipping company suing its insurer for refusing to pay under the policy. He knew the law, the shipping business, the judges, courtroom politics, and he knew how to take insurance companies to the mat.

Gary had asked Jonathan to join the case three months earlier, mostly to depose the defendant's witnesses. Jonathan had a knack for bringing out the truth, or, if that didn't work, sniffing out the bullshit that often spewed from the mouths of witnesses. He had left an indelible impression on Gary in an earlier trial, having grilled a Port of New Orleans inspector with such zealousness that the man confessed on the stand to receiving a kickback. Gary was eager to use him again. And now that Jonathan's caseload had lightened a bit, Gary felt it was the right time to bring in his prizefighter.

"All right, now," Gary said, resting his hand on Jonathan's shoulder, "don't dilly-dally on trivial points with that fella. He didn't become a naval officer by being stupid. You heard him in direct; he'll be just as tough in cross. If you get stuck, I'll jump in."

Jonathan nodded, but he sensed Gary's warning served another purpose. Gary wasn't about to cede control of this litigation to a younger gun, and his words were a roundabout way to delineate the turf.

Gary leaned into Jonathan again. "You've carefully reviewed the transcripts, right?"

"Yes, till three in the morning."

"Good, there's no sense in getting sleep when we're about to lose our largest case," Gary whispered within earshot of his client's CEO—the other Gary—seated immediately behind him with his eyes opened wide.

*Oh no*, Jonathan thought, *not again*. He had often warned Gary, who wore a hearing aid of questionable quality, that trying to whisper was not a good idea. But then again, Jonathan's call earlier that morning had been an equally humiliating faux-pas.

The door to the courtroom opened and a stocky, brown-haired man dressed in a white naval uniform, his hat tucked under his left arm, walked down the center aisle. He sat down on the bench behind Peyton, who then quickly signaled the clerk to summon the judge.

The fossil threw a hostile gaze at the officer when he reentered the courtroom. He looked ready to spit out one of his notoriously spiteful rebukes—preciously rationed for such moments—when Peyton preempted him.

"Your Honor," Peyton said, "I appreciate your courteous patience. Our witness is ready to take the stand."

"Yep," returned Judge Breaux from the side of his mouth. "Let's get the jury in here and get this trial goin'."

The naval officer stood up and headed to the witness stand as the jurors sluggishly proceeded to their chairs.

Jonathan, now at the podium, reviewed his notes, which were filled with important salvos for the battle that lay ahead. He looked up at the officer's bright uniform, decorated with rows of colorful patches and wide black epaulets, each embroidered with four yellow bands. Jonathan knew he faced a hardened opponent, and juries tended to look highly on military men. He had to purge his mind of all wishful premonitions that this man would in any way capitulate under cross-examination.

Jonathan waited purposefully for the air of authority to dissipate and for the jury to gather the real role this uniformed buck was to play: that of a mere civil servant at the mercy of cross-examination in a case that had nothing to do with supporting the troops but rather a multi-million dollar melee between a shipping company and a powerful maritime insurance carrier.

"Good morning, Captain," Jonathan greeted. "Please state your full name and profession for the record."

"Captain Donald Tucker, sir, commander of the *USS Meecham*, a U.S. Navy recovery vessel based in Norfolk, Virginia."

"How long have you been in the service, Captain?"

"About eighteen years, sir."

"Explain your role as captain."

"I'm responsible for the crew's safety and the vessel's ability to fulfill its missions."

"What is the pennant number of your vessel?"

"RS-56."

Allen walked behind Jonathan and placed a poster-sized photograph on an easel.

"Please take a look at this, Captain," Jonathan said, "and tell the court if this is a photo of your ship."

"Yes, it appears to be."

"And it shows the pennant number *RS-56* in white letters on the starboard bow of the ship, correct?"

"Yes, sir."

"And when did you take command of the ship?"

"In December, 1988."

Jonathan glanced at the jurors. One woman in the first row fought to keep her eyes open. The man next to her stared at the floor, perhaps hoping he could lay on it and not wake up until deliberations. Then again, most of the jurors looked like patients awaiting euthanasia.

"Captain, are you aware that two experienced sailors have testified that your ship collided with their vessel, the *Cajun Star*?"

"Yes."

"Are you aware that they testified that after the collision your vessel took off, ignoring their call for help?"

"I'm aware of their mistaken claims."

"So you deny that your ship was anywhere near the *Cajun Star* that Sunday night of March 19, 1989?"

"Correct."

"Can your ship be in two places at the same time?"

"Of course not."

Allen again walked around Jonathan, carrying another large display. He placed it on the same easel.

"Do you recognize this map?" asked Jonathan.

"It's a map of northern Europe—the North Sea and the Baltic, Scandinavia, as well as the Netherlands, northern Germany, Denmark and the east coast of England."

"And the place you claim to have been that night is here?" Jonathan asked, pointing to a large dot in the North Sea, between Scotland and the Norwegian coast. The spot had been marked in prior testimony.

"Yes, around there."

"How are you so sure?"

"My own recollection and my ship's log."

Jonathan drew a circle around the dot with his marker so the jury could see it well. To the jurors sitting ten feet away, the location the captain claimed to have been and the alleged collision site seemed fairly close—an advantage for Jonathan—but they were about a hundred miles apart. They also represented differently trafficked routes in the North Sea. The alleged collision site was in an area used by ships headed to or from the Baltic Sea through the Skagerrak and Kattegat straits, while the captain claimed to be farther west, in an area dense in north-south traffic, much associated with oil platforms.

"Why were you there, Captain?"

"A training mission."

"Why would you pick such a busy area for training?"

"It's as good as any other place in the North Sea."

"Uh'huh."

Jonathan did his best to be confident, but he had an impossible task. Somehow he had to show that the *Meecham* was closer to the alleged collision site than the captain claimed, and to best do that, he had to find some connection to Baltic-related traffic, but he had seen no evidence of it in anything he had read or heard.

"Have you ever taken the *Meecham* into the Baltic?"

"Objection, Your Honor," Peyton said, springing from his chair as if his seat were suddenly on fire. "As stated in your ruling this spring, Judge, that issue is irrelevant and delves into matters of national security."

The judge reclined in his chair, the squeaking sounds

of stressed leather echoing loudly. "Overruled. The witness can answer, but I caution you, Mr. Brooks, to tread lightly."

The captain looked at the judge as if he had called him a dirty name. "Yes, I've been there."

"Did the *USS Meecham* sail into the Baltic in 1989?"

"Objection."

"Overruled, Mr. Peyton," the judge said loudly. "I think you're being trigger-happy with your objections."

Jonathan tried hard to contain himself. Raw energy was buzzing inside him like a power line. He had Peyton on edge.

"We sailed into the Baltic later that year."

"And when you did, did you pass by where the *Cajun Star* was located on the night of March 19, 1989?"

"You'd have to."

"And why did you head to the Baltic?"

"Objection!" Peyton blurted out. "Your Honor, this is irrelevant and restricted subject matter under—"

"Sidebar!" the judge said, interrupting Peyton. "I need to straighten you boys out, I guess."

Jonathan knew it was time for punishment, though he hoped to leave ground zero less bruised than his opponent. And anything was possible with this feisty judge.

The two lawyers stood shoulder to shoulder below Judge Breaux's warm breaths. The judge pushed aside his mike and leaned forward, his pointy nose taking on the attributes of a bazooka. "You two are gonna stop these shenanigans. Mr. Brooks, your questions regarding Navy operations must only relate to the alleged collision. Neither the captain nor the Navy are defendants in this case, remember?" The judge then turned his gruff stare at the defense counsel. "And you, show me you can do more than yell 'objection' like a nutty parrot. And your demeanor is awful these days. During our lunch recess I suggest you go find a pleasant personality and return to my courtroom wearing it. Now, get going."

Jonathan always made it a point to leave sidebars with a smile, no matter what. It would dispel any notion that he may have been admonished. Peyton, however, looked as if he'd been sodomized by a linebacker.

The caution had shaken Jonathan. It was his nature to play fair, no matter how tempting it was to stray across boundaries when faced with opportunity. One thing was clear: he was not to delve into facts that could reveal naval intelligence sources and methods. But this wasn't the first time the bench had articulated this point.

The issue had raised its ugly head long before that morning. A litany of briefs and memoranda had passed under the judge's eyes in the preceding months. Even as far back as 1990, when the first trial began in a German court, the plaintiff's prior lawyers had requested in discovery every imaginable document relating to the *Meecham*. The same demands were made after the case was moved to New Orleans. If the *Meecham* had indeed collided with the *Cajun Star*, there was little evidence to show it. Without it, the jury would certainly believe the defendant's claim that there was no collision and that the damages were caused by the reckless conduct of the *Cajun Star's* captain, in which case the insurer could count on the policy exclusions to avoid indemnifying a single penny.

Peyton wasn't alone to restrict discovery of Navy records. He had been helped by a Judge Advocate General attorney named Joe Tillerman. Together, they did everything possible to curtail Gary's access to the *Meecham's* sailors, its deployment records and electronic data, like radar tracks and electronic messages. As a result, Judge Breaux allowed access to only a handful of government documents, many of them with large portions redacted. And to make matters worse for Jonathan's side, the Judge allowed only one sailor—Captain Tucker—to be subpoenaed.

"Your Honor," Jonathan said, "I would like to rephrase my prior question, as you suggested."

"That wasn't what I said," the judge retorted.

Peyton stood up and pointed his finger at Jonathan. "Your Honor, he's aiming for irrelevant information again," he protested.

Jonathan and Peyton quickly began talking loudly over one another.

"Mr. Peyton, please be quiet!" Judge Breaux yelled as he hammered the gavel several times. "Mr. Brooks, is it your wish to wait for the captain to retire before you ask your next question?"

"*You* should retire," Jonathan mumbled to himself, but he instantly realized that the microphone had picked up his words, shattering all forms of deference. "I'm joking, Your Honor."

The courtroom fell dead silent. The judge stared at Jonathan, no doubt weighing the responses available in his ferine arsenal.

"Counselor, I'm sanctioning you five hundred dollars for that remark. Give a check to the bailiff today."

"But my comment was—"

"Please resume your questions!"

Jonathan returned to his map, taking in a deep breath. An entire minute passed in silence.

"Captain, how far do you think your vessel was from the *Cajun Star* at around 19:00 local time that night?"

The Judge allowed the witness to get a closer look at the chart, which the captain did.

"About a hundred nautical miles."

"And what's the *Meecham's* normal cruising speed?"

"About eighteen knots," he said, returning to his seat.

"So it should take your ship approximately five or six hours to cover that distance, right?"

"Yes, about that," the captain murmured.

Before moving to the next question, Jonathan glanced at his client, Gary Moore, CEO of Victory Lines, the owner of the *Cajun Star*. Moore sat with his arms crossed, staring blankly at the jury. He was a pedantic loser who showed off the attributes of an undeserving tycoon while also leading the once vibrant shipping line onto a path of financial destruction. How he was still head of the company left Jonathan dumbfounded and pondering the question lawyers often ask themselves at some point in any trial: does this client deserve my effort?

Perhaps most lawyers would have answered no. Moore was not only a reckless executive, he was a jerk. Not worthy of Jonathan's time or intellect. But Jonathan's ardent advocacy wasn't aimed at saving Moore's ass. What mattered was saving the hundreds of local jobs that hung on the line as a result of the litigation. And one man in particular—Captain Mitch Glengeyer—had struck Jonathan as the poster child of this noble effort.

Glengeyer was the *Cajun Star's* seasoned skipper, a calm, humble man who happened to have sailed every ocean. But now, he was without his ship and his judgment was under close scrutiny. It had been his call to obey the order from headquarters to sail from Hanover, Germany, despite news of an incoming storm. But the cable from Victory Lines was hardly the sort of message he could have blown off. The shipment was on a tight schedule to reach Helsinki, Finland, and Glengeyer was expected to click his heels and sail.

Now, a courtroom seven thousand miles away and seven years after that fateful night was the venue chosen to dissect Glengeyer's decisions and observations, which stood in sharp contrast to Captain Tucker's. One of them was a liar. And Jonathan was convinced it wasn't Glengeyer.

"Your Honor, I'd like to go over Plaintiff's Exhibit Fifteen, the redacted log of the *USS Meecham* on the evening in question." It described only the general location of the vessel—logged every two to four hours—and named the watchman on duty at each interval.

Peyton briefly examined the three-page document before nodding approvingly.

"Captain, is this a copy of your ship's log?"

"It's a redacted version, summarizing the information about our location, heading and other events."

"Is there an original document?"

"Yes."

"Which one is more trustworthy?"

Peyton instantly objected, but he was nervous doing so.

As anticipated, the judge sustained it. Jonathan was pushing to discredit the redaction by showing that there was a more accurate, original document, even though Judge Breaux had prohibited its use because of a perceived risk to national security. The judge had told jurors to treat the redaction as equivalent to the original.

In a futile gesture meant only to preserve the issue for appeal, Gary Green stood up and restated his objection to the exclusion of the original log, but the judge overruled him before he could finish his sentence.

Jonathan handed the document to the captain. "Isn't it true that according to the entries at seven and eleven-thirty, your vessel could have been anywhere in a 600 square mile area?"

"Only if you completely disregard other evidence."

"It's a yes or no answer, Captain. Based on this redacted information, your vessel could have been much closer to the *Cajun Star* that night, correct?"

"Uh—"

"Isn't it possible based on this sanitized log?"

"It's not sanitized; it's redacted."

Jonathan asked the judge to make the officer answer.

"Let's not quibble, Captain," said Judge Breaux. "You can't invent a third choice to a yes or no answer."

"Fine, yes," the captain said with a scowl.

Jonathan grabbed his red marker and drew a large circle on the map, representing the area delineated by the redacted log. It put the site of the alleged collision potentially far closer. He then gleamed proudly at Gary and Allen. He'd made the naval officer buckle, at least a bit. No one had expected anything more than a stalemate. But Jonathan's balloon of optimism was short-lived. It wasn't enough to show that the *Meecham* was closer to the *Cajun Star*, but rather that it collided with it. That meant convincing the jury that the radar and navigation data on the multimillion-dollar military vessel was wrong. Worse yet, photographs of the *Meecham* taken in Norway six days after the alleged collision showed no damage at all—not a scratch. The *Cajun Star* had a twenty-foot gash in its hull.

"In the days following March 19, 1989, where did your vessel sail?

"We continued our training and then made port in Bergen, Norway."

As Captain Tucker answered, the heavy-set bailiff stepped away from the wall and wandered to the center of the proceedings, staring vacantly at the ceiling for a few seconds.

Jonathan gazed at him.

The man then collapsed, his head jolting violently. He began foaming at the mouth.

Someone near the jury shouted, "Call a medic!"

"Not again," Judge Breaux groaned into his mike.

This was the second time the bailiff had interrupted the proceedings with an epileptic seizure.

Jonathan immediately went to his assistance. He loosened the man's collar and turned his head to the side to make sure he wouldn't choke.

"Counselor, take that gun away," the judge added.

Jonathan, now on his knees, removed the firearm from the bailiff's holster and handed it to the clerk. As Jonathan stabilized the man's head, a wave of vomit exited the man's mouth and splattered across Jonathan's lap.

*I'm having a real bad day*, Jonathan thought.

The judge ordered an early lunch recess.

# 2

FEDERAL COURTROOMS ARE AUSTERE PLACES THAT RARELY provide entertainment. But the Victory Lines case had not ceased to do so, in the form of the most bizarre delays Jonathan had ever seen.

He walked out of the courthouse shaking his head in disbelief. His pants were soaked from a hasty rinse in the restroom, but the stench wasn't entirely gone. Jonathan set his briefcase down and gazed up, taking in the humid air. The sky was a bright shade of blue, something it hadn't been in weeks. He glanced back at Gary, who was in the lobby on his cell phone bickering with the firm's accountant.

Jonathan leaned on a wall at the edge of the steps, closed his eyes and faced the sun, his cheeks warming gently. With little sleep to think straight, his mind wandered off a bit until it settled on something familiar: the first day of the trial.

It had been Gary's moment to shine, and Jonathan

was merely a studious third-chair. Gary had meticulously presented his opening argument before asking the *Cajun Star's* skipper, Glengeyer, to take the stand.

Gary and Jonathan had prepped Glengeyer over the prior weeks. But it had been a delicate process because juries distrust witnesses who appear excessively coached. Besides, Glengeyer's greatest asset was his aura of sincerity—something neither lawyer wanted to jeopardize.

Gary had the instincts of a gambler and the subtleties of a surgeon. His direct examination of Glengeyer had painted a picture of a veteran sailor who had made the right decisions in the face of insurmountable odds.

Gary paused frequently. Long pauses. To Jonathan, this passive style was a sign of shrewdness rather than age. But not everyone admired his style. A native of Shreveport, Gary's Southern accent and mellow ways could be a curse on any juror prone to daydream. A reporter once called him "Plato," and not as a compliment.

Captain Glengeyer, under oath and in a suit and tie for the first time in his life, had responded calmly and methodically. He was a great witness overall, but his eyes betrayed a fear, perhaps of becoming the fall guy for his employer. Everyone in the industry knew Victory Lines' reputation for mistreating its employees: no sick time, low wages and shipments on schedules so tight the crew hardly ever had shore leave. It was the worst shipping company Jonathan had ever encountered, and even worse than the military, he'd been told. So it would not have surprised him if Glengeyer were sacrificed the moment Victory Lines saw an advantage in doing so. And neither Jonathan nor Gary had any duty to fight for Glengeyer's best interests if that happened.

"The storm had been raging for hours," Glengeyer had recounted under oath, the deep lines on his forehead accentuating his somber demeanor. "The massive swells rocked my ship as if it were a toy."

It was true. The *Cajun Star* had entered a storm about two hours after leaving the port of Hanover, Germany. By early evening Glengeyer was in his cabin, but he was well aware of the storm's strength. "Everything that wasn't nailed down had moved or fallen over," he had said.

Glengeyer's recollection of the night was crucial to the plaintiff's case. At around 9:20 P.M., Glengeyer recalled for the jury, one of the *Cajun Star's* lookouts caught a glimpse of a red light off starboard. The sailor couldn't tell the distance, but he reported the sighting to the bridge, which then alerted Glengeyer via intercom. Less than a minute later, the bridge once more notified Glengeyer that another lookout had spotted lights some distance away.

"I raced up the stairwell to the bridge. The watch team was pretty tense," Glengeyer had said. "Understandably so. An hour earlier, the powerful winds had knocked an antenna mast onto the main radar, damaging it beyond repair. We were sailing blindly into the stormy night."

Gary masterfully continued to pave the way for the jury to understand what had happened that night, to which Glengeyer responded perfectly.

"I told my first officer to look hard for the other vessel, and I grabbed a pair of binoculars myself. I told him to send two crewmen, Martinez and Solano, to help look for the other vessel. I also turned on all auxiliary upper deck lights and the aft searchlight—every bulb on the ship—so as to be seen." Glengeyer's eyes were wide open as he described the tragedy that unfolded. "I then threw on my coat and stepped onto the bridge's starboard outer deck. The raindrops hit my face like bullets. The wind was so strong I had to grab onto the handrail to stay on my feet. I couldn't see a thing. The first officer pointed his searchlight in various directions, but all that was visible was a wall of rain and some of the whitecaps of the giant swells nearby."

Jonathan had glanced at the jury repeatedly. Everything looked good. They were fully tuned in to the skipper.

"I was worried that we were on a collision course with another vessel, so I ordered the helmsman to pull back to eight knots and signal six short blasts on the ship's whistle—as required under international maritime rules—but it just didn't seem loud enough in the midst of the raging storm. I then ordered left full rudder, all the time hoping to steer clear of the danger. I knew that if we had a collision in that weather, we'd be dead in no time. For starters, no helicopter would be able to rescue us, and we didn't have the most modern lifeboats, if we could even get to them in time." Glengeyer had momentarily gone off-script, but he glanced at the plaintiff's table as if to acknowledge that he'd pointed out one of the ship's flaws. Fortunately for Gary and Jonathan, that was his only mistake during direct examination. He didn't mention the unreliable thirty year old diesel engines that powered the *Cajun Star*, nor the lackluster training given to his crew, nor the old navigation instruments and radios.

"I waited with the others on the bridge," Glengeyer had said. "Patiently waited. Five minutes, I think. Or perhaps six or seven. And then I felt things were fine. We hadn't seen anything, so I told the helmsman to resume our original course." Glengeyer then sat back in his chair and shook his head. "But then, suddenly, one of our lookouts—perhaps Martinez—shouted into the intercom. 'Vessel incoming, ten degrees starboard, two hundred meters,' I remember hearing." Glengeyer paused to wipe his brow with his handkerchief. "I heard the first officer yell to turn left full rudder again. The searchlight moved to point at about two o'clock from the bridge. And that's when I saw the scariest thing a sailor could ever see: the bow of another ship appear out of nowhere and head straight for us. The vessel sliced through a massive swell at great speed, and with no lights."

The room had become so quiet, all that was audible was the gentle typing sound from the court reporter's station.

"At that moment," Glengeyer testified, his voice tiring, "I was fixated on the top deck, where some of the heavy cargo was situated. A cable had just snapped, and then another and again another. They whipped about like crazed snakes. The three, twenty-ton turbines they held in place began to shift as our ship listed to the port side. And a dozen thirty-foot metal tubes next to them also moved abruptly. I spotted my crewman, Martinez, and clenched the handrail. He was running back toward me, but he was midship some eighty feet from the bridge. He ran faster, his handheld flashlight bobbing up and down from his efforts, his body bumping a few times into the railing as he tried to make it to safety. 'Run, run!' I told him, but it was too late. I could only watch in horror."

Glengeyer paused again, and Jonathan sensed it was unrehearsed. Gary had told the old skipper to be himself, even if that meant being upset in front of the jury. Glengeyer had earlier told the lawyers how he cared for his men. Martinez was one of forty-three crewmen on the *Cajun Star*. "He was a normal, quiet guy, a native of El Paso, with a daughter and a pregnant wife at home. He'd celebrated his fifth anniversary with Victory Lines the week prior to that night."

Glengeyer appeared to be choked up for a moment before resuming his testimony.

"The vessel swayed in the other direction," he went on, "and the turbines collapsed from their support and screeched across the deck. Martinez disappeared under the first one. The cargo plunged into the sea. I turned to starboard and saw the other disaster in the making. The other vessel was closing in rapidly, though it began to turn as a last-ditch maneuver. I grabbed the handrail again, ducked behind the metal railing and braced for the impact. Suddenly two powerful searchlights on the other vessel beamed in our direction, blinding everyone on the bridge. That's when a loud thud resonated, followed by a high-pitched screech—like nails on a chalkboard, but a thousand times louder. The hit knocked me down, but

I quickly got up and looked at the gray-hulled ship pass just feet away from me. I squinted, my eyes burning from the strength of the lights pointed at us. I couldn't understand why they were doing this. First, they'd approached without a single light on and then they were blinding us. I simply gazed at the vessel as it disappeared into the wall of rain, its searchlights finally fading in the darkness. The ship was gone as if nothing had happened."

At that point Glengeyer had reached the pinnacle of the plaintiff's case: the identification of the mystery vessel. Gary had been salivating for it to come out just right. If the jury believed him, they would rule that Martinez's death, the lost cargo, and the damage to the ship was caused by another vessel, and not by Glengeyer's negligence, and thus the defendant insurance carrier would be forced to pay. It was as simple as that.

"And what did you see?" Gary asked at that tense moment.

"A military ship for sure. And its pennant number—*five-six*—which I later found out was the *Meecham*."

"And then?" Gary pressed on.

"Immediately after the collision, I ran down to the starboard deck with two crewmen to search for our man overboard, although I knew it was an impossible task. But God, we tried. I sent another crewman down to check for flooding, and I leaned over the side of our ship to inspect the damage. I could barely see through the rain, but what was there wasn't pretty: a huge gash in the bow, just above the waterline."

Gary's questioning had left everyone in the courtroom on the edge of their seats—a first for a jury that since *voir dire* had shown little interest in the subject matter of the litigation. And that's when he guided Glengeyer to explain the traffic rules at sea. Under the International Regulations for Prevention of Collisions at Sea—the so-called COLREGS—a vessel's duty to give way depends on how the vessels approach one another. Since the *USS Meecham* had sailed in an angle sufficient to be deemed a "crossing" situation, the rules required that the Navy ship yield to the *Cajun Star*. In other words, according to Glengeyer's testimony, the Navy was squarely to blame for the collision.

Glengeyer's testimony that first day of trial was a chilling account, and it was etched in Jonathan's mind as if it had happened an hour ago. But it hadn't, and Jonathan worried that the jury would not have a solid recollection now that weeks had gone by.

The sun continued to warm Jonathan's face. It was a peaceful feeling, accompanied by the sounds of traffic and a light breeze that carried the odor of diesel fuel.

Gary finally came out to the courthouse steps. He put on his large gold-rimmed sunglasses. "Why didn't you go home to change clothes?"

"It's okay. I got most of it off," said Jonathan, glancing at his left pant leg, still soaked from the knee down to the cuffed bottom. "It's only vomit; let's grab lunch."

"If I can ignore the smell."

*       *       *

THE two lawyers sat in a corner booth at the Palace Café on Canal Street. They aired their frustrations at the morning's proceedings. And a pair of Ketel One and tonics soon appeared in their hands to help them along.

"It's really too bad," Gary said.

"What?"

"Our best moment was Glengeyer's testimony, now weeks ago—an eternity for a jury. But then again, Peyton cross-examined him quite effectively."

Gary was right. Peyton had carved up the old skipper's testimony into small, digestible pieces, and poked enough holes in the plaintiff's case to drive a semi through it, particularly the most glaring weakness: if there had been a collision, why did the *Meecham* show no signs of damage? Worse yet, Glengeyer was the only person on the *Cajun Star* who claimed to have seen the *Meecham's* pennant number.

"Here's to your first sanction," Gary said, raising his glass over the table. "Just don't get too many; I need you in this firm."

"Cheers," Jonathan said timidly, his mind wrestling with something else. Something even more troubling. A fact that Gary had dismissed long ago, in one of their first conversations about the case. And it was itching to come out again, even though he knew Gary wouldn't want to revisit the issue. "I still don't understand," Jonathan said. "Why is the Navy so feverishly denying the incident ever happened? It just doesn't make sense. The statute of limitations has long passed. We can't sue them now."

"You're right," Gary said after a long pause. "In other collision cases, the Navy never categorically denied being involved, and they've never been so tight-fisted with their records, even when they've been defendants."

Jonathan knew this well. He had researched ample collision lawsuits brought by commercial and private vessel owners against the United States. In almost every case, evidence of the ship's course, radar readings and related records were made available with little or no resistance, and the Navy rarely made a fuss about its crewmen testifying.

Gary took a long sip of his drink and then looked into Jonathan's eyes. "There's no point rehashing this. Breaux made up his mind and that's that."

"I'm still troubled."

Gary's gaze didn't budge. "Maybe they're full of shit."

"Who?"

"Our client!" said Gary as if Jonathan should have known. "Moore, Glengeyer, the whole lot."

"What are you saying?"

"What if Glengeyer made up the whole incident to cover his bad judgment? Maybe that's why the insurance company and the Navy are fighting so hard. Have you thought about that, Jonathan? What if the *Cajun Star* crewmen are nothin' but liars?"

"I hardly think Glengeyer is that sort of man."

Gary frowned. "Don't be too sure."

His words left his junior partner speechless for a moment. Jonathan had never considered this possibility. Not once. When it came to the old skipper, Jonathan had long ago set aside his natural lawyerly skepticism. He believed Glengeyer with a passion.

"I know you better than that," Jonathan said. "You would never have accepted this case if you didn't believe Glengeyer's account to be true, or at least highly probable."

Gary shook his head and cracked a smile. "Victory Lines is an old client of ours, Jonathan. I couldn't turn them down, even if . . ."

Jonathan studied Gary's expression. The thought of being complicit to a contrived incident of such magnitude was abhorrent.

"But even if our clients are lying," Gary suggested after a long sip of his drink, "there are still several things pointing to a collision, like the seismic readings."

"True," Jonathan said, downing the last of his alcohol until the ice cubes tumbled to the tip of his nose. "But did you see the way most of the jurors reacted to Mikkelsen? They were bored to tears! I was tempted to lob my chair at them to wake'em up."

Dr. Høgaard Mikkelsen was a seismologist from the Technical University of Denmark. Gary had flown him in to testify as an expert witness to show that some sort of seismic activity indicative of a collision had occurred on the night of March 19, 1989. In his testimony, the professor explained various seismic recordings taken from Denmark's National Survey and Cadastre seismograph stations, which, although designed more for registering large earthquakes around the world and tremors from nuclear tests, were perfectly suited to monitor smaller man-made tremors. Dr. Mikkelsen had stressed that although the alleged impact of the two ships was an impulsive event—where only a fraction of the resonance manifests itself below sea level—the seismograms he used definitely showed an event consistent with a vessel collision.

It all sounded quite logical, but the jury had a hard time, given Mikkelsen's thick accent and quirky body language, not to mention a topic so tedious it would drive clergy to drink. The jurors became notably restless when Mikkelsen buried them in technical jargon. Fortunately, when it came time for Peyton to have a shot at the professor, he couldn't debunk Mikkelsen's claim of a collision. And his own expert had neither the credentials nor the wherewithal to do it.

Jonathan sat back in his seat and sipped his espresso.

"I'm just an old fart," Gary said as the waitress arrived with the check. "I'm not sure we've made the right decisions in this case."

Jonathan didn't respond.

It didn't take long for the lunch crowd to vanish. The busboys toiled like drones to restore the restaurant to its orderly environment. Jonathan stared at his empty cup, his thoughts filled with the dreaded reality of having to return to the courtroom.

As the two waited for the waitress to bring back change, Jonathan noticed a beefy man taking a seat at the bar. He wore a tan-colored tweed jacket, which had earlier caught his eye in the courtroom—the back row. But it wasn't the first time he'd seen the stranger. As Jonathan thought harder about it, he recalled seeing the guy on at least two other occasions. The man was in his late thirties or early forties, with short blond hair.

"Do you know that fella?" Jonathan asked his partner, who then turned with a raised brow.

"He was in court this morning," Gary answered. "But I don't know him."

"A reporter, maybe?" Jonathan suggested.

"Hardly. This trial has a tough time attracting lawyers, let alone the press."

Jonathan was uncomfortable with the man's presence, although he couldn't quite put a finger on it, but he wasn't about to annoy Gary with his vague suspicions.

The two walked back to the courthouse just in time for the resumption of proceedings. But to their surprise, the afternoon session didn't last long. Judge Breaux allowed Peyton to redirect Captain Tucker for about forty-five minutes before ordering a recess till the following day on account of an urgent motion in another case. It was yet another unexpected interruption in the trial. But this time Jonathan welcomed it. He'd done his best with the scant evidence at his disposal, but he hadn't really damaged the naval officer's credibility. He had tonight to scour documents for anything else he could use to reduce his chances of defeat.

"See you in the mornin'," Gary said as he left the plaintiff's table. "We need to come up with a break in this case. Captain Tucker is leaving town tomorrow."

Gary was asking for magic.

*       *       *

THE passenger side of Jonathan's car was filled with trial papers, some stashed in two vinyl satchels and a leather briefcase, while the rest covered the floor and filled the door bins and other nooks in the front compartment. Gazing at the pile of materials, he added the hours needed to re-read them and quickly realized he was in for another long night. But his endurance was better than most lawyers. Linda had trained him well. He'd gotten used to late nights. As lead anchorwoman on Channel 6's ten o'clock news, Linda rarely got home before one in the morning on weeknights. And she had done this for four years.

Jonathan drove out of the parking garage onto St. Charles. As he passed the first block from the garage, he spotted the blond man in the tweed jacket slip into a green Toyota sedan parked in a metered space. The streetcar ahead slowed, and the traffic backed up, giving Jonathan more time to observe the man through his rearview mirror. The Toyota pulled out and was about ten car lengths behind.

Jonathan was headed home, but first to a flower shop in New Orleans' west suburb of Metairie. It was a habit he'd picked up after his brother died, to give Linda a bouquet each month. Lilies, stargazers, or irises, but never roses—too pedestrian.

He turned at the next light and noticed that the Toyota made the same turn. After crossing the next intersection Jonathan was convinced something wasn't right. The man seemed to be on his tail, way back. By the time Jonathan reached Tulane Avenue, there was no more doubt. His nervous glances toggled between the side and rearview mirrors, studying the Toyota's every move.

*Why the hell would someone be following me?*

Jonathan's palms began to sweat. His anger fermented. He clenched the steering wheel and shook his head.

*Gary Moore, maybe? Checking on his lawyers? He'd be capable, that ungrateful bastard.*

Jonathan became angrier. For a split second, he considered stopping, getting out of his car and confronting the stranger. But he quickly tempered his instinct with a good dose of caution.

The Carrollton Avenue light ahead turned yellow. Jonathan, seeing an opportunity to lose his tail, floored the accelerator. He hoped the man trailing him would be forced to stop at the red light. Jonathan cleared the intersection and gazed into the mirror. But the Toyota also sped up.

"Stubborn bastard," Jonathan said, his eyes glued to the mirror.

A truck suddenly appeared out of nowhere and slammed into the Toyota. Jonathan heard the thud, followed by the sound of screeching tires and then a loud bang.

"Christ!" Jonathan said, instantly letting off the pedal. He threw his head over his shoulder, but there was no sign of either vehicle, except some debris scattered over the road.

He quickly drove around the block and parked at the far end of the shopping center facing the intersection. He walked a few feet before catching sight of the scene. The mangled car rested partly over the sidewalk, its left quarter panel twisted around a concrete bench. The truck was some fifty feet away, its grill smashed and spewing steam. The smell of gasoline seeped into his lungs.

He cautiously approached the Toyota. All the windows were shattered. When he walked around to the driver's side, the serious condition of the vehicle was even more apparent. The driver's door was smashed nearly all the way to the center console, and the man behind it was a bloodied mess.

Jonathan leaned in. "Can you hear me?" he asked, not expecting the driver to answer. He stared at the man's left eyeball which was halfway out of its socket.

Jonathan pressed his hand over the driver's nose and chest. The man wasn't breathing. Nor did he have a pulse.

At that moment, a bystander claiming to be a nurse opened the door on the other side and jumped into the front seat. She quickly straightened the victim's upper body.

"Help me loosen his clothes," she said to Jonathan. She hurriedly unbuttoned his blood-soaked collar as Jonathan unbuckled the man's seatbelt. She too checked for a pulse.

The crushed car was not an ideal place to give CPR, but she tried anyway, repeatedly pushing on the man's chest. She then shoved her pudgy fingers into his mouth to clear his airway.

"I'll tilt his head," Jonathan said, leaning farther into the car.

The woman continued her efforts, but she could barely move her arms. Her chubby body was wedged between the victim and the wrecked dashboard.

She threw a gaze at Jonathan. "This won't work! Let's get him to the ground." She then yelled over her shoulder for someone to call an ambulance.

Jonathan couldn't help but find a sliver of humor.

Only hours earlier he'd given first aid to another man, the courtroom bailiff. *I'm acting out an episode of M.A.S.H.*, he thought just as reality quickly set in again. He removed the man's jacket and loosened his legs from under the dash as the woman pulled the man's body toward her. That's when two other people helped her extricate the victim from her side of the car.

Jonathan stepped back and observed the nurse. She bobbed up and down, as did her melon-sized breasts. She was determined to resuscitate the victim. She persisted for several minutes. But it was a pointless exercise. He was unresponsive. His blood gushed uncontrollably from his temple and neck and oozed over the pavement.

Jonathan glanced at the tweed jacket he had removed from the victim. The crimson-stained garment rested over the shattered remnants of the driver's door. This was an opportunity he wouldn't pass up. He dug into the inside pocket and pulled out a wallet. His driver's license was from Maryland, and his name was Anthony Gordon.

Jonathan shook his head. "Come all this way to see a boring trial and then die. What bad luck."

Just as he returned the wallet, a shiny, odd-shaped object on the front passenger floor mat caught his eye. He craned forward for a closer look, suspecting it was a camera. It wasn't.

"I'll be damned," Jonathan said as he stared intently at a chrome-plated handgun nestled in a black leather holster. He then gazed at the man's body lying on the pavement. "You've just made me *very* curious."

# 3

JONATHAN COULDN'T FEND OFF THE REVOLTING IMAGES OF the crash scene. The crushed skull, the broken jawbone protruding out of the man's ear, and that loose eyeball. And all that blood. Jonathan's clothes were covered in it. He had stayed at the intersection a while, well after the nurse threw in the towel, and after the ambulance left. He was troubled that an armed man had been following him for no apparent reason. He had to find out why.

Once home, Jonathan sprinted upstairs and wasted no time dialing the number he had in mind.

"Eighth District, Royal Street, Lequesha here."

"Is Derek in?"

"Who ju'say, seh?" the receptionist asked, the crunching sound of food echoing after her words.

"Lieutenant Derek Ashton."

She swallowed whatever it was, sighed and asked, "And yow name?"

"Jonathan Brooks."

"One momen'," she said, followed by another slow sigh.

A second later, Derek picked up and answered in his usual hurried tempo. "Yeah, what's up?"

"I was wondering if you could do a little favor for your kind and thoughtful brother-in-law."

"Kind and thoughtful, my ass," Derek said, chuckling. "Okay, what d'you need? And make it quick—it's busy tonight. A drunk tourist just got stabbed on Dauphine, a huge amphetamine bust is underway in Armstrong Park and I just got word of a balcony brawl at the Conti—damn college brats. So, let's have it."

"I need information on someone named Anthony Gordon." Jonathan gave Derek the Maryland address he had read off the driver's license and the license plate information, and added, "The guy died in a car crash today on Tulane Avenue—I witnessed it. And he had a gun in the car."

"So what? Everyone's got a gun."

"He was following me."

"You're probably imagining things."

"Can you pull up any info on him?"

"I suppose, sometime tomorrow."

That was all Jonathan wanted to hear. He hung up, threw a pillow on his chair, sat down and flung his long legs over his cluttered desk. His eyes circled the room, gazing at the inordinate memorabilia—frames, trophies, ornaments, and photographs—that was stuffed in its confines. Linda had insisted that none of it stray to other parts of the house. Trophies from archery and crossbow were the most ostentatious and covered many of the

shelves on the far wall. There were also framed professional certificates, awards and degrees, which he chose
to display here rather than in his office downtown. And
for good reason. This was home, and he preferred to
savor his trinkets of accomplishment in the quiet comforts here. By day, his window offered a slice of the
Mississippi, with ships passing by the distant tree-lined
levee. At dusk the view was just as serene.

                    *        *        *

EVEN at midnight, the evening was still young. In front
of him lay a hastily prepared sandwich, and around it an
endless amassment of legal papers—all of it from the
Victory Lines litigation. For several hours, he had
refreshed his memory by rereading transcripts and notes,
some from depositions, some from earlier testimony at
trial. As tempting as it was to simply go to bed, he knew
his team depended on him to extract something more
from the mountain of evidence.

Jonathan wasn't alone in conducting this chore. He
picked up the phone and dialed Allen at home.

"Did you recalculate the distances?" Jonathan asked,
referring to the gap between the collision site and
alleged location of the *Meecham*. Though Jonathan had
previously measured the charts, he was aware that his
legal skills did not extend to mathematical formulations.

"You're in luck," Allen said. "I just crunched new
numbers moments ago."

"How do they look?"

"Not good. The distance is still about seventy nautical miles under the most favorable interpretation."

Jonathan sat back in his chair and sighed.

"But," Allen came back, his voice hinting of better news, "if somehow we can time-shift the other data, in particular the radar tracks, we could bring the distance down to twelve miles."

"Twelve?" Jonathan asked. He dropped his sandwich and held the handset with both hands.

"You got it."

"But what exactly do you mean by time-shifting?"

"If for some reason the time-stamp on the radar data was off by two hours, the data coupled with the redacted log would show that the *Meecham* could have been as close as twelve miles from the *Cajun Star*—"

*Which could be helpful to sway the jury*, Jonathan thought. "Well done. But how on earth can we prove the radar data was wrong?"

"Faulty calibration, perhaps."

"Maybe," said Jonathan, "but that's a stretch. We'd be better off claiming it was manipulated." He wasn't sure, but it was a sliver of good news in what had otherwise been an unproductive day. "Can't you find out more from that radar expert—that former Navy technician we talked to a few months ago?"

"Will do."

They hung up, and with food back in one hand and a transcript in the other, Jonathan returned to his tedious reading.

\*          \*          \*

A faint buzzing sound crept through a deep dream and mutated into a recognizable noise. It was Jonathan's cell phone, laying face down on the nightstand. It kept vibrating as he simply stared at it, shaking its way toward the edge of the furniture. He hadn't been asleep long, having scrutinized mounds of transcripts and other records until nearly two-thirty in the morning, about an hour after Linda had returned from the station.

His languid hand reached forward, grabbed the device and brought it to his ear.

"Brooks," whispered a sleepy-eyed Jonathan, his jaw restrained by his plush feather pillow.

"Good morning, sir," said a young woman with a British accent. "I have Barrister Paul Higginbotham on the line. He would like to speak with you. It's rather urgent."

Jonathan sat up quietly and headed out of the bedroom so as not to wake Linda. "Can't this wait till later in the morning?" he asked, but she had already patched him through to a beeping tone.

"Mr. Brooks, I'm dreadfully sorry to wake you," said the Englishman, his accent an intoxicating resonance of aristocracy. "I know it's awfully early on your side of the pond, but I thought you might want to hear the news as quickly as possible."

Higginbotham was the local barrister Gary had hired to unearth records of the *Meecham's* call on the Royal Navy base at Portsmouth, on England's southern coast. The vessel had docked there for a few weeks before leaving for the North Sea, just prior to the alleged collision. Jonathan had never spoken with him before and had just about forgotten about him since nothing meaningful had come out of the London firm's research.

"Good news, I hope?" asked Jonathan, as his tired head replayed Gary's frequent complaints about the barrister's steep fees.

"I'm not sure quite what to make of it, really," the barrister said. "My associate got his hands on a rather interesting document last week. It was a good bit of luck, I say. May I read you the pertinent part?"

"Please," Jonathan said, quietly closing the bathroom door behind him.

"It's cryptic, but I'll explain," Higginbotham said. "It says '*Courier changeover to P-R slot, USN-divert, CDel-Bergen.*'"

Jonathan was expecting more, of course. "What the hell does that mean?"

"It's a dispatch order from the Royal Mail service at Portsmouth naval base."

"So?" Jonathan asked, irritated that Higginbotham had woken him up to share this crap.

"Well, as you know, after the *Meecham* left the U.K., its next scheduled stop was Bergen, Norway. But this dispatch—dated March 20th, the day after the alleged collision—diverted the mail back to Portsmouth!"

"But the ship did make it to Bergen. We have ample evidence."

"Yes, Mr. Brooks, but it did something strange first."

Jonathan started to add things up and suddenly felt an exciting rush flow through his veins.

Barrister Higginbotham cleared his throat. "This Royal Mail dispatch seemed awfully peculiar—and I'll spare you my personal sentiments of our country's mail service. But suffice to say I hurried my colleague to

Portsmouth yesterday afternoon to investigate. You may want to sit for the rest."

*Go right ahead*, Jonathan thought, as he sat on the toilet seat cover and listened for what he hoped would be music to his ears.

"He looked around, asked questions and then . . . he struck gold."

"Paul, you're leaving me hanging like a ripe berry on a steamy plantation orchard. Will you *please* get to the point."

"Are all you Yanks so impatient?" Higginbotham asked, chuckling. "My colleague got word of a local whose life is centered on, get this: ship-spotting."

"And you dare call Americans strange?"

"Apparently this man does this for a hobby, spotting ships from his village on Gosport, across from the naval base. He's got quite the reputation for photographing everything that floats, military and civilian. He's won prizes, too. Now, as I understand it, he saw the *Meecham* enter the sound at dusk on March 21, 1989."

Jonathan's jaw just about fell to his lap. He quickly calculated the time interval. "Yes, yes . . . that's about thirty-eight hours after the collision. Is this ship-spotter reliable?"

"I can't vouch for anything right now, but I'll know more soon."

"Can we make him testify?"

"We're not there yet. But there's even better news. Our little hobbyist took a photograph, so I'm told. He apparently caught a very interesting picture of the *Meecham*. I should have it very soon, and I can send it to you air mail."

"Does it show any damage to the Meecham?" asked Jonathan.

"I'm not sure," replied Higginbotham.

"I need it right away," Jonathan said. "Have it couriered on the next flight out of London. And please fax me a copy as well."

There was no time to lose. Jonathan would not be able to extend Captain Tucker's cross-examination much longer, and this incredible piece of evidence could, if proven true, be the miracle he so desperately needed in this pitiful case.

Higginbotham agreed to hurry. He seemed proud of his feat, though Jonathan was tempted to remind him that he'd charged over five thousand dollars for his services over the prior six months and had until now produced zilch.

Jonathan was ecstatic, nervous and completely unaware of the time until he looked up at the clock high on the bathroom wall. It was five-ten. Damn early, but Jonathan was on an adrenaline rush that he didn't want to lose.

He went downstairs, fixed some toast and plopped a legal pad on the breakfast table. He started writing the questions he would ask Captain Tucker; questions he hoped would impeach the naval officer once he had a copy of the photograph. Only then would the jury give the plaintiff's team the credibility they deserved.

# 4

No matter which way he drove toward downtown, there were reminders of Matt. Reminders that six years was still a short time when it came to losing his brother. As he eased to the stop sign at Leake Road and Broadway, he gazed at the levee some distance away. And what a simple, unassuming structure it was, built of earth and shaped in an uncomplicated form to suit its judicious purpose—to keep the waters around New Orleans from inundating its many neighborhoods that stand below sea level.

A plainly constructed oeuvre, a levee need not rise more than a dozen feet above level ground. At its summit, one can always find a beaten path where the grass struggles to grow, its sandy soil revealing the faint tread of sneakers and bicycle tires. And how diverse the vantage seems from such an unassuming perch. On one side flows the lifeblood of countless industries, with a veritable armada of rust-colored barges and foreign-flagged freighters guiding their loads to destinations afar. The acrid, peppery scent of the Mississippi glides over the embankment, filling the air and reminding those on the other side that a mighty river is near. Levees are as much a part of the Big Easy as are jazz, brothels-turned-bistros and jambalaya. But they possess subtle traits, their splendor oft overlooked and only rarely glorified for their utilitarian qualities on those terribly rainy days. No one could call New Orleans home without having had at least one memorable moment on a levee's crest, whether it was a sweetheart's first kiss, a favorite pet's first glimpse at a body of water, or an endearing stroll with a lifelong companion. Surely, if these barriers could speak, they would recount many tales. For Jonathan, these tales would be of a cherished childhood.

Reminders crept forth as he gazed out the window at the long stretch of grass that formed the front slope of the levee. It was where he'd played Frisbee with Matt. Where their dad's excited Dobermans, Justice and Damage, ran wild. It was a place where time could have so easily stood still.

As Jonathan veered left onto Leake Road, he honed in on the familiar spot. The past now threw itself at him uncontrollably.

"Oh, man," Jonathan whispered to himself. "Why is it still so hard?"

And the heavens did their bit, too—divine whispers of sorts in the form of familiar sounds that brought back memories of him and his brother as children: the barking dogs frantically circling Matt, his body contorting as he was about to throw the Frisbee Jonathan's way.

"When I grow up, I'm gonna be an astronaut," shouted Matt, giggling.

Jonathan laughed before answering. "It's a little early to think about that."

Justice raced ahead of Damage. The canine duo, their tongues wagging to one side, charged across the overgrown grass toward Jonathan, who caught the toy with one hand as if it required no effort at all. He loved to show off.

"Then why do you keep saying what *you* plan to be?" asked Matt.

"Because I'm grown up. I'm fourteen! You're just a pip-squeak."

"Then, why does mom pack your lunch everyday?"

"Because it saves time."

"She puts milk in your lunchbox and says it's cuz you're a growing boy."

"I throw the milk away."

"That's cuz of the *girls*."

"No, I may still be growing, but mentally I'm already all matured and ready for life, brat."

"Nah'ah. Mom says you're still a kid."

"If I were a kid, I wouldn't think about becoming a lawyer, like dad. I'd be like you, wanting to reach the moon or the stars."

The levee was a wonderful spot. A place near home where kids can be kids, and the rest of the world disappears, if only for a short time.

But there was yet another place where Matt and Jonathan found even greater pleasure and mischief, a place where they never took the dogs, only their bikes and brave spirits. It was an abandoned lighthouse on the north end of town, on the shores of Lake Pontchatrain. It was hallowed ground. Jonathan hadn't returned in years. He could not face the pain.

*        *        *

GARY and Allen were standing in the lobby of the courthouse when Jonathan walked through the door.

"Why are you smiling?" Gary asked, his hands resting on his hips. "Is it because you're on time for a change?"

"Gentlemen," Jonathan said, raising a manila folder to Gary's chest. "In here is the torpedo that will sink Captain Tucker's credibility."

After Jonathan explained to his co-counsel the gem he had gotten from Barrister Higginbotham, he pulled out the faxed photograph he had just picked up at the office on the way to court.

At first, his colleagues were amazed, but Gary quickly opened the folder and began to scan the document. A veil of skepticism ran over his face.

"This fax is *junk,*" Gary said. "It's a dark and grainy image. Breaux will never allow this in."

"Perhaps not," replied Jonathan. "But the original will be here by mid-afternoon. It's being delivered by courier."

"That's too late," Gary said bluntly.

He had a point. The courier's flight was scheduled to arrive at two-thirty, but by the time he found this way downtown, it would be closer to four. Jonathan knew Judge Breaux would not easily extend Captain Tucker's availability beyond the morning.

"We *must* try," Jonathan stressed. "If *I* ask the bastard, he'll definitely say no. Gary, why don't you give it a shot? Breaux likes you."

Gary chuckled. "He doesn't care much for me. I just don't give him as much grief as you do." Gary again glanced at the fax. He then headed to the elevators. "Fine, we'll see what happens."

Jonathan waited in the lobby while Allen headed into the courtroom. Jonathan checked his watch nearly every minute. Without the photograph, the case was doomed. With it, he could butcher the defense beyond repair. How he craved to be a fly on the wall in the judge's chamber.

Nearly thirty minutes passed before Gary reappeared. His smile gave it all away. "We've got till four, and not a minute more."

"Fantastic," said Jonathan, though he really wanted to scream for joy. All he needed now was for the courier to arrive on time.

In the meantime, Gary offered to work on a new motion dealing with defense exhibits. This gave Jonathan a bit more time to prepare. Gary also asked Allen to wait for the courier at the airport and race back to the courthouse once he had the picture.

*       *       *

THE noble triers of fact plopped down their large posteriors for the late afternoon session. Their seats creaked and squeaked for an annoyingly long time, until the last juror finally settled into a comfortable position. But they were all vicious and restless. Their faces could not have shown greater disdain for the legal machinations surrounding their civic duty. The women looked especially resentful. Hatred beamed out of their eyes every time they glanced at the attorneys, most notably Peyton.

It didn't matter that they'd eaten lunch. Steak sandwiches, he had heard, from one of the finest delis downtown. Nor did it matter that the day before, the judge had handed them free tickets to the aquarium, the nicest thing he had ever done for jurors in his career. They simply didn't want to spend another second in that courtroom. *Bitches.* For a fleeting moment, Jonathan wished they had been sequestered instead, just to punish them. Or worse, that the bailiff, now recovered from his epileptic episode, would simply shoot them out of their misery.

Standing at the plaintiff's table, Jonathan checked his watch. It was going on four-ten. He glanced at the courtroom door, hoping Allen would walk in before the judge. But Allen had not answered his cell phone minutes ago. Unless he got back from the airport with the photograph, Jonathan was resigned to use the faxed version, which would most likely be excluded. He checked his watch again as the judge took his seat and nodded to his clerk to get the show on the road. There was no more time.

Just as Jonathan called Captain Tucker to the stand, he heard the door open behind him. *Thank God.* It was Allen, and he'd come in giving a discreet thumbs up at Jonathan, who then returned to face the naval officer.

"Good afternoon," Jonathan said to the Navy captain as Allen placed the eight-by-ten black and white photograph on the podium. "You should put on your seatbelt; it's going to get bumpy."

"Counselor!" Judge Breaux barked, quashing a few chuckles from the jury box.

Jonathan nodded an apology. But it had gotten the jury's attention, something of a miracle. Now was the time to bring out the artillery.

"Captain Tucker," he said, "you have testified that on March 20, 1989—one day after the alleged collision—your ship headed north-northeast toward the port of Bergen, Norway, arriving there four days later. Is this correct?"

"Yes."

"And you headed there directly, making no detours or port calls between March 19 and 24, correct?"

"Yes, sir."

"If your vessel had gone elsewhere, and someone were to have taken a photograph of it, you'd be able to tell if it was your vessel or not, correct?"

"I'm sure," the captain answered before giving Peyton a subtle, puzzled look.

Jonathan glanced at the photograph and suddenly noticed something odd. The picture was a wider image than what had appeared on the faxed page. Wider because it showed something strange behind the *USS Meecham*. An odd-shaped object. Jonathan crowed his head forward to examine it more carefully. His hands gripped the edge of the podium as he realized what it was. Shivers ran down his spine.

*A barge, a fucking barge.*

Jonathan's mind ignited a whirlwind of thoughts. He

was piecing it all together faster than he could scribble words on his notepad.

"Your Honor," he said, grasping the significance of what rested before his eyes: proof not only that Tucker had lied about his ship's whereabouts, but damning proof of the actual vessel that hit the *Cajun Star*. "At this time, I'd like to ask the witness to identify this photograph."

"Please show it to defense counsel first," the judge said, and Jonathan did as he was told.

Peyton stood up but didn't say a word. He casually glanced at the photo, but he didn't seem to spot its relevance, so he calmly sat back down.

Jonathan walked closer to the witness and held up the photo a foot away from him. "Is this the *Meecham*?"

Captain Tucker's face seemed to rapidly lose its color. It was a glorious moment that Jonathan wished he had captured on film. The man was dumbfounded, frozen in his chair, nervously licking of lips, his eyes shifting edgily—all tell-tale signs of a lying scoundrel. And slowly a response finally exited the man's mouth. "I think it is."

"Your Honor, it'd like to introduce this picture into evidence."

Peyton seemed to sense the captain's discomfort and so he asked for a sidebar, which Judge Breaux granted.

But before Peyton could say a word, Jonathan walked to the bench with enough adrenaline to get himself another sanction. "Judge, we just received this image from a witness who saw Captain Tucker's ship at a time and place that contradicts his testimony. So, we're about to impeach this witness and set the record straight in this case. We have been lied to for months, and now, Your Honor, we respectfully ask that you remove the smokescreen and let these jurors see for themselves."

"This is out of left field," Peyton complained, gesturing like a man about to be put into a straitjacket. "He can't spring this on us like this, Judge. They didn't produce this in discovery, and—"

"May I explain?" Jonathan asked, leaning forward and raising his voice to a loud whisper. "This original photograph shows the *USS Meecham* entering the port of Portsmouth, in the United Kingdom, during the same time our dear Captain Tucker is trying to convince the court he was headed to Norway."

Peyton's eyes were as large as balls on a pool table.

"And we can get a signed affidavit from the photographer confirming its authenticity and timing. He is also ready to testify in person. The photograph is electronically time-stamped on the film itself, and we have a Royal Mail document corroborating our claim."

Judge Breaux was silent for an agonizing thirty seconds, but his eyes intently examined the photograph. *He must be equally shocked*, Jonathan thought. As a judge and former Marine, Breaux didn't tolerate dishonesty. For Jonathan, this case would live or die by Breaux's next words.

The judge handed the photograph back to Jonathan and said, "I don't like this."

Peyton's patently offensive smirk returned to his face, as he seemed to think the judge would side with him.

Jonathan knew better.

"I'll allow it, if done properly," the judge said. "Proceed."

"But Your Honor . . ." said Peyton. "We have no way to verify this. This is grossly unfair."

"You'll have your chance to challenge the assertion later," the judge said and then turned to Jonathan. "Will plaintiff produce the witness this week?"

"That's our intent," replied Jonathan. "Friday, I think." Jonathan knew that was a stretch. He hadn't yet gotten a definite answer from Higginbotham, let alone from the photographer. But it was imperative that he nail the captain to the wall, while he still could.

Peyton flung a poorly camouflaged look of disdain at his opponent before he returned to his table.

Jonathan was now free to unleash his inquisition. After describing the photograph for the record and circulating the copy to the jury, he again held it in front of the captain and asked, "Do you recognize this ship?"

"The *USS Meecham*."

"And when was this taken?"

"No clue," Captain Tucker said without even looking at the photo.

Jonathan held it even closer to the man's face. "It has the time-stamp on it. What date does it show?"

"March 21, but I can't be sure."

Judge Breaux immediately butted in, telling the witness only to answer the question, not comment on whether or not the time-stamp was accurate. And he struck the captain's words from the record.

"And where was this picture taken?"

"I don't know."

Jonathan was coming in for the kill. "Do you know that this picture was taken in Portsmouth harbor, on England's southern coast?"

"No." The captain began raising his voice. "I can't tell by looking at it."

"Taken on the 21st of March. And what is your vessel towing? Is that some sort of barge?"

"Look at the picture before you answer, Captain," the judge said in a bellicose tone. "May I remind you, you are under oath."

Jonathan held it in front of the witness for a few more seconds and then walked past the jury box as he returned to the podium. He felt an electrifying charge of confidence run through his body, almost enough to make him levitate. The witness was on the defensive, his testimony about to be torn to shreds—a man in uniform on the verge of being branded a liar.

His eyes not leaving the jury, Jonathan asked, "Captain, isn't that a barge you are towing as you entered Portsmouth harbor? Isn't that what collided with the *Cajun Star*? And isn't that why your ship shows no signs of damage?"

"Objection, objection, objection!" Peyton stood up with his arms wide to his side. "He's badgering the witness."

The judge shook his head, but it was anybody's guess what he was really thinking.

*Another sanction, perhaps?* Jonathan mused.

"Mr. Brooks, one question at a time, please."

The captain's neck had turned blotchy. Jonathan was

eager for the *coup de grace*.

"Captain, is your vessel towing a barge in this photograph?"

After a long pause, the captain answered, "Yes."

"Have you previously testified about a barge?"

"No, but I wasn't asked."

Jonathan was pleased with his answer. At best it would make the captain appear like a smart ass; at worst, it was an admission of guilt of devastating proportions. But the best was yet to come.

"Please read to the jury the time-stamp exactly as it appears on the photograph."

"17:34, March 21, 1989."

Luckily for Jonathan, the captain was not as quick on his feet. Jonathan had feared that in his defense he would have argued that the photograph time-stamp was off by a week, since the vessel had indeed been in Portsmouth harbor before sailing to the North Sea and colliding with the *Cajun Star*. Peyton would surely bring that up later, in redirect. But for now, the damage was done, and Jonathan gave Gary a wink.

Allen then handed Jonathan a few pages of testimony from the previous week. The judge allowed the witness to read from it.

The perfect posture the captain had kept throughout the trial had vanished. He was slouched forward, shifting his legs every few seconds.

Prompted by Jonathan, Captain Tucker read from the transcript. "On March 21, 1989, we were headed north about sixty-five nautical miles off the Scottish coast." The captain read his own words as if he were ingesting arsenic. "We were headed 020 toward Norway."

"Don't you mean *no way*?" Jonathan asked off the cuff as he neared the first row of jurors.

The jury erupted in laughter. If they had gotten the joke, they had surely grasped the captain's lies.

*Slam dunk.*

Jonathan laughed as well, as he imagined how spectacular the saying "No Way to Norway" would sound in his closing arguments to the jury, perhaps even rivaling the legendary "if it doesn't fit, you must acquit."

Jonathan slowly strolled back to the podium, feeling lighter than air.

"Captain, you've said it yourself in this courtroom: you can't be in two places at the same time. So, were you near Portsmouth at that moment, or, as you've claimed, hundred of miles north sailing to Norway?"

Jonathan glanced at Peyton, who was looking down at his notes, his hand covering his forehead.

"We were at sea."

"Meaning?"

"We were headed to Norway."

Jonathan knew that the captain wanted to evade the answer as best he could. Perjury would not help his career. Granted, a legal scholar would probably agree that sailing to a British port for less than a day could still be deemed heading toward some place else. But juries aren't scholars. For laymen, a quibbler is a liar. And a liar in uniform is as good as hung.

"There is *no way* you could be headed for Norway," Jonathan said with a grin, "if at the time you were pulling into the harbor at Portsmouth, isn't that so?"

"All I can say is that we were at sea."

Jonathan held the photograph in the air and gazed at the jury. "Wouldn't you agree, Captain, that seeing is believing?"

Not surprisingly, Peyton objected, and the judge sustained it. But Jonathan's shot across the bow had devastated the defense. And to really rub it in, he went through the motions of introducing into evidence the Royal Mail dispatch, showing that mail destined to the *Meecham's* crew had been diverted to Portsmouth.

Jonathan re-examined the photograph, focusing again on the barge. Only part of it was visible, the rest cut off from the print. It appeared like any other barge, not much higher than a dozen feet above the waterline. But it was carrying something. Jonathan held it at a different angle, avoiding the glare from the lights above. A large tarp covered part of the barge's cargo. But the judge didn't give him more time. He had to move on with his questions. And he did. Questions about the barge: where the captain had picked it up, what cargo it was carrying and loads of other questions, each one prompting the captain to answer "I don't recall." It was the officer's best possible tactic, as pleading the Fifth was not an option in a civil trial. His credibility was shattered beyond repair.

Finally, Jonathan was done. He'd get no more from this man, not now anyway. "Your Honor, at the moment we have no more questions for the captain, but we wish to retain his availability in the week ahead so that—"

"Granted," said the judge before Jonathan could finish.

Jonathan took a close look at the jury. They appeared attentive. He hoped they would now give the testimony of Captain Glengeyer a hell of a lot more weight.

But Judge Breaux looked troubled. After announcing a thirty-minute recess, he turned his eyes to Jonathan's table. "I want to see counsel in my chambers right now. And you too, Mr. Peyton."

# 5

WAITING OUTSIDE THE JUDGE'S CHAMBER FELT A LITTLE like being sent to the principal's office. Peyton showed up a few seconds after Gary and Jonathan had entered the waiting room.

Jonathan had no clue what Breaux wanted, and now that he was on a roll, he didn't appreciate the recess. He was eager to see if the defense would rest, since Captain Tucker was their last witness. This would give Jonathan a chance to bring Glengeyer back on the stand.

The judge's assistant answered her phone and quickly got up and crowed her head into the demon's office.

"Let'em in," Jonathan heard the judge say. The assistant ushered the lawyers in.

Judge Breaux was standing behind his leather chair. It was a fairly large room but had very little floor space because of the crowded furniture. Bookcases lined every wall, and three stuffed chairs and a small couch encircled the judge's cluttered desk.

"Gentlemen, please sit. Let me cut to the chase. I want the ship's logbook and radar return data delivered to my office in the next forty-eight hours." He then gazed at Peyton, nudging his reading glasses farther down his nose and asked, "Are you prepared to comply?"

With an irritable scowl, Peyton leaned back in his chair. "Your Honor. First, that's short notice. Second, I believe the current redacted version is sufficient for—"

"Save it, Counselor. I think you should use your efforts at making sure your witness, Captain Tucker, is able to tell fact from fiction in my courtroom."

Peyton looked like a man seated on a bed of nails.

"I will conduct an *in camera*, *ex parte* review of the logbook and radar data," said the judge. "And it's your responsibility to get the cooperation of the Department of the Navy."

Peyton's shoulders seemed to melt into his chest. "Would you be so kind as to allow counsel Tillerman to conference into this meeting?"

"Dial nine," Judge Breaux said gruffly, pointing at the phone at the edge of his desk.

Peyton's fingers trembled a bit as he dialed. Things were definitely going to heat up. Peyton had misdialed. He tried again and this time managed to reach Tillerman, informing him of the judge's demand for the original records, and telling him plaintiff's counsel were in the room.

Tillerman's hollow voice echoed from the speakerphone. "Good morning, Judge, counselors."

The judge leaned back. "I want the originals."

"Your Honor," Tillerman said, "with all due respect, you must first allow us to provide a new declaration or affidavit in response to your demand, as we've done before."

Jonathan quickly chimed in to back the judge. "The Navy's initial declaration, the one filed late last year, covered the contents of the logbook, and after Your Honor's hearings on this issue, the Court ordered the redacted version, which we've shown today are falsified documents. Our client is now entitled to review the originals. We are prejudiced by any further delay. There's something there that would clearly benefit us, and they don't want us to find it. It's all very fishy."

"The conduct of the witness and the Navy is sanctionable as well," Gary added.

"The declaration was submitted for different purposes and referenced the logbook in a different light," Peyton argued. "This is an entirely new request."

"What I heard in testimony only minutes ago shows me the information is *false*," Judge Breaux said brashly, scratching his chin. "And remind me what the classification is for the logbook itself."

"Your Honor, the files are Top Secret, Sensitive Compartmented Information, with a codeword that I am not privy to," Tillerman answered.

"And the radar data?"

"Secret."

"Uh-huh, that's what I thought," the judge said, sliding his chair back and slowly getting to his feet. "I've made my decision. I want those materials in my possession no later than four P.M. on Thursday."

"Then I have no choice but to file an interlocutory appeal," Peyton declared sulkily.

Jonathan wasn't too worried. He knew it was a long shot for the Fifth Circuit Court of Appeals to put the brakes on the trial and deny the judge's request.

"That's entirely your choice," said the judge. "But for now, my order stands."

Tillerman mumbled something inaudible, but then cleared his throat and added, "Your Honor, in accordance with security requirements, classified Sensitive Compartmented Information may only be stored in a certified SCI Facility, and I don't believe your court is such a facility."

Jonathan knew he had a point. Documents of that nature had to stay in secured locations. All he wanted was for the judge to see the originals. He couldn't have cared less where they would be kept. It was simply another delay tactic.

"I don't care much for logistics," Judge Breaux replied in a fatigued tone. "Just provide the documents on time. Forty-eight hours."

Peyton shook his head and stood up.

*       *       *

THE quietest lawyers are those who have just lost a battle. Peyton sunk into the far corner of the elevator, avoiding eye contact with Jonathan and Gary, silently choking on the ashes of what remained of his ego.

Jonathan had won a significant victory and had at the same time embarrassed the defense. But he had to plant his dagger in a little deeper into the lanky man. As the lawyers left the elevator in the lobby, Jonathan turned to Peyton. "The truth *will* come out."

Peyton stopped and craned his neck forward, his face only inches away from Jonathan. "I wouldn't be too brazen, if I were you. You're playing with fire. There are some on my side of the aisle who scare the living daylights out of me. I'll be glad when this case is over." He turned and walked off.

Jonathan's feet froze to the floor. He felt a cold sweat crawl over his chest. He had expected a smug response, or none at all, but not this kind of answer. It didn't seem like Peyton was trying to frighten him, but rather warn him.

Gary leaned into his colleague and said in a sage voice, "Maybe he didn't know."

"What?"

"Perhaps the Navy didn't tell him the truth. That Tillerman fella may be pulling more strings than we think."

Jonathan watched Peyton pass through the glass doors. He replayed his adversary's disquieting remark over and over again. He realized later that he should have pressed Peyton right then and there about what he had meant. It was Jonathan's first grave mistake.

*             *             *

WEDNESDAY morning at the office had started with a message on Jonathan's voice mail. It was welcome news. A clerk for Judge Breaux informed him that the judge had received a hastily prepared declaration from Navy counsel regarding the secret documents, had reviewed it and stood by his decision to see the original unredacted logbook and radar data. The government had attempted but failed to reassert a secrecy privilege, a legal tool that if approved by the court would block access to all documents falling within its scope.

This was followed moments later by a call from Peyton. He was brief and frosty. "We're filing an inter-locutory appeal with the Fifth Circuit today to halt the court's request."

Clearly, Peyton and his JAG cohort were going to fight this out to the bitter end. To Jonathan, the defense's actions were indicative of some wrongdoing, something he was now determined to uncover.

Jonathan was called into the firm's main conference room to review materials with Allen.

"What's all this?" Jonathan asked Allen, who had been there a while.

"Just research files," Allen replied. He had covered the conference table with stacks of trial documents.

"And that thing?" asked Jonathan as he gazed up at a poster-sized chart pinned to the wall. Names, dates and locations were scribbled in black marker ink, and vari-ous arrows connected some of them.

"Last known addresses of the sailors who served on the *USS Meecham* in 1989," Allen said. "I've located one hundred-sixty so far. Another two hundred or so to go."

Jonathan looked at Allen for a moment, guessing how much work he must have put into collecting the data—fifty hours over the last few weeks, perhaps. With little or no help from the Navy, he was sure.

Allen was a heavyset man in the making. Not quite obese, but heavier than chubby. Two things were as much a part of him as his pager: beignets and anything with Remoulade dressing. And whenever he sat down, got up, or did anything else that required more than a few bodily movements, he would sweat profusely. A pouring sweat, at times so abundant he would have to excuse himself to find the nearest roll of paper towels. But Jonathan had given up lecturing him on his diet. Allen was a good man who happened to have succumbed to the great culinary temptation that was New Orleans, and so, when he took a seat at the head of the table, his lungs wheezed an unhealthy cry for help. And his dress shirt was soaked, having labored on this assortment of documents for hours.

"How many are in Louisiana or in neighboring states?"

Allen sighed, wiped his brow with his handkerchief and opened a folder in front of him. "Looks like fifteen are in Louisiana, six in Mississippi and twenty-four in Texas."

"Good job," Jonathan said, realizing, however, that Judge Breaux had yet to change his mind on whether they would be allowed to subpoena former or current sailors under the command of Captain Tucker. Gary and Jonathan had so far failed to convince Breaux that this was necessary, but now that the court had seen the bold-faced lies from Peyton's witness, Allen's grueling research was more likely to be admissible.

Jonathan took a seat and opened the folder with the photograph of the *Meecham* in Portsmouth. He hadn't looked at it since he had impeached Captain Tucker in the courtroom. He gazed at it, examining every detail of the ship and the barge it had in tow. His eyes then migrated to a large tarp covering the barge and immediately saw something strange. He quickly headed to his office, dug into his desk, retrieved a magnifying glass and returned to the conference room, all the while feeling almost angry that he hadn't spotted it earlier. He passed the loupe over the photograph, over the ten-foot-high tarp that covered whatever was being carried in the barge.

"Allen," he said excitedly, "take a look at this."

His colleague, comfortably slouched in his chair, did not seem to immediately gather the urgency.

"Come, come," Jonathan insisted, staring at the photograph strongly enough to burn a hole through it.

As Allen leaned his head over the image, Jonathan tapped it hard with his index finger.

"I've already seen it," Allen said, still not getting it.

Jonathan passed his pen along the outline of the tarp and said, "What does this look like? This part of the tarp that rises here and then slopes down?" Allen took too long to answer. "The tail of an airplane! And look at this very small portion that's not covered. It's dark, gently rounded."

"You mean a plane's horizontal stabilizer."

"Whatever you call it," Jonathan blurted. "Isn't it? Don't you think? Huh?"

Allen took the magnifying glass and leaned his face in front of Jonathan. "I'd say . . . you're *right*."

Jonathan got to his feet. Something Allen had dug up

months ago now popped into this mind. "Find me that article from Sweden. Remember, the story about a plane that went down in the Baltic and a pilot was rescued?" He looked at Allen, whose body was leaning over the table with his pudgy hands pressed to a pale color under the stress of his weight.

"Sure," Allen said, suddenly galvanized into action. "I think it's in one of the folders over there."

It was. Allen plucked it out of a binder and gave it to his colleague. The newspaper article dated back to March 8, 1989. It was written in Swedish and was stapled to a translation they'd gotten soon after Allen had been given the document by Victory Lines' prior counsel in Germany. In less than two minutes, Jonathan had convinced himself that there was a link between an aircraft going down in the Baltic, the tail of a plane on the barge and the probable course of the *Meecham*. Jonathan had no idea what it meant, but it was an astounding coincidence—and worth examining with a fine tooth comb.

Allen gazed at Jonathan, perhaps waiting for some enlightened guidance.

Jonathan stared into the air for while and then said, "I need to go there."

"Where?"

"Sweden."

Allen tilted his head to the side. "A little impulsive, don't you think?"

"It would take me only a few days, and it could be well worth it."

"Try convincing Gary," Allen said, his face grimacing.

"I'll tell him when I'm on my way there," Jonathan replied, realizing Gary would ask too many questions, particularly now that Victory Lines was increasingly nerve-racked by the skyrocketing cost of the litigation. "I have a hunch, and I'm not letting go."

Allen shook his head but didn't say anything.

"In which paper was this published?" asked Jonathan.

"A newspaper in Visby, Gotland—an island off the coast of Sweden."

"Ok, I'm heading there as soon as possible. And while I'm at it, I'll stop over in D.C. to surprise Tillerman in-person."

"Why?"

"He's a liar, and I want to see that jackass face-to-face," said Jonathan. "Besides, there's something strange going on. I feel it. You remember me telling you about that car crash—the guy following me?"

Allen nodded.

"His car was registered to a contractor at Bolling Air Force Base, in Washington, D.C."

"And what does that mean?" Allen asked.

"Not sure," Jonathan said pensively. "My brother-in-law called me with this information a short time ago."

Jonathan left the room energized by his discovery. He quickly made arrangements to travel to Stockholm to dig up as much as he could on the air crash.

*       *       *

MULTITASKING was never Jonathan's favorite part about practicing law. It was a life interrupted—constant interruption—combined with a requirement to know as much as possible about any given case at any moment and for any reason, important or not. He was engaged in a profession that demanded endless juggling acts with cases, some small, some large, many dull, most demanding a high level of attention necessary to retain client satisfaction and not instigate a malpractice claim. The Victory Lines matter was not the only litigation on his plate. It was one of many, and almost every moment at the office was devoted to tedious multitasking.

For Jonathan, the demands of his career came as no surprise. Growing up, he had seen the strain in his father's eyes. It had become the norm for him as well as he followed in his father's path. Normally, he felt it was a small price to pay to be able to do the work he loved. But for no apparent reason, while at his desk, his office door closed, he thought of Linda and questioned if it was all worth it—if being a lawyer was sufficient reason to give up so many hours with her, with her family, with their friends, with oneself. A life forfeited by interruption and distraction.

Jonathan drove home but couldn't shake off the disturbing question. He had never considered it before with such intense reflection. By the time he parked his car in the driveway, he had forced himself to let the question die unanswered, but it just wouldn't, no matter how hard he tried. It lingered as he entered the house and saw Linda on the couch, dressed in a pale blue suit with a glass of Chablis in her hand.

She had that look she always had at seven, her mind elsewhere—a customary early evening downtime before heading to the station for the nightly broadcast. This was the only time she enjoyed spending alone. A time in her day that was entirely hers, and Jonathan never dared disturb her moment of tranquil reflection, taking her satisfied world into a surreal suspension.

*I love this woman*, he told himself as he gazed at her from the foyer.

She smiled up at him, serene and peaceful, and pointed to the second glass next to the wine bucket.

Jonathan's question lingered in his mind, but he was not going to pester her with it. He suspected the thought had materialized as a by-product of his exhaustion, rather than a lucidly gathered one.

"You look stressed," said Linda, her head tilting to one side.

"I'm fine, honey," he replied. "I don't want to bug you." Jonathan had *de rigeur* always thought himself as skilled at camouflaging any tension in his trial work. But Linda was an equally skillful observer.

"Tell me," she insisted, her welcoming smile pushing him to be more open. "What's wrong?"

"I'm just struggling to line up new evidence in the Victory Lines trial."

"Something new?" she quizzed, resting her wine glass on the coffee table.

Jonathan told her about the battle that had gripped the court earlier in the day. He explained his victorious cross-examination that left Peyton and his star witness tongue-tied and begging for a hole to crawl into and perish.

Linda was intrigued. "Sit with me."

"I'm also trying to get other Navy crewmen to testify, but it's not easy tracking them down. Many are retired. Some are in Louisiana, and some in New Orleans, I'm guessing."

"How badly do you need them?"

Jonathan nodded. "Like I need a drink."

"Have some," Linda said, raising her glass to him. "Maybe you need some help."

Jonathan gazed at her but said nothing. He'd later realize what her comment meant, and how foolish he had been to have overlooked its significance.

"I know I've asked you this once," Linda said. "But has it been hard for you to work on that case, knowing the incident happened around the time of Matt's death?"

She had asked that when Jonathan first joined the Victory Lines case, and he remembered that the coincidence with his brother's accidental death was somewhat trying in that it was yet another reminder of those dark days. "I'm fine with it now, I guess. I think of Matt a lot, regardless. I miss him."

"I know," Linda said.

"I love you," Jonathan said, wanting to change the subject and contemplating again the question he had asked himself earlier. He gazed into her eyes.

"You're acting a little odd," she said as her hand gently caressed his hair. "What is it? It's not only the trial, is it?" she asked with an inquisitive frown.

"No," replied Jonathan as he took her hand into his and leaned into the couch. "I don't know if we're spending enough time together." His mind spoke without his logic intervening. "You know, with your work and all.

And with mine. I feel like our lives are shackled to our Outlook calendars." But he suddenly began feeling silly about having brought it up. Jonathan respected her career, not because lawyers like media people, but because she was a woman who had stolen his heart nineteen years earlier. The passage of time had instilled an immense respect and devotion since their days as high school sweethearts, and throughout their marriage of nine years. "I'm sorry," Jonathan mumbled and shrugged his shoulders. "I don't want to sound—"

"If you want me to give up the nightly news, I would do that," said Linda without an ounce of hesitation in her words, as if it had been negotiated long ago and all that remained was a formal request from Jonathan.

He was stunned. He had never imagined asking her to do such a thing. She was her own person, a local icon, a pillar of strength who had always valued her commitment to professionalism, not unlike Jonathan. And neither had ever floated the idea of asking the other to give up anything of the sort. He was embarrassed but also excited. It was a question he had never dared think, nor ask, but he adored her answer.

"You would do that?" Jonathan asked, his thoughts suddenly bouncing wildly with the idea of mutually giving up everything—his law partnership, her anchor work—and blindly going off to unknown horizons with a lot less money but far more time to stay around in each other's company.

"Yes, darling, I would," she said, Jonathan now convinced that her words had not left her mouth lightly. It was in the way she looked at him. She didn't blink. She had put away her smile for that statement, a gentle seriousness he had often seen but in other contexts. And even after so many years, it comforted him to hear her declaration of devotion to their relationship, to him.

He approached her slender face and gently kissed her supple lips. He ran his hand along her neck, cheek, temple and through her soft hair. They kissed again, and again. Their tongues touched. Her breaths moved more air. Jonathan unbuttoned her blouse. Her breasts were warm to his delicate caress. Her nipples were hard and he pressed his mouth on one and then the other.

"Would *you*?" asked Linda between breaths. "Would you give up something as equally important to you, if I asked?"

A lawyer, like an animal, always guards one's instinct of preservation, a permanency about one's self-worth, one's attachment to what is familiar. And Jonathan felt that intimacy with destiny collide with that little thought that had bothered him since this afternoon. And he did not know how to answer. His love demanded fairness, that what she had offered needed reciprocation. *I must be fair*, he told himself, while expunging the notion that he would ever go through with giving it all up. He kissed her neck and unzipped her skirt. "Of course I would."

Jonathan's hands slid along her thighs. He kissed her with all the passion a man could have for a woman he loved and marveled at her extraordinary beauty, both on the surface and in depth. As he slowly removed her nylons, their mouths locked again in heated motion. Her skin perspired just enough to tell him the surrender was entirely mutual. His fingers explored inside her. They began to reach for each other. They bumped into the table, the wine glasses falling to the carpet as the couch slid across the floor. He put himself inside her, and nothing else in the world mattered. Not the Victory Lines case. Not another God- or man-made thing. Nothing but Linda.

# 6

THE RIDE ACROSS THE POTOMAC FROM NATIONAL AIRPORT
to the Washington Navy Yard took less than fifteen minutes. Jonathan checked his briefcase, making certain
which documents he had at his disposal should the meeting with Tillerman become as challenging as he feared.

He pulled up in his rental car to the security gate on
Dahlgren Avenue and asked the Navy guard on duty to
contact Tillerman's office.

"Your name?"

"Brooks, Jonathan Brooks."

Jonathan had no clue how Tillerman would react to
an unannounced visit on his turf. They had only agreed
to a conference call for nine o'clock, and it was ten till.
That didn't mean he would accept to meet in person, but
for Jonathan, a face-to-face offered a better chance to get
things moving in the case. It was also an opportunity to
gauge Tillerman, a seemingly worthy opponent who had
yet to set foot in the New Orleans courthouse.

The guard closed his window to make the call. He dialed, waited, and then spoke. The man then raised his brow and glared in Jonathan's direction. Judging from the guard's frown, Tillerman was probably laying into him.

He then hung up, opened the window, and said, "Sir, you'll have to park in that lot over there and walk the rest of the way. And please wear this pass on your jacket." He gave Jonathan directions to Tillerman's building on Patterson Avenue.

Jonathan was exhilarated, though he anticipated Tillerman's displeasure.

The six-story office building was two blocks away, squeezed between a large parking garage and a brick edifice. It was the seat of the Office of the Judge Advocate General's Admiralty and Maritime Law Division, one of the largest such practices in the world, with hundreds of lawyers representing not only the Department of the Navy, but its various divisions, its fleets, bases and installations worldwide, as well as the Marine Corps.

Tillerman had solid credentials and was fairly high up the totem pole in the Division's litigation practice, which for the most part worked closely with lawyers from the Department of Justice. And many in the division were, like Tillerman, not naval officers, but rather attorneys with prior practices in prominent law firms.

Once out of the elevators, Jonathan made his way to suite 3043, apparently Tillerman's office. As soon as he opened the door, he was greeted by an assistant, a petite woman in a dark navy uniform, her hair frizzy and her smile non-existent. "Mr. Tillerman will be delayed, sir," she said with a snippy voice. "He's had an unexpected call, which may take some time."

So Jonathan waited. And waited. It would have been nice if she had offered coffee or water, especially after Jonathan had spent nearly forty minutes waiting in an ergonomically inhospitable wooden chair in the corner of the stuffy room. Jonathan realized Tillerman was probably yanking his chain. But it did not matter. Jonathan was there, in the flesh, to survey the enemy and raise hell if needed.

The phone rang at the woman's desk. She answered and glanced at Jonathan. "He will see you now," she said coolly and then pointed to the door, as if Jonathan had not read Tillerman's name etched on it in four-inch letters. She then resumed her paper shuffling.

"Is this the way your firm conducts telephone conferences?" were the first words out of Tillerman's mouth.

"No, but this isn't a normal case, is it?" Jonathan replied as they shook hands. He sat in a chair facing Tillerman's oversized desk.

"I took the liberty of calling someone in for our talk," the Navy lawyer told Jonathan. "He should be here momentarily."

Jonathan didn't like the sound of that and asked, "Who?"

"I'll let him introduce himself. I suggest we work hard to reach some sort of agreement. He will not agree to give you additional sensitive documents, but perhaps there are other things that could put you at ease in this case. But he's not the kind of person who plays games, and he's no push-over in this town. And neither am I."

"Well, then we're all alike," Jonathan said, mockingly. "Three stubborn advocates standing on a pile of false evidence." He had no intention of letting Tillerman get any kind of upper hand, and certainly not when it came to chest-thumping. It was then that a fleeting thought made him smirk: the way lawyers posture. He'd seen every insult and arrogant gesture in the book, and what he had seen in the last few seconds was one of the better examples of archaic, pointless, shallow and hysterical bravado that educated men should know to avoid.

"For us," Tillerman began, his head tilting back on his chair, "your little case is an annoying and useless expenditure of taxpayer money. And if you believe there had really been a collision, you should have sued the Navy when you had a chance."

"What our clients and their prior lawyers did or didn't do back then is irrelevant now. I'm here to talk about fabricated evidence and witness tampering."

As Tillerman was about to say something else, probably just as pointless as his earlier comment, his secretary knocked and peered in. "Sir, Vice-Admiral Scar—"

"Yes, yes, I'll be right there," Tillerman snarled, interrupting her. He stood up, gave Jonathan a condescending glance and quickly left the room.

Jonathan surveyed their silhouettes through the frosted glass. Tillerman seemed agitated, but there was no sense in reading into it. Perhaps he was just the cocky jerk that he appeared to be from the first day Jonathan had spoken with him by phone some months ago.

An entire minute passed, and then the two men strolled in.

"Good morning, I'm Vice-Admiral Scarborough, Defense Intelligence Agency," said the man walking ahead of Tillerman. He was a brawny guy, in his fifties, his face tanned and heavily wrinkled around the eyes. He wore a spotless dark Navy uniform with rows of patches sewn across the left side of his jacket, no doubt portraying an illustrious career.

"Pleased to meet you," Jonathan said. He shook the vice-admiral's hand and returned to his seat, attempting to appear unfazed by his presence. But underneath his calm demeanor, Jonathan was quite troubled. He could not understand why someone from the DIA would have anything to do with this case. It didn't make sense from the mountain of evidence Jonathan had gathered since pre-trial proceedings began. Jonathan was familiar with the DIA only because it was headquartered at the nearby Bolling Air Force Base, where his brother Matt had once served as a translator with the 11th Wing before being transferred to the Pentagon.

The vice-admiral took a seat next to Jonathan and crossed his arms.

Jonathan told himself to start things off with a bang. "Gentlemen, perhaps this is a good opportunity to restate the obvious dilemma in this case. The evidence points to a deliberate attempt on the part of the Navy to conceal the actual course of the *USS Meecham* during the period in question. This is a huge problem for us, for the court, . . . and certainly for the jury."

"Now listen here," the vice-admiral said with an icy

stare. He turned his chair a bit more toward Jonathan and cocked his head back. "I don't give a damn about your claims against the defendant insurer. From my standpoint, you can bleed them dry to your heart's content. But what I care about most, and where you'll have nothing to gain in fighting us, is to venture into matters that have nothing to do with your client and everything to do with keeping our nation safe, which is what I do every single day, along with many brave men and women. I will not compromise on that. Am I clear?"

Jonathan wasn't falling for this crap. "Let me get this straight, Vice-Admiral. A Navy ship rams my client's vessel, killing a sailor. Then the Department of the Navy submits false records to a federal court. Captain Tucker, perhaps with some nudging from higher ranks, lies in depositions, lies on the stand, and falsifies logbook entries in an attempt to conceal the whereabouts of his ship. Now, you're telling me this kind of rogue conduct makes our nation safer? That's hogwash."

"You're making some pretty serious accusations." Scarborough perched himself on the edge of his chair and gazed sternly into Jonathan's eyes. "Don't play with fire, Mr. Brooks."

"You're being awfully cavalier with your use of our court system, and it's clear you've got something to hide."

Scarborough's face turned a bright shade of red—redder than Santa's ass.

Jonathan wasn't done. "And why was someone from Bolling Air Force Base following me?"

"Don't be ridiculous," Tillerman said, his eyes not

even aimed at Jonathan. "We have better things to do with our time."

"Maybe you need to check on him, a certain Anthony Gordon," said Jonathan, sitting back in his chair. "He won't be reporting for duty."

"We don't have all day to move this case along," said Scarborough, glancing at his Navy colleague. He seemed to be recalculating whatever he had planned to throw Jonathan's way.

Jonathan stood up. He knew he was not going to get anything more out of them. Besides, what Jonathan had really wanted from this visit was to see Tillerman in the flesh, to gauge his eyes. And now he suspected that Peyton and Tillerman were puppets of a far more powerful person. He looked sternly at the vice-admiral. "I'm headed to Europe in a few hours and before I leave I want your answer as to why the evidence has been tampered with. Here is my card, my cell phone number is on there. If I don't hear from you, then all hell will break loose."

Neither the vice-admiral nor Tillerman said a word. It was as if Jonathan had said nothing. Tillerman swayed gently in his chair, his fingers shuffling through a stack of papers. Scarborough crossed his legs and sighed again.

After more than a minute of silence, Scarborough finally spoke up. He cleared his throat and said, "If we go along with your allegations that the *Meecham* was in fact the proximate cause of your vessel's damages, and the crewman's death, will you cease to pursue this matter as it concerns the Navy or any other government agency and simply settle with the insurance company?"

Jonathan caught Tillerman's expression as the vice-admiral was in mid-sentence. Tillerman appeared astonished—even appalled—at Scarborough's semblance of compromise. Perhaps they weren't on the same page. Jonathan now was convinced Tillerman didn't know everything, and that someone—possibly at the DIA— was playing him like a fiddle. Jonathan couldn't be sure. Tillerman and Scarborough were one and the same: liars.

Jonathan was tempted to agree. *Gary would be delighted*, he thought. The Navy's admission would surely force the insurance company to settle and his client would be vindicated. But Jonathan couldn't accept. The fact that such an enormous lie had been concocted showed him something far more sinister could be at play. It was a question of principal.

"You'd better explain what really happened that night in question, because I'm going to the depths of the earth to uncover what you're hiding." Jonathan, however, realized they had little reason to admit anything at this point. Tillerman would risk contempt of court charges, or worse, disbarment for tampering with evidence. The vice-admiral, too, risked his career if he was involved in some cover-up.

"Then I retract my earlier offer," Scarborough said as he slammed his fist onto Tillerman's desk. "If it's war you want; war you shall get. You will pay a price for your stubbornness, Mr. Brooks."

Jonathan picked up his briefcase and headed to the door. "I simply want the truth, gentlemen. My client deserves it, as does the family of the dead crewman."

"Gary decides at your firm, not you," Tillerman quipped. "We'll only deal with him from now on."

Jonathan responded only by shaking his head.

"You're wasting your time going to Sweden," were the last words Scarborough said as Jonathan left the room.

Jonathan was all too pleased to be leaving the lying duo. But by the time he reached the elevator, his heart just about stopped. He suddenly realized he had never told Scarborough that he was headed to Sweden, but only to Europe.

"*Jesus* . . ." Jonathan whispered to himself as the realization sank in deeper. Obviously, Scarborough knew about his airline reservation. Jonathan's fighting instinct egged him to return to Tillerman's office and confront the vice-admiral head on. He thought hard during the elevator ride down. *Bastard.*

By the time he reached the ground floor, the adrenaline was flowing like a river. But he didn't want to fumble. And fumble he might if he headed back upstairs. The vice-admiral was capable of much more than threatening words. He had power, knew more about the case than he let on, and didn't appear to be the kind of man who either loved lawyers or the rule of law.

Jonathan strolled to the exit. By then he had convinced himself Scarborough had not accidentally uttered those words. He wanted Jonathan to feel the crosshairs crawling over him. It was disturbing. Frightening even.

Walking toward the parking lot, Jonathan's heart pounded in his chest. He felt an imminent danger. And it was no trivial feeling for a man who had grown up in

New Orleans, a city where rich, middle-class and poor neighborhoods are adjacent to one another, which trains you to be vigilant and wise about spotting trouble.

An eerie feeling lingered as Jonathan drove away from the naval base. He crossed the Potomac once more, but this time headed to Dulles airport, a thirty minute ride northwest of the city.

About half-way to the airport along I-66, he glanced in the rearview mirror and saw a large, white sedan speeding along the left lane of the divided highway. It was traveling at over eighty miles per hour, he guessed. There were two people in the front seat. He continued to glance back as the car gained momentum and then suddenly he spotted the person in the passenger side hold what looked like a pistol with a long barrel.

*A gun! . . . A silencer!*

He tightened his grip on the steering wheel and held his breath. The white car was flying up the highway and had pulled up behind Jonathan's rental Oldsmobile. Before Jonathan could spark another thought, the armed passenger had rolled down the window and pointed the weapon in Jonathan's direction. Jonathan craned his neck over his shoulder to see the threat directly, as if the mirror might have been lying. It hadn't. The car was about to pass Jonathan's when it suddenly decelerated to match his speed.

As Jonathan slammed on his brake pedal, his side window suddenly shattered into tiny pieces. The glass sprayed over this body and across the dashboard.

*Jesus!* he exclaimed as he frantically swept the glass pebbles off his face with one hand.

The other car also braked, its tires venting thick white smoke, but it had overshot Jonathan's compact by two car lengths. Jonathan swerved into the left lane, behind his pursuers, just as they sliced across his path into the right lane. In the rapid crisscross, Jonathan unintentionally tapped the rear bumper of the attacking vehicle, causing it to slide left. It slid further, and the car lost its rear traction. The car spun right, the loud sounds of shredding rubber tearing through the air.

Jonathan quickly swerved to avoid hitting the car again. He narrowly missed it as the front end spun past him. He glanced over his shoulder, his eyes never leaving the other car. The assailants who had nearly ended his life a split-second ago spun out of control into the grassy median. Their car began rolling. Two of the doors instantly flew open, ejecting one man into the air as it twisted violently into a huge ball of metal, asphalt and soil. Jonathan kept going and stared at the rearview mirror at the wreckage as it came to a standstill in a cloud of dirt.

Jonathan sped up. "Holy crap," he uttered, now thinking only of getting the hell out of Dodge. Fortunately, there had not been another car nearby, and no witnesses to jot down his license plate. His heart was racing.

A couple miles before reaching the airport, he exited the highway to clean most of the glass off the floor. The bullet had come close, finding its resting spot in one of the center console's adjustable vents.

He drove to the Hertz lot and told the attendant the window was broken and that it had not worked after he'd rolled it down. Jonathan quickly headed to the terminal, assured that by the time the rental car staff noticed that the window was not there at all, he would be comfortably seated in his plane.

Jonathan had been lucky. He had made it safely to the plane, albeit with only two minutes to spare, but an overwhelming sense of confusion, fear and disbelief haunted him as he waited for the airplane to leave the gate. He was convinced Tillerman and Scarborough were behind this attempt on his life. Before boarding, he had tried to reach Gary, but all he could do was leave a quick message on Gary's voice mail, telling him about the incident and warning him that anyone associated with the case was in mortal danger. The long flight to Sweden would be filled with perplexing thoughts about his near-death experience. Nothing would be the same again.

*      *      *

NEWS anchor desks are the antithesis of a newsroom. They are spotless, brightly lit places where persons trained in the art of speaking flawlessly inform their communities of the good, the bad and the absurd.

But cameras never show the real newsroom, the loud, chaotic motor at the heart of Channel 6, where insults and bad English fly freely, where yelling is the norm and where almost everyone indulges in self-importance while also secretly harboring a desire to do something vastly more fruitful with their lives.

"Five minutes to airtime," yelled a woman somewhere behind Linda, who was waiting for the last draft of a story to pop up on her screen, while at the same time concentrating on the plan she had concocted.

"Where the hell is Charles?" another loud voice rang out.

Linda laughed and turned to the evening weather anchor next to her and said, "You know there's a problem when the makeup guy can't be found and our co-anchors are bald and old."

Seth shook his head and grinned. They were the only two on the Ten O'clock News team who weren't.

"So, you want to hear my segue for tonight?" he asked, as he did every night.

"Let me guess . . .," Linda said, turning her head sideways and holding back giggles. "Given that the last news bit will be about that two-headed snake found in the back of a taxi, I'd imagine you could be quite inventive."

"Uh-oh, is that the last piece?" he asked worriedly. "I thought it was the story about that truck towing the double-wide trailer under a bridge and ripping the roof off."

"Nope, it got tossed."

"Damn, I had the perfect line . . . *And tonight you won't need a roof over your head either, since the weather will be clear.*"

"Gag!" Linda said, shaking her head. "Thank God we won't have to hear that one."

"I can still do a lot to segue from the two-headed snake."

"Three minutes!" the same woman yelled.

"You're outta time," Linda replied, hoping he would simply drop the segue, if just for tonight.

Linda leaned left and glanced past her monitor at the assignment desk—the command post—where the loudest person in the station stood, his elbows spread wide and his hands planted on his large waistline.

"Okay, let's hustle," he barked, and then turned to his attentive cadre of interns, who followed him like flies.

"Are we cleared for the Hammond baby-switching story?" Linda asked her newscast producer at the center of the octopus-like assembly of tables.

He returned a thumbs-up.

"Done," she uttered and hit the enter key, prompting her printer to spit out the last couple pages of the script, freshly uploaded from the copy editors, who were glued to their monitors ten feet away.

One last thing. She picked up the phone and dialed Tim, the all-around helper, whose most appreciated skill was to work the teleprompter, and to do it perfectly.

"You know it's not in there, right?" Linda asked him. "Remember what we talked about?"

"Sure, no problem," Tim replied. "I'll work around it."

Linda smiled. "You're my hero."

She stood up, yanked the pages from the printer and headed to the anchor desk at the far end of the room. As she took her seat, two staffers swarmed around her. One quickly attached her microphone and the other directed the cameramen to test each shot.

Linda inserted her earpiece and immediately began hearing three or four voices stepping over each other to form a chaotic chatter. Her producer was asking about the satellite feed. The director was telling her to leave

out the "T" when pronouncing the name of the convict-
ed murderer George Faggot. The associate director was
complaining about the lighting. And for some reason the
audio operator was humming an Elvis tune until another
voice yelled at him to stop.

But the showpiece of this evening came to Linda as
a complete surprise. Brett, her co-anchor, appeared out
of the dark perimeter of the stage in a mustard-colored
suit, with a bright red tie to boot. Under the bright lights,
and with his pasty skin and large bald head, he looked
like a giant french fry, with a touch of Catsup.

*Someone should yank his clothing allowance*, she
thought, before reminding herself that he was one of the
best in the business. A great voice, that is. A stocky man,
ten years her senior, he never hid his desire for her cov-
eted lead anchor position. *Not with that suit, you won't.*

Several more lights came to life. The director gave
the cue, the theme music echoed from the speakers overhead, and the little bulb above camera two glowed red.

"Good evening from the Channel 6 Newsroom,"
Linda began. She started with the grim news of the day:
a suicide at a downtown high-rise, the accidental elec-
trocution of a teen in the Ninth Ward and a liquor store
heist gone real bad. The first set of commercials passed,
as did her next segment, and the second commercial
break, and then her co-anchor introduced the fluffy news
of the day.

As she followed the teleprompter, she knew her cue
was coming up. Any second now. And, regardless of
what *el commandante* in the control room might think,
she was going off-script, come hell or high water.

The teleprompter stopped, as she had requested of Tim. The french fry basted under the lights, his deep voice carrying his story about a recovering one-legged pelican as if it would profoundly influence the lives of the station's two-hundred-thousand viewers.

She gazed at him as one would at a circus act turned dull. She skipped her segue to give herself more time. A ninety-second window was all she had, and every word lined up at the tip of her tongue.

"It's not every day when a commercial case in Federal District Court downtown draws the attention of the media," she said, turning away from Brett to face camera four.

"What's going on . . ." someone said loudly into her earpiece.

She ignored it. "But over the past couple of days, the case of *Victory Lines v. Sentinel Insurance Group* has exploded into a bizarre mystery fit for the movies. In testimony over whether there was a collision between a New Orleans-based freighter and a U.S. Navy vessel, the captain of the military vessel lied under oath. And he was caught."

A screaming match erupted in Linda's earpiece. The boys in the control room had a rogue anchor in their midst. She had done it before—once. Today, she reminded them she could do it again. *That'll teach them to turn down a story I find important*, she reasoned, relishing her audacious rule breaking.

"Attorneys for the shipping company are looking for your help," continued Linda, pulling her earpiece out as the tirade became unbearable. "If any of you viewers served in the Navy in March 1989 in the North Sea or Baltic Sea, please call us here at the station."

She glanced at Brett, and that's when she just couldn't resist something more. "We've asked the pelican, but he was in the Gulf at the time."

The weatherman was convulsing in laughter, as was the sports anchor, who had just taken his seat. The teleprompter kicked in. She smiled and the next *approved* story exited her lips as if nothing had happened. Such misbehavior. It was a perk of being the star anchor, though she'd still have to go through the motions of being scolded by the paper tigers.

*          *          *

JONATHAN took his place in line at Swedish passport control. He was tired, having changed planes in London, which made the trip seem even longer than he'd feared. But his greatest concern was for his safety. He wondered if his arrival in Stockholm would be as delightful as the drive-by near Dulles.

During the flight, Jonathan had questioned his decision to travel so far to inquire on a small newspaper article about a crash, given that he was nearly killed. He was tempted to take the next plane back and call the authorities. But something inside him persuaded him to follow his gut. If indeed Scarborough and Tillerman were behind the whole thing, they had felt compelled to try to stop him from going to Sweden. And if that was the case, he was surely onto something big.

At the terminal, he again tried to reach Gary. His secretary said he had gotten Jonathan's earlier message, but was in court and not reachable by cell phone.

"Is there a number he can call you at?" she asked.

"No, I'm still traveling. I'll try again later." Jonathan didn't want to tell her where he was headed. "Just tell Gary to ask Allen where I'm going." The message had to be cryptic, since he feared the phone lines were tapped.

Jonathan had planned to take a shuttle south to Stockholm's smaller airport, Bromma, and head from there to Gotland. But now he needed to cloak his path with anonymity. Fortunately, he had not booked a continuing flight to Gotland, so there was no way anyone would know of his intention to reach the island. He realized a ferry ride would offer him a more discreet mode of transportation, but he had to ensure no one at the airport would follow him to the dock. After claiming his luggage, Jonathan quickly headed to an information desk and asked about the ferry. It left from Nynäshamn, a town about a forty-five minute drive south of Stockholm. Scanning his surroundings with great care, he headed to a cab at the curb and asked to head into town. As the cab pulled away from the terminal, Jonathan eyed the traffic behind him. There were other cabs, a few private cars, a minivan, and a bus. A few minutes passed.

Jonathan continued to peer through the rear windshield. "Please use a smaller road for the rest of the way," he told the driver.

"Is there a problem?" asked the baffled driver, his English surprisingly good.

"Yes," replied Jonathan, focusing his sights on one car—a dark blue Jetta—some hundred yards back. As feared, it followed Jonathan's cab through the same highway exit.

"I don't want trouble," said the driver, lobbing a nervous look at his passenger from the rearview mirror.

Jonathan instantly felt his cab slow down a bit.

"Drive faster, please. There is someone following us," Jonathan said anxiously, and then to calm the man, he added, "It's not the police, trust me."

The driver looked over his shoulder and gave Jonathan a disturbing stare down.

"Please, can you lose them?" Jonathan asked. "I will pay you whatever you want—the largest tip you've ever had."

The man shook his head. "You better be telling the truth, sir." He picked up his radio mic and spoke to his dispatcher, her replies echoing from the speaker below the dash.

Jonathan was now deeply worried. The gap between the two cars was closing rapidly. He leaned forward and asked, "What are you—"

The driver quickly raised his hand to interrupt his passenger. He spoke again to the dispatcher and then looked at Jonathan through his rearview mirror. "I call the station and say for her to call police for drunk driver behind us."

Jonathan nodded and smiled. "Perfect."

The driver resumed a higher speed along the suburban road. Jonathan glanced periodically over his shoulder to gauge the Jetta's distance.

"There, you see," the driver suddenly said, excitedly slapping his steering wheel.

A police car approached from the opposite direction. It passed them, and not a moment later slammed on its brakes and made a U-turn. For a split second, Jonathan thought the driver had called the police to stop him instead of the Jetta. But a moment later, the police car pulled up behind the speeding Jetta, flashed its high-beams and turned on its blue gyro light. Jonathan's pursuers slowed to the side of the road and stopped.

"You like?" the driver asked, his wide grin taking up half the mirror's surface area.

"Yeah, excellent." A huge sense of relief oozed through Jonathan. "Now, take me to Nynäshamn. And please hurry, my boat leaves in one hour."

The *M/S Tjelvar* was a huge ferry, painted white, with a bright red smoke stack. It had everything: restaurants, a small movie theater and shops. But Jonathan sat the entire five-hour trip gazing out the window at a calm, unimpressive Baltic Sea. A dreary gray sky hovered above.

Jonathan smiled momentarily. He was lucky to have once more evaded his enemies—whoever they were. But a fear inside him brewed: he might not be so fortunate the next time.

Jonathan had skimmed through a tourist pamphlet of Gotland, getting the skinny on a place he had never heard of until a few months before trial, when Allen had blathered an exhaustive Geography 101 of northern Europe. The island, situated in the middle of the Baltic Sea, some fifty miles west of the Swedish mainland and eighty miles from the former Soviet Baltic States, was apparently a favorite holiday destination for mainland

Swedes—a bit like Pensacola or Biloxi for those from the Big Easy, Jonathan mused, only possibly not as warm.

Upon arriving in Visby, the island's largest town, Jonathan rented a car and headed northeast along Gotland's winding rural highway 148, past the quaint towns of Tingstäde and Lärbro. He then caught another ferry at Fårösund for a short ride to yet another island, Fårö, for the last leg of the journey to the tiny village of Hammars.

At the ferry dock, Jonathan asked an attendant for directions to the bed and breakfast he had been recommended in Visby. It was also the only guesthouse in the area. The man didn't speak a lick of English, but he knew where to point. It was a matter of two long turns through a wooded area before Jonathan reached the place, a spacious L-shaped row of a half-dozen pristine square cabins, most painted white, one peach, and all illuminated by several outdoor gaslights.

Jonathan drove up the dirt road to the circular driveway. A quick knock at the door prompted a stocky, elderly man to answer, greeting his guest in English with a docile Swedish accent.

"*Välkommen*. Welcome to Gotland and to Stora Gåsemora Gård. I'm Hark, the owner. You must be Mr. Brooks."

"*God dag*," Jonathan replied, using one of a handful of Swedish words he had picked up in the last twelve hours. "I'll be staying one night, perhaps two."

"Stay as long as you wish. This is off-season, so we're extra happy to see visitors." He then lowered his bifocals, and added, "I must apologize. There is no phone in your room. But you can always use this phone on the wall."

"No problem."

"I say this because I assume Americans want all the comforts possible."

"I just want a bed," Jonathan said with a hearty chuckle. "And maybe a stiff drink."

"Ah, I've got just the medicine for you. When you're all settled in, come back here for one of our local drinks that will put hair on that young face of yours, eh?"

"You bet."

Hark led Jonathan to the two-story peach-colored cabin. The second-floor apartment was a cozy nest, with a large bedroom, antique furnishings and a modern—if somewhat sterile—Scandinavian kitchen.

After freshening up a bit, he went down, armed with his thirst and a copy of the news article.

Judging from his glassy, red eyes and toxic breath, Hark had taken a shameless head start.

"I'll give you a choice," Hark said, lifting two bottles from behind the counter. "This one is my very own *Gotlandsdricke*—malt, brown sugar, hops, yeast, juniper twigs, only enough water to make it flow, made into a thick paste called *lännu* and then fermented. Don't mind the color, it's fairly safe—it's only brewed here. Illegal on the mainland."

"And the other," Jonathan asked of the bottle with a semblance of a label.

"*Brännvin*, local vodka made from corn and potatoes and flavored with more spices than you can imagine."

Vodka it was. Hark poured it into schnapps glasses.

After a touch of small talk and a few toasts of the wicked brew, Jonathan placed the article in front of Hark.

"Can you tell me more about this incident?" Jonathan asked. "I understand that a pilot was rescued by a fisherman from here."

"Huh? This was years ago," Hark said, his eyes as surprised as they were red. He adjusted his glasses and began reading, holding the paper at eye level. "Ah, Ragnar, the poor fellow." He slowly shook his head. "He was a good man, a strong lad, beautiful children. He came back from fishing one night with a pilot—rescued, barely alive. He immediately took the man to Ingrid, our village nurse. The pilot apparently spoke a few words of Russian to Ragnar before becoming unconscious. Ingrid called for a doctor in Visby and in Ljugarn, but no one was available to travel so far north that night, not until the next day." He put the article down for a moment.

"What happened to Ragnar?" Jonathan asked.

"Yes, . . . it was very, very strange," Hark said, gazing at Jonathan, and then returned to the article. "From what I heard from others in the village, Ragnar and Ingrid stayed up late in the night taking care of the pilot, but they got very sick, and Ragnar especially. And I remember later that morning seeing a large helicopter fly right over my head and land just south of town, along the shore. It had a red star on it—Soviet Army, no doubt about it." Hark then chuckled and added, "An invasion, I thought. But then again, those crazy Russians already invaded Gotland in the early Nineteenth Century, and only stayed for a few weeks, I think."

"What was the helicopter for?"

"To take the pilot away!"

Jonathan was taking copious mental notes, unfazed so far by the potent vodka gushing recklessly through his veins.

"Not much later," Hark continued, "an ambulance finally arrived, but it wasn't for the pilot—he was already on his way home. It was for Ragnar and Ingrid. The medical team tried to save Ragnar, but it was too late. I was told he had a high fever and died."

"But he was fine before rescuing the pilot?"

"Yes, of course. I think that's why a coroner from Stockholm visited the village for a day or two, asking lots of questions, but then he left, and—" Hark suddenly interrupted himself, put his half-empty glass down and lobbed an odd stare at his American guest. "Why are you so interested in this . . . this *old* incident?"

Jonathan sensed Hark's uneasiness, as if suddenly the man realized that a total stranger had come from so far away to ask questions about what might be the strangest thing ever to take place on his tiny island.

"Well, I'm a lawyer working on a maritime case back home, and for some reason what happened here might help my client."

"Uhuh," Hark said, scratching his chin. "Hmm . . ."

"My firm has been trying to piece together information, but we keep coming up against a brick wall, mostly because of the government, the military in particular. So we have to pursue every possible lead we find. I'm not yet sure how this piece of information fits in this puzzle, but I'd be very grateful if you would give me more details."

"I see," Hark replied, nodding a few times. He then smacked the counter with the palm of his hand. "I'm happy to help."

"So, weren't you curious about what happened?" Jonathan prodded.

"Of course, Mr. Brooks."

"Call me Jonathan, please."

Hark nodded. "You know, Fårö is a quiet place—has been so since the Stone Age! It's the most remote part of Gotland, with a hundred square kilometers and less than six hundred locals with very simple lives. And only a few thousand visitors each year come by to give us something to talk about. So yes, when a pilot is taken away by a Soviet helicopter and the rescuer dies mysteriously, we don't soon forget, and we get terribly curious."

Jonathan could not quite understand why the pilot was so quickly turned over to the Russians, before he'd been given proper medical care. "Is Ingrid still in town. I would like to ask her—"

Hark raised his hand. "Unfortunately, no." He glanced again at the article, fidgeting with his bifocals. "What this leaves out is that Ingrid died a week later— mysteriously, just like Ragnar. They are both buried at Fårö Kyrka, a church near here. It's a beautiful place. Our most elegant landmark. Can I show you tomorrow?"

"Yes, that would be nice. Did you see the pilot?"

"No, but I know someone who did. She's our well-known orchid grower, and she hears, sees and repeats everything. She's . . . oh, how do you say in English?"

"The town gossip?" Jonathan suggested.

"Yes, that's it," Hark said and laughed. "I'm forgetting some of my English these days. I'm trying my best to keep up—rereading my old collection: Hemingway, Frost, Kipling, Russell. So, would you like to meet this talkative woman? She could be helpful."

"Yes, please."

Since arriving on Gotland, Jonathan had been tempted to call Gary. But he knew using the phone would be risky. Nothing was beyond the reach of America's eavesdropping capabilities, and he feared Scarborough had the means of tracking him down if he so much as dialed a number back home. Jonathan had been lucky to roam about the island without being followed or hunted down, and he wasn't about to jeopardize this relative safety.

# 7

THE SKY WAS GRAY, AND FAINT DROPLETS OF RAIN SLID down the windows. Jonathan took his key and small notepad and slowly headed to the main house. Despite a long sleep, he felt drained from the trip, from the stress of the assault near Dulles airport, from being followed in Stockholm and from Hark's local vodka, which had just about dissolved his liver and left him with a hangover that would have killed a small animal. Not even this tranquil bed and breakfast could help him unwind.

Hark looked like he had been up for hours. His husky arms were busy flinging logs over a stone wall near the front steps.

"*God morgon*," Jonathan said, experimenting again with his limited knowledge of Swedish.

"Hello," Hark answered. "Had a good night?"

"Perfect." Jonathan didn't mention the hangover or the fact that his stomach was threatening to revolt.

"I've arranged a breakfast meeting with Tantina at

ten at the bakery. You know, the orchid woman."

The words were good to hear. Jonathan was not only eager to ask the woman questions but also to munch on anything at the bakery that would absorb into and soothe his stomach after the harsh vodka he had guzzled the night before. The last thing he wanted to do was to be remembered as the American who came, asked crazy questions, vomited and left.

As soon as Hark was done with his chore, he waved at Jonathan. The two hopped into Hark's old two-door Volvo station wagon, a 1959 Duett, he called it. Orange, dented and festering with the scent of manure, the car was his proud possession. Hark wouldn't stop raving about it: from which relative he had bought it, where it was made, how many pigs and other animals he had carried in it. And so they headed toward the village.

"Those are Gotland's very own breed, dating back to the 13th Century," Hark said, pointing at two horses behind a fence. "Known as *Russ*. They are still wild."

"Are there other animals common here?"

"Lamb. Sixty thousand on Gotland—as many as people! We also have many, many hedgehogs and cows."

Hark slowed down as he approached Fårö Kyrka, the church he had mentioned the night before. Its facade was a tall, square, four-story stone tower with a wooden spire. The church was surrounded by an old stone wall.

"Inside, there is a wonderful painting called *Stora kuta tavlan*, from the 17th Century," Hark said. "It's about seal hunters who were stranded on a small iceberg in the middle of the Baltic; they were rescued and lived to tell their story."

"Unlike Ragnar, huh?"

"Yes, he's buried in the cemetery behind the church. Ingrid too."

The smell inside the car was getting unbearable and made his stomach even more uncomfortable, so Jonathan cracked open his window.

"Gotland is full of these churches, many Romanesque and several Gothic, mostly built by early German merchants," Hark explained as he checked his watch. "We should hurry, we're a little late."

Hammars was a quaint coastal hamlet—essentially one street, lined with small one- or two-story buildings. The gentle sound of waves washing upon the rocky coastline came their way.

At the bakery, Hark introduced Tantina, the orchid lady, a rosy-cheeked, thick-boned woman in her mid-sixties. She gave Jonathan a firm handshake and uttered words in Swedish until Hark stopped her. They made themselves comfortable at a table near the window. By then the drizzle had turned into a downpour.

Tantina flicked her curly, grayish-blond hair off her brow and talked with Hark while Jonathan sipped his *kaffe* and picked his way through an assortment of cheeses and meat.

"Try the *filmjölk*," Hark suggested. "It's like a blend of sour-milk and yogurt."

Jonathan obliged though he feared he might not be able to keep the stuff down.

"Tantina welcomes you to the island," Hark said, translating for Jonathan's benefit. "She also wants to show you her orchids."

Jonathan laughed.

"What's so funny?" Hark asked.

"Oh, nothing," Jonathan said, not wanting to explain that back home, "orchids" is also a euphemism for someone's privates.

Hark handed the woman the news article, as Jonathan had asked.

"Can she describe the pilot—what he looked like, his uniform and any other details she remembers?"

Hark chatted with her, but judging from Hark's expression, she seemed to go off on a tangent. Hark sighed and turned to Jonathan. "She really wants to show you her orchid collection. She says you can't visit our island without seeing the huge variety of orchid species—some are even unique to Gotland." Hark then shrugged his shoulders. "She insists."

Jonathan smiled. "Fine, fine. But I need to ask her several questions first."

Tantina picked up the article but only glanced at it before setting it down. She spoke fast, as if she had mastered the details of the incident, and was now professorially speaking to Hark. Of course, Jonathan didn't know Swedish, so she might still have been yakking about her damn orchids, for all he knew.

As Tantina continued to talk, Hark helped himself to Jonathan's notepad and began jotting things down. Hark's face gave an air of renewed interest, as if she had told him something unexpected. He wrote some more as Tantina paused and took a long sip of her coffee, the steam rising over her face.

"After Ragnar brought the pilot to Ingrid's house,

Ingrid called Tantina for help," said Hark to Jonathan. "Remember, no medical doctor was available. By the time Tantina arrived, Ragnar was removing the pilot's wet clothes. He then carried him to the small examination room—nothing elaborate, like at a doctor's office. As I told you before, Ingrid's home was also our village clinic.

Jonathan, still feeling his hangover, sipped his drink from the warm mug and listened to every word Hark said.

"She says the pilot had short, brown hair and had a broken arm. He was unconscious but breathed on his own. Ingrid was hesitant to give him any medicines until she had a better sense of his condition. She was not equipped for much. No x-ray machine. No laboratory. Only simple things. Tantina held the oxygen mask over his face for a while. And she said Ingrid stood ready to give him a dose of morphine for his arm if he regained consciousness. It was a terrible fracture."

Despite his increasingly upset stomach, Jonathan listened with the ears of a fox. But he wanted more. "Did the pilot say anything?"

"Just a few words. Russian, I guess."

"Is she sure? Would she know Russian from Greek or Chinese?" asked Jonathan. "Wait, don't translate what I just said."

Hark shrugged his shoulders, asked her and then translated her reply. "She said Ragnar had heard him speak some Russian on the boat, before they came ashore. The pilot never said anything to her."

"Did Ragnar know Russian?"

"Probably not," Hark replied. "Does it matter?"

"Perhaps," Jonathan replied. Of course it did. What if it wasn't Russian at all, but rather English? Maybe it was an American pilot or a sailor the *Meecham* was sent to rescue. Anything was possible. That could have been the reason to send the ship into the Baltic. But then again, the *Meecham* was a recovery vessel, not a rescue ship in the truest sense of the term. Jonathan knew he was going down a path paved with speculation, something neither Judge Breaux nor the jury would find plausible or relevant.

Hark gazed at his notes. "Tantina left Ingrid's house to grab towels and blankets from home and returned around . . . eh, four-thirty in the morning. That's when she found Ragnar sick—terribly sick. He had thrown up several times and looked pale, fatigued and wasn't his usual talkative self. Ingrid, too, looked unusually pale, but she was busy taking care of the pilot, who by then had lost a lot of blood and whose temperature was still very low, despite her efforts."

"And then?" Jonathan glanced at Hark, who continued to ask Tantina questions and note her answers.

"At around five in the morning," Hark said, "a hospital administrator from Visby telephoned. Tantina answered. The man said not to worry, that a Soviet medical team was coming at any moment to pick up the pilot. But by then Tantina was worried about Ingrid and Ragnar. Both began to appear worse than the pilot. They weren't just tired; they were deathly sick, but she could not understand why."

Jonathan let his mind wander for a moment, trying to

piece together the little there was. "What about his uniform? Did she see anything unusual?"

Hark turned to her and asked.

Her vivacious voice echoed around the small dining area of the quaint bakery. Her hands crossed over the table, while her eyes glanced occasionally at the ceiling and walls. She was nutty, all right.

"She says that his uniform was plain dark green, absent of any insignia, flags or indication of rank. It was wet and torn, with blood on it. Ragnar had cut apart the pilot's life vest and shirt with scissors."

"What happened next?"

Hark translated her reply. "She was there when the helicopter brought the Russian medical team. There were three people, all of them wearing plastic lab coats, gloves and face masks. They went straight into the house to pick up the pilot. She was very angry that they came in like storm troopers, so she demanded to see their identification.

"She did?" Jonathan grinned, imagining the old woman raising hell with the Russians.

"Yes, she says she argued with them. Apparently, when they first refused to cooperate, she threatened them with a frying pan from Ingrid's kitchen."

Jonathan raised his eyebrow. Hark was dead serious.

"Finally, one of the men showed her an ID card. He was a Soviet Army general and she wrote his name down as well as the names of the other two in his team."

"What was the general's name?" Jonathan asked.

Hark asked Tantina, who then murmured what was probably a curse word or two.

"She says his name was General Yakovlev . . . Andrei Yakovlev—about fifty years old, with black hair."

"What did the Russians do?"

"She says they wheeled a stretcher from the landing spot all the way to the house, picked up the pilot, gave him an IV and took off. At that point, she was very worried for Ingrid and Ragnar. When the ambulance finally arrived nearly an hour after the helicopter had left, the doctor tried frantically to revive Ragnar, but he died."

Tantina shrugged her shoulders and then took a pastry from the basket in the center of the table. She didn't have much else to add, other than to say that the ambulance crew took Ingrid away. Six days later, she too was dead, and no one knew why.

Jonathan pulled out his wallet to pay the bill and turned to Hark. "Please thank her for the information. So, tell her I'd love to see her orchids—unless you can find a polite way to postpone this for another day." He opened the wallet flat on the table to find the right Swedish currency when suddenly Tantina leaned forward and let out a loud gasp.

"*Åh, Herregud!*" she said excitedly, immediately stabbing Jonathan's open wallet with her index finger. She started pulling at a picture that stuck out above his driver's license.

"*Vad tar du dig till?*" Hark said to her, nearly shouting. He leaned into her and asked something, and then cocked his head back. "She wants to see it."

Jonathan threw his hands up and let her have it.

Her thick fingers plucked the wallet photo out, and she turned it her way and intensely examined the picture.

"What is it?" Jonathan almost shouted, his stomach turning.

Tantina was agitated. She rattled off words to Hark, who sat wide-eyed, his jaw falling.

"What is she saying?"

"*Jag förstår inte*—" Hark replied and then interrupted himself, realizing he'd just spoken to Jonathan in Swedish. "Sorry. She is saying that, . . . *this* is the pilot."

"Impossible!" Jonathan felt his stomach ball up. "It can't be. This is a picture of my brother, and . . . he's been dead seven years." Jonathan interrupted himself, realizing, as if for the first time, that the *Meecham's* collision with the *Cajun Star* and his brother's death both occurred in the spring of 1989. But it wasn't the first time. Linda had first mentioned it in passing when they'd talked about the case over a year earlier, and most recently two days ago.

*But it makes no sense*, Jonathan pondered. His chest suddenly felt cold.

The woman uttered something else, and Hark quickly translated. "She says she never forgets faces."

*She's a nutcase*, he instantly thought, but he could not convince himself that she really was. Her face was too honest, her demeanor too confident, and her gaze at Hark too intense to simply brush her off as a senile old hag with a screwed-up memory and a freakish passion for orchids.

She continued to speak to Hark, holding the picture under her hawkish stare. She nodded a few times and then slowly handed it back to Jonathan.

Hark listened to her and turned to his American

guest. "Tantina says she's certain this is who Ragnar rescued that night, but if you say it can't be true, then she's obviously wrong."

Jonathan breathed in deeply and looked into Hark's eyes, feeling completely baffled. "For Christ's sake, my brother died a couple of weeks *after* the date of this incident. And he died in the North Atlantic, near Iceland, nowhere near Gotland. And he was not even a pilot."

"I understand," murmured Hark.

Jonathan was so upset, he jumped to his feet, his wallet slipping from his hands and falling to the floor. His thoughts ran a hundred miles per hour. *It can't be. But then again, Matt's remains arrived in New Orleans nearly three weeks later.*

"She *must* be mistaken," Hark said in an appeasing tone.

"My brother was only a linguist—a Pentagon translator, nothing more," Jonathan added, his voice nervously jumping from word to word. But Matt was proficient in Russian, as well as Polish. And he had been to Europe several times, though he never shared great detail about his deployments. Jonathan's skin felt as if it was crawling off his body, and he was now fighting to keep his food down.

He ran for the door just as he heard Hark shout his name. When he reached the curb, it all came out. The cheese. The sausage. The *kaffe*. White blobs of *filmjölk*. And perhaps even the remnants of the vodka from the night before. The ugly American had marked his spot in the annals of Hammars history. He'd come, he'd caused an argument, he'd thrown up, and surely he'd leave.

Hark quickly came to his aid, handing him napkins and apologizing profusely for Tantina's comments.

"I'll be fine. I think it's just jet lag."

Tantina stayed inside, perhaps embarrassed by her claims.

Jonathan went back into the bakery to use the washroom, where the moment he saw the toilet he threw up again, this time in the bowl.

"*Tala med Ralf i den stora vita telefonen,*" he heard Hark say as he followed him into the restroom.

Jonathan got up and rinsed his face in the sink. "What did you say?"

"You speak to Ralf in the big white telephone," Hark said, laughing.

"Ahah," said Jonathan, splashing more water on his face, "or, as we Americans say: you pray to the porcelain god."

Jonathan wasn't nauseated anymore, but he was overcome with grief and anger. He could not dismiss what Tantina had said, as outrageous as it was. *How could this be?* he now asked himself. And that's when the words of Vice-Admiral Scarborough and Captain Tucker seemed to echo over one another. Jonathan's head was spinning as all of a sudden a dark realization captured him. What if Tantina was right? What if the military had lied about Matt's death? And about the *Meecham*? Captain Tucker had no qualms about lying through his teeth, so why wouldn't they all? And if they were behind the attempt on Jonathan's life back in D.C., they'd be capable of nearly anything.

Jonathan's rage boiled inside him, though he tried to

collect himself. He tuned Hark out as he walked by him and headed to the street. He simply gazed at the passing cars, but his mind wandered off deeper into the past, arbitrarily replaying images he didn't want to revisit. Images of that day when the men came. Their shiny green Caprice pulled up into the driveway while Jonathan was mowing the lawn. It was a Sunday in April. Two men in Army uniforms walked calmly toward him. Jonathan was horrified. He had only seen this in the movies, its devastation so incalculable. Every detail had soaked in: the bible in one man's hand, the cross on his lapel. But not a word could exit Jonathan's lips. Nothing but a harsh breathing and a strong but hopeless wish that it was all a mistake. A wrong address, perhaps; a wrong name.

But it was not so. Like a bullet jammed in the chamber, not a word could leave his lips because he knew. He knew from their faces, made to look somber but which only showed that they had performed the ritual hundreds of times before. It was time to share the news no one ever wants to hear. *Your brother has died in an aircraft accident on his way to Brunswick, Maine,* Jonathan remembered the man saying. And the rest played itself out. The disbelief. The sorrow. The formal letters. The elaborate funeral. And the flag, neatly folded. Everything was made to appear so proper, so collected. And he had never thought to question what they had said. Never. Not until now. Not until this very second.

# 8

THE RAIN HAD STOPPED. A DESOLATE, ROCKY COASTLINE and cool breeze had brought back a sense of tranquility. Jonathan sat quietly on a stone wall, gazing at the sea. It was a welcome distraction from what he had tackled at the bakery.

Hark was behind him, by the car. He had not said a word since they left Tantina and drove to this quite corner of Fårö.

"I'm sorry if she offended you," Hark said.

Jonathan didn't answer right away. He rubbed his eyes and shook his head. "She didn't."

"Is what she said even possible?" Hark asked hesitantly.

"I want to say no, but I can't be certain."

Hark offered to take Jonathan anywhere he wanted, but there wasn't much else to see. Ingrid's relatives had long ago sold her home, and Ragnar's family had moved to the mainland and sold the boat that brought the pilot to shore. No one else could corroborate Tantina's story.

Hark drove around for half an hour, showing Jonathan other scenic parts of the little island. After they returned to Hark's bed and breakfast, Jonathan used the phone at the front desk to call home, knowing the risk that that entailed.

Linda answered, her voice hinting that she'd just woken up—it was eight in the morning in New Orleans. "Sweetheart," Jonathan began, his jumbled thoughts scrambling to line up correctly. But he quickly told himself not to alarm her. "Honey, I need you to find some documents and give them to Gary at the office as quickly as you can."

"What's the matter?"

"Nothing to worry about," Jonathan replied, knowing, however, that Linda had a paranormal disposition to decipher his thoughts. "Please give Gary the last two letters from Matt, and the letter of condolence from his unit commander, and the circumstance letter."

"What's going on?"

"Nothing, . . . I'll explain later."

"Are you okay? Are you still in Sweden?"

"Yes, and everything's fine. I'll give you all the details later. I promise."

"Okay, honey," Linda said, her alarm clock ringing in the background. "I'll take care of it later today. When are you coming home?"

"In a day or two."

"I love you," she said.

Her words comforted Jonathan, though he felt a twinge of guilt for not confiding in her. She had always been there for him through the worst of times: when his father died, when his mother passed, and, finally, when Matt died.

"I love you, sweetheart," he said, somewhat surprised that she hadn't probed deeper. "And thank you."

The day had brought back memories Jonathan had not expected to explore. Fear and sadness were intermittently shaking his psyche throughout the long afternoon and into the evening.

At Hark's suggestion, he took a walk through the nearby forest to help him relax. The smell of pine, mixed with the gentle scent of the sea that came in with the breeze, filtered through his lungs. He listened to the soft crackling sounds of twigs breaking below his feet. It was strangely peaceful. In the morning he'd head to Stockholm to enquire further on the incident, as he was certain Swedish authorities had investigated the event.

*        *        *

LOUD footsteps jolted Jonathan out of his deep sleep. Someone was racing up the stairs. A hard knock shook his door. Jonathan craned his neck to see the clock. It was a little past six in the morning.

"Open quickly!" shouted a man who sounded like Hark. The knocking continued unabated.

He sprung out of bed, put on some pants and answered the door. Hark's expression told him something was terribly wrong.

"There's an urgent telegram for you," Hark said, looking flabbergasted. He handed the envelope to Jonathan. "I opened it, not knowing that it was for you."

The message was from Gary, and it read:

A FIRE AT YOUR HOUSE. LINDA IN SERI-
OUS CONDITION AT CHARITY HOSPITAL.
I AM WITH HER. NO CELL SERVICE AT
HOSPITAL. PLEASE CALL ER ASAP.

"My god." He jumped up and gazed around wildly.

"I'm sorry," Hark said. "You are welcome to use my phone to call home."

"It must have happened . . ." Jonathan murmured, checking the timestamp of the telegram and then his wristwatch, "a few hours ago."

Hark glanced at his own watch. "Isn't it nearly midnight in New Orleans?"

"Yes." His heart began racing.

Hark grabbed Jonathan's arm. "Come with me. We'll make the calls."

Jonathan went along, but his mind was numb. Linda was all he could think about.

At the lodge's reception, Hark quickly placed the phone on the counter. "It's all yours."

"How did this telegram come to you?"

"Oscar, our postman. He got it this morning when he arrived at work."

By the time he dialed Gary, Jonathan's mind was swirling with suspicion that this was no accident, and certainly not after what had happened in D.C. He called the hospital, knowing that by doing so, he risked being tracked down. But he had no choice. The switchboard patched him through to the ER, where a man answered.

"I'm calling about my wife, Linda Brooks, she—"

"Oh, yes," the man said, interrupting Jonathan. "I'm Dr. Crowley. I'm sorry to say . . . your wife has serious injuries."

"How bad?"

"Third degree burns on about thirty percent of her body, mostly her legs and lower abdomen, and less severe burns on her chest and left arm. She also has head trauma, possibly from falling down."

Jonathan felt his body turn cold. "What exactly happened?"

"I was told a house fire."

"Doctor, is there a Gary Green there?"

"Yes, I saw him earlier; I will tell him you called."

"Thank you."

Jonathan heard himself breathing, almost panting. His elbows kept him up against the counter. He felt Hark gently take the handset from his hand and hang up the phone. He couldn't move, though his body wanted to race out the door. His mind quickly recalled the words he had heard Linda say, and her playful eyes that morning before he left for Washington, D.C. Her voice had jazzed up his whole day. A horrid notion then interrupted his train of thought: *those words might be her last. Forever*. The thought made him move. Fast. Back to his room, where he packed his things and returned to the front desk.

The only thought that swarmed in his head was of getting home, but all the hurrying in the world would not change the predicament: he was in the middle of nowhere on a Monday morning. The fastest way home was by plane from Visby. *Oh, no*, he then came to another realization. *The ferry service doesn't begin until eight.* He picked up his tickets and returned to the phone, where he dialed the airline demanding to change his transatlantic flight from Stockholm.

"Dammit!" Jonathan said as he hung up the phone. He glanced at Hark. "Even if I make the morning flight out of Visby, the best they can do is get me on the first flight to New York on *Tuesday* morning."

Jonathan was a bundle of nerves. Before receiving the telegram, he had programmed himself to ignore everything except the disturbing claim by the nutty orchid lady. But now, Linda's life hung by a thread. If that was not tormenting enough, another frightening thought came to him. If the fire had been deliberately set, then they might try to harm her again. He had to try to get back today. He thanked Hark, paid him and left.

Jonathan was one of the first to pull up to the station in the nearby village of Broa. At eight o'clock sharp, the gate opened, and he drove onto the five-lane-wide open ferry, a large yellow-colored vessel with the words KAJSA-STINA painted on its side.

The drive back to Visby was aided by Jonathan's lead foot. But speed made no difference. The flight to the capital was delayed. He didn't board until almost twelve-thirty, and, as feared, the flight arrived at Bromma Airport well after he could make any transatlantic connection from Stockholm's main airport north of town.

He was resigned to the fact that he would stay the night in Stockholm. To take his mind off Linda, he cast about for a productive way to make use of the enforced delay. But he also needed to keep a low profile for his own safety. Everything seemed to be turning on its head, and no one could be trusted.

Before leaving the airport, Jonathan arranged a reservation at a budget hotel. An attendant with limited knowledge of English had helped him find one well off the beaten path. But when Jonathan arrived by cab and stared at the accommodations, he realized the language barrier was to blame for this terrible selection. It was quite a change from Hark's quaint rural oasis: a floating hotel sitting alone on a dock off an industrial park at the foot of a forested hill topped with a cluster of high-rises. The barge was some seventy feet long, with about ten rooms and a grossly tattooed man—a cross between a biker and a Viking—manning the front desk and apparently surprised to see a guest.

Jonathan's only solace was that this temporary abode was the perfect hideout, as few humans with any standards would ever crawl on board this pit. A creepy, dark hall led to Jonathan's room, a place fit for shooting second-rate porn flicks and hiding fugitives. The room was half below the waterline, and the stench of mildew blended with the pungent odor of cigarette smoke that emanated from the linens, curtains and woodwork.

Jonathan couldn't sit or lay down or pace. He had tried. Silence brought his collapsing world closer, an intimacy that was driving him nuts. He had to do something. Anything. Finding answers was the goal. And being the capital, Stockholm harbored government offices that surely had some sort of records relating to the plane crash. The problem was deciding where on earth to begin.

From his hotel room, he phoned the Consular Section of the U.S. Embassy. But it took only a few minutes for him to wonder why his tax dollars were supporting such shamefully incompetent and unfriendly civil servants, none of whom were the least bit interested in helping him.

He also had little luck with the transportation ministry and the foreign affairs ministry. But by chance, the Swedish Ministry of Defense offered hope. At least a little. After being accidentally disconnected, he was transferred to a man named Otto Johannsen, who not only spoke perfect English, but also seemed to take an interest in Jonathan's claim. He was in charge of aviation safety for the ministry's Department of International and Security Affairs.

Jonathan wanted two things in particular: information about the pilot and any records of the plane crash off Gotland. Jonathan explained to Otto much of what Tantina had said and added the relevant dates. But after some twenty minutes on the phone, Jonathan sensed that Otto was stalling.

"Let me get back with you next week or so," he said to Jonathan, even though Otto knew the American would be gone in the morning. "That's the best I can do."

Jonathan was angry. He realized nothing more would happen unless he pressed his case with Otto in person. He hung up but didn't tell the man he would be right over. Instead, he simply gave him his contact information in New Orleans. He also gave him the phone number to his trashy barge, something he later realized was an imprudent move.

The sky was darkening at four, and judging by the heavy clouds, Jonathan was prepared to see more snow by evening. Bundled in his thick coat, he left the hotel by cab, heading to the Ministry of Defense headquarters on Jakobsgatan Street.

Stockholm was a sprawling maze of waterways. He crossed several bridges, most of which were built low over the water. He crossed another one, this time to Galma Stan, the largest island in the city. Both sides of the street were filled with restaurants, bookshops, souvenir stores and antique dealers. The street passed by the Royal Palace and led to another bridge and onto a built-up area dominated by ornate office buildings, many of them with greenish copper roofs. The driver circled a spacious open square across from the elegant Royal Opera House. An equestrian statue dominated the middle of Gustav Adolf Square. The driver then veered right, past a medieval church, and stopped at a six-story building facing the square.

The Ministry was a stylish copper-roofed building, nothing like Jonathan had expected. It wasn't monstrously austere like the Pentagon, which his brother had once shown him on the day of his promotion to Second Lieutenant. And he was amazed at how simple it was to enter the building. No metal detectors. No band of zealous armed guards. Just one unarmed, fat-bellied security guard, no more intimidating than a bellman.

At the reception desk, Jonathan asked to speak with Otto, although he was not brazen enough to pretend he had an appointment. He simply said it was urgent and that they had spoken earlier. Surprisingly, Otto agreed to meet in a third floor conference room overlooking Gustav Adolf Square, but the Swede did not take kindly to Jonathan's intrusion. He shook hands roughly but did not invite Jonathan to sit down. Jonathan began explaining more details about what Tantina had said, but Otto interrupted him.

"I'm not sure we can find this information. This happened a long time ago and when—"

"For God's sake," Jonathan cut in as he swept some papers off the table. "There must be someone here who knows that a Soviet army helicopter landed in your country. This sort of thing doesn't happen every day, does it? Are you such an idiot that you can't understand the seriousness of what I'm telling you?"

"There is no reason to get angry," said Otto with the calmness only a Swede could pull off after being insulted.

"Yes, there is!" Jonathan blurted out, clutching the edge of the heavy wood table as if the next move was to dislodge it from its legs and crush Otto's skull. "My brother may have been kidnapped on Gotland, and I want answers."

Otto rolled his eyes, which angered Jonathan as much as if it had been a physical assault.

"Why do you stand there as if this isn't important?" asked Jonathan, once more slamming his hand on the table and secretly wishing this Nordic block of ice would respond with either an ounce of cooperation or a manly fighting stance. Jonathan threw his arms into the air and stormed out of the room. "Someone else will have to help me."

"*Lugna ner dig!*" Jonathan heard Otto say from the room, but by then there was no stopping him. He remembered reading on the English language directory at the reception desk downstairs that the defense minister's office was on the top floor, so he quickly followed the signs to the stairwell and headed upstairs.

He exited the stairwell, turned the corner and headed straight for the door at the far end of the hallway. *This has to be it*, he thought, spotting the Swedish flag on one side and a coat of arms mounted on the adjacent wall.

Without a second thought, Jonathan barged into the office and spotted a mustached man standing a few feet away, reading a document, and a woman—probably his assistant—sitting at her desk. She got up and moved toward Jonathan as he drew nearer.

"Are you the Minister?" Jonathan asked. "I apologize for my abruptness, but I desperately need your help."

The man took a few steps back but said nothing.

"Please, sir, I've asked Mr. Johannsen for help, but he is not interested. My brother is missing and—" Before Jonathan could finish his sentence, he felt a huge force bear down on him from behind. His body collapsed face-down under the weight, his chin hitting the floor before he could even make a sound. Jonathan struggled to free himself, but he felt yet another person jump on top of him.

"I'm only asking for help!"

"*Du ska få igen, din jävel!*" shouted a man that

sounded like Otto. "*Kalla på vakterna!*"

After a few more seconds of struggle, Jonathan could no longer move his limbs and could barely breathe. He was in a headlock, his arms and legs pinned down by at least two men. And all he could see was a beefy arm around his throat and the parquet floor inches from his face. Several people spoke loudly to one another in Swedish.

"Get up!" said the person who held him in a choke-hold. He felt another man frisk his pants pockets and jacket.

Jonathan managed to look up at the man he thought was the defense minister, or at least someone much higher up the food chain than Otto. "I'm not trying to cause problems; I'm only asking for help. My wife has been attacked, I'm being followed, and my brother is missing. I beg you . . ."

Jonathan felt the grip around his neck loosen. He was brought to his feet, his hands now cuffed tightly behind his back. Otto thrust his face forward. "This is *not* the way to get help, you stupid cowboy."

Jonathan spat on Otto's face and then tried to wrestle his arms free. But the men dragged him out into the hallway. "Okay, okay!"

Otto was furious. He wiped his face with his sleeve, pointed angrily at Jonathan and cursed in Swedish.

The two men who had custody of Jonathan shoved him into the elevator, whisked him through the downstairs lobby, butted him up against a wall while they unlocked the handcuffs and then threw him out onto the sidewalk like a trash bag.

Except for a bruised knee, a sore neck and a torn collar, he had fared well enough to walk upright, flag down a cab and head back to his floating hotel with a semblance of dignity. He later realized how fortunate he was not to have ended up in jail.

From a payphone some distance from his hotel, he called the ER to check on Linda. Her condition had not changed.

*          *          *

JUST past midnight, Jonathan was awakened by a phone call. It was the front desk.

"There's somebody heah to see you, sah," the man said in English, his accent Indian. "He says it's urgent."

"Who?" Jonathan asked, imagining for a moment that it was Otto coming with the cavalry to even the score. *Perhaps Swedes have it in them to shed their genetically imbedded passivity for a healthy dose of revenge.* But Jonathan quickly sensed renewed fear that perhaps it was not the Swedes at all. *What if . . . it's Scarborough's killers?*

"I do not know, sah," the man said in English. "It's *not* the police," he added as if he was accustomed to saying this to his guests. "He said he has information about what you were asking at the Ministry."

"Can you pass him the phone?"

"Sorry, he's waiting outside now, sah."

Jonathan scratched his jaw, his lucidity coming to him quickly after the abrupt awakening. He wasn't sure what to do, but it now sounded as if it could be Otto. He didn't want to leave the relative safety of a nasty hotel to be beaten or killed. *But if it is Otto?* Against his better judgment, he got dressed and left the room, but not before placing his lucky fountain pen in his sock. It was the only weapon he could come up with. He walked down the barge's narrow, smelly hallway, passing the front desk, where the man behind the counter pointed to the dock.

"Out there, sah." He sounded as if he wanted to say something else. *Good luck*, perhaps. Or *don't come back in here if things go south.*

Jonathan stepped into the glacial air wearing only a sweatshirt, jeans, socks and shoes. A tall man in a dark trench coat stood by the large dock cleat to which the barge was moored. Jonathan at first felt strangely disappointed and nervous that it didn't appear to be Otto.

"Who are you and what do you want?" Jonathan asked from a safe distance, his warm breath steaming out of his mouth.

"Please come with me to the car," the stranger said in English, his Swedish accent intoxicating. "Someone has information about your incident in Gotland."

Jonathan hesitantly complied.

A black Saab sedan idled at the dimly lighted end of the parking lot, vapor spewing from its tailpipe. As he got close enough to hear the low-pitched hum of its engine, the man suddenly turned, pulled Jonathan forward, grabbed his belt from behind and expertly frisked him with one hand. The man then opened the front passenger door and waved Jonathan in.

Jonathan noticed that the inside dome light was not functioning as he sat in the warm seat. The man quickly shut the door and circled around to the driver's side, only to stop and light a cigarette. Suddenly, from the corner of his eye, Jonathan saw a dark figure in the backseat.

"Don't look, please!" snapped the man behind him, preempting Jonathan's instinct to turn all the way round. The man's English was better than his colleague's.

"What's going on?" Jonathan asked, quickly grabbing the door handle but stopping short of pulling the latch.

"Please face forward; you don't need to see me."

"Who are you?" Jonathan asked, slowly reaching for his ankle to grab the pen.

"Call me Erland. I'm here for two reasons. First, I have information to give you—I assume you are still interested, since your visit to the Ministry of Defense can hardly be called a success. Secondly, I have a request."

Jonathan heard a loud click. *The cocking of a gun?* he asked himself. He took a big gulp of air and slowly leaned back in his seat and stared out the windshield, calculating an escape route should the meeting turn uglier than it already seemed. His hand discreetly clenched his pen, but he left it in his sock for now.

"Must you point a gun at my back?" Jonathan asked.

"One can never be too careful," Erland responded coldly. "Not after your tantrum earlier today."

"I'm an attorney, I'm unarmed, and I have no interest in hurting anyone. I assure you."

Erland sighed. "Perhaps."

Another clicking sound came from behind; perhaps he'd uncocked the weapon, but Jonathan wasn't sure.

"Your spectacle today was foolish. Expect that our state security services will be watching your every movement for the rest of your stay in Sweden."

"I'm leaving tomorrow anyway."

"Well, at least you did your circus act in Sweden," said Erland with a chuckle. "Imagine what would have happened to you if you had entered the Pentagon, stormed into the defense secretary's office, and spat on one of his senior deputies. *Imagine.* I think we Swedes are a bit more forgiving."

Jonathan grinned in spite of himself. "I suppose you're right."

"Like most Scandinavians, I'm pragmatic. So, I'd like to make a mutually convenient arrangement with you."

"First, tell me who you are."

"I'm with the *Militära underrättelse- och säkerhetstjänsten*—our military intelligence service—in Uppsala. I also collaborate with the *Försvarets Radioanstalt*, our signals intelligence directorate, located in Lovön."

"So what *arrangement* are you proposing?"

"I have answers to your questions. But I need two promises in return."

"Promises?" asked Jonathan incredulously, crossing his arms.

"First, that you will not return to Sweden looking for trouble."

"If you give me truthful information, I'll have no reason to return," Jonathan said gruffly. "And the other promise?"

"That if you travel to Russia, you will obtain information for us, on an unrelated matter of interest to me."

Jonathan was tempted to accept for the sake of expediency. *What can he do to me anyway, once I leave this country? Send me poisoned Swedish meatballs? Sabotage my Swedish furniture?* He nodded and replied nearly child-like, "Okay, I promise."

Jonathan felt a tap on his shoulder. It was the edge of a folder.

"Here, take a look," said Erland. "It's the radar track of a transport or reconnaissance aircraft, I believe American, but it is possible it was British. It crashed on March 7, 1989."

Jonathan, his pulse quickening, plopped it on his lap and unfolded the large chart inside with both hands, tilting it at an angle to gather the best light from the nearby lamppost.

"Coincidentally," Erland said, "the Pentagon had relayed to our embassy in Washington a dozen flight plans for that month. These were routine flights, some VIP, but most signal intelligence missions—usually by either a U.S. Air Force RC-135 or a U.S. Navy P-3 *Orion* aircraft. The planes usually departed from West Germany straight up the Baltic, then they either turned back or headed west, flying over our airspace and continuing to Norway, and then to Iceland or the UK."

"Was there a flight plan for this plane that went down?"

"Yes, supposedly a transit flight by an *Orion*. You see, the plane's course is extrapolated from the series of red dots, each representing a hit from one of our long-range primary radars. The black line represents the flight plan, which starts in Germany, heads north past Gotland and then turns westward to Stockholm and then on to Norway. But what is unusual is that the radar first detects the plane off the Latvian coast, not Germany. The aircraft flew fairly low, at about eighteen-hundred feet at that moment. It slowly gained altitude. But less than twenty minutes later, it began a rapid descent. The aircraft never used its transponder, which means it was trying to keep a low radar signature, and it never communicated with our air traffic controllers. Notice the multiple returns in the flight's last five minutes. That's because it was breaking apart."

"It crashed, right?"

"Looks that way to me," Erland conceded.

"Why are you so sure it was an American aircraft?"

"Because a pilot speaking English signaled a mayday and gave his call sign on a scrambled channel, which we decrypted a few weeks after the incident."

"What was the call sign?"

"Raven Five-Zero."

Jonathan shook his head grimly. Certainly this information was not conclusive, but it was the best he had gotten to confirm the orchid woman's claim. Matt *could* have been on that plane. Possibly. But if he was, nothing gave Jonathan any clue to the reason the Pentagon would lie about Matt's death.

*Why? Was there something so secretive about the flight that warranted such immense deception?*

"So is it true that Russians picked up a survivor from this crash?" asked Jonathan.

"A Soviet helicopter was cleared to fly to Gotland."

"Why did you let them?"

"At the time we believed it was a Soviet aircraft. And the Americans never contacted us."

Jonathan was angry. Angry that the Swedes had been so naive. That they hadn't made any independent verification. But his anger toward the U.S. military was greater. If the allegations were true, they'd deliberately abandoned one of their own.

The climate control kicked the heater into high gear, and the vents blew out the warm air with renewed strength.

Erland cleared his throat.

Jonathan folded the flight chart and returned it to the folder. "Can I keep it?"

Erland laughed. "Impossible. You're lucky I'm showing it to you."

The man outside—nearly seated on the warm hood of the car—glanced at Jonathan, checked his watch, turned his back again and lit another cigarette. That's when Jonathan noticed the bulge of his coat at waist level, a tell-tale sign of a concealed firearm, for sure.

"If your brother was indeed on board the plane, and he survived, then the answers you seek are in Russia, not here. You *must* go there. And when you do, I would like something that would help me."

"I'm listening."

"There are unusual parallels to your situation— another aircraft incident. It happened long ago. 1952. One of our military DC-3s was shot down by a Soviet fighter jet somewhere over the Baltic. We'd like to know where the wreckage is located before anyone else does. There is already a privately financed search team scouring the sea bottom to find it."

"Why do you want to keep this secret? It happened so long ago."

"We have our reasons. They'll find it eventually, I'm sure. We think it is possible that one or more of the eight-man crew survived—we've heard that two parachutes were seen descending shortly after the plane was hit. We can't know this yet, not until we examine the wreckage. Although Russian officials have admitted privately that they downed the plane, they've never said more than that. While in Russia, you may stumble on something that could help us."

"What on *earth* can I do that your government can't?" Jonathan asked as he concurrently asked himself the same question.

Erland didn't immediately answer. "You have balls, Mr. Brooks. You're persistent, even pestilent. You showed that today."

"I thought you said I was foolish."

"That too."

Jonathan scratched the top of his head. He admitted to himself that there was no more important place to go than Russia. And he would go there right this minute if it wasn't for Linda.

Jonathan returned the folder to Erland, who then slipped him a business card containing only the initials T.E.S., a post office box and a phone number.

"Call me if you find something useful," announced Erland. "I wish you luck."

"You know, my life is probably in danger."

"Oh."

"Someone had me followed when I arrived, and now my wife and my home have been attacked."

"Who's doing this?" enquired Erland.

"If I told you, you will think I'm crazy."

Erland chuckled. "Try me."

"U.S. intelligence services, or perhaps our military," Jonathan said angrily. "I'm not sure yet."

"My driver will pick you up tomorrow and take you to the airport. It's all I can do to help."

"Thank you," Jonathan said, surprised at the offer. "Every little bit is appreciated."

Jonathan opened his door. He felt uncomfortable having to avoid eye contact with the man known as Erland. But the restriction came with the territory. *Spooks will be spooks*, he thought, *even when it seems quite ridiculous*. He headed back to his room in the floating pit, feeling a deep sadness displace his adrenaline rush.

# 9

NOT A MINUTE OF THE FLIGHT FROM SWEDEN WAS FREE OF
worry about Linda. The plane could not have flown fast
enough. Everything seemed to pass in slow motion. Just
prior to boarding, Jonathan had spoken to her supervising doctor, and things were grim.

Jonathan found Gary waiting for him at the airport.
Gary appeared both worried and relieved, and as
Jonathan had expected, dozens of questions came his
way. There was so much Jonathan wanted to share with
his law partner, but he didn't have the strength to revisit
it all. He only briefly told him about the shooting in
Washington, D.C., and simply asked that they talk about
the details later. Right now, all Jonathan had on his mind
was Linda.

Gary drove him to Charity Hospital, the city's
largest, with Louisiana's best burn unit and the state's
densest concentration of trauma physicians. Jonathan
headed upstairs while Gary parked the car. He held his

breath as the petite nurse pushed into the heavy door of a private room adjoining the intensive care ward. Linda lay on the bed, her eyes closed and most of her body covered by a metallic sheet.

"She's heavily sedated," the nurse said, checking Linda's IV and monitors. She then picked up her chart at the foot of the bed.

"I understand," Jonathan uttered, the reality of the horror sinking in quickly as he resisted the impulse to rush to Linda's bedside and gather her up in his arms.

He stripped off his jacket, draped it over a stool by the bed and sat down. He rested his palm over her hand. Her skin was cool. Her face at peace. Jonathan had always found Linda beautiful, even without makeup. Those cute freckles, and her fine, blond eyebrows. He stared at her face, its chiseled contours, its stillness accentuated by an eerie calm that enveloped the room. Calm because it was silent. Calm because all the screams and commotion—from victims and rescuers alike—that he imagined would resonate at the site of a raging fire were quelled. Calm because her injuries were hidden under the sheets that covered her. Disturbingly calm.

"How has she been in the last few hours?" Jonathan asked the nurse after explaining that he'd spoken to the doctor before his flight.

"Unchanged," she replied solemnly, her face contorted by anxiety. "I'm afraid she has a tough fight ahead of her."

"Well," Jonathan said, suddenly feeling tears clouding his vision, "she's strong enough to prevail."

"The doctor will be in around five," she said before walking out.

Alone with Linda, the tears poured down his face. He begged for Linda to forgive him for putting her in jeopardy. He could hear her voice in his mind. A voice that was real only in spirit. Her lips didn't move. Her eyes stayed shut, her entire body motionless. The only sign of life was the mild rising of her chest as she breathed, assisted by a supply of oxygen through small tubes in her nose.

There was nothing he could do except believe in her strength. He leaned forward and gently pressed his mouth to her ear and whispered, "I love you. Everything will be fine."

It wasn't long before Gary joined him. He put his arm around Jonathan, which was comforting in that it was so unlike Gary, the son of a plantation owner, old school and as detached from human emotion as his aristocratic roots were to the plight of slaves. But that didn't mean he wasn't a good man, just that not all good men know how to display emotion. For Gary, it had been at rare moments, like at Matt's funeral and at Jonathan's wedding to Linda. And Jonathan knew Gary loved Linda in his own way. Sure, Gary loved his tawdry stripper-wife, but as a lawyer, he respected Linda's strength and grace and her quiet commitment to anyone important to Jonathan.

"Why don't you get some rest," Gary suggested. "She's in good hands, and we won't know much about how this happened until the morning."

Jonathan quickly began thinking of the places where

he ought to be, attempting to place some order of priority with each place, until, finally, he'd decided. He abruptly rose, put on his jacket and headed to the door. "I need to see the house."

"Let me drive you there."

"That's all right, I'll take a cab. I'd feel better if you would stay with Linda until I get back."

Gary nodded and smiled.

Jonathan arranged to meet his brother-in-law, Derek, at the house. He simply had to know whether the fire was deliberate or not, though he had already convinced himself it was arson.

As his cab pulled up, Jonathan had trouble believing his eyes. Only one wall and the chimney of the two-story house remained in recognizable form. Everything else was a pile of debris. Derek's patrol car was already in the driveway.

The smoky stench seeped into Jonathan's lungs the moment he stepped out of the cab.

"I'm sorry," were Derek's first words. He gave Jonathan a strong hug, patting his back. His eyes were bloodshot and puffy, his face unshaven. He told Jonathan that he'd stayed at the hospital the first twenty-four hours straight. It was no surprise. Linda and he were the youngest of six. The closest, too.

The slab of concrete that formed the home's foundation was blackened by the fire. Above it lay what was left of wooden beams, insulation, roofing and other structural debris. All the furniture was destroyed. Their paintings. Their photographs. Everything.

Jonathan and Derek stepped through the charred

remains of the once-elegant home, one of the nicest on Pine Street.

"This is where the fire started," Derek said, pointing to an area near the fireplace, in what was the north side of the house. "A short in the power lines leading to the air conditioning unit."

"So it started outside the house?"

"That's what the investigator told me," Derek said and then leaned down, motioning with his hands at a small opening in the brick wall. "It was a freak accident. An electrical short here ignited an insulator mesh that then burned through the wood exterior, and the flames shot up the siding to the second floor, and to the roof and then engulfed the whole house. Apparently, it went real fast. It's a miracle Linda got out alive."

Jonathan leaned his broad shoulders on what was left of the fireplace and looked up at the covered sky. "This was no accident."

"What're you saying?"

"Someone did this."

"Not in this neighborhood," the confident officer said, shaking his head disapprovingly. "Who on earth would do this?"

"Someone who wants to kill me, or send me a warning."

"The fire investigator looked at this carefully. I've worked with him before, and he's good. He tested for accelerants and found nothing. It was a faulty wire, I tell you."

Jonathan knew Derek would have a hard time believing him. All the more because Derek was a decorated, know-it-all cop, with little tolerance for conjecture, less so from a lawyer's mouth. So Jonathan went on to explain Vice-Admiral Scarborough's threatening words and the drive-by shooting on his way to Dulles airport. He also told him what Tantina, the orchid woman, had said about Matt. He told him everything he knew about the Victory Lines trial.

"*Jesus*, man," Derek said, his eyes wide open. "Are you kidding me?"

"This is all true," Jonathan said.

Derek was shaken by the revelation.

"My trial is masking something far more sinister, but I can't put my finger on it yet."

Derek stood with his hands at his hips. "You honestly think the Navy is behind this?"

"The Navy, the Defense Intelligence Agency, the Defense Department . . . who the hell knows? What's clear is I've stirred up a hornet's nest, and whoever wants me off their backs has gone after Linda, probably to bring me home from Sweden before I discover anything more." He clutched the edge of the red-brick mantle until its gritty surface began flaking into his palm.

Derek scratched his jaw and looked deep in thought for a moment. "So *that's* why the guy—the one in the car accident—was following you, huh?"

"To keep an eye on me, or to kill me. Perhaps I'm being watched right this moment. Now, nothing would surprise me."

"Just a moment." Derek flipped open his cell phone and started dialing.

Jonathan listened. Derek called his precinct and

demanded that an officer be posted immediately to Linda's hospital room.

"Thank you," said Jonathan, puzzled that the thought had not come to him first. "You're right, she could still be in danger."

"What about you?" asked Derek, holding his thumb on the keypad ready to dial again.

"I'm in their crosshairs, all right," replied Jonathan as he walked toward where the kitchen once stood. The refrigerator was toppled to one side and charred. The stove was covered by a slab of rooftop, the shingles still nailed to their support. The countertops and cabinets had vanished.

"Where are you staying tonight?"

Jonathan initially thought a hotel. Or at his office. Or even at Gary's place in Mandeville. But then all those places felt unsuitable. "I don't know."

"Stay with us. Caroline will cook you a good meal."

Jonathan wanted to accept. *No one will attack a cop's house*, he thought. Not a guy like Derek, who wasn't shy about the way he slept: naked with a 45-caliber handgun under his pillow. How Caroline put up with it was a mystery.

"No thanks, Derek," Jonathan said. "I'll probably stay at the hospital." He didn't want to tell him the real reason: if indeed Scarborough was behind this, there would be no police force strong enough to protect him. They'd kill Derek and Caroline and Nick and anyone else they thought was in their way. Jonathan could not allow the already tragic circumstances to metastasize.

Derek took Jonathan to his place in Metairie only to

give him his car, which he'd parked there for safe keeping after the fire. It had been in the driveway and survived with only a few scratches. Linda's car, on the other hand, had burned in the garage and been towed away.

*       *       *

NOVEMBER in the Big Easy is often sunny and mild, a time when the air usually feels less humid and people more tranquil. But today, none of this would prove true. Jonathan drove under the dark, cloudy skies, his mind rehashing everything he'd tackled in Sweden, compounded with visions of Linda laying on her intensive care bed, fighting for her life. It was a wonder he could concentrate enough to drive his car. But he knew exactly where he was headed. His burning desire to discover the truth had identified the most pressing destination of all. He'd already pondered the wisdom of the difficult demand he was about to make, and he'd already made up his mind half a dozen times since his plane landed. Now it was merely a matter of making it happen. And without delay.

Metairie Cemetery was the final resting place for many famous people, such as JFK assassination lawyer Jim Garrison and Civil War General Pierre Gustave Beauregard, along with former Louisiana governors and senators. More importantly for Jonathan, it was the venue he'd chosen for Matt's grave and those of his parents. Jonathan had set foot there on five occasions since Matt's death, the last time nearly a year ago. The experience was too painful to make it a more frequent ritual. And this was the first time he'd come without Linda.

The cemetery was filled with graves, all above ground, as New Orleans' high water table required such practice. His parents were buried near a large oak tree on Avenue M, at the south end of the property. Their graves were neither ornate nor large. No towering marble to send a pretentious posthumous message to passersby. No gaudy statues. No Italian marble. They were just right. Simple above-ground stone tombs with names and dates. Plain enough to symbolize the modest lives his father and mother had lived despite having accumulated great wealth. Jonathan briefly remembered his father's voice as he was succumbing to cancer. "I'm no national hero," he'd said. "I'd rather my ashes be sprinkled over a bayou." Jonathan hadn't done that, at his mother's insistence.

Matt's grave was a short distance away. Jonathan walked more slowly. The scent of flowers and freshly cut grass filled his lungs.

1965 to 1989. He read the dates, but for the first time his gaze at his brother's tomb was accompanied by hope. An infinitesimal speck of hope that this grave was not necessary. Somewhere in his mind he heard Tantina speak, and Hark translating her words. He pictured her finger pressed against Matt's photograph, her stunned expression burned into his memory. *Perhaps it was Matt that she had seen. Maybe the Soviets spared his life.* But there were so many maybes.

He stared at the grass at the base of the tomb and as if divinely ordered to do so, he quickly gave his decision a final blessing.

The cemetery's business office was what one would

expect: neat, quiet, with no one pressed for time. Jonathan asked to see the manager, a portly man in his mid-fifties, who greeted him in the waiting room.

"I'm having Matt's body exhumed," Jonathan declared in an authoritative tone, as if he needed to make himself feel more convinced of his decision. "And I'd like your cooperation."

"What?" the manager asked, his face so surprised it told Jonathan he'd never been asked that before.

"I'm not sure the person buried there is my brother."

The man returned an incredulous sneer. He crossed his arms but didn't say anything. Not until Jonathan told him he'd make sure it was done in the coming days.

"Now, hold on," said the manager, turning to his assistant's desk for a paper and pen. "What's your name again?"

"Brooks."

"And your family member?"

"Matt Brooks. You don't have to do a thing yet. I'm making arrangements today and the forensics team will be in touch with you."

"I think you'll need court approval to—"

"I'll do what's necessary," said Jonathan as he walked out. Whatever approval there was, he knew it was a mere formality.

That afternoon, he called AGI Forensics, a private forensics group best known for using DNA technology to clear up paternity disputes. He'd heard they were the best and had also used state-of-the-art polymerase chain reaction technique to assist New Orleans crime scene investigators in high-profile cases. They promised him they'd make all the arrangements and have an answer in ten days or less. That was still a long time to wait, but he accepted.

Jonathan also called Matt's former dentist. Luckily, the dental records were still available, albeit in storage somewhere near Baton Rouge. They promised to furnish Jonathan with x-rays in the coming week.

*       *       *

TELEPHONES always seem to ring louder, and more often, when you're already full of bad news. Jonathan didn't know who it was, but he answered his cell phone on the fifth ring. It was Brett, Linda's co-anchor.

"I'm glad she's alive," Brett said. "It's a tragedy, but we'll manage as best we can without her."

Jonathan was stunned. He knew Brett well, and as the husband of his star co-anchor, he'd expected to hear a little more hope for Linda's full recovery.

"We'll make a formal announcement this evening that someone will fill in for me and I'll take the lead for the time being. And hey, hopefully things will turn out fine and she'll be back in no time."

Brett's words didn't sound like a man concerned about a valuable colleague he'd worked with, side by side, in front of New Orleans' largest television audience. And it would have been nice to hear at least an ounce of concern for Jonathan exit his lips, rather than an impersonal voice uttering words as if they came from a press release.

Jonathan held his tongue. He instead gave the man time to redeem his callous attitude. Time to praise Linda;

to pave the way to Jonathan's ear with how much her smile, charisma and humor were missed at the anchor desk. But no, not a word. Not one uttering of the immense selflessness that radiated from her soul. Jonathan now understood what Linda meant when she said that Brett was a shallow, calculating man. Although he was somewhat shocked by the revelation, Jonathan realized that he should have expected this from a psychiatrist's son who had grown up with a silver spoon so far in his mouth it came out his ass. He owned one of the largest homes along the levee in Algiers, a mixed-race, mixed-class neighborhood on the other side of the river. From a game room on the second floor, Jonathan once heard him utter in a sour-drunk state that "he could see the teeth of every damn nigger working nightshift" at the chemical plant across the water in Arabi. To him, the noble white race—rich whites, in particular—deserved the spoils of this great city, and they needed to take it back, neighborhood by neighborhood. One could only imagine his popularity if his racial views were ever aired publicly.

"You know, I was a little rough on her going off-script that one night—about that court case of yours—but I've already put that behind me. Just between us, Jonathan, your work has no business in our station. But, hey, that's in the past."

"What are you talking about?" asked a surprised Jonathan.

"You mean, you don't know?"

"No."

"She went off-script and told viewers about that

Victory-whatever case you're handling and that viewers should call in if they had any information."

The revelation hit Jonathan like a bat to the head. "Oh my god." He was horrified. It all made sense now. *That broadcast was probably the catalyst to the attack on our home.*

"The other reason I'm calling," Brett said, "is to tell you that a man was asking for Linda. Some black dude. He came by the station when she wasn't here. Apparently responding to her request for information on your case. He left a short note for her and said it was urgent."

"What's it say?" Jonathan asked.

"I don't know; it's at the office. I won't be there until later this evening."

Jonathan asked him to call back as soon as he had the note.

*         *         *

LOYOLA Law School was on Pine Street, the same street as Jonathan's home, about a quarter mile south, toward the river. The neighborhood was a tree-lined sanctuary where in summer the birds chant, law students graze between classes and life seems ideal. Novembers are not much different, though the air is a bit cooler and students somewhat more stressed as finals approach.

Jonathan had become a faithful alumnus of this renowned Jesuit institution that had given him his law degree, cementing an everlasting bond with the profession he loved.

Ten years had gone by quickly, even more so because

he hadn't really seen the place in so long, only occasionally using the library for research or attending an alumni function. But the school was unchanged. It took only a short mental leap to remember scurrying down the hallway with classmates toward the dreaded first year classes, like torts, civil procedure and obligations.

Jonathan took the elevator to the fourth floor, all the while feeling a pleasant nostalgia creeping into him. The roster of professors had familiar names, though he expected them to look older.

Professor Defleur's office was where it had always been, with the familiar odor of cigar smoke seeping out from under the door. As the most-traveled professor at the school, his door was decorated with his latest tacky international souvenir, this time a coaster from a bar in Budapest. He'd been to Moscow and St. Petersburg as a visiting faculty member as far back as the mid-1980s, and again a few times since the Soviet Union collapsed. If there was a man who could give him a useful contact in the Russian capital, it was Defleur. A Post-it note next to the coaster indicated he was in the courtroom downstairs, so Jonathan headed there.

The school's mock courtroom was on the ground floor, in the center of the building. A circular room, complete with a jury box, judge's bench, classroom seats and desktops and a glass-divided audio-visual control room at the back from which the lawyerly theatrics could be filmed. The room was a stage that Jonathan had enjoyed back in the day, learning the tactics that helped him become the litigator he was today.

Before knocking, Jonathan brought his eye to the

peephole and immediately caught sight of his old professor. There were no students in sight.

"Professor?" Jonathan said, peeking in timidly.

"Come in," a raspy voice came back from Defleur, his body whipping around. When Jonathan had been a humble L1, the lowest level in a law school's food chain, next to the janitor and groundskeeper, Professor Miles Defleur was the most witty, feisty, and often plain cruel tenured professor on campus. He was as old as Louisiana's *Code Napoleon*. His face was rawhide. Ten more years had turned him into a dinosaur.

Defleur raised his chin, his eyes locking onto Jonathan with an arresting power. "And who are you?" he asked before seeming to remember. "Oh, Jonathan, of course. Back for a refund, are you?"

His gritty humor was still there, a trait that had survived decades of attempted character assassinations from terrified students.

"No," said Jonathan with a smile. "I just want to tap into your brain." He walked to the center of the room and gazed at the familiar surroundings.

"You've got five minutes," said Defleur as he took out his trademark lecture notes: a single sheet of paper, folded in half long way, its sloppily perforated edge indicating that it had been torn hastily from its pad. The man didn't need notes. A former judge, he embodied the holy grail of myriad courtrooms. *A bit like Gary*, Jonathan thought, *but with more vinegar*. "My classes start on time, as you recall," the old academic added.

"I need a lawyer in Moscow," Jonathan said, realizing he didn't really have time to explain why and knowing damn well Defleur would ask.

"Really?"

"Yes, a smart lawyer."

"And I need a new fishing rod," Defleur uttered, chuckling, as he unfolded his note and pressed it flat on the defense table. "What on earth for?"

"You said I have five minutes," Jonathan murmured, "so it's not enough time to explain to your satisfaction."

"Uhuh," said Defleur, scratching his cheeks, bristly with whitish hair and deep wrinkles. "I can think of a few . . . a law professor who's an unparalleled genius during his five hours of daily sobriety, but useless otherwise; a wealthy oil and gas lawyer with an addiction to corporate kickbacks and call girls; a criminal defense lawyer who lives his life like Casanova; and a young judge turned Mafia hunter—ensuring for himself the lifespan of a goldfish."

Jonathan laughed and clarified, "I'm looking for a smart *and* dependable lawyer. Now that I've had the naive scholarly optimism sucked out of me by the practice of law, I feel like you've just described most of my New Orleans colleagues. Since law school, we've all transformed into the same corruptible, cynical, skeptical subspecies, Professor. Don't you think?"

Defleur's eyes were wide open. "I hope you never tell that to a jury." He then erupted in laughter. "You have one minute and thirty seconds."

"Okay, I'll take the Casanova, if those are the only ones to choose from."

"They are," the professor murmured. "I have vetted them from a larger group, if you can believe that. The fella's name is Alexandre Ivanovich Abramov. I met him last year during my last visit. He taught a class to my visiting students. And he's well connected, if that is useful to you, although I hear he is pretty busy these days. I'll e-mail you his contact information later today."

Jonathan thanked the professor, gave him his card and left satisfied that he had a name in Moscow, but apprehensive that Alexandre might not be as reliable a lawyer as he'd need.

# 10

A TWENTY-FIVE MINUTE DRIVE NORTH ACROSS TOWN TO Terrace Lake may not seem like much, but for Jonathan it was an arduous occasion that required him to take on a tough skin, something he could not so easily do when it came to his brother. But today, he gathered the courage to face the past—to venture for the first time in years to the hallowed grounds of the Milneburg Lighthouse, a place which he and his brother shared with no one else, not even their Dobermans.

It was no ordinary lighthouse. Built in 1855, it became the landmark of a now non-existent amusement park on Lake Pontchartrain. And as daring, mischievous kids, Jonathan and Matt had made it their secret turf to explore adolescence and build a bond stronger than most siblings ever experience. Of all the memories Jonathan had of Matt, none were more cherished than those from the lighthouse. And none were so vivid, etched into memory with frightening clarity.

Jonathan parked his car in a cul-de-sac off Elysian Fields Avenue. As he got out, he saw the bright facade of the lighthouse, illuminated by the nearly-full moon. He picked up a six-pack of Abita Amber from the back seat and walked a couple hundred yards across the wet grass, property of the University of New Orleans, and the place where the brick tower lay orphaned for decades several thousand feet from shore. But that's why it was so special—an abandoned lighthouse nowhere near the water, in the middle of a barren field.

As children, Matt and Jonathan rode their bikes along the edge of City Park, all the way to the lakefront to their hideaway. It was there that Matt had first smoked a cigarette, with Jonathan providing both the incentive and the pack of Marlboro Reds. This oasis was also where Jonathan fabricated his first homemade rocket, having assembled it over a period of five months. They had chosen a clear Saturday afternoon to launch it. Concerned that his own engineering skills were still in development, Jonathan convinced Matt to light the fuse. The resulting explosion lifted nothing into the air except Matt. With slight burns to his right hand and a blackened face, Matt had learned the first rule about brotherhood: never to follow instructions. The blast had dug a two-inch hole in the cement floor of the lighthouse and quickly drew the attention of a patrol car. They'd escaped, but just barely.

A month later, they succeeded in launching the second rocket, a seven-foot long monstrosity, painted black and white to resemble the Apollo spacecraft. It blasted so high they could hardly see it. They never knew where it landed, but they watched the news that night—something their parents surely found bizarre—and prayed it had not landed on someone's head.

One summer, Jonathan and Matt had traveled back and forth to the lighthouse to bring half a dozen old couch cushions, crib mattresses and oversized pillows, piling them at the base of the structure. The objective was nothing short of foolhardy: to jump from the top and land without breaking bones—quite a challenge from twenty-five feet up. All had gone well for a few hours, and then, unfortunately, Jonathan broke his ankle, and by the end of the week, Matt his wrist.

Milneburg Lighthouse had become the citadel of Satan's rascals and a way to become accustomed to orthopedists, and neither had ever told their parents the truth about where and how they'd been injured. They had taken a vow of silence that remained unbroken long after they'd stopped frequenting their prized hideout.

Seventeen years had made a difference. There was a whole lot more grass, weeds and shrubs than Jonathan had remembered. He climbed over the short fence and headed to the concrete base of the tower. He grabbed a metal handle and pulled himself up to the door that stood some five feet above the weeds.

He pushed on the door and felt it give a bit. A second, harder push made it open with a protracted screeching sound. Jonathan gazed into the familiar belly of the beast, the damp, acrid air filling his lungs but without bothering him.

The inner chamber was exactly as in the past, only its confines now felt smaller. He climbed the narrow, spiral metal stairs to the top and emerged into the open air almost short of breath. The old lantern, dating back to the 1880s, was still in its proper place, attached to its clunky rotating mechanism. Jonathan smiled, soaking in the warm feeling of familiarity.

The breeze pushed on his face with gentle strength. He gripped the cold metal handrail and stared at the distant shore. He smiled as the voice of Lucky Lucy, as he later called her, suddenly trampled over his fond recollections. Not a voice carrying words, but rather moans. Loud moans of pleasure like nothing he'd ever heard before. This Tower of Babel had also played a vital role in propelling Jonathan to manhood. Lucy's arms stretched across the floor of the circular balcony where he now stood. Her breasts, the largest his virgin eyes had ever seen or dreamed of. Those fleshy, perfectly round masses took up his entire field of vision. Her methodical, nearly musical chants broke the silence of the memorable night before his fourteenth birthday. He'd learned two tricks in one evening: how to talk a woman into sex and *not* call her the day after.

Jonathan had heard much later that Lucy had also helped Matt leap out of his virginity that same year. Though he had to pry it out of Matt, the confession detailed the same woman, the same breasts, the same pleasantly traumatic reaction to that hypermoaning sexual predator ten years his senior. And to be kind to Matt, Jonathan never told him he'd already taken her for a spin.

"I miss our crazy days, Matt," Jonathan said loudly, staring out at the dark sky, exhaling a mild alcohol breath from his sips of beer. "We were so *free*."

He stared at the bright moon. Everything valuable in his life had now been taken away or held in jeopardy. And it was a miserable acknowledgement.

Before heading back to the hospital, Jonathan went to his office and sent a fax to Alexandre in Moscow. He was brief and to the point. He wanted information about General Yakovlev, and he wanted it as quickly as possible. Jonathan didn't know if he could go to Russia, though he wanted to. But to do so would mean leaving Linda behind, something he quickly dismissed. He would not leave her. Not until she was out of danger.

# 11

LITIGATION FIRMS, LIKE AUTOMOBILE ASSEMBLY PLANTS and steel mills, never close. And certainly not Jonathan's. With twenty-nine high-powered lawyers— two-thirds of them partners—you'd be sure to find at least one in the office at any moment of the night.

Jonathan knew the nocturnal routine well, though these days the firm's young associates tended to know it better. From the time the paralegals and secretaries leave, these legal machines press on, reading documents with the speed of a supercomputer, free from the nuisances of senseless meetings, ringing phones, and petty questions from clients. Even at ten or eleven, their efficiency only mildly downgraded, they churn out their paperwork and impel their analytical skills with amazing ease. It's only by one or two in the morning that the engine starts to taper off. At that point, they either head home or hunker down at their desks for the night until the staff returns, the latter choice often leading to the gradual onset of a vegetative state that can bring an attorney to the brink of malpractice.

It was not yet ten and Jonathan knew he didn't have it in him to stay all night. The stress had beaten him down. Besides, he needed to be with Linda. He glanced out his window and saw the bright lights along Canal Street. His eyes felt glassy. For over three hours he had stared at the monitor on his credenza, analyzing video-taped depositions of Captains Glengeyer and Tucker, as well as other witnesses.

The phone rang. It was Brett, Linda's co-anchor. He had picked up the letter she'd received. Jonathan asked that he read it over the phone, which he did.

"*Shiit*," Brett uttered, "why can't these people learn to write?"

Jonathan knew exactly what this bigot meant.

"It says 'Dear Ms. Brooks, I'm writing about your report the other night on that court case. I was in the Baltic, and I saw something real strange going on. It may be useful, I don't know. You are a nice lady and I enjoy you on the news. Let me know if I can help. God bless, Sammy Dupree.'"

"That's it?" asked Jonathan, hoping for a lot more and suddenly feeling an uncontrollable rush of frustration take hold of him. *Come on, spit it out!* His patience with everything was wearing thin because he was exhausted. He wanted things to be so much simpler, with far more clarity, requiring less of an arduous mental crawl, which he would have to muster in his sad state.

"Yep, and a phone number," the jerk replied efficiently. "Oh, there's more: five calls on her voice mail from other people also claiming to have been there, and they left their contact info."

Jonathan wrote down the numbers and hung up.

It was still difficult to believe Linda had done such an incredibly selfless act. Sure, it was thoughtful. But now she was paying a heavy price for her on-the-air query. The troubling thoughts prompted Jonathan to call the hospital. He spoke with the head nurse. Linda was stable, asleep, but still in a grave condition. He would be with her soon. But it was late and he first had to make his calls before doing so would be rude.

By ten-thirty, Jonathan had called all those who had left a message with Linda, with the exception of Sammy Dupree, who he thought might take longer than the others. But none of their accounts appeared useful. Either they had served on the mainland, in bases located in Germany or the Netherlands, or they had been in the Baltic during periods that were irrelevant to Jonathan's case. *Perhaps Dupree will be more useful*, he thought.

The phone rang a couple times before Dupree answered, and Jonathan explained who he was.

"Man, I'm sure sorry 'bout cho wife," Dupree said, his voice deep and sedate. Jonathan felt a comforting sincerity in the man's words.

"So, you were in northern Europe?" Jonathan asked.

"Sure was," Dupree said and then a long breath caught Jonathan's ear, as if the man was smoking. "Now, I don't want no trouble, you know. And I don't want to go to court, or nothin' like that."

"You don't have to," lied Jonathan. "I'm only looking for leads."

There was silence on the other end for several seconds—enough hesitation for Jonathan to tell himself not to be too pushy.

"I was there, around the middle of March, 1989," Dupree said. "I 'member real well, cuz som' strange happened. I didn't even know the details until days later, when my shipmates told me. What I know is just what I hear. I didn't see nothin' from down there."

"Down where?"

"The galley."

Jonathan didn't understand. "Galley?"

"In the sub," said Dupree as if Jonathan should have known. "I was chief cook on a submarine."

"Which one?"

"I'd rather not say on the phone," Dupree replied, his voice withdrawing, followed by a long exhale telling Jonathan he was nearing the butt of his cigarette. "I'm a simple man and don't want no problems, you know."

"I promise," assured Jonathan. "I can keep everything you tell me confidential. And if it's helpful, I'll gladly pay you for your trouble."

"Well, okay then. Can we meet tomorrow?"

They arranged the rendezvous for the next morning.

Jonathan left his office and headed out through the side door of the building, hopping into a waiting cab in the dark alley. Every move he made was designed to minimize exposure to those who wanted him dead.

During the five-minute drive to Charity Hospital, Jonathan replayed Dupree's words. He did this again on his walk from the lobby to the elevator and to the ICU. Every word. He was excited. With luck, whatever

Dupree would have to say would have some link with
the *USS Meecham* or the plane crash. But his excitement
quickly vanished when he saw the cop standing outside
Linda's door. The seriousness of the moment had set in,
even more so when he entered the cold room and
stepped to her side. He gazed at her blank expression,
her eyes closed, her body silently struggling to survive.
*It'll be another long night*, he told himself.

*          *          *

THE next morning, using Allen's car as a precaution,
Jonathan left for his meeting with Dupree, taking a
lengthy, convoluted route to make sure he wasn't followed.

He spotted the hangar-shaped bus maintenance depot
on Magazine Street and parked in the adjacent alley. He
walked to the corner and waited by the storefront of a
tobacco shop, as Dupree had asked.

There were few cars on the street. The sidewalks
were vacant. The desolation made him nervous—more
than he already was. And after all that had happened, he
wasn't about to blindly trust anyone, not even Dupree,
no matter how sincere he had sounded on the phone.
Jonathan gazed at his car, calculating the seconds it
would take to run to it, unlock the door, jump in, start the
engine and bolt out of there, *if* something went wrong.

At eleven, nothing had happened. Eleven-fifteen the
same. By eleven-twenty, Jonathan was convinced the
man would not show up. He glanced westward. Not a
soul in sight. And then he glanced toward the east, where
a man headed his way waved from a block away, on the

other side of the street. He was black, wearing a long white apron, jeans and a dark T-shirt. Jonathan suspected he was employed in a nearby restaurant. The man casually waved again at the suited lawyer as he began crossing the street.

"You're Dupree?" asked Jonathan not yet letting go of his nervousness. He felt better when the man nodded and returned a wide, gap toothed smile.

They shook hands. Dupree's was warm and felt coarse.

"Call me Sammy." He checked his wristwatch, then eyed each end of the street and turned to the alleyway. "Let's walk over there, outta the spotlight."

"Can I drive you somewhere and buy you a coffee?" Jonathan asked, hoping it was a better option than to walk down a small side-street with a total stranger. "My car's right here."

Dupree walked ahead of Jonathan. "No, I'm on break and need to get back in a few minutes."

Jonathan didn't insist and simply accompanied the man to the narrow street behind the bus depot. Dupree, seeming quite at ease, patted Jonathan's shoulder and said, "So you a lawyer, huh?"

"That's right. That should make me a good listener."

"That's not what I hear 'bout them lawyers."

Jonathan chuckled, "Whatever you've heard is probably true—good and bad."

"I thought so, and mostly bad," said Dupree with a deep laugh. He stopped and leaned against a stack of wooden crates.

"This lawyer is all ears. Tell me what happened."

"What I got may be completely useless to you, so I ain't promising nothin'."

"Understood."

"I served on the *USS Bergall*, a Sturgeon Class nuclear-powered fast attack submarine. We were on a Northern Run—what we call our deployments in the North Atlantic and Arctic. We sailed from Norfolk to Europe and stayed submerged for about forty days with very little action. But then, I remember sometime in the middle of March, something horrible happened. I was in the galley preparing meals for the crew when all of a sudden the lights started flashing—the signal for going all-quiet."

"All quiet?"

"Yeah, when a Soviet vessel was in the area, we needed all hands to stop making noise. So the lights were the signal for us to clamp down. In the galley, that meant turning off the ovens, securing the pans and cookware, putting everything back in the refrigerators. And, of course, the guys in the dining area headed to their stations."

Jonathan didn't think this too unusual, given what he had read about the cat and mouse games between NATO and the Soviets.

Dupree rubbed his curly, graying hair and added, "We stayed like that for about an hour and then we *surfaced*—something a sub on patrol only does if it's on fire or it's reaching port. We were neither. I knew something was wrong. But it was later that I discovered how wrong."

"Where were you then?"

"In the Baltic—that too I found out later. Keep in mind, a cook *always* finds out—just never right away."

Jonathan crossed his arms. "What happened?"

Before answering, Dupree looked over his shoulder, gazed at the other end of the alley and then stared at Jonathan with his large close-set eyes. "We surfaced so we could shoot down a plane. We had two sailors with Stinger missiles combing the sky in the pitch black night looking for the damn thing and, if that wasn't weird enough, we also had a radio operator trying to contact the aircraft."

"What?" asked Jonathan, finding that awfully contradictory. "To tell the plane what? That you were about to destroy it?"

"No," Dupree uttered, shaking his head. "To make sure they were American."

Jonathan was shocked. What he'd just heard brought some sense to the picture he'd painted in his mind from the moment Tantina had made her farfetched claim. *An American crew blown out of the sky.* It was still baffling, but beginning to sound more believable.

"We were about to shoot down one of our own."

"Are you sure about this?"

"You bet I am," Dupree said, pushing himself away from the crates. "Half the crew knew about it before breakfast. Worse yet, at first the captain refused the shoot-down order when he found out it was an American plane."

"But they *did* shoot it down, right?"

Dupree rubbed his jaw and shook his head. "They sure did," he said solemnly. "They blew it out of the sky.

I also heard that the officers on bridge had picked up the pilot's distress call. Let me tell you, there were some confused faces on board. They were just kids, you know. Most of them eighteen, nineteen. Kids from Iowa, from small towns in Kansas and Georgia, where you still worship the Star Spangled Banner, eat apple pie and trust your government. So for all of us, weird stuff like that is hard to swallow. Things got worse. About a week later we surfaced again, in the middle of the Atlantic and the captain was replaced."

"Replaced?"

"Yeah, for initially refusing the attack order. I heard it first in the officer's mess. A helicopter came by, plucked the guy out and dropped off a new asshole. That's how screwed up it got, man. When we returned to Norfolk 'bout a month later, a Navy lawyer and another mean-looking guy in a suit questioned us—the whole crew, one by one—and made each of us sign a paper that said we wouldn't talk about the incident, or else we'd go to jail."

"A confidentiality agreement."

"Whatever you call it," Dupree said, shaking his head. "Them bastards. They knew they'd done something real bad."

Jonathan's thoughts were scattered by the complexity of Dupree's revelation. If there was anyone who'd corroborate Dupree it was Erland, back in Sweden.

*       *       *

NOT far from the French Quarter, on Broad Street, Jonathan pulled into the parking lot of a small office building. It was the location of AGI Forensics, the private company Derek had recommended as the city's most reliable independent lab to perform tests on remains.

Jonathan sighed as he gazed out the windshield at the entrance and then looked down at the front passenger seat, where lay a red baseball cap. It was Matt's from high school. Derek had found it among his things years ago, after Matt's death. The lab had told Jonathan to bring anything that could still have Matt's hair fibers. And since nothing had survived in Jonathan's burnt home, he was especially thankful that Derek had kept the cap.

The technicians took the hat and then asked to take samples from Jonathan. They drew his blood, plucked some hair fibers and took a swab from his mouth. The whole thing was done in less than twenty minutes, but everything seemed to pass slowly. Jonathan was overwhelmed with grief and stress. Mundane things had morphed into colossal challenges. And there was nothing he could do about it except to be brave and pursue the truth.

As Jonathan headed back to the hospital, he answered his cell phone. "Who did you say you were?" he asked, barely able to hear the voice through the poor signal.

"Michael with AGI. We're here at your brother's grave, sir. We just wanted to let you know we're about to load the remains and should have them at our lab in the next hour or so. Someone will contact you as soon as we know something."

Jonathan acknowledged the man and hung up. He took a deep breath and rested his head back. "I just want to know the truth," he whispered to himself. "Forgive me, Matt, if I've made a mistake." His eyes began to water, and the entire drive to Linda's hospital was filled with memories.

# 12

UNLESS YOU ARE ILL, HOSPITALS ARE AWFUL PLACES TO sleep. If it's not the smell of disinfectants, it's the bright lights or the crappy attitudes of overworked, underpaid and underappreciated nurses and nurse's aides. For Jonathan, the horribly uncomfortable old chair was another reason. And for the price of medical care nowadays, he ought to have been laying on a bed of ivory, padded with ostrich feather pillows and the finest Egyptian cotton. Jonathan had just woken up when the door opened.

"I'm Officer Gantreau," whispered the uniformed woman, peaking her head into the room. "I'm the new shift and just wanted to say a quick hello."

He nodded and smiled and then gazed back at Linda, his guilt setting in again. She was asleep, the serenity of her face immediately warming his heart. She had made it through another night. The battle wasn't over, but she was winning.

Jonathan had turned on the television, but left it muted as the local morning news played. He gazed at the screen, his mind drowning in the morsels of traumatic emotions that seemed to take up every part of his cranial cavity.

Suddenly, a grainy picture popped up over the shoulder of the anchorman—a picture that looked awfully familiar.

*Oh, no! Sammy!* Jonathan jumped to his feet and turned up the volume. He stood in disbelief, his chest seizing as if it had been instantly frozen. Dupree was dead, his body discovered floating in a canal under the Filmore Avenue bridge, on the city's north side. It wasn't Dupree's neighborhood. He'd told Jonathan he lived in Gretna, on the south side of the river.

"Police are investigating the cause of death," the anchorman said before switching to another story.

Jonathan turned off the television. He hurriedly dialed Derek at his precinct and counted the seconds before his brother-in-law picked up the phone. In the most abbreviated way possible, Jonathan explained to Derek what he knew about Dupree and that they had met to discuss evidence linked to the Victory Lines case.

"This is getting completely out of hand," Derek said loudly. The empathetic tone he'd had a day earlier was gone. "Meet me right now at the crime lab." He gave Jonathan directions to the Scientific Criminal Investigation Division, as the new facility was officially called. It had opened just two months earlier.

Jonathan had arrived as quickly as he could, about twenty minutes after his call to Derek. He'd never set foot in such a place. As he headed through the lobby of the lab, he conjured up scenes from movies and television shows.

Derek was standing against the wall in the lobby, and he greeted Jonathan with a concerned gaze. "Come with me." Derek led Jonathan through a set of double-doors and down a long hallway. "I already spoke with the supervising deputy coroner. The autopsy will take place in the next day or two."

"But we—"

"Hear me out," Derek said, interrupting his brother-in-law. "But I've arranged for another of the coroner's staff to take an initial look at the body right now. It's not as thorough as the autopsy, but it will give us some clues on the cause of death."

"Good."

"Are you sure about your suspicions? I mean, people die everyday and—"

"I promise I'm not making this up. Just like Linda has been targeted, so was this man. Someone has gone to great lengths to silence him."

Derek introduced Jonathan to Tony Molina, deputy coroner and toxicology analyst. If it weren't for Molina's lab coat, his unshaven face and disheveled hair made him look more like a car mechanic.

"You're here for the guy brought in early this morning, right? Dupree, that's his name, right?"

"Yes, yes," Jonathan said, trying to conceal his eagerness to get things rolling. "This is important."

"Uh-huh." Molina checked his watch, his jaw contorting with his steady gum-chewing. He seemed unfazed by Jonathan's sense of urgency. "All right, come with me." The deputy coroner led his guests through another set of doors, at which point the temperature dropped significantly.

They entered a large room with six metal tables evenly spaced in the center, three of them topped with supine cadavers—one black man, shirtless, with what looked like a huge gash in his chest, and a black woman, still clothed. Dupree's body lay on his back on the farthest table. On shelves along the wall were two other cadavers, Caucasians—one fairly bloodied—wrapped in see-through plastic, tied at their feet with white string.

Dupree was naked. The skin of his face was shrunken, his eyes taped shut. A white tag with his name scribbled in black marker ink hung by a string tied to his big toe.

"He was murdered," Jonathan declared, gazing at Molina and then at Dupree. "I'm sure of it."

"Well, it would be just one of ten murders this week, and, hell, over three hundred so far this year," Molina replied with a grin, seeming rather blasé about Jonathan's claim.

Molina put on examination gloves and picked up a chart on the wall behind Dupree and returned to the body. "71 inches, 189 pounds, black male, aged 41."

"The decedent was found partially floating on the banks of the canal," said Derek. "I guess he'd been dead a few hours."

"I know," Molina said. He raised Dupree's left arm. "Other than this small abrasion on his palm, there are no other abrasions or bruises anywhere else on the body. No

puncture wounds either, or any signs of blunt trauma."
Molina lowered Dupree's arm and met Jonathan's gaze.
"It doesn't appear like a murder to me. The decedent's
clothing was not damaged, and x-rays revealed no broken bones or other internal injuries. Body surface and
discoloration of the skin is consistent with drowning."

"Didn't the paramedics report an odor of alcohol?"
asked Derek.

Molina scoffed. "Many drowning victims are intoxi-
cated, which explains why they're careless in the first
place. We're waiting on preliminary toxicology results,
but the final results will come only after the autopsy."

Jonathan shook his head and glanced at Derek. "I'm
confident there was foul play."

"It doesn't look that way right now," Molina said,
now sounding cocky and impatient. "The medical exam-
iner will conduct the autopsy and make his own conclu-
sions, but from what I see this is a classic case of drowning, perhaps combined with alcohol intoxication."

Jonathan left the crime lab a little before eleven.
Despite Molina's claim that there were no initial signs of
foul play, Jonathan was already convinced Vice-Admiral
Scarborough had his goons do the dirty work. But he
worried that Derek was not yet persuaded.

*          *          *

NAPOLEON Street, just past the intersection with
Baronne Street, is the home of Pascal's Manale, a his-
toric Garden District Italian-Creole hangout. For
Jonathan, it had always meant a welcome break from
busy court hearings to indulge in barbecued shrimp and

savor a few bottles of Abita Amber with his buddies. Today, he'd try to bring back some semblance of normalcy. He walked in and strolled straight to the bar, the last stool. The smell of garlic and seafood filtered through his lungs. It had been a while.

He had barely finished his plate when his cell phone rang. It was Gary, and he sounded anxious, his words barreling in too fast for Jonathan to catch them.

"What are you saying?" Jonathan asked, holding his finger in the other ear to block out the loud conversation of his fellow bar patrons.

"I said Judge Breaux's chambers were broken into last night. I left a message on your voice mail a short while ago."

"My God," Jonathan spat out, quickly sensing this was no coincidence. "I didn't get your message because I was at the crime lab."

"Crime lab?"

"I'll explain later," Jonathan said, now gripped with dread. "What happened?"

"The judge had kept in his safe the original ship's log and other documentation the Navy had turned over yesterday. And today, I hear it was stolen. The safe was pried open like a can of tuna."

"They did it!" Jonathan declared. "The Navy, the government, don't you see? They were forced to turn over the evidence, but then they stole it—it's brilliant."

Gary paused. "I'm not sure it's so clear, but I am suspicious."

"What do you mean, Gary? It's clear as daylight. Who the hell would do this? And who would have the skills to get into a federal building and pop open a vault, for crying out loud?"

"I understand," Gary replied. "but if they did it, I'm sure they've covered their tracks quite well."

He was right. Jonathan knew there was little chance the break-in would create a trail back to Scarborough. As silence took over the phone line, Jonathan came to grips with the worst realization of Gary's news: these were original documents, and with their disappearance, Scarborough and his legal crony, Tillerman, had all the excuse they needed to say they had no other copies. *How perfect*, Jonathan thought. *How damn convenient for those bastards*. He was furious. He shoved his empty plate forward, slamming it against the beer taps. "I'm heading to the office. Can you meet me there right away?"

"Sure, Jonathan, sure." Gary sounded exasperated. If this case was killing Jonathan, it was no doubt ulcerating his law firm partner.

*          *          *

JONATHAN arrived at the office to find Gary sitting quietly in the main conference room, the phone line stretched to his corner of the table.

"Have a seat, please," Gary said, his voice barely audible, his eyes never leaving the closed folder in front of him, which told Jonathan something else was wrong.

"What is it?" Jonathan asked.

"We're settling this case."

"But we can't!" Jonathan bounced back on his feet. Gary raised both his hands. "Wait, wait, wait! We have no choice. We don't have the logbooks, there are still too many open questions, and . . ."

"And what?" Jonathan asked angrily.

Gary sighed. "And the insurance company is offering 6.5 million, to which our client said yes. They can't afford to fight this any longer. You know that."

Jonathan walked off.

"It doesn't mean I don't believe you," said Gary. "For God's sake, Jonathan, you're the best lawyer I have."

Jonathan stopped at the door and looked back at Gary, wanting desperately to believe this was all a joke, that Gary was just pulling his chain, that the case would go on. That victory was near. But it wasn't so.

Gary slowly got up and held up the folder. "It's all here: the settlement agreement and a fax from our client instructing us that they have no objections." Gary lay his hand on Jonathan's shoulder and gazed into his eyes. "The moment you nailed Captain Tucker with his lies about the *USS Meecham's* whereabouts, this became a battle on two fronts. We may have surrendered on one, but the other is still there, and I am on your side, my friend. I will not let you down, nor will I let Linda down. Let's get the assholes on our own terms, and we don't need our clients to do it."

Jonathan felt as if he could kiss the old man, but he was still weighed by disappointment that the case would end on such terms. He knew it would be infinitely harder to press the Navy for anything now that there was a settlement.

"Thank you, Gary. I do need your help, your wisdom

and your patience. Let me tell you what I've discovered so far." Jonathan explained to Gary everything he knew and suspected.

"You're a good man," Gary said, as Jonathan finished and they walked out of the conference room. "Do what you need to do."

"When Linda is a little better, I'm going to Russia," Jonathan said. "And I'll need your help back here, including your help to keep Linda safe. These people have gone to huge lengths to derail a legal case, to silence me and my wife, to kill a witness. They could do much more. They could come after you. After Allen."

"To them I say, *bring it on!*" Gary said loudly, waving his fist.

*        *        *

JONATHAN didn't turn on the television the next morning. He didn't want any more surprises. He crawled out of his chair, stretching the stiffness out from his limbs and reached for Linda's hand. Today, he hoped she would be more lucid, as her dosage of pain medication had reduced just a bit. He wanted to hear her voice, to speak with her. And to his delight she turned her head toward him.

"How are you, my love?" he whispered. "I am so glad you are pulling through."

Linda's eyes cracked open. Her soft voice mumbled something but she didn't have the strength to speak any louder or more clearly.

"I love you," Jonathan said, gazing at her serene expression. "I have always been yours, since we were kids. Remember those days, in my parent's backyard. 'Member all those times you beat me up with that plastic chair of yours? How many bruises do you think you gave me?"

She swallowed and gathered her strength. "It explains . . . the brain damage: you became a lawyer." She smiled, as did Jonathan.

"You must be getting better. Your humor is coming back."

Jonathan kissed her hand and held it between both of his. "When you are better, I must go to Russia. I think Matt survived the plane crash and was taken there against his will, and that he still may be alive. Everything you and I were told was a lie. I am sure the remains we buried are not his. And I'm certain they did this to you."

"Matt's alive?" Linda breathed, her voice weak.

Jonathan held her hand to his cheek. He felt he was about to cry, but fought it off. He couldn't appear weak, when what she needed the most was strength. "I don't know what I will find, but I am desperate for the truth."

"Go now. Don't wait." Linda took another deep breath. She looked in pain. "Please, do what needs to be done." Linda tilted her head toward Jonathan. She seemed in even greater pain than a few moments earlier, her breaths now short and deep. Her hand gripped his tightly. Her other hand gripped the bed sheet.

"I'll call the nurse?"

"Please." Linda's face cringed and her eyes closed.

Jonathan returned with the nurse, who quickly injected the painkiller into Linda's IV.

"Go, go find Matt," she whispered as the effects of the medication rapidly sent her back to sleep.

*     *     *

GARY had urged Jonathan to stay at the hospital over the weekend. Now that Jonathan had his Russian travel visa and had made arrangements with the Russian lawyer Professor DeFleur had recommended, there was no need to risk being out of police protection, so Jonathan stayed with Linda. As the hour of his departure approached, his anxiety mounted over leaving her alone, but Derek had ensured that the police presence outside Linda's room would stay as long as Jonathan asked for it. Derek had also promised that he and Caroline would continue to come by a least once a day.

Gary had come by earlier and dropped off a guide to Moscow as well as a map. He'd also brought him a suitcase full of clothes and personal effects, traveler's checks and several thousand dollars in cash. Jonathan would soon be on his way to Russia, armed with not much more than hope. Gary had also promised Jonathan he would contact the FBI, and more importantly, Senator Labenne, a former law school colleague of his. "Surely, they couldn't be webbed to Scarborough's conspiracy," Gary had said, which Jonathan hoped would be true. Anything was possible.

# 13

JONATHAN'S PLANE LANDED JUST BEFORE NOON AT Moscow's Sheremetyevo Airport. The exhausting twelve-hour flight was compounded by a ridiculously long wait at the passport control, located in a dark hall filled with the pervasive odor of armpits. The booth that had to process three hundred fatigued, impatient passengers was manned by only one officer. This wasn't the welcome Jonathan had expected of mighty Russia.

As he entered the arrivals lounge, a man approached him.

"Transport," the lanky guy said loudly with a heavy Russian accent. His eyes locked onto Jonathan's, and that's when he grabbed the American's luggage cart. "Transport. City. Cheap, cheap."

Jonathan shook his head and was about to give the guy the finger, when out of nowhere a large-framed, goateed man the size of an armoire stepped forward, swatted the annoying fellow aside and greeted Jonathan.

"Meestar Brooks, *da*?" he asked in a deep voice.

"Yes, are you Alexandre?"

"*Nyet*, I take you to Alexandre. Me driver, Boris." He had high, pointy cheekbones and slightly bronze skin that told Jonathan he was not an ethnic Russian, or Slavic for that matter. *From the southern republics*, Jonathan thought.

Jonathan followed him outside. The place was a madhouse, with drivers vying for a prized spot at the curb, their horns blaring, with hands gesturing and words that sounded unfriendly in any language. Boris led the way through a pack of travelers arguing with police and onto the far end of the drive-up area, where a boxy, white car idled.

Boris was such a large man, his knees hugged the steering column and his head rubbed up against the car's ceiling. *If he scratches his ass, the car will simply rip open at its steel seams*, Jonathan observed.

The first ten minutes of the ride gave little indication of the bustling metropolis Jonathan was impatiently expecting. Instead, vast snow-covered fields extended as far as the eye could see. But the view quickly changed after the airport road crossed over a wide divided highway and veered onto a huge, busy boulevard.

"Germans stop here—the limit," said Boris, pointing to a strange object in the distance. "Moscow defense."

Jonathan leaned forward as his Russian driver again pointed at the object. It was a large six-pronged, metal tank obstacle. Jonathan gathered that it was a monument marking the farthest point of the Nazi incursion into the city during World War Two.

"No mess with Russia, huh," Boris said with a playful frown and then swiped his hand across his neck in a slashing gesture. He then laughed.

They crossed dozens of spacious intersections busy with foot traffic on the wide, crowded sidewalks. Jonathan was in awe at the massive concrete buildings that lined the streets. He'd never seen so many, and certainly not in New Orleans. Some appeared to be apartment blocks, while others had the austere look of government offices.

"Alexandre is not ready until one hour, so I take long way, okay?" Boris asked. "For you see city good, *da?*"

Jonathan nodded, watching Boris rotate the steering wheel with his octopus-sized hands as if he were driving a bumper car.

They continued along an eight-lane avenue, its sidewalks wide enough for a herd of elephants.

"At left is famous Ukraina Hotel," Boris said pointing over his shoulder at a colossal square structure crowned by a central tower some forty stories high, its architecture resembling a '30s-era New York high-rise. As they approached a bridge, he then pointed at a large white building on the other side of the river. "White House—*Rossiisky Parlament*, and this here, Moskva River."

The curvy banks along the calm waters were heavily trafficked and lined with old, mid-rise buildings. But what struck Jonathan as odd was the lack of billboards, neon and other advertising clutter that he was so used to seeing back home.

Boris was a fast driver. Though he seemed eager to

show off his city's landmarks, he didn't slow down long enough for Jonathan to observe each one with any degree of detail.

"Kremlin," Boris blurted out before pointing his pudgy finger over the steering wheel.

Jonathan spotted the Kremlin's maroon-colored fortress walls some five hundred yards away. As the car drew nearer, Russia's citadel of power rose from the ground even more impressively. Several cone-shaped towers were built into the massive wall. Boris continued along a wide street that ran parallel to the back of the Kremlin.

A few more large buildings passed before Jonathan heard another familiar name.

"Bolshoi," Boris said, pointing at the world-renowned theater, its Roman columned façade standing elegantly about a hundred yards away. "And here, your hotel—Metropol."

"Wonderful," Jonathan said, gazing at the sprawling five-story hotel. Its grandiose windows, wrought-iron balconies and elaborately painted tile roofline were clear signs that this was no run of the mill address. Jonathan had seen more world-class landmarks in the last forty minutes than many of his N'awlins buddies had seen in a lifetime. The excitement had momentarily made him forget his exhaustion and all the other stresses that were pulling him apart.

Boris headed to the back of the building and pulled up under the glass canopy, where a bellman quickly appeared. Boris said a few words to the bellman that quickly brought the hotel employee to an even more formal demeanor. "I told him you are a guest of Alexandre, so he will take good care of you. Wait in your room."

Jonathan nodded and watched as the giant man defied the laws of physics by re-entering his compact car. Jonathan then checked in and went up to his third-floor room, which could easily have passed for a presidential suite. The cherry wood furniture, with golden accents, was meticulously crafted. He strolled to the window, cracked it open and soaked in the splendid views and sounds of the bustling goings-on. To his right, across the busy ten-lane boulevard, was the Bolshoi and in front of it a large fountain at the center of a pedestrian square. To his left was a snow-covered park that took up an entire block. The cool breeze wrapped around his face and the scent of diesel fumes seeped into his lungs as his thoughts once again migrated to troubled ground: Linda. He pictured her lying in her hospital bed. The same solemn gaze. The same helplessness. Her life hanging by a thread.

After unpacking his things, the phone rang, and he immediately answered.

"Hello," a male voice said in English. "This is Alexandre Ivanovich. I am in the hotel lobby." He spoke Jonathan's language with a hybrid accent that sounded part Canadian, part American, with a tinge of Russian.

Jonathan was delighted. "I'll be down in a few minutes."

Wanting to start things off with as much goodwill as possible, Jonathan took with him a bottle of Jack Daniels he'd purchased at New Orleans airport for that very purpose. "Russians are born drinkers," Gary had told him.

Jonathan would later realize how right his partner was.

Alexandre was not at all what Jonathan had expected. He was clean-cut, pale-skinned and wore an expensive suit. When Professor Defleur had told him he'd hook him up with an energetic Moscow criminal defense attorney, he'd instantly pictured a bounty hunter. The surprise was reassuring, to say the least.

"*Priyatno poznakomitza,*" Alexandre said. "It means 'nice to meet you.'"

"The pleasure is all mine," Jonathan replied, shaking hands with him and adding, "*Da,*" the only Russian word he'd picked up so far. He then handed him the gift box, with the clear plastic front showing the bottle inside.

It was as if Alexandre had seen a bullion of gold. His eyes lit up, and a huge smile emerged on his young, rosy face.

"Your English is excellent," Jonathan remarked, thinking how fortunate this was. Absent that, Jonathan would have been in a hell of bind. The Cyrillic alphabet on everything he'd seen since the airport had already made him feel as if he'd landed on an entirely different planet.

"Thank you," said Alexandre proudly. "I was always interested in languages, so I learned English and French at the same time as my juridical studies at Moscow State University. It was not easy."

"I can imagine," Jonathan said.

"I mean not easy because the school did not like me learning English, particularly. Unless it was for a special purpose, like for the government or military, the school administration reacted with suspicion, you understand? So, much of my learning was after class."

"We Americans prefer to stay monolingual to make things simpler," Jonathan said.

The two men laughed. They headed to the hotel's coffee shop, and after ordering tea and pastries, Alexandre got to the crux of the meeting.

"So you are looking for General Yakovlev, is that right?" Alexandre asked, his tone hinting that he already had answers.

"Yes."

"Well, I found only one person by that name and rank: Major-General Yakovlev Andrei Matveyovich."

"Fantastic!"

"Well, not really," Alexandre said with a sigh. "He's dead."

Jonathan's smile faded. "Oh?"

"He died in 1993, during the parliamentary revolt in Moscow. He was one of the high ranking communist officers who took over the White House—our parliament. He was killed when the army retook the building floor by floor. It was a bloody affair."

"Yes, I remember seeing that on television. Didn't a tank attack the building?"

"Many times. Half of the White House was on fire." Alexandre put his hands together, his large gold watch emerging from under his sleeve. "I tried to call you before you left to tell you the general is not alive, but it was too late. Your secretary told me you had already taken your flight. I didn't want you to waste your time coming here if this man is dead."

"Are you sure he's the right person, and there isn't someone else with a similar name."

"Positive, Mr. Brooks."

"Call me Jonathan."

Alexandre took a sip of his tea. "Okay."

"Do you have more on Yakovlev?"

"This is what I found." Alexandre dug into his brief-case and pulled out a plastic file folder. "His last posting was as chief intelligence officer at the Gagarin Air Force Academy, not far from Moscow. Before that, he served briefly as a senior analyst with the GRU—Soviet mili-tary intelligence. And prior to that he was with the Third Main Directorate of the KGB in Leningrad and also in Afghanistan, but it's not clear what exactly he did in any of these posts."

"What is the Third Main Directorate?" Jonathan asked.

"Principally counterintelligence and security, but it doesn't exist anymore under that name. Everything was reorganized after 1991."

Jonathan had many more questions, but he was frus-trated that the general was dead. He realized that the task of finding anything remotely useful would now be infi-nitely more problematic.

Alexandre flipped through the pages of his file and said, "I came across his name in many documents relat-ing to the parliament uprising. Coincidentally, I repre-sented over twenty officers, mostly mid-level, who were charged with treason and other crimes relating to the revolt. General Yakovlev is definitely dead."

Jonathan hadn't come all this way to simply turn

back. Alexandre had been quite resourceful in quickly finding the general's background. That meant he would be able to dig up a whole lot more if he had additional time. But then again, Jonathan wanted to approach things as methodically—and as prudently—as possible. His near-death encounter after his meeting with Tillerman and Vice-Admiral Scarborough had left him with a deep distrust for anyone with authority. It was entirely possible that despite Defleur's recommendation, Alexandre too was untrustworthy. *What if they're all in cahoots*, Jonathan thought anxiously, before dismissing his concern as a momentary spell of paranoia. But he was in a huge city known for its extreme corruption and danger, and being cautious was something he'd have to take seriously.

"Since I'm here, I would like to know more about Yakovlev. And I'm willing to pay for your services at your normal rates."

Alexandre seemed unsettled. "Well, it's easy for me to charge fees. But I'm not sure what I can do for you."

"I need to know Yakovlev's activities around 1989. He must have had people working with him. Someone, somewhere must have known what he was doing." Jonathan wasn't prepared to give Alexandre details about what he'd learned in Gotland.

"I see," Alexandre said. "That's possible. I have many more documents at the office, and I can make more calls as well."

"I would be very grateful," Jonathan said.

"Why do you have such an interest in this general?"

"I will gladly explain this to you later," Jonathan

said. He wasn't comfortable giving this stranger any more details than he had to.

Alexandre appeared surprised but simply shrugged his shoulders. "No problem."

The waitress brought another tea.

Jonathan was curious about Alexandre's legal practice, and so he asked, "Tell me, what do you do?"

"I've been a criminal defense lawyer for about ten years, defending a wide range of clients, many of them former city officials, military officers, and, on occasion, some violent criminals." He raised his brow and added, "But I have avoided defending certain *businessmen*, if you know what I mean. In this city, it is not uncommon for those kinds of clients to kill their lawyers if they don't like the result."

"That's less of a problem where I come from," Jonathan said, smiling. "Clients simply don't pay their bills."

Alexandre returned the grin. "Russia is in transition, and things are a mess. Many vital laws are either new or not yet enacted, and enforcement is difficult, arbitrary and susceptible to unfair influence. It's not a pleasant environment, but I hope things will improve."

"Criminal defense is a challenging practice anywhere, Alexandre. Not every attorney has the stamina for it."

"Let me give you an insight into today's Russia, with this joke . . . Clinton and Yeltsin arrive at the gates of hell. They are given a choice to reside either in the American zone, where you must eat one bucket of shit every day, or the Russian zone, where you must eat two a day. So, Clinton, wanting less shit, picks the American zone, and Yeltsin, drunk as usual but retaining a modicum of wisdom, picks the Russian zone. A few weeks later they meet again, and Yeltsin asks how things are. 'Great!' Clinton says, 'you devour the bucket of shit in the morning, and then you're free to do anything you want the rest of the day. How about *you*?' Yeltsin shrugs his shoulders and answers, 'Same as always—they never make the shit or, if they do, there are no buckets to go around.'"

Jonathan laughed. "Things aren't perfect anywhere."

"That's true, but my pessimism is growing."

"Have you ever been to America?"

"Once, two years ago to visit a cousin in New York. It was amazing—the architecture, all those big buildings in Manhattan in such a tight space."

"Yes, it's a crowded and fast-paced city."

"The traffic in New York was terrible, though, worse than here," Alexandre said. "And the subway was not reliable, not like the *Metro* here in Moscow. Our *Metro* is an amazing work of art. What about in your town, New Orleans?"

"The day someone proposes a subway is the day I'll quit paying taxes."

"What do you mean?"

"Half the city is below sea-level."

Alexandre laughed. "I see."

"But then again, in New Orleans, our affinity for corruption makes even the absurd entirely possible."

Alexandre paid the tab and headed out. "I will call you this evening."

The two parted ways in the lobby. Jonathan went back to his room feeling relieved that he'd met a man who seemed quite reasonable and astute. But he quickly became overcome with grief over Linda.

*        *        *

THE crimson-colored Kremlin with its tall towers was an impressive site. The fiery sky, cast by the sunset behind its fortifications, amplified its striking features. Jonathan couldn't think of a single building in New Orleans that could make such a powerful statement.

Jonathan had left the Metropol some twenty minutes earlier, and the only thing on his mind was to unwind, if only for an hour, before his scheduled dinner with Alexandre. He'd also called Charity Hospital for a status on Linda. He'd caught her awake and they had exchanged a few mutually encouraging words, which gave him strength to continue his efforts in Moscow.

Bundled in a heavy coat and carrying a small map, Jonathan strolled through the twin-towered Resurrection Gate to the wide expanse of *Krasnaya Ploschad*, the famous Red Square, in the shadows of the Kremlin. The vast cobblestone place was nearly deserted. A lone police car was parked along the GUM, the large department store on the east side of the square. Jonathan kept walking, observing Lenin's mausoleum, which resembled a rust-colored marble wedding cake. It stood ominously at the base of the Kremlin fortifications. Above and behind the wall was an elegant yellow and white building with a snow-covered rotunda topped with the tricolor flag of Russia, brightly illuminated by floodlights. The majestic St. Basil's Cathedral stood nearby with its ornate, multicolored onion domes. The cold breeze brought the smell of exhaust fumes from the heavily trafficked embankment behind the cathedral.

Jonathan had much on his mind as he took his long walk from Red Square to the banks of the Moskva River. Seven Kremlin towers rose from the ground under bright floodlights. Each faced the water's edge and was topped with a radiant ruby-red five-pointed star. He wished Linda was there, by his side, taking in the strikingly beautiful sights.

He strolled to Alexandrovski Gardens, a narrow park that ran along the west side of the Kremlin. A thin coat of snow covered the pristine grounds. He strolled by the tomb of the unknown soldier, where a guard watched over a permanent flame that burned from the raised stone foundation. To his left was the construction site at Manezhnaya Square—the finishing touches to a new Western-style underground mall.

The cool air filled his lungs and chilled his face, even with the collar of his coat raised high. He headed back toward his hotel. The surreal calm was invitingly deceptive. He felt something was wrong, as if an evil presence surrounded him, its cursing eyes tracking his every move—a hatred, an anger, a desire to harm burned through his skin.

Jonathan eyed his hotel a block away, feeling anxiety and disappointment. His first day in Moscow had yielded less substance than lukewarm borscht. He returned to his room, feeling more restless than when he'd left. He hoped Alexandre would find much more on Yakovlev.

For now, his trip was a potentially dangerous yet wasteful fishing expedition.

*       *       *

JONATHAN answered the phone on the first ring, perhaps because he was hungry: for food, for information, for news. For hope, too.

"I have interesting news," Alexandre declared, nearly shouting. "It seems Yakovlev had a loyal subordinate. Apparently they were inseparable at the Academy."

Jonathan felt excited yet skeptical, but he didn't want to dampen Alexandre's enthusiasm. "Tell me more."

"He could help answer your questions."

"Can you arrange a meeting?"

"Yes, I already have."

"Good. Where?"

Alexandre chuckled. "In prison."

"What?" Jonathan asked, moving to the windows carrying the clunky rotary phone in one hand and the handset in the other.

"He's in jail waiting for trial."

"For what?" Jonathan asked as he glanced out the window. Large snowflakes cut across his view of the street and seemed to hover a bit.

"For fraud and battery on an officer of the *Militsa*. I found his lawyer, but he's not representing him any more. He arranged the meeting, but only if we agreed to pay him a small fee—I hope that's okay with you."

"For setting up a meeting?" Jonathan asked, finding that completely ridiculous.

"Five million rubles—that's over 800 dollars."

Jonathan was irked at this poorly camouflaged act of thievery, and he entertained the thought that Alexandre was partly to blame. But he accepted, reluctantly. "So, who is this person?"

"Second Lieutenant Vladin Bornikov—an instructor at the Academy whose specialty was aviation munitions. I'm expecting a complete dossier early in the morning."

*Aviation munitions?* It didn't mean anything to him.

"We must be at the jail at nine-thirty in the morning," Alexandre stated. "Will this work for you?"

"Of course."

Alexandre now seemed in a hurry to get off the phone. "You can either take a taxi directly to Butyrka Prison, at forty-five Novoslobodskaya Street, or I can pick you up at the hotel, whichever you prefer." But before Jonathan could answer, Alexandre took the choice away. "Never mind. It's better that I pick you up. Nine, okay?"

Jonathan agreed.

Alexandre also cancelled his dinner plans with Jonathan on account of an urgent personal matter on which he didn't elaborate. After hanging up, Jonathan called the hospital again. Derek answered and said everything was stable and that Linda was asleep, heavily sedated.

Jonathan headed downstairs and dined alone under the immense vaulted glass ceiling of the hotel's main restaurant, one of the best in the city. But every second was consumed with thoughts of his beautiful wife.

# 14

JONATHAN HAD BEEN STANDING OUTSIDE FOR LESS THAN A minute, but the frigid air felt as if it was about to freeze every inch of his body. It was colder than any place he had ever been in his life.

Luckily, he didn't have to wait long. Alexandre pulled up in a black Isuzu Trooper and waived a thumbs-up.

Jonathan jumped in. His Russian host was quite chatty from the outset, even friendlier than the day before. Jonathan took it as a good sign. A less positive sign was Alexandre's liquored breath—and so early in the day.

"I must warn you that your visit to this prison will make you want to go home on the next plane out," Alexandre said, shaking his head and cracking a smile. "Our entire penitentiary system is a disaster, and no one knows how to repair it—or even manage it."

"You should see the prisons in New Orleans," Jonathan replied, reminding himself of countless times he'd visited inmates as part of his *pro bono* work in law school and beyond. "I think our prison systems have much in common."

"Perhaps," Alexandre said with a scowl. "But in Moscow, we have several prisons, called SIZO—prisons that serve to hold pre-trial inmates as well as convicts. But the overcrowding is awful, inhumane. I have two clients at Butyrka, four at SIZO NUMBER 2 and a woman at SIZO NUMBER 6. I also have three clients at the federal Lefortovo prison—an ugly place. My clients at Butyrka have to take shifts sleeping, because there is only one bed in the three-by-three meter cell and four prisoners. Can you believe this?"

"Terrible."

Alexandre cracked open his window and lit a cigarette. "It is 1996, but in many ways we are still in the age of the Gulags. Pre-trial prisons here are still based on the large dormitory concept. I know in your country and in Western Europe this is not the case. There are much more individual rights for prisoners, with more private space. It is very rare to have individual cells in Russia. It is mostly for punishment."

Jonathan listened, thinking about the infamous Angola prison in Louisiana. It was no paradise hotel either, with violent inmates crammed together like sardines. He'd been there three times during his law school days, helping his professor and a team of civil rights lawyers interview clients who had been victims of abuse and retaliation by prison officers. He'd even seen the notorious Camp J, known as the "dungeon", the prison's punishment unit, where inmates are under lock-down and subjected to grossly inhumane treatment in cramped, poorly ventilated cells.

"Several of my other clients are in cells made for twenty but that now house about fifty prisoners." Alexandre was an even faster driver than Boris. He weaved through traffic as if he were in a rally. He turned left and pulled up to a gate. "All right, we're here."

Jonathan suddenly opened his eyes wide. The building straight ahead at first glance looked like an abandoned factory. It's outside walls looked battered, as if a remnant of urban warfare. "Don't tell me that's—"

"Shocking, huh?"

"It looks like it's taken a few artillery rounds."

Alexandre nodded and laughed. "A treasure from 18th Century Russia—"

"You mean ruins."

"And home to about four thousand prisoners," Alexandre said as he pulled up to a spot in the small parking lot adjoining the narrow gated entrance.

"Four *thousand*?" Jonathan blurted, completely baffled. The main building was a long one-story structure with what appeared to be a couple of annexes behind it not much larger than a strip mall. That so many inmates were housed here seemed a physical impossibility. It looked like it barely had room for a few hundred.

Just before leaving the car, Alexandre cautioned Jonathan about speaking. Prison guards were notoriously skittish when it came to foreigners, he said, particularly now that human rights groups had converged on Russia to shed light on every conceivable violation. "If a guard asks you anything, I will tell them you are an exchange lawyer working with my firm and nothing more, okay?"

Jonathan nodded. "No problem."

The smell of mold was the first thing that greeted Jonathan as he followed his colleague into the jail through the gate.

Alexandre seemed to know at least two of the four guards loitering around the atrium, one of them behind a makeshift wooden reception area. The formalities were much simpler than Jonathan had experienced back home. Alexandre signed in for himself and Jonathan and waved an ID to the guard. They then walked to another guard, who carefully inspected them with his handheld metal detector before letting them through a steel door behind him.

The place was essentially a single long hall, with red and yellow tiled floors, yellow walls, and a white ceiling, the paint peeling and cracked from neglect. On the left side were the cells, their metal doors large, with tiny slits at eye level. On the other side were large windows, many with the glass panes missing or broken, and with thick bars on the outside. The rancid smell, perhaps from unbathed inmates or rotting sewers, was overpowering. A guard was positioned every thirty or so feet along the corridor. How they withstood the odor was a mystery.

Alexandre had secured the meeting with Vladin for a maximum of thirty minutes, though he'd mentioned the guards would likely allow more time if asked.

A guard waved the guests into a room the size of a two-car garage at the far end of the hall. The furnishings were sparse: two tables, each with two benches, a metal ashtray at the center of each table, a large garbage can in the corner and two bulbs on a five-foot cord dangling from the filthy concrete ceiling. The resident rats were probably there too, in the numerous large cracks and holes in the walls.

"They will bring him here any minute now," Alexandre whispered to Jonathan, after the guard had said a few words to him and left the room. He and Jonathan took a seat on the same side of the table closest to the door.

"Are we free to speak here?" Jonathan asked, pointing at the ceiling, "or can they listen?"

Alexandre snickered. "This prison is lucky to have electricity. I don't think there are any listening devices here." Alexandre then scratched his forehead and leaned into his colleague, adding, "Now, let's be careful. Inmates here have AIDS, hepatitis, tuberculosis and other diseases. It's a very sick place."

"I promise not to kiss him," Jonathan said mockingly.

"Maybe he will use his tongue on you! We may be his first visitors in months."

"You've got the humor of a Southerner," said Jonathan. "Just not the mullet or bad teeth to go with it."

"What is a mullet?" asked Alexandre.

Jonathan grinned. "A bad haircut."

The door opened and a handcuffed prisoner, dressed in a gray one-piece outfit resembling mechanic's overalls, was escorted into the room by the same guard that had led the lawyers to the place. Vladin was a skinny guy with brown hair, brown eyes and a pale, freckled face that made him seem younger than his forty-three years. But he also had an eerie poise.

Alexandre stood up first and greeted him in Russian and then introduced Jonathan by name only. They exchanged polite nods. Alexandre had told Jonathan that he would first make Vladin think they were investigators, not attorneys, so that he would be more intimidated and thus more cooperative.

The guard unlocked the prisoner's right handcuff and secured it to a metal brace that extended a couple inches from under the tabletop. The guard then took one last glance at the three men, uttered a few words at Alexandre and headed out. The loud thud of a deadbolt jarred the silence in the room.

Alexandre wasted no time. He spoke fast, his tone and gestures indicating he was explaining what Jonathan was after.

The prisoner gazed dispassionately at Alexandre and then at Jonathan. Vladin's disinterest could be translated into any language.

Alexandre talked a storm, but Vladin returned only a vacant stare.

Jonathan took out his pocket notepad, his thoughts gathering the right order of questions to ask.

The freckled man cocked his head back, stared coolly into Jonathan's eyes and said in fluent English, "So, an American who wants to speak with me."

Jonathan and Alexandre glanced at each other with the same look of astonishment.

"Yes, I speak English," Vladin said. "Does that surprise you? You must either be retarded or you work for

Canadian intelligence not to know this."

"Unlike you, we're not stupid enough to be locked up," Alexandre retorted feistily in English.

"Why are you here, and what will I get if I cooperate?" Vladin asked. "As you can see, this place is not fit for an animal, let alone a human."

"How about a cigarette for now," Jonathan said, nodding at Alexandre to hand him one. "And maybe you'll get more if we find your information useful."

Alexandre cut in, "You're charged with embezzlement and assault on an arresting officer. I think you can use all the help you can get."

"Fabrications!" Vladin barked back. "I didn't do anything."

Alexandre glanced at Jonathan and said, "They all say this—I bet in your country, too."

"You're right."

"These are serious charges," said Alexandre, his voice hardening as he peered at Vladin. "And even your lawyer has given up on you. Why should we think you will be any more cooperative with us, if we decide to help?"

Vladin's eyes lit up in rage. "My lawyer dropped me because I didn't pay him, and I didn't pay him because he was useless. Lawyers are nothing but worthless whores. Worthless! I've been in this place over nine months without trial, no hearing, no idea about my status. I'm told I have the right to make one phone call every three months, but there are no telephones. To contact my shit lawyer, I had to get permission to send a telegram, and then, one month later, he contacts me with a *letter*. He then visited me here once, for five minutes! Lawyers are the scum of the earth, I tell you."

Jonathan gazed calmly at Vladin and said, "*We* are lawyers."

Vladin raised his chin, his eyes round with surprise. "Oh."

Alexandre handed Vladin a cigarette and lit it for him.

"In March of 1989," Jonathan began, "General Yakovlev flew to Sweden. What can you tell me about that?"

"I didn't know," Vladin replied.

"Can you tell us anything Yakovlev did during that time period?"

Vladin looked up for a moment and seemed in deep thought. And whatever his thoughts, his face and neck began to sweat in the cold room. Vladin peered around the room, his eyes momentarily scanning the wall behind Jonathan. Then, he sat back and smiled. "I know what you're after. It's all about the farm, isn't it?"

"Farm?" Jonathan asked.

Vladin's smirk evaporated and a look of distrust stretched across his face. "You're nothing but spies. I know where you are going with these questions."

Jonathan didn't want Vladin to get the wrong idea. "We have nothing to do with the government. I am working on a legal case in the United States, and I will tell no one what we discuss today." Jonathan didn't want to mention anything about Matt, as it would complicate things. A legal case was far more abstract than a missing person. Besides, he hadn't yet told Alexandre.

"Why should I believe you?"

*I could beat the crap out of you until you do*, Jonathan thought, wanting the man to get rid of his attitude and start talking. But now he saw fear in Vladin's eyes.

Alexandre jumped in. "I could speed up your hearing if you help my friend. I have good connections."

Vladin was silent. He took a long drag of his cigarette and exhaled protractedly. "I suppose I have nothing to lose. Can I count on your word?" he asked, staring at the American. "Because what I know could have me killed in a second."

"Yes," Jonathan said. "He will help you. I assure you."

Vladin took a deep breath. "In March that year, I was promised something extraordinary," he said, shaking his head. "And Yakovlev let me down."

"What are you saying?" asked Alexandre.

Vladin tapped his cigarette over the ashtray and then brought it back to his lips for another long drag. "I don't remember the exact date in March, but Yakovlev had called me to his office, a few buildings away from where I was training new recruits. When I arrived, a woman was there. I instantly didn't like her. She looked both dangerous and beautiful, with hypnotic, snake-like eyes that told me she could seduce me and kill me all at the same moment. She asked me questions about my qualifications, my family, my background, as if I were under interrogation. And she didn't like the fact that I was Ukrainian by origin. The bitch."

"Who was she?" Jonathan asked.

"Someone who needed to get fucked."

"What was her name?"

"Not sure, but I may have heard Yakovlev call her Marina, but he never introduced her to me by name. He only said she was an official from the Ministry, without telling me which one. Yakovlev and the woman told me to take supplies to an airstrip. He also asked if I was willing to travel to the West with him for awhile. I was tempted to say I would never return, but, of course, I pretended to be only mildly interested. I hoped, however, that it was a genuine offer. That I would be able to get the hell out of this country. He didn't give me much to go on, but he said that if I helped him deliver some equipment, he and I would be paid well for it and would be allowed to travel to Austria and other parts of Europe and that the operation was approved by the KGB." Vladin leaned back and rubbed his fingers over his greasy scalp. "Now, before I say anything more, what can you do to help me?"

"I'll pay to defend you," Jonathan proposed.

Vladin glanced at Alexandre, probably waiting for confirmation. But Alexandre apparently had another card to play. He took out his cell phone and placed it in the middle of the table. "I'll let you use this when you're done speaking. You don't have much time."

Vladin gazed at the phone as one might a life raft on a sinking ship. Jonathan could feel Vladin's struggle.

"*Da, da,*" said the inmate. "I didn't have a clue about what Yakovlev and that woman had planned. But the next morning, I was told to wait at a football field near the Academy's sports center. A helicopter landed and picked me up. It was an uncomfortable three-hour flight on the aircraft's hard metal floor. The pilots dropped me off in a wheat field and told me to wait for a ride at the nearby road. I waited a long time, until finally my contact pulled up in a military vehicle. We traveled for over an hour, arriving at dusk at a vast farm complex. It was a strange place."

"Where was it?" Jonathan asked.

"Somewhere near the border with Belarus. That's all I know. The place looked like a farm, with tractors and barns and everything you would expect at a farm, but the only animals I saw were rabbits and squirrels, thousands of them in rows upon rows of cages. Most cages were stacked in covered sheds, but some were out in the open, covered only by canvas tarps. There were no horses, no cattle, no pigs, just those damn rodents. When I got out of the vehicle, I spotted that same wicked woman from the day before. She was there, arguing with two men in white lab coats. Yakovlev was there as well, but he was some distance away, smoking near his car. He ignored me completely. And when the witch saw me arrive, she walked to Yakovlev and they both got in the car." Vladin then gestured for another cigarette, which Alexandre handed over, along with the lighter.

"Then what happened?" Jonathan asked.

"The men in lab coats signaled for me to join them in a large shed. Parked inside was a big army truck. One man—the fat one—introduced himself as Comrade Vadenko—I think that was his name. His skinny, mustached colleague was Comrade Karmachov, but he didn't talk to me other than to tell me his name. They were either physicians or scientists and both were agitated, probably because of their earlier confrontation with that bitch. Vadenko gave me a map and instructed me to drive the truck to the designated coordinates and to be careful with the cargo—not to drive fast. By then, I saw Yakovlev's car leave the property in a hurry."

Jonathan took notes. "Please, don't stop."

"I made it to the airfield that night. I remember that cranky bastard Yakovlev complaining that the plane was late, his raspy voice echoing from behind the truck as he took a piss," Vladin said, his face twisted with disgust. He then took another drag of his cigarette. "'American pilots,' he'd said, 'they hate rules.' I told him they were trying to delay the great victory of socialism. The bastard took my statement as if I meant it. How absurd."

Vladin put out his cigarette and immediately reached into Alexandre's pack for another one and lighted it.

"Yakovlev was old fashioned," Vladin continued, "cursed with delusional patriotism gained through blood, sweat and shrapnel in the Cold War's worst battlefields—Angola, Nicaragua, Chad, Afghanistan. You name it, he was there. But his warrior days were gone by the time I got to know him. Yakovlev became nothing more than a glorified pencil pusher at the Academy. He was an ethnic Russian wedded to the Communist Party apparatchik, so he possessed all the expected traits."

"What do you mean?" Jonathan asked.

"Corrupt, shallow, drunk, rude, ruthless and fond of hookers," Vladin replied. "Everything I despised."

"I thought you were friends," Alexandre said.

"No, he was my ticket to other things. He still wielded much power, so I had to kiss his ass. Thank goodness for the fall of the Soviet Union. That's when I severed the ties. But back then, I tolerated him by thinking about the lighter side of it all. My humor is what kept me from killing the asshole. For whatever reason he turned me into his vassal, a truly miserable existence. And he always insulted my Ukrainian heritage. He hated all non-Russians: Jews, Armenians, Chechens, the whole lot."

"What happened at the airfield?" asked Alexandre.

"I was a nervous wreck. I'd been at the abandoned airfield for over an hour; he'd gotten there much earlier. So much was at stake, most importantly my freedom. For once in my life, I had my hand on the future I wanted. If all were to go as planned, I'd be sipping Guinness in an Irish pub by the following week. Yeah, freedom. I remember him saying '*Tovarisch*, you will be a very happy man in a few days.'" Vladin's shoulders drooped as he took another drag of his Marlboro. "As you can see, I'm not in Ireland."

"What went wrong?" Alexandre asked, now sounding a little impatient.

"General Yakovlev and I were waiting for the American plane and it was more than fifty minutes late. Every second that passed meant that my chances at a new life were slipping away. I scanned the pitch-black sky, hoping—begging—for that damn thing to show up. But there was simply nothing but a cool breeze and the sound of crickets. Yakovlev was nervous too, perhaps because he knew the consequences of failure. 'This mission is for the Motherland,' he reminded me, as if I didn't appreciate its importance. But motherland my ass. I didn't know the nuts and bolts of Yakovlev's plan, nor for that matter the real players involved, but I'd learned long ago not to believe a word out of the general's mouth. He was doing it for himself, just as I was doing it for my own interests."

Jonathan glanced at his watch. "We don't have much time left, so please get through the most important information. We can discuss other details at another meeting."

"Americans," Vladin said mockingly. "Always in a hurry. A stay in a Russian prison will make you a more patient man."

Alexandre raised his head and looked annoyed.

"Fine, fine," Vladin uttered. "You should have seen Yakovlev. He wore tall, polished black boots, flared breeches, and rows of overlapping medals on his inflated chest. His regalia looked more appropriate for a May Day parade down Red Square, only it wasn't May and no one that night would give a damn what he looked like. I was tempted to tell him he looked like a clown. So, this dressed up pig and I stood by the truck, waiting for the damn plane. And then, then . . ." Vladin suddenly raised his hands excitedly. "I finally heard it. What a beautiful sound. A faint whine at first that soon turned into a growl as it approached, and then a loud roar echoed when it landed. The sounds of freedom. I was so happy, I almost hugged the bastard."

Vladin took a long drag of his cigarette and let out a thick plume of smoke from between his lips as Jonathan quickly scanned his notes.

"The cargo aircraft's dark silhouette slowly appeared," Vladin continued, "its lights turned off except for the cockpit, which glowed red, probably from its instrument panel. I quickly walked to the truck. That's when that bastard general told me to stay put. That was because he didn't speak English. So, I stepped into the cab of the truck and signaled the pilots with a flick of the headlights."

"Weren't there other planes around?" asked Jonathan.

"Nah," said Vladin. "Twenty years ago, it was crawling with MiG fighter jets, but by then those days were long gone. It was a perfect venue for this clandestine rendezvous."

Vladin was now on his fourth cigarette since their meeting began.

"It was a C-130. The aircraft's engines idled noisily as a door on the port side popped open and two pilots stepped out. They headed at a fast pace toward us. I got out of the truck and signaled to them again, this time with my flashlight. The general asked me who they were with. If he hadn't been drinking, he'd know. These pilots sported crew cuts and one-piece flight suits, but neither carried any insignia—not even name patches, unit badges or indication of rank. The taller of the duo stopped in front of me and saluted. 'I'm Major Travis,' he told me in a deep voice. And he introduced his colleague as Lieutenant Blake. Of course, I quickly translated for the general's benefit and returned a salute, but I forced myself not to laugh. Major Travis was exactly like officers in those bootleg Hollywood movies. The swagger. The rolling R's. The cocky, hawkish gaze. I had never before met an American, so I was delighted that the major appeared just as I had imagined. Yes, the great enemy of Mother Russia." Vladin then raised his chin at Jonathan and added, "No offense."

"None taken," Jonathan replied. "Not all Americans are like that. Just like not all Russians are chain smokers or crooks."

Vladin smirked. "Frankly, I was fascinated. I remember the major had a large, shiny wristwatch, flashier than anything I had ever seen. By then, General Yakovlev was about to lose his mind. He shouted that they had only fifteen minutes to turn the plane around and that the radars at Andreopol and Ostrov were on, meaning the flight plan had changed. As I translated the general's words, I was also hoping to deflect attention off Yakovlev, who had nearly a liter of vodka in his blood. I was sure the Americans would know a drunken babble even if they didn't understand Russian. But it was too late. The pilots stared at the general until all the English words had cleared my lips. Major Travis then asked me if my commander had been drinking, to which I responded 'Yes, look at his chest—one medal for each bottle.'"

Jonathan and Alexandre joined Vladin in laughter, but the lawyers knew there wasn't enough time for anecdotes. They needed more facts, faster, before the guards would bring their meeting to a close.

"General Yakovlev waved for everyone to follow him to his black Volga sedan, parked a short distance away," explained Vladin. "Although the pilots probably had never seen one before, and would mistake it for an ordinary car, it was one of our military's prized perks, with tinted glass, leather seats, a car phone and privacy curtains in the rear compartment. And I tell you, that loser Yakovlev didn't deserve it."

"Tell us the important information," Alexandre said, sounding frustrated.

Vladin casually saluted with his cigarette between his fingers. "Okay, okay. As we walked toward the car, I spotted a hand pulling the curtain back for a second and then quickly closing it. I hoped the Americans behind me had not noticed, but the major had. He asked who was in the car. I told him it was the general's assistant and that she was probably on the car phone. That wasn't true, of course. As I told you a moment ago, I didn't know that bitch's exact title, but she was trouble. I had avoided her all evening, and it was just as well she stayed in the car."

Alexandre too lighted a cigarette, filling the air over the table with smoke.

"The four of us huddled over a map stretched across the hood of the car," Vladin said. "I held a flashlight above the general's shoulder as the Americans were informed of the new flight plan. We explained that after takeoff they would have to fly a heading of two-one-zero toward Belyy and not northwest as previously planned. They would then head to Lake Dvin'ye, then turn toward the Sivera Lakes and onto the Daugava River. The path would take them past Viesite and Bauska and then to the Baltic. I told them that they had to fly low—no higher than two hundred meters, or six hundred feet—to avoid the radars. Unfortunately, my drunk general kept burping and the odor of booze glided past me, toward the Americans. I could only imagine what they were thinking. How on earth could they be comfortable with this drunkard's low altitude flight plan designed to dodge our surface-to-air missiles across hundreds of miles of hostile territory? And then Yakovlev babbled even more nonsense, saying radar operators in that part of the country had little to do except stare at their consoles, drink, and fuck whatever moves—even deer. I translated, but I left out the animal reference to preserve some self-respect for myself and my military."

"Tell us more about the pilots," asked Jonathan.

"I told you, they were arrogant, especially the major. When I pointed out a mobile radar site on the map, he cut me off, explaining that he knew exactly what were the capabilities of the *P-15M Squat Eye* radar at that site. I remember him saying, 'I know your backyard as if it were mine,' and that he had flown into Soviet airspace many times and that our radar operators were narcoleptics! Yes, he was a real cowboy, that pilot. Full of machismo. He paraded a cockiness I had seen all too often in our military, at the Academy. And many of those confident faces never returned from their tours in Afghanistan."

"Did the pilots speak any Russian?"

"No."

Jonathan checked his watch and realized time was fast running out. "Hurry, tell us more."

"The pilots pulled out a thick envelope and tossed it on the hood. It contained our airline tickets, forged passports and some cash—dollars and Swiss francs. There was also a bank deposit confirmation made to a numbered account in Luxembourg—I assume in the general's name. I counted the notes, about seven thousand dollars, and several thousand francs. I had never held so much cash in my life, and I was promised a cut of what had been deposited in the bank, as well. It was mesmerizing. So much so that my anger at General Yakovlev, at the system, at everything that had tormented my adult life quickly vanished. I tell you, it turned that dreary night into a carnival. I began to imagine what I could do with it. I saw refrigerators, cartons of American cigarettes, a Madonna concert, a Cadillac—no, a Porsche, a Ferrari, a Mercedes. All I needed was a place to spend the money, a place as far away as possible from the Soviet prison-state I craved to escape. The major gave us the name of our contact in Vienna. He was to meet us at the airport, after our transit through Budapest, where our counterfeit Yugoslavian passports would make travel easier. From Austria, we would then be separated for our own safety. That was music to my ears. Separation from the old bastard.

"After that, the pilots returned to their plane, and I drove the truck to the back of the aircraft. As I approached, the plane's cargo door began to lower. I got out. The engines were still on, throwing up dirt that hit my face like needles. The plane's cargo bay was huge and lit up like a stadium. I then saw four people march down the ramp dressed like aliens—baggy, white plastic protective suits with black rubber gloves and gas masks. The first two crewmen were black. They walked right past me as if I wasn't even there. They held small electronic devices, pointing them at the truck and checking the readings every few seconds. One of them jumped onto the bed of the truck and examined the large wooden crates up close.

"What were in the crates?" Alexandre and Jonathan asked simultaneously.

"Yakovlev had never mentioned the contents. After seeing what the crew was wearing, I became worried. But I tried to think of a more favorable explanation. Just paranoid Americans, I tried to convince myself. Or blacks, they're more afraid—that's what we were taught in high school. But those men didn't seem frightened, just businesslike, and I never believed that garbage anyway.

"Finally, I decided that I should rest on the fact that if anything were that dangerous, Yakovlev would have been the first to wear protective gear. Besides, he was an expert at it, just like me."

"Expert at what?" Jonathan questioned.

"What, you don't know already?"

"No."

Vladin sighed. "Yakovlev was very knowledgeable with special weapons, chemical and biological weapons in particular. That's why he had been in Afghanistan, although he never told me more details than that. And that's why he was at the Academy—to handpick cadets for the special weapons groups around the country. And I was a special munitions tactical instructor for helicopter pilots. That's why, when I saw the protective suits, I became concerned."

"Were there such weapons in the cargo?"

"I don't know. I gestured for the Americans to remove their masks, but they ignored me. The cargo is safe, I again told myself, probably because it was easier to think that way. As a Soviet officer, my instinct was to never question the questionable. It was a survival tool I wasn't about to alter that night."

"Can you tell us more about the crew?" Jonathan asked, again checking the time.

"Another crewman finally approached me," Vladin said. "I brought with me the cargo manifest in a sealed envelope. General Yakovlev had forbidden me from opening it. Just as I handed it to the man, he replied in Russian. He said '*Spasibo*.'"

Alexandre leaned into Jonathan. "That means 'thank you.'"

"I was surprised," Vladin went on to say. "I asked if he spoke Russian, and he answered that he did and when he opened the envelope he asked me a few questions about the size and weight of the crates. He spoke nearly fluently. And then I asked him why he and his colleagues wore the protective gear, to which he simply said, 'Shouldn't you have one on?' I was not amused, as you can imagine. The other crewmen unloaded the crates with a forklift. They positioned them in the center of the cargo bay and secured them all with multiple cables and a huge net. The crew then fastened the forklift to the floor and the ramp rose to its locked position. And that was it. The plane took off a few minutes later."

"What about the general and that woman?"

"The bastard patted me on the back when I drove

back to where he was. He was all excited to share the news with the bitch in his car. I remember him tapping on the glass, the curtain moving back and the tinted window rolling down just enough for us to meet the woman's fierce gaze. The general told her the transfer of the crates went well, but her steel blue eyes stayed frigid. She was evil, all right. I never wanted to see her face again." Vladin shook his head. "And then . . . then . . ." He took another drag of his cigarette.

"What?" Jonathan asked. "Tell us."

"She shouted at the general something like 'fine, don't just stand there like an idiot. Drive me out of here!' He was so nervous that he bumped into me as he jumped into the driver's seat, slammed the door shut and took off."

"Who was this woman who could turn a top general into a chauffeur?"

"A real bitch."

Alexandre raised his chin. "What's Marina's full name?"

"I told you, I don't know; I'm not even sure her name was Marina," Vladin said, extinguishing his cigarette in the ashtray and reaching his hand half way to the cell phone. "Can I make my calls now? *Pozhaluysta*."

Alexandre glanced at Jonathan for approval, after which his American pal shook his head. "No, I want more information first."

"Please, let me at least make one call," Vladin asked, nearly begging. "Just *one*."

Alexandre waved his hand and said something in Russian.

Vladin grabbed the cell phone and started dialing as fast as he could.

Jonathan sympathized with Vladin, a man cut off from the outside world for months, unable to get adequate help.

"*Natasha!*" Vladin said, his voice suddenly sounding as if he was about to cry with joy. "*Eto Vladin! Gdye moya sestra?*"

All of a sudden, the loud noise of the door unlocking surprised them. The guard staggered in, his large set of keys dangling from his clenched fist, and immediately addressed Alexandre in an authoritative tone, after which Alexandre stood up and joined him at the door. All Jonathan knew was that they were arguing, with the guard's voice twice as loud as the Russian lawyer's. Things didn't look good.

Alexandre turned to Jonathan with a resigned look. "The interview is over."

"This is crap," Jonathan said angrily, checking his watch and realizing the promised thirty minutes had not yet elapsed. "Why is he cutting it short?"

"He's not telling me why."

"Did you ask?"

"Yes," Alexandre answered, appearing exacerbated. "He simply said time's up, and that's it."

"Can't we have five more minutes?" Jonathan pleaded. "Or pay him off?"

"Too risky; I don't know this officer."

Jonathan needed every bit of self-restraint to avoid yelling at the guard, but Alexandre's empty stare was enough to convince Jonathan that insisting was pointless. The guard escorted Vladin out as Jonathan looked on, frustrated.

*        *        *

ARBAT was one of the hippest neighborhoods in Moscow. At least that's what Alexandre had told Jonathan. Located in the west-central part of town, it was host to the parliament, foreign embassies, the elegant Ukraina Hotel, countless Russian government offices and a pedestrian street known for its cafés, bars and street-side entertainment.

"Look over there," Alexandre said.

Jonathan gazed to his right. A woman was holding by a leash a dark animal that at first looked like a furry dog. "Jesus, is that a bear?" he asked as he walked closer. The small brown bear, probably only a few months old, was rolling over onto its back on the cobbled street surrounded by several tourists taking pictures.

"Yes, it's a beautiful animal," Alexandre answered as if it were perfectly normal to have one there. "They don't have bears in your shopping areas?"

"Eh, no."

Alexandre took Jonathan to lunch at one of the area's trendy Italian restaurants. Interestingly, he'd told Jonathan it might not be around long. Apparently, three other Italian eateries had burned down since the summer, the result of a feud between local Italian mobsters and a new, more violent Russian mafia family.

They dined and talked as friends would, though Jonathan didn't really know this Muscovite, this stranger, who had so far been quite hospitable. But

Jonathan felt far more at ease to tell him about the Victory Lines litigation, about the fact that the U.S. Navy was hiding evidence and manipulating testimony. However, as tempted as he was to tell all, Jonathan was not yet comfortable to divulge anything else, whether about Matt, about Tantina's wild claim or about his meetings with Erland in Sweden and the late Sammy Dupree. And he certainly didn't want Alexandre to feel that his own life was in danger. So he chose not to tell him about Linda and the car chase that nearly had him killed. This was all better left unsaid for now.

Alexandre listened, but not once did he appear shocked by the twists in the court proceedings. Perhaps in Russia, the game is played that way all the time. Alexandre patted the American's shoulder.

At that moment, Alexandre's cell phone rang. He answered and then turned to Jonathan. "A fax has arrived for you at my office."

Jonathan immediately realized what this could be. "Can we pick it up right now?" he asked.

# 15

THE FACSIMILE FROM HOME LAY ON THE COFFEE TABLE, on top of his city map, beside crumpled chocolate wrappers and an empty can of Baltika beer. The two-page fax from AGI Forensics had been sent to Gary, who then sent it on to Moscow. Jonathan had immediately called AGI for a verbal confirmation.

His hand shaking, Jonathan wiped the tears off his cheeks and rubbed his bristly jaw. He reclined further into his hotel room sofa, his eyes randomly surfing the surroundings. Nothing he'd ever experienced could have prepared him for how he felt. He glanced at the fax once more and shook his head. Suddenly his mind filled with the voices of Tantina and Linda and Gary and Judge Breaux. And then young Matt, and the jolting sounds of the 21-gun salute at Matt's funeral. The fluttering of feathers as Linda released two white doves into the air, accompanied by the bugler playing Taps. And the sound of his sobbing as the casket was lowered into the ground.

And now those magnified memories were eclipsed by the truth: the body was not his brother's. With an error probability of one in two billion, the test on the remains proved they were not those of his brother. He finally knew, though it gave him less comfort than he had hoped.

The phone rang, and Jonathan crawled out of the plush sofa to answer it.

"How did you do it?" a man asked agitatedly, his English voice not immediately recognizable. "Tell me!"

Jonathan realized it was Alexandre's. "Do what?"

"How did you bail him out?"

"Who?"

"Vladin!" Alexandre said, this time sounding angry.

"I don't understand."

"You mean . . . you didn't arrange his bail?"

"No!"

"*Der'mo!* About an hour after we left the prison, someone paid one million rubles for his release."

Jonathan quickly converted the currency. "That's about 8,000 dollars, right?"

"Yes."

"Who paid it?" Jonathan asked.

"The clerk told me a man speaking English came with a government lawyer and had a private meeting with one of the judges."

"Did Vladin leave with them?"

"No, Vladin wasn't there. He was released directly from the prison and the guard I know saw him walk to a nearby *Metro* station."

"Where would he go?"

After a long pause, Alexandre replied, "I tracked down the woman—Natasha—he called using my cell phone. I think she's his aunt, and I have her address. Perhaps he went there? But when he called her, he also asked her about his sister. Anyway, I don't believe he has many places to choose from."

Jonathan felt his heart pound rapidly in his chest. "Someone bailed him out to shut him up. He's in danger. We must go there now if we want the rest of our answers. Where is it?"

"322 Vernadskogo Prospekt," said Alexandre. "It's in the Yugo-Zapadnaya district, southwest of town. I can pick you up in thirty minutes."

"No, there's no time," Jonathan said. "This has all the signs of something bad, *real* bad."

"Okay, then go. It will take you about twenty minutes to get there by taxi," Alexandre said. "Look for the name Natasha Davydov on the mailboxes. This will tell you which floor the apartment is on. I'll join you as soon as I can. But don't cause any trouble."

"Perfect."

*       *       *

ALEXANDRE was exactly right about how long it would take to get to the place. The taxi stopped at the front of the apartment block—a dreary concrete structure some fifteen stories high that seemed to have been haphazardly erected in the snow. The building had an uncanny resemblance to the Fischer public housing complex back home. A heap of discarded furniture lay nearby, as did an overturned garbage cart.

The dimly lighted lobby reeked of urine, probably animal, but he couldn't be sure. The concrete floor was littered with wrappers, plastic bags and empty vodka bottles, and the walls were covered with graffiti.

Jonathan scanned the row of mailboxes for the name Alexandre had given, remembering that in Cyrillic the letter *N* was an *H*, *D*'s looked like a hat and the letters *A* and *T* were the same as in English. He carefully read the name plates one after the other until the second to last one made him stop for a double-take.

"Jackpot!" he uttered excitedly, his finger tapping on the name. Next to it was written the number 10. *The floor*, he instantly deduced.

He exited the elevator and entered the narrow common area. There were four apartments, and one door was cracked open, which drew him to it. The name Davydov was etched onto a wooden plate above the doorbell.

He slowly pushed on the door and discreetly peeked in. The entry hall looked clean, with small framed pictures on the wall and an elegant rug over the hardwood floor. He leaned into the door a bit more and walked in but stopped in his tracks the moment he heard the faint sound of someone weeping.

*I don't have a weapon*, Jonathan reminded himself. *Don't be too brave.*

He moved stealthily into the apartment's cloistered foyer. Creeping cautiously forward, he peered into the living room and saw an old woman, presumably Vladin's aunt, seated on the couch, shaking, her mouth taped, her hands tied in front of her. She was crying, and her gaze was locked onto something or someone outside of Jonathan's line of sight. He quickly took a step back so she wouldn't spot him. Suddenly, he heard heavy footsteps from the direction in which the woman was staring.

Jonathan slipped into the dark kitchen on his left. Instantly, he caught sight of a man passing by the small window that overlooked the balcony. He quickly ducked and huddled near the stove. Sweat started to pour freely under his wool turtleneck.

The stranger was noisy with whatever he was doing on the balcony. It sounded as if heavy objects were being thrown about. Boxes perhaps, or books. Jonathan squatted forward, grabbed the edge of the countertop and lifted himself up just enough to sneak a quick look out the window. Indeed, the man was emptying drawers onto the balcony and sifting through clothes, papers and personal effects.

Jonathan could only see the back of the man, but then he glanced at the other end of the balcony. "Shit," he whispered loudly. Vladin's motionless body was sprawled out face down on the cement floor.

The stranger then walked rapidly to Vladin, crouched down and emptied his pockets.

Jonathan quickly glanced behind him, searching for anything he could use as a weapon. On top of a bread box was a huge rolling pin. He leaned forward, grabbed it firmly in his hand and crawled out of the kitchen.

He'd have to be quick. The woman was his first problem. If she spotted him too early, she'd make noise and give the stranger time to react. Jonathan assumed the man was armed with something more powerful than a rolling pin. So, timing would be key.

He moved out of the shelter of the entryway and looked directly at the woman, placing his index finger over his lips, signaling her to stay quiet. She stared at him for a few seconds and then looked away. He then peeked around the corner, through the open glass doors leading to the balcony. The stranger was squatting down, examining some papers scattered around Vladin's body.

Jonathan raced toward him, raising his kitchen utensil high above his head. The stranger never saw it coming. The impact was loud and hard. The man instantly collapsed head first over Vladin's legs.

Jonathan quickly checked the man's neck for a pulse and ripped an empty clothesline down from the balcony and then tied the man's hands together behind his back. He patted the man down and felt a weapon—a small pistol with a silencer. He quickly removed the magazine, emptied the chamber and tossed the weapon to the far end of the balcony.

Jonathan glanced at Vladin. He had fared worse than the stranger. A pool of blood stretched from under Vladin's stomach to the edge of the balcony.

Hysterical moans erupted behind Jonathan. He turned to face the woman but had no idea what to do with her. Her horrified gaze was aimed at Vladin. He raised his hands, signaling her to wait. She was now on her feet, racing his way and desperately trying to free her hands. He quickly turned Vladin's body over. He had been mortally wounded in his chest.

As the woman ran toward him, Jonathan grabbed her, removed the tape from her mouth and untied her hands.

She then threw herself over Vladin and burst out crying.

Jonathan watched as she stretched her arms over Vladin's shoulders and rested her head on his bloodied chest, mumbling in Russian and sobbing loudly.

Jonathan quickly pulled the stranger's body aside and searched his pockets. He pulled out a wallet and, to his amazement, two passports. One was maroon-colored with the words United States of America and OFFICIAL PASSPORT printed on it, along with the eagle emblem. The name on the document was Frank Corrigan and the photo matched the man that lay at Jonathan's feet.

*Aren't they blue?* he thought, having never seen an American passport in any other color. The other passport was Swiss, with the same photograph, but had a different last name, Urwil.

Jonathan slipped both passports into his own pocket, grabbed the man by his feet and began dragging him out from the balcony into the living room.

"*Tvoyu mat!*" Jonathan heard someone yell behind him. It was Alexandre, and he looked as anxious as Jonathan felt. "What's going on?" He then said something to the woman, but she was too overcome with grief to respond.

"I'll explain later," Jonathan said, dragging the assailant's lame body past Alexandre.

"Is he . . . dead?" Alexandre asked with a disgusted expression.

"No, but Vladin is."

"Let's get out of here," Alexandre said, his voice now trembling.

"First, tell the woman to call the police, or this guy

will kill her when he regains consciousness," Jonathan said loudly, after which Alexandre quickly spoke with her, though she was still too distraught to pay him any attention.

"Tell me what happened," Alexandre said to Jonathan.

Jonathan ignored him and let go of the feet and grabbed the man by his arms instead, pulling him through the hallway and into the elevator.

"I want to leave this fucker downstairs," Jonathan said. "Away from her long enough for the police to arrive."

"Who the hell is this guy?" Alexandre asked.

"I'm not sure."

"Did you do this to him?"

"Of course!"

"And you don't know him?"

"Right."

"*Idiot*," Alexandre mumbled, shaking his head while holding the elevator door open. He then squeezed in behind Jonathan, his feet avoiding any contact with the unconscious man. "We must hurry!"

Jonathan pressed the button, but the elevator door wasn't closing. He pressed it again and again.

Suddenly, one of the woman's neighbors popped his head out of an adjacent apartment and shouted something, prompting Alexandre to yell back in Russian. The man shut up and slammed his door shut. The elevator finally headed down.

Jonathan glanced at Alexandre. "What did you tell him?"

Alexandre grinned. "I said we're from the Federal Security Service—like your FBI. Open your door again and we'll throw you and your family in jail for a year."

"You have an evil side, Alexandre." Jonathan laughed.

During the ride down, the stranger began to regain his senses. Jonathan leaned forward and began grilling him. "Who sent you here? Who are you? Who wanted Vladin killed? Answer me!"

The man's eyes stayed closed, but he mumbled incoherently.

Jonathan grabbed the man by his collar and shook him firmly. "Answer me, dammit! Who sent you?"

"Stop!" Alexandre grabbed Jonathan's arm. "This is crazy. What if he's with the police?"

Jonathan waved off Alexandre's hand. "He's no cop. He's American or Swiss or both, and he killed Vladin!"

"Please, let's just get out of here."

Jonathan continued to interrogate the man as the elevator slowly descended the ten floors. "Why did you come for Vladin?"

"Don't do anything stupid," Alexandre pleaded.

"He killed Vladin!" Jonathan said. "I walked into the apartment, found the woman tied up, and this piece of shit going through Vladin's belongings."

Jonathan grabbed the man's feet, dragged him out of the elevator through the filthy lobby and dumped him behind the adjacent stairs.

Both of them now running, Alexandre led Jonathan to his car in the parking lot, and they took off with lightening speed.

"We are not in a Western film," Alexandre shouted. "You can't just beat up whomever you want. You can't play policeman either. You could get yourself killed."

"I didn't have a choice."

Jonathan was scolded the rest of the drive back to his hotel, but he refused to admit he had done anything wrong.

As Alexandre zoomed into a spot in front of the hotel, he turned unfriendly eyes toward Jonathan. "I will not speak to you again. You are completely nuts."

"Please, I understand the whole thing back there didn't look good, but I need your help."

"No, I can't risk my career for your insane pursuit. And all for what? A fucking lawsuit?"

Jonathan was grasping for words. He needed Alexandre. Desperately. "It's not only about a lawsuit. I'm looking for information about my brother. He may have been taken to Russia long ago."

"I don't care about your stories," the Russian said, his face bright red.

"I must tell you the real reason I'm looking for Yakovlev," Jonathan said. He told him everything he knew about his brother, about what had happened in Gotland, and Tantina's claim, about the attempt on his life back in Washington, D.C., and about Linda.

Alexandre appeared to listen, but he was still angry. "Your claim seems outrageous."

"I swear, it's all true. That's why I'm here. I really need your help."

"Then find someone else! Now, get out."

"Please, Alexandre," Jonathan pleaded, his hands in

the air. "I just need a little more help from you."

"No." Alexandre then threw his chin up, again signaling the American to get out of the car.

Jonathan reluctantly stepped out. He watched as Alexandre's Isuzu sprinted through the parking lot and disappeared into traffic.

# 16

A STREAK OF DAYLIGHT BEAMED THROUGH AN OPENING between the crimson velvet curtains. Jonathan rolled out of bed and squinted at the bright sliver of light. He pushed one curtain aside. The sky was pale blue, which was a welcome surprise. It added color and warmth to an otherwise gloomy start to his day. Despite the comfortable hotel bed, he'd had a restless night, with only intermittent sleep between nightmares. And now that Alexandre wanted no part of Jonathan's search, things looked rather bleak. What would he do now, on his own, in a city as unwelcoming as he could possibly imagine? Without Alexandre, it was hopeless and he knew it. Worse yet, he had no protection from whoever wanted him dead, the first one probably being a rather sore and vengeful Frank Corrigan. He thought about what he could have done differently at the apartment where Vladin was killed. The possibilities seemed endless in retrospect, if only he hadn't been so scared. Had he gone overboard by attacking the stranger, who hadn't threatened him directly? Perhaps someone else had killed Vladin before the man had arrived. Perhaps they'd been on the same side. *God knows.*

Jonathan cracked open the window, bringing in the orchestra of traffic into the quiet room. He checked the clock. It was about one in the morning back home, too early to call Derek or Gary, so he quickly dialed the hospital to check on Linda. The nurse on duty told him nothing had changed.

After pulling out a can of orange juice from the small refrigerator, he noticed a piece of paper under his hotel room door. He quickly picked it up. The handwritten message read:

> Let's meet at eleven. Go to a place called Bryusov Pereulok, not far from your hotel. Make sure you are not followed. First, walk toward the Hotel National, then turn the corner and go up Tverskaya Ulitsa. After the central telephone and telegraph office and the McDonald's, you will see to your left a building with a tall archway. Pass under it, toward the Church of the Resurrection straight ahead of you. A cab will be waiting, unless you have been followed.
>
> Alexandre

It was ten-thirty, and Jonathan wanted to believe that this was good news. Perhaps Alexandre had changed his mind and was willing to help. He wasted no time doing as he was told. He quickly got dressed and headed out.

It was a short stroll to the National, another of Moscow's pristine hotels. Every few seconds Jonathan glanced over his shoulder, assessing whether anyone was on his tail. But it was nearly impossible to tell—too many pedestrians on both sides of the street.

He headed up Tverskaya Ulitsa, a wide, bustling boulevard. There, too, crowds filled the sidewalks. There were shoppers, old folks, kids, tourists and laborers. The McDonald's along the way was packed. He again peered around him, attempting to spot anyone remotely suspicious, but there were still far too many faces to gauge whether he was in any danger.

After a quarter mile stroll up the busy avenue, past the telephone center, Jonathan arrived at the tall Bryusov Pereulok archway, built into a large building, with four floors rising above it.

It was just before eleven. He stopped and again observed passersby on the sidewalk behind him. No one seemed to stop or look at him unusually, neither on his side of the avenue nor the other, but just to be safe, he crossed the street and crossed back. Satisfied that he likely had not been followed, he walked under the wide archway, each side adorned with a row of granite pillars. Just as the note had indicated, the church was straight ahead, a few hundred yards down the gently sloping street.

He waited.

There were a dozen parked cars, but no cab. At ten after eleven, he headed toward the church, looking over his shoulder one more time. If the cab wasn't there, he knew what that meant. And being followed would guarantee that he wouldn't again hear from Alexandre.

He checked his watch. It was eleven-twenty. Suddenly, a car screeched to a halt right beside him. It was a yellow cab. The driver waved for Jonathan to get into the backseat, which he did.

"Are you—" Jonathan's words were cut off as the man floored the car with such abruptness that it almost gave him whiplash. "Are you taking me to Alexandre?"

The man replied first with a dismissive wave of his hand and then uttered something in Russian. Obviously, he was not interested in making Jonathan feel at ease about this clandestine rendezvous. Jonathan only hoped he hadn't just made a huge mistake.

The driver did not say another word. He simply headed north, through heavily trafficked streets. After another ten minutes, Jonathan was getting extremely worried. He was no longer in the city center, and he couldn't be sure that the driver had good intentions. He gave himself another five minutes before he would confront the man for an explanation.

Fortunately, he didn't need to make a scene. The car drove over tram lines and headed toward a large square, when the driver suddenly stopped. Jonathan looked out his window and saw a massive free-standing arch, five times the size of the one he'd seen earlier. At the top were statues of a man and a woman, brandishing sheaves of wheat. Jonathan gazed at it and then beyond it, at what looked like a theme park of sorts.

The driver pointed at the entrance and rudely motioned for him to get out.

Jonathan again looked up, this time observing a large sign above the ticket booths that read ´~˝°. He deciphered the Cyrillic and remembered reading about the place in a hotel magazine. It was the VDNKh—a national exposition center used during the glory days of the Soviet Union to showcase industrial innovation from its various republics.

Jonathan stood in a short line, quickly searching his wallet for enough Russian currency to pay for a ticket. But before he could make it to the attendant's window, a heavy hand landed on his shoulder and pulled him back.

"I have your ticket," the deep accented voice said in English as Jonathan turned. It was Boris, the gentle Chechen giant with bad teeth. "You go dere, to big fountain—Fountain of the Friendship of Peoples. Alexandre wait for you."

Jonathan nodded and took the ticket from Boris' hand. "I wasn't followed, right?" he asked almost jokingly.

"*Nyet.*"

The snow covered the grounds, and leafless branches swayed in the breeze. The cold air seeped into Jonathan's skin. *Summer is probably a wonderful time to visit this place*, Jonathan imagined as he walked toward the fountain.

And there Alexandre stood, alone, bundled in a thick fur coat that at a glance made him look like a grizzly bear. The fountain was empty, the surrounding area desolate.

"Do you know about this place?" asked Alexandre.

"A little."

"That building over there was a pavilion for home appliances, and that glass one over there for agricultural equipment. For years, this whole place was an elaborate showcase for inferior Soviet hardware that no Westerner would want, except in a museum."

Jonathan laughed and patted Alexandre on the shoulder. "Why are we meeting in such an open space? I thought you would want more secrecy, given what we went through yesterday."

"Boris has the eyes of an eagle. We are quite safe to discuss things now."

"What do you have in mind?"

Alexandre sighed. "I am not keen to help you after what happened with Vladin, but, against my better judgment, I will do so anyway. I didn't know that you had a far more personal reason for being here. You should have told me much sooner. I can imagine this is very painful."

"It is, and I need closure," Jonathan said, filling his breath with the cool air. "There have been so many lies. It's possible that my brother was taken to Russia, and if he's alive, I need to find him. And whoever tried to kill Linda did so because I'm after the truth."

"I understand, but let's not repeat what happened yesterday. You have now seen what a Russian prison looks like. Neither of us wants to end up in one as an inmate, right?"

Jonathan nodded, feeling a little relieved. "I promise to behave."

"And how is your wife doing?"

"She is struggling, but she's alive. It wasn't easy to

leave her behind to come here. I keep thinking I should be by her side, rather than pursuing an uncertain trail of clues in this city."

"I will do my best to help you, so you can return to her quickly."

Jonathan placed his hand on Alexandre's shoulder. "Thank you." He was comforted to know that the Russian lawyer seemed to genuinely care.

Alexandre lighted a cigarette. "I have a contact—a very important person who can find more information."

"From the face you're making, I have a feeling this will be complicated."

Alexandre's gaze was dead serious. "You are correct—complicated indeed." He looked away from Jonathan, seeming to gauge his words before speaking.

Jonathan followed his gaze up at the fountain. It was gold plated, its ornately decorated central tower rising some thirty feet. "Well, tell me."

"When I defended several former Soviet officials implicated in the Parliament uprising, I turned to this informant for all kinds of information. His name is Nikolai. The documents he found helped exonerate two of my clients. In three other cases, what I learned from him helped reduce prison sentences by many years. And in yet another case, the information was so disturbing to the authorities that I got my client to be pardoned by Yeltsin himself."

"Who is this Nikolai?" Jonathan asked.

Alexandre hesitated as he studied Jonathan's gaze. He threw his cigarette down and extinguished it with his boot. "He is the Kremlin's chief archivist."

"Wow." It was an unexpected revelation, and Jonathan was grateful that Alexandre had offered such a potentially valuable informant. "I assume I'll have to pay him handsomely."

"Whatever you must have heard about Russians, Jonathan, I must tell you he's a special case when it comes to money."

Jonathan began to worry about how much this would cost him. "I'm not a millionaire, you know."

Alexandre raised his brow. "No, you misunderstand. Nikolai isn't after money. He's a very kind, gentle man—an intellectual confined for twenty years to a profession that requires seclusion. It is entirely by luck that I stumbled on him, and I am thankful for all he has done for my legal cases. And to this day, no one has ever discovered how I was able to get all the information. And he did it because he believed what I was doing was right. He is a friend, without being a friend. It's hard to explain. So, don't worry, he's not after your wallet."

"But he still wants something, right? I mean what Russian wouldn't—" Jonathan interrupted himself, realizing he was unintentionally about to insult Alexandre as well.

Alexandre tilted his head to the side. "I helped his mother get into a better hospital. I bought him a German refrigerator, and last year I got him a cat."

"A cat?"

"Yes, a nice Persian cat, something you can't easily find in Moscow. It's not about *money*, I tell you. It's whether he believes that what you ask of him is the morally right thing to do. So, he'll want to know why you want the information, and you can't easily fool him."

Jonathan was suddenly embarrassed, realizing how callous or pompous his statement must have sounded. The fact that it came from an American probably made it worse.

Alexandre rubbed his chin and added, "Now, I've heard he is looking for a new Japanese television."

*I knew it*, Jonathan told himself, shaking his head.

Alexandre crossed his arms and raised his chin. "Even if he accepts to help you, there is still a problem."

Jonathan frowned. "What exactly do you mean?"

"Nikolai will not allow his documents to leave the Kremlin. He doesn't photograph or copy them either, and he'll never let anyone else do so. But he does let you read them."

"But I don't know Russian."

"Not to worry. His English is fair—not perfect—but fair, if he's not drinking."

"Drinking?"

"Yes, Nikolai is a big drinker. A shy man who makes love to his vodka almost all day long."

Jonathan started so see this getting really messy. "And let's assume for a moment that he agrees, and that he hasn't drunk himself to the floor, and that I buy him a television, how exactly I am supposed to meet him?"

"Yes, that's the most complicated factor. But not to worry—it's safe. However, it's not the most pleasant way to visit the Kremlin."

Jonathan shook his head, waiting for him to spit it out.

"You can only meet him in the Kremlin, and only on Thursday—the day the place is closed to tourists."

"So, I'm supposed to climb the walls and find his office?" Jonathan asked, chuckling.

"Not exactly," said Alexandre with a grin. "You will enter by a secret tunnel!"

He sensed Alexandre's suggestion was sounding like something between bungee jumping and Russian roulette. "Is this your sick way of turning me into a client, so you can defend me?" asked Jonathan, shaking his head in disbelief.

Alexandre didn't seem humored by Jonathan's comment. "There are numerous tunnels and passageways under and around the Kremlin, some of them built centuries ago. It is an entirely safe way to get in, if you know what you're doing."

Jonathan's receptiveness was wearing thin. "I am neither an archeologist nor a miner. I'm a lawyer, I'm claustrophobic, and I don't feel like getting shot."

"I've used the passageway before, and I had no trouble," Alexandre said as if he'd done so many, many times. But then he added that he'd used it only once.

"I'm not crazy, Alexandre."

"The tunnel begins in the Russian State Library. It's about two hundred meters long, and Nikolai will be waiting at the other end."

"If he's sober enough to remember," Jonathan retorted grimly. "I would feel safer if Boris accompanied me."

Alexandre chuckled. "He would not fit through the tunnel."

"Have you spoken to Nikolai?"

"A little."

"And what could he show me?"

"KGB files, transcripts of government meetings, secret reports, that sort of thing. He could find more information about Major-General Yakovlev. He also has access to certain files of the old Central Committee—the former Poliburo of the USSR."

Jonathan was tempted to ask that Alexandre go with him, but something, perhaps pride or bravado, didn't let him. Either way, Alexandre hadn't volunteered, or he surely would have if he really wanted to go.

Coincidentally, as if he'd read Jonathan's mind, Alexandre said, "It's better that you go alone. It will make Nikolai nervous to have two guests. Besides, you know all the right questions to ask."

To Jonathan, it was a lame excuse, but he chose not to debate Alexandre. Jonathan raised his chin. "What is the worst that could happen to me if I get caught?"

"Someone shoots you."

"And the next worst thing?"

"Someone shoots you but doesn't kill you."

"And the next?"

"Imprisonment in a jail like Butyrka for five to ten years."

*Fabulous.*

They walked toward the pavilion that represented the Soviet Union's accomplishments in air and space travel. Two large rockets and a medium-sized airliner sat on display outside the large, austere expo building. They stopped at a concession stand, where Alexandre bought his American colleague a beer.

"Well?" Alexandre asked with his glass held high, shall we toast to your upcoming secret rendezvous, or are you not willing to accept the risk?"

Jonathan stared into Alexandre's eyes, weighing his options. "Okay, I'll do it," he declared firmly.

Alexandre nodded. "Good. I will contact Nikolai this evening and confirm everything."

Jonathan walked with Alexandre for a while longer, but they left aside any further serious discussions. Instead, Alexandre talked at length about his latest conquest: a twenty-two-year-old cashier named Karina he had met while shopping at the Benetton store in the GUM shopping mall. Ironically, he'd been there to buy a gift for his prior flame.

They walked across the vast park that was the VDNKh. The cool air filled Jonathan's lungs. It was strangely peaceful. As they strolled out of the grounds, Alexandre signaled for Boris, who was kind enough to drive Jonathan back to the Hotel Metropol.

*       *       *

COLORFUL pastries decorated a small plate that a waiter brought to Jonathan's table. The American sat in a cozy circular booth in the hotel's Confectioner Cafe, the same place he'd first met Alexandre. The quiet voices of Englishmen and louder ones of other Americans echoed from the three other occupied tables near the window that overlooked *Teatralnaya Ploschad*, Theatre Square.

Jonathan was re-reading his notes from when he'd interviewed Vladin at the prison. He needed to know more about Yakovlev, but more importantly the woman

Vladin had suggested was in charge of the whole operation at the farm and at the airfield.

Suddenly, the waiter returned to Jonathan's table rather hurriedly and asked, "Sir, are you Mr. Brooks?"

"Yes."

"There is a call for you," he said and then pointed to his right. "You can use the phone over there."

"Thank you," Jonathan said and quickly headed to the phone at the far end of the elegant, mahogany-walled café. He had learned to become fearful of unexpected calls, especially if they were from home. That's why he felt an immediate relief when he heard Alexandre's voice on the other end of the line.

"Did you know that there is a U.S.-Russia commission on prisoners of war and missing persons?" Alexandre asked excitedly.

"No, I didn't."

"The commission formed a Cold War Working Group a few years ago in part to research cases involving U.S. military reconnaissance aircraft lost over or near Soviet airspace during the Cold War. As I understand it, they have already recovered the remains of several aircrew members from incidents in the 1950s."

Jonathan immediately realized this committee was something to look into more closely. "Then I will contact them. Is the commission here in Moscow?"

"Yes. But the reason I'm calling is that the American head of that working group will probably be at a reception tonight, and my very good friend Lena is invited. She's number two at the Ministry of Culture—a nice, charismatic lady, widowed and harmless. She was a friend of my mother's. She would be willing to take you. She owes me a favor. Well, what do you say?"

"What's the reception for?"

"A military choir from your country is in town, so they are performing tonight. I think there will be several military and political personalities."

"Where?"

"At the Spaso House, the U.S. Ambassador's residence," Alexandre said. "It's in the Arbat area, where I drove you around yesterday. It may be a better opportunity to meet one of the heads of this commission and get their attention more quickly than if you start with the lower ranks at your embassy."

"I don't know if that's such a good idea, given that I almost killed an embassy official."

"Embassy official?" Alexandre asked, his enthusiastic tone suddenly evaporating.

"Frank Corrigan, that dirt bag from yesterday, had an official, diplomatic passport. He was American." Jonathan had asked Allen to research what it meant to have a maroon-colored passport with the OFFICIAL PASSPORT designation. Only government officials carried that kind of passport, which was different than the blue-colored ones like Jonathan's.

"We shouldn't talk like this on the phone," Alexandre cautioned. "Go to the reception. Trust me. You'll be fine. She will pick you up at six-thirty."

*       *       *

LENA'S chauffeured Mercedes pulled up to the hotel entrance, where Jonathan had been waiting. Lena was in her late fifties and elegantly dressed, wearing an haute couture suit and a pearl necklace that no doubt cost a fortune, if it was real. Her English was nearly flawless, a result of working as a consular official in Ireland in the mid-1980s.

The short drive to the Spaso House didn't give Lena much time to ask Jonathan many questions, though her curiosity led her to try as best she could. Alexandre had told her only that Jonathan was trying to meet a few American officials for a legal case, and nothing more.

Spaso House was a huge mansion, with tall white Roman columns decorating its peach-colored facade. As they pulled up to the entrance, Lena leaned into Jonathan and said, "It was built in 1914 by a wealthy industrialist named Nikolai Vtorov, and, believe it or not, your government is only paying about $50 per year in rent."

Jonathan was astonished. "Fifty?"

"The lease was signed in 1985 at a fixed price, before the fall of the Soviet Union, and now the value of the ruble has dropped so much that they ended up with a great deal."

A doorman ushered the arriving guests into the pristinely decorated lobby with a soaring domed ceiling from which hung an ornate crystal chandelier.

"Do you come to many of these events?" Jonathan asked Lena.

"Only when I have nothing more pleasant to do. Look around. Most of these people, whether Americans or Russians, they think they are better than everyone else. More knowledgeable, more noble, richer and more powerful. I think I'm invited because they are tired of the other senior diplomats at my Ministry. They are as dull as their English is poor. Frankly, I don't think many at your embassy are all that interesting either, and I'm certain they don't give a damn about Russia's cultural programs."

"You are an interesting woman, Lena," Jonathan said, smiling. "I can see exactly why they would invite you."

Jonathan did his best to eavesdrop on each conversation as he casually walked around the room.

The hundred or so guests gathered into the domed room as waiters handed out drinks. The Ambassador spoke for a few minutes and then introduced the ten members of the U.S. Air Force Academy show choir, which was in Russia for the first time. Their performance was short, which suited Jonathan, as his interest was in the VIPs wearing military uniforms and no one else.

"You said you're interested in senior military officials, right?" Lena whispered, to which Jonathan nodded. "Then, over there, the one with the uniform," whispered Lena from the side of her mouth, sipping her champagne. "He's General Forester, the American military attaché."

"You know him?"

"A little," Lena said, smiling. "From what I hear, he's gotten into a lot of hot water with his bosses back home. He's got quite a thing about Moscow girls, if you know what I mean."

"Uh-huh."

"Shall I introduce you to him?"

"No, no," Jonathan said, thinking how absurd it would be if he, as an American, were to be introduced to the attaché by a Russian official. "I'll do it myself."

Jonathan strolled across the blue and beige carpeted floor toward the general, who stood at a hors d'oeuvres table with his back facing him.

"Good evening," Jonathan said. "Are you General Forester?"

"Yes, I am."

Jonathan realized he had the attention of one of the most senior embassy officials, and every word out of his mouth would have to be calculated and flawless. And he wasn't about to use his real name. "I'm Sylvester Johnson. I've been working with Frank Corrigan on an investigation."

"Oh, Jesus," the general said, almost dropping his cheese-laden cracker from his hand. "I'm terribly sorry to hear about what happened."

"Yes, very serious," Jonathan said, though he had no clue about Frank's condition. "It has hurt the whole team."

The general frowned. "I imagine so . . . but C.J. Raynes is not the sort of man who'll just sit there. I hope he can nail whoever assaulted Frank. "

"Yes."

"Are you working with anyone else in C.J.'s group?"

Jonathan shook his head, realizing the general had just given him a huge bit of information. C.J. was the head of Frank's group, whatever their role was.

"Is C.J. coming tonight?" Jonathan asked.

The general smirked. "He would come to this kind of

event only at gunpoint. Besides, as you must know, he doesn't mingle much with us folks."

"You got that right," Jonathan said.

"So what kind of investigation are you heading?"

"An old missing persons' case, dating back to the late 80s."

"I see."

Jonathan spoke to him for a few more minutes. He'd learned that the so-called Cold War working group focused on finding airmen who disappeared in the '50s, '60s and '70s, but no investigations related to any later period.

He mingled with others at the reception, including a consular official and the embassy's press officer until it was time to leave. He got no additional insight into the identity of C.J. Raynes, but he was thankful that Lena had given him such an opportunity. He'd gained a small piece of information, and with it he hoped to dig into Vladin's murder. And he would do it soon, in the cleverest way he could think of.

# 17

Moscow streets were wide and busy, but Jonathan was amazed at how easy it was to park, nothing like the hassles in downtown New Orleans, especially in the central business district and in the French Quarter.

Alexandre had promised to take Jonathan to a place that would help give him a new perspective of post-communist Russia. It was a small park, divided in half by a narrow trail cleared through the snow.

"What's that over there?" Jonathan asked, eyeing a set of red-brick buildings that took up the entire block across the street.

"The back of your country's embassy."

The two walked along the icy sidewalk at the perimeter of the snow-covered park.

Alexandre strolled a few paces ahead and then turned to Jonathan. "This is a sacred place for many of my countrymen, those who miss the Soviet Union, and the security, the social order, the pride and the respect that came with it. Three years ago, Communists, both young and old, many of them from the military, including our dear General Yakovlev, took over the parliament to save the empire from the perils of a new democratic order. This park is where their opponents—the troops under Yeltsin—gathered for a final assault on the building to end the rebellion. Hundreds of soldiers were assembled here with tanks and armored cars. They waited, loading their ammunition, until they got the signal. And then they attacked. The rest is history. The parliament has been rebuilt and most Muscovites have conveniently discarded this from their collective conscience. And now, all that's left are these bulletin boards. Crazy, isn't it?"

Jonathan gazed at the strange makeshift memorial, no more glamorous than a series of job posting boards. Their facades were filled with photographs, notes, letters, ribbons and a few wilted flowers. So many young faces. Kids in uniform, from all branches of the military. Nearby were worn wreaths and more ribbons, partly covered by snow.

"And all for what?" Alexandre asked. "It didn't change a thing. They died believing they were defending a legitimate government from an illegitimate one."

"But they revolted against Yeltsin?"

"Yes, but he had illegally abolished parliament, taking power for himself under the guise of democracy at a time when no one understood what democracy really meant. He didn't have the authority to do what he did, but he eventually received the support of key generals, which in this country ultimately determines if you win or lose. The sad truth is that we *all* lost."

Jonathan saw pain in Alexandre's eyes. "And which side were you on?" he asked, his tone deliberately non-judgmental.

Alexandre leaned forward and swung his arm at the corner of the closest billboard. "Dmitri, my nephew," he said, tapping a small black and white photo of a short-haired boy who looked not a day over eighteen. "I was both on his side and on Yeltsin's."

"Torn loyalties?"

"Yes," Alexandre said, reaching into his pocket for a cigarette. "Torn by pragmatism, pessimism and the faintest of hope for the future. You see, we're all Russians. One thing we have done so well, for so long, was to kill our own people, to create irreparable tragedy to our own identity. We don't seem to learn from the past."

"Now," Alexandre began. "I must prepare you for your Kremlin visit." They drove a few blocks until he pointed at a building. "There, we'll quickly go in, and then we'll head to the library."

The two men faced a nondescript concrete block, which had what looked like a small store at street level. As the men strolled into the store, Jonathan realized it was something of a cross between a liquor store and a bar. He observed the dozen men lining up at the counter, not a single person speaking.

Alexandre leaned into Jonathan and whispered, "Watch this." He walked a few steps further to the edge of the counter, glanced at the patrons to his right and then brought his middle finger to his neck. He tapped the side of his neck twice and then raised two fingers in the air. Another man, standing a few feet from Jonathan, then raised his index finger high above his head and then looked at Alexandre.

The man working the counter approached with a bottle in hand. Alexandre paid him and the stranger next to Jonathan paid Alexandre for the portion of the bottle he wanted to drink, their only communication being eye contact and money changing hands.

Alexandre pressed his thumb against bottle. "There, one-third," he whispered to Jonathan before bringing the bottle close to his face. He then chugged the drink until the liquid had emptied to the level marked by his thumb. "Now, your turn," Alexandre said, handing the bottle to his American colleague. "It's okay; it's only vodka."

Jonathan gazed at the bottle. It was early afternoon and the last thing on his mind was to risk losing his faculties. Especially knowing that he was about to sneak into the Kremlin in a matter of hours.

Alexandre grabbed Jonathan's hand and made him hold the bottle just as he had seconds ago. "Mark the spot and drink. This man next to you is thirsty. He gets the last third of the bottle. Now, drink."

Jonathan did as he was told. The alcohol left a burning trail down his esophagus, and his stomach began to warm. "I'm not used to drinking like this," Jonathan said.

Alexandre chuckled. "I wanted you to see a typical way that older Russians get their drinks."

Jonathan exhaled as if he were a dragon, the smell of alcohol permeating his immediate surroundings. He looked around and saw everyone else doing the same thing: chugging but not conversing.

"Drinking is a serious thing here, my friend."

Jonathan shook his head and followed Alexandre out to his car.

*          *          *

"EVERYTHING will be fine," Alexandre said, putting some change into the parking meter.

As much as Jonathan distrusted Alexandre's blind optimism, he was willing to accept it today, just this once, to tame his anxiety about the risky plan they had concocted.

Jonathan had slept barely three hours, his sleep interrupted by nightmares about Linda. He had paced about his room to wear off the tension. He remained perplexed. Fearful. He'd spent the early morning piecing together what he'd collected so far. *Perhaps he's still alive*, Jonathan thought, before feeling skepticism retake the helm of his confused, tired mind.

To paint an even rosier picture, Alexandre pulled out a letter from his jacket, waved it proudly at Jonathan, and said, "This is all we need to get into the right part of the library. Trust me." But Alexandre then told Jonathan it was a forgery. The letterhead was a cut-and-paste work by a part-time graphic artist and the text was drafted from memory based on an original Alexandre had used a year earlier.

"And if they find out it's fake?" Jonathan inquired.

Alexandre smiled. "I'll bet you the person working the front desk is either an old woman who can barely see her hands or an incredibly horny *biksa* who is damn tired of her man, if she has one, and will overlook anything in return for attention."

"*Biksa?*" Jonathan asked.

Alexandre scratched his chin and thought for a moment. "A woman who, you know, goes around."

"A slut," Jonathan said, happy to add to Alexandre's English lexicon.

They walked one block, turned the corner, and headed to the end of the next block.

The Russian State Library was at the intersection of Vozdvizhenka and Mokhovaya streets, a heavily-trafficked area facing the Alexandrovski Gardens adjacent to the Kremlin's northwest wall.

Jonathan had a good picture of the layout etched in his mind. Alexandre had also made it a point to drive twice around the block to further familiarize Jonathan.

"The underground passageway runs under there," he'd said, pointing over the car's dash while on Mokhovaya Street. "About twenty to thirty meters below. The area is full of passageways—sewer systems, drainage tunnels and bomb shelters, in addition to the Metro tunnels. Some of them are makeshift homes for gypsies, refugees, drug addicts and other squatters."

He'd also passed onto Jonathan the rumor that buried somewhere under the Kremlin was a medieval library built by Tsar Ivan the Terrible for his wife, a princess from the last Byzantine emperor, after which Jonathan reminded Alexandre that he was claustrophobic and didn't care to know how deep, secluded or small the labyrinth of tunnels were.

Alexandre and Jonathan walked briskly over the snow-covered sidewalk. The air was chilly, but the wind had died down from earlier in the day.

Alexandre led the way up the steps to the library as Jonathan gazed up, observing the deeply austere, hard lines of the 1930s-era edifice. The concrete facade was lined with tall, narrow columns, some clad with black marble. *Perhaps the dreariness of the architecture had a purpose at one time*, he mused. *Most likely to suppress the Proletariat's urge to read, which might have helped them educate themselves out of communism.*

"It says *Biblioteka Imeni Lenina*—the Lenin Library," Jonathan heard Alexandre say as he fixed his eyes on the gold-leafed lettering above the columns. Below it, intricately carved stone figurines depicted male and female laborers.

As they reached the heavy entrance door, Alexandre turned to Jonathan. "Don't say a word," he reminded his American cohort. "I will do all the talking." He had already explained the rules twice. How to act, when to speak, where to go and what *not* to do.

"Yeah, yeah," Jonathan whispered. He understood that he was to keep his mouth shut, walk in Alexandre's shadow the entire way, avoid eye contact, stay serious, and wait until their butts were planted in a chair in Reading Room B before uttering another word. The room was reserved for authorized guests only, Alexandre had said, and it was the perfect spot from which to enter the adjacent restricted gallery, an area off limits to civilians—no exceptions. It was the only room that led to the underground tunnel.

The library's atrium was immense but dreary—even more so than the building's facade. The concrete floor sealed in the coldness, giving the feel of a mausoleum.

"Now watch me," Alexandre whispered.

Jonathan watched him discreetly undo the top two buttons of his shirt and snake his way across the atrium to the reception desk, apparently on a charm offensive. He honed in on the two female attendants, one in her late thirties, the other not a day over sixteen.

Jonathan wasn't a woman, or a Russian, or an expert in international cultures, or even an aficionado of courtship. But he considered himself qualified enough to assume that the way Alexandre swaggered forward with his artificial smile, his gold chain and chest hair crawling into daylight like a marsupial, that no woman on earth would fall for his charade.

Jonathan gazed at the Russian gigolo in action, which made him even more nervous. He waited, fully expecting a rebuff of humbling proportions, so severe it might send Alexandre to a monastery.

To his astonishment, the wooing progressed with amazing speed. The echoes of flirtatious giggles ricocheted off the stone walls. The women were hooked. Alexandre had proven himself a player. *I'm not jealous*, Jonathan told himself, perhaps not so convincingly. He waited. The older woman joked, and Alexandre responded exuberantly, his gestures energetic and his smile so wide it nearly encircled his head.

The younger attendant, her own smile competing with Alexandre's, took his forged letter and, amazingly, nodded affirmatively without even reading it. The elder woman playfully pinched Alexandre's cheek and headed back to her files. That's when Alexandre turned to Jonathan and winked.

The young attendant walked out of sight, and Alexandre strolled back to Jonathan's side.

"She's getting the key to the reading room," said Alexandre.

It pained Jonathan to see Alexandre prevail so flagrantly. He shook his head. *He must have known her*, he thought, but didn't care to ask.

"Sometimes it can be tricky," Alexandre said, barely above a whisper. "The staff is still not accustomed to unofficial visitors, particularly civilians. Prior to the fall of the Communists, this library was off limits to most Muscovites, and those allowed in could not freely roam the floors. You had to order your book at the counter. Things have changed now, but some departments still offer only limited access. Keep in mind, this is an important place. Since the 1920s, the building was the country's main repository of military books—now some 114,000 items in all. And as of last year, it officially became the Central Library of the Armed Forces of the Russian Federation." Alexandre raked his hand through his short, brown hair, and shifted his gaze at the counter. "Ah, here she comes. Her name is Nadia."

"*Biksa*," Jonathan whispered back mockingly and grinned.

Nadia was just plain hot, a descendent of Scandinavian nobility, one would have guessed. Fair skinned with long, red hair, rosy cheeks and slender arms. And now that she had walked around the counter toward the center of the atrium, the rest of her real estate came into view: her long legs, and a rear end that not only tested the endurance of her tight skirt's fabric but also mesmerized both men sufficiently to shut them up momentarily.

"Let's go," Alexandre whispered, falling in behind her.

Her stiletto-heeled shoes stabbed their way along the worn faux-Persian rugs that lined the trek to the stairs at the back of the building. Alexandre and Jonathan followed her like puppies.

They headed one floor up, to the Department of Military Literature, where the prized reading room was situated. Unlike the lobby, the second floor had all the attributes of a distinguished library: bookcases made of ornately crafted wood, decorated ceilings and elegant furniture. Jonathan stared in awe at the endless amassment of crammed shelves and display cabinets that made the room feel like a cocoon. The place was filled with myriad books, binders and journals, but Jonathan couldn't spot one that was titled with Western alphabet.

*One of the largest libraries in the world*, he thought, *and I can't read a damn thing!*

Nadia and her two admirers headed down a long corridor until she stopped at a set of double doors. She unlocked them and waved the men in with a come-hither pose, her flirty gaze locked on Alexandre. She pointed to the bookstalls in the center of the large room, said a few words to him and then politely moved her steamy silhouette to an oversized metal desk by the windows.

Alexandre took Jonathan by the arm and casually

walked to a nearby table. "Behind you is the restricted area, where you'll go when I tell you."

There was a doorway all right, but no door. It looked like another reading room, but with fewer tables and many more stacks. Jonathan turned and glanced at Nadia. She was reading a magazine, her long scarlet hair draped over her shoulders. Though she sat only twenty feet away, the restricted room wasn't in her line of sight.

"Let's sit here and wait for the right moment." Alexandre pulled a chair back and waved for Jonathan to take a seat. "I'll be right back."

The air was stale, saturated with the smell of old paper. Walls of unreadable books surrounded Jonathan, who in the back of his mind wondered if this excursion would be worth the trouble.

Alexandre returned with three large books under this arm. "I told Nadia you are a renowned professor, so you must look studious," he whispered, sliding the smallest book to Jonathan, and adding, "Pretend to read this one. It's a manual about constipation on the battlefield."

In keeping with Alexandre's instructions, Jonathan didn't respond or even crack a smile, though he wanted to. He stared at the book's engraved title, trying to decipher the Cyrillic letters to see if Alexandre was pulling his leg. He then scanned the pages, thinking that drawings of intestinal tracts or photos of soldiers shitting in bomb craters might confirm Alexandre's assertion. There were none, only more Cyrillic.

*Constipation, my ass.*

Alexandre took a seat across the table from him and began reading one of the other books, and seemed awestruck by its contents. To Jonathan's consternation, Alexandre sat there for almost fifteen minutes without looking up. By then, Nadia had walked away, perhaps returning downstairs.

"Psst," Jonathan said, wanting to get the ball rolling. He glanced at his wristwatch. It was just shy of three-ten.

Alexandre casually put his book down, his demeanor not unlike someone on holiday. As if that's what you're supposed to act when you're about to help someone illegally infiltrate the Kremlin, a place guarded by a thousand armed Russians.

*He's fucking with me*, Jonathan's mind declared before he whispered, "For cryin' out loud, can't I go now?"

"Shh!" Alexandre snapped. "It's not time."

Jonathan returned an indignant snivel, his patience reaching an end.

Another nerve-wracking nine minutes passed before Alexandre finally unglued his butt from the chair and headed to the reading room doorway, his head peeking into the hall. He then turned and nodded at Jonathan.

"Okay, go!" Alexandre whispered loudly from the corner of his mouth. "Be back here no later than five."

As planned, Jonathan walked out of the other end of the reading room to the adjoining area, past the fifth row of bookstalls. He glanced left, at a door on the far wall. He headed briskly toward it, making his way around a display case containing several leather-bound books.

The door wasn't locked and no alarm rang as Jonathan stepped across the threshold into the confined space that led to the concrete stairwell. Parroting in his mind was his own voice, repeating the sequence of steps and directions he was to follow to reach the tunnel. He spotted the stairs, as Alexandre had described. The air was stuffy and cool, and by the time he got to the bottom of the stairs, some three flights down, it had dipped twenty degrees. He stopped to put on his coat and continued through a dark basement of some kind. As the path ahead of him darkened further, he pulled out the flashlight Alexandre had given him.

"First right," he whispered to himself, the beam of his flashlight illuminating a large room filled with generators—large industrial generators the size of tractors. A quarter-inch-thick coat of dust covered the equipment. Alexandre had told him the room had been used as a backup source of power for the Kremlin and the two closest Metro stations but was now abandoned. Jonathan kept his sights on the third generator. It was behind there that Alexandre had promised he'd find a manhole, though he warned of the possibility that it might have been sealed over the past year.

Jonathan directed the light at the metal cover. He dropped to his knees for a closer inspection, praying he would still be able to open it. He slid his hand into a slit in the cover and pulled it with all his strength. The cover slowly lifted at one end, but his arms began to tire quickly from the strain. It must have weighed sixty or seventy pounds. He slid it to one side and let it fall ajar.

He made his way down the shaft, some fifty feet deep, as a rancid smell became stronger. At the bottom, he reached the beginning of a tunnel, no wider than three feet and only a couple of inches higher than his head and about an inch deep in water. He pointed the flashlight ahead of him. The tunnel seemed to go on forever into the pitch-black distance. The air was thick and the walls so close, so confining. *Stay calm*, he told himself, knowing that his claustrophobia could easily get the best of him in such a horrible place. His chest began to sweat, his hands too, despite the near-freezing air.

He quickly walked across the slushy surface of the tunnel, breathing out of his mouth to avoid smelling the stench. He kept going, until some thirty yards ahead, he saw a dim light. As he drew nearer, he noticed it came from the floor of the tunnel. He stopped at the edge of the concrete and looked down through the metal cage floor and saw two sets of tracks some twenty feet below. *The Metro*, he thought. He looked ahead and realized this part of the tunnel was a walkway of sorts. Alexandre had told him the tunnel passed over the secretive *D-6 Metro*, a system of subway lines built by the military in the '50s to evacuate Kremlin officials to bunkers and airports in the city's outskirts, in case of an attack. Part of the line was supposedly constructed adjacent to the civilian *Metro* to help hide its development and expansion.

Just as Jonathan was about to cross the walkway, the loud sounds of laughter suddenly jarred the quiet surroundings. He kneeled down and turned off his flashlight. He heard male voices coming from one end of the subway line, but he couldn't see anything except the tracks directly below him. The voices and footsteps grew louder. He then saw them, two uniformed men holding assault rifles. They casually strolled under his tunnel and stopped. One guard suddenly looked up.

*Shit*, Jonathan thought, and almost said it out loud. He quickly jolted back. Luckily for him, the guard had not flashed his light up until a second later. Jonathan squatted motionless, his heart beating rapidly, a few inches away from the beam that pierced the floor and illuminated the ceiling of his tunnel. Then, one guard spoke to the other, but he didn't sound alarmed. And when Jonathan heard one of them laugh again, he knew he was safe for the moment.

Jonathan sighed. He waited until the guards had walked away, their voices now faint, before he slowly and quietly crossed the twenty-foot-long metal floor and continued through the tunnel. He then rubbed his arms and hands to warm himself.

With his flashlight back on, he walked at a fast pace until he reached a fork in the tunnel. He turned right, as Alexandre had instructed. And then he counted the large wooden doors that appeared on his left. *It's the fourth one*, Jonathan told himself, recalling what Alexandre had said. He examined the surface of the door with his flashlight and then knocked three times, also as Alexandre had told him.

A noisy clanking of keys resonated from behind the door, and then the lock snapped loudly. The door creaked as if it hadn't been opened in years, and immediately a flashlight beamed onto Jonathan's face.

"Are you Mr. Brooks?" whispered a man with a Russian accent. He seemed agitated.

"Yes," Jonathan replied. "You are Nikolai?"

The man lowered his flashlight and nodded. "Please, please," he then said, motioning for Jonathan to come in. Nikolai quickly shut the door behind Jonathan and locked it.

Jonathan gazed around the small, stone-walled room, which was illuminated only by a gas lantern atop a pile of wooden crates at the far end of the room, next to another door. Except for the half-dozen crates, the room was empty.

"Are we safe here?" asked Jonathan.

"It is an abandoned cellar from the late 19th Century," Nikolai answered. "I don't think anyone has taken the time to see if it still exists. We are safe, unless you were followed." His breath reeked of alcohol, but it didn't seem to impair his English.

"I'm sure I was not followed."

"*Kharasho, kharasho,*" Nikolai said, sounding relieved. He sat on one of the crates and pointed to the one next to him. "Sit, please."

Nikolai pulled two documents out of the top of the stack of papers, the first paper clipped, the other stapled. He rested the papers on his lap, licked his index finger and flipped past the first few pages."

He seemed excited, or perhaps nervous, or both.

Jonathan kneeled down and opened his notebook over his lap, his pen ready take down any information of value.

Pulling his wide-framed reading glasses away for a second, Nikolai wiped the sweat from under his eyes and quickly jostled the paper below Jonathan's nose. "Very difficult, but I find helpful information about Yakovlev."

"Good." Jonathan took a deep breath.

"I am sure it is your Yakovlev," he said and then began reading the text, translating slowly. "'Item Six: Concerning attempts by United States intelligence services to acquire Soviet weapons.' It is a handwritten transcript of the working notes at a meeting of the Politburo."

Jonathan nodded impatiently. "What is the date?"

"Twenty-two October, 1986, and all the big men were present, it seems," he said, his eyes wide open, as he spat out some of the names, "It looks like Gorbachev, Gromyko, Zaikov, Ligachev, Ryzhkov, Shevardnadze, Dobrynin—the full house! But it looks like each minister has a number, so I'm not sure who was saying what."

He then began a verbatim translation, starting with one of the ministers:

NUMBER 7: We need to exchange opinions concerning measures in connection with the hostile action by the USA administration intelligence services. As stated earlier, the events after Reykjavik shows that they are doing everything to inflame the atmosphere, covertly and publicly. As I understand it, they are aggressively pursuing our biological weapons capabilities, and one of our trusted groups has uncovered a potential danger to us. We have learned that one of their agencies is attempting to acquire some of our special weapons.

NUMBER 3: Is it the CIA?

NUMBER 4: I have been told no, but no one is

sure. What is most dangerous is that they are trying to take possession of the weapons, not merely the plans, drawings and other information. They are using several agents in our military and at Biopreparat laboratories, in an operation they have codenamed "Tranquility."

NUMBER 3: Yes, Comrades, another example that they are acting like bandits from the big road.

NUMBER 7: Can we shut their operation down? And should we make it public?

NUMBER 1: We cannot allow a public response in this case. In this extremely complex situation, we need to be clever and not simply reach for propaganda points. This problem risks damaging our credibility and our positions on disarmament.

NUMBER 6: Perhaps we can do something else. As I already reported to the Politburo, we discovered many eavesdropping devices in our offices in the USA. This fact should be made public in order to expose American espionage, and a press conference should be called with a demonstration of American espionage's eavesdropping devices. This may make them nervous and stop their latest operation.

NUMBER 7: That will not stop them. They seem committed to stealing our most sensitive weapons.

NUMBER 2: But we must stop them. We have weapons that are more advanced than theirs, thanks to our two newest laboratories.

NUMBER 8: I agree, but let us find a better way, a way to turn their plan against them, without damaging us.

NUMBER 4: There is a group already working on this.

NUMBER 6: What is this group?

NUMBER 4: People at Yasenevo, mostly T and RT Departments, with assistance from the Institute of Applied Molecular Biology, as well as KGB Major-General Yakovlev at the Air Force Academy. Apparently, he is one that is being targeted by the Americans, no doubt because of his access to special weapons facilities and experts.

NUMBER 8: I have heard of Comrade Yakovlev Ivanovich. Are we sure he is a trustworthy person to pose as a double-agent?

NUMBER 4: Yes, the group is under the tight control of Comrade Zhumavik. I suggest giving her even more room to be creative.

NUMBER 6: Is this the infamous Mariya Zhumavik, of the Line Five operations last year?

NUMBER 4: Yes, a brilliant, shrewd mind.

NUMBER 2: Well, I must caution using her in this effort. May I remind the Politburo that she is Minister Zhumavik's daughter, and any misstep would be highly embarrassing? The Americans would rejoice at such negative publicity.

NUMBER 8: I am sure Mariya will do a fine job.
NUMBER 1: We should have this group work as
quickly as possible.
MEMBERS OF THE POLITBURO: We agree.

"Is this real?" Jonathan asked as his eyes scanned the
Cyrillic text of the paper.

Nikolai returned a look that could well have been a
slap. "Of course. I don't collect fake documents."

"Sorry," Jonathan said, shrugging his shoulders.

Jonathan immediately wondered if Vladin's recollection of the woman named Marina was in fact this
woman, Mariya. Vladin had not been completely certain
of her name, he recalled.

Jonathan glanced at the document once more and
asked, "Who are the people at Yasenevo?"

"Yasenevo is the name of the area. It is where the
SVR is located."

"SVR?" Jonathan asked.

"The *Sluzhba Vneshney Razvedki*, our external
reconnaissance services. It is like your CIA."

"I thought that was the role of the KGB."

"It is the same in your country. You have many intelligence departments and groups, and sometimes they
work together, but more often not. I think in this case the
SVR was handling the operation. And Mariya is most
definitely SVR. I have heard of her."

Nikolai turned to another document, flipped the
cover page over and pointed to one line, half-way down
the page.

"This is a dispatch to SVR headquarters from the

Ministry of Health, sent on March 22, 1989."

Jonathan looked into Nikolai's eyes, waiting for him to translate the content of the note.

"It's not clear who sent it, but it was sent to Major-General Yakovlev," he said, looking up with a cracked grin. "It says 'We must quarantine Patient Number 12 far from Moscow. Arrange for transport to Ministry clinic No. 211 until such time as we establish protocol. Authorization was never given for you to accompany specialists to Gotland, and we need debriefing on retrieval operation. Please report to Deputy Director.'"

The words were providing the pieces of the puzzle Jonathan so desperately wanted to cement together. It made sense, he guessed, but was he supposed to hang his hat on Matt being this patient number 12?

"Does patient number 12 have a name?"

"No," Nikolai said. "There are some more indirect references in some of these other documents, but those two papers are the best ones."

"I need to know more about this Mariya woman."

Nikolai suddenly looked annoyed. "I spent much time looking for Yakovlev materials; no one ever asked me for information on her."

"I suppose," Jonathan said calmly, although he wanted to grab the man's head and shake it like one would a misbehaving pin ball machine. *Doesn't he understand that I need new leads?* And Mariya was the one who managed the operation described in the Politburo transcript. *She has to know.*

Nikolai began digging through the pile of papers on his lap. He then pulled out a black and white photograph.

"Here, here. This is Mariya." He handed it to Jonathan, who then examined the image of a woman in uniform posing in front of two military men. "This is a few years ago." Nikolai then chuckled. "But you won't find her in a uniform now. I hear she is now completely . . ." He finished his sentence my motioning a nutty gesture with his hand. "Crazy lesbian sex parties. Heavy alcohol and drug use. She's lost her head."

Jonathan gazed at the photograph a bit longer. "Where can I find her?"

"I heard she's got a permanent room at the Baltschug Kempinski Hotel."

He and Nikolai then took a few more minutes to examine the remaining documents, but nothing new of interest came up.

Jonathan asked Nikolai to fetch more documents about Mariya Zhumavik when suddenly he realized that he also owed a favor to Erland, the Swedish intelligence operative who had given him some useful information about the crash near Gotland. "I have one more request. I need anything you can find about a Swedish DC-3 that was shot down by the Soviet Air Force in 1952."

Nikolai raised his brow. "You know, it takes time to find these documents. We are not in your country, where I am sure there are centralized computer systems to locate every document. Here, I do most of it by hand."

"I understand."

Nikolai tilted his head to the side and cracked an unexpected smile. "Well, I know about that incident because I helped to reclassify an updated report. The plane was shot down. Everyone knows that."

"But where is the wreckage?"

Nikolai's expression told Jonathan that he knew. "Apparently, it came down a few kilometers east of a small island off Sweden's coast."

"Gotland?"

"No, another one." Nikolai scratched his head and frowned. "I think it was called Sandon. Yes, that's it, Gotska Sandön, north of Gotland. If I remember correctly, one of our submarines spotted the wreckage in the late '80s. It was little more than a hundred meters below sea level."

"I would greatly appreciate if you could obtain more information on this." Jonathan was amazed that this man could remember such detail. *But then again*, he thought, *archivists are paid to scrutinize details.* Jonathan then remembered what Alexandre had said: to give Nikolai a reason—a morally justifiable one. "It's for the families of the pilots, you know. They want closure. After all these years . . ."

"I will see."

Jonathan patted Nikolai on the shoulder and sat back and stretched his arms. In doing so, he suddenly caught sight of a snakelike object that seemed to twist itself forward under the wooden door. *A camera?* Jonathan grabbed the kerosene lamp and held it up high, lighting up the far end of the room. The object seemed to have a glassy tip.

"What is it?" Nikolai blurted and then he too turned his attention at the object.

"It's a camera!" Jonathan's heart began to race and his legs tensed up like concrete poles.

A loud thud shook the door. And again. The camera whipped back under the door.

"Dammit," Jonathan barked, staring at Nikolai. "They're trying to come in?"

"Who is it? What do you want?" Nikolai shouted, jumping to his feet. "This can't be. No one knows about this place."

"You're obviously wrong."

The door shook again from the force that was pounding on it from the other side.

"Where does this lead?" Jonathan asked turning to the room's only other door, the one behind Nikolai. "Quickly."

The thuds continued, but the door seemed to hold, its thick structure buying Jonathan and Nikolai a little time.

"Let's go!" Nikolai quickly opened the door as Jonathan ran out of the room, holding the lamp ahead of him.

Suddenly, another loud thud crashed through the air. The wooden door swung open from the force. Before Jonathan could turn all the way round, Nikolai's head split open, flesh splattering across the wall and over Jonathan's shoulder.

Jonathan instantly darted down the dark corridor. He lost his grip on the lamp, and it shattered over the stone floor. He was now racing down a completely dark passageway. He'd left his flashlight back in the room. He heard yelling—possibly two or three men had stormed the room. Suddenly, a muffled series of pops echoed from far behind him, followed by the screeching bullets ricocheting off the tunnel walls.

He guessed that he'd been running about a hundred yards, and he wasn't about to stop. Not now. Not with the heavy sounds of footsteps and bursting gunfire so close on his tail. He continued to run, his hands stretched out in front of him to help shield him should there be a sudden turn in the abyss.

Jonathan again heard a series of loud crackles, then the echoes of bullets ricocheting off the stone walls somewhere behind him. Suddenly, a ripping pain burst through his right shoulder. Still running, he threw his left hand over his shoulder and felt a tear in his jacket. The needling pain tore through his arm.

*I've been shot!*

He ran as fast as he could, trying to ignore the pain and praying he would find a way out of this labyrinth.

Another shot rang out.

# 18

THE TUNNEL WAS COMPLETELY DARK UNTIL SUDDENLY, Jonathan spotted a faint light some distance away. He continued to run as fast as he could, but he needed to find a way out to street level. The sliver of light came through what looked like a ventilation outlet on the ceiling. He stopped momentarily. Sweat beaded on his forehead. He stood on his tiptoes and peeked through the opening, trying to gauge what was on the other side and deciding if he could crawl into it somehow. But it didn't look good. There was nothing to see, only an amorphous light, which was barely able to give his human eye the most minimal view of the tunnel ahead of him. He took off running, hoping he'd find another exit somewhere else along the dark tunnel.

Rapid, gritty-sounding footsteps resonated loudly, and though he estimated his lead at about fifty yards, if he didn't run like hell, he'd get his brains blown out like Nikolai. Panting wildly and nearly out of breath, he continued his race down the cobblestone tunnel, his thighs and calves burning, and the soles of his dress shoes barely able to keep any traction.

*If I fall, I'm dead.*

Another loud bang rang out behind him, followed by a crackle—the bullet again hit the stone walls. He kept running, his arms and shoulders brushing violently against the bulbous stones that made up each side of the tunnel. It was about four feet wide, but there was no telling how much further it went on—or if there were steps or a sharp turn anywhere ahead.

*Jesus!*

Jonathan's right foot clipped a ledge, hurling him forward uncontrollably. His knees planted first.

*Fuck!*

His body rolled once, twice and a third time as he brought his arms around his head to protect himself in the final tumble of his cascading journey over the cold, wet stone floor.

Jonathan took a deep breath as spindles of pain shot up from his legs and arms, but he could still move them. He again heard footsteps. He held his breath, got back up and stretched his arms wide open to find the right direction and bolted.

The tunnel was now completely dark, and with every lunging step he risked another chance of wiping out. The alternative—a bullet or two in the head—was an entirely unacceptable choice. Another shot rang out, the bullet finding only a stone near Jonathan.

Even with the darkness surrounding him, he ran with all the speed he could muster, praying that he'd avoid another fall. But he knew he had to get out of there soon. He couldn't see anything ahead of him.

He ran, rubbing his hand along the stone wall as he desperately sought to find a door or another passageway. Suddenly his wrist banged into a handle. He stopped and raced back to the door. He hastily twisted the latch and then attempted to shake it open.

*Dammit!*

He then stepped back a few feet and rammed the left side of his body into the door, the pain from his shoulder tearing across his back. When it didn't budge, he realized how thick the wood was. Another gunshot rang out, the lead scraping the stone wall just inches above his head. He ducked and darted down the pitch-black path, his thoughts jumping to the realization that he might indeed die, right here in Moscow's murky kingdom of Hades.

The moldy air surged into his lungs. He needed every bit of strength—and oxygen—to run farther, faster. But Jonathan suddenly crashed into something—something metallic—and then another rod-like object. He stumbled and rolled to the floor, as did the shattering pieces of whatever he had crashed into. He felt his hands plough through the cold, sandy soil. The stone ground had vanished. He crawled forward, and the soil became clumpy. Feeling his way ahead, several objects, perhaps tools, littered the ground. As he moved further, trying to get back up, his injured shoulder bumped into what felt like furniture. The object collapsed and a protracted sound of thumps followed. So did his excruciating pain. He'd just knocked over a bookcase, maybe two. He quickly turned, remembering what he had just touched seconds earlier—what had felt like a lamp, the kind you see on construction barricades. Now on his knees, he desperately searched the ground, his fingers feeling everything in arms' reach to find the light. He lunged forward, the throbbing pain in his shoulder exploding. He felt warm blood dripping down his right arm.

He finally grabbed the light, examining its surface with his fingers. He depressed the switch and the yellow bulb illuminated his surroundings. Jonathan quickly glanced at the myriad antique bookstalls that covered the walls. Hundreds—thousands—of dusty leather books littered the shelves. *The library*? he asked himself as he remembered Alexandre repeating the rumor that there was an ancient Byzantine library buried somewhere under the Kremlin. *Amazing!*

From the looks of it, the place was an archeological site, with excavation equipment, including ladders, netting, brushes and other tools all over the ground.

The sounds of his pursuers echoed from the tunnel behind him. Jonathan glanced ahead, at what looked like another passageway. He quickly dimmed the light, held it close to his chest and sprinted over a mound of dirt to the other side of the vast room.

*"Finally!"* he hissed upon seeing a faint light directly ahead. He was again on a stone floor. Like earlier, the light came from a ventilation duct in the ceiling. He jumped and punched it loose, the loud clanging sound echoing down the tunnel. He jumped again, this time miraculously popping it completely loose from its brackets. Once more he jumped, grabbed the ledge that

circled the opening and pulled himself up. His shoulder now felt on fire, the pain crisp.

Jonathan continued to grab the sides of the shaft to pull himself upward. The lamp that he had secured under his shirt fell and smashed on the stone ten feet below him. He looked up and saw another metal cage, but this time, a lot more light appeared through it. His arms barely sustained his weight, but he persevered. Three feet. Two. One. Then, his head butted the cage loose. He grabbed each side of the opening and pulled himself out of the shaft. His hands felt a thin layer of carpet as he rolled his body out of the manhole and over onto the floor, his exhaustion freezing him in place. He breathed in deeply.

Jonathan knew his escape was far from over. He was in a hallway illuminated by a row of half-lit incandescent lamps on the ceiling. But he was probably still in the Kremlin, and when he again heard noise rising from the shaft, he realized he was still being pursued.

He got up and raced into the hall. He spotted glass display cabinets and larger display windows lining both sides of the corridor. *A museum.* He shook his head and scanned every direction, seeing mostly extravagant gowns, hats and ceremonial flags dating back to the 18th Century. *I'm in the fucking Armory Museum.*

Jonathan had to get the hell out. At any moment, the men chasing him would pop out of the same hole he'd crawled out of and resume their shooting. Jonathan walked rapidly toward another gallery. He found himself in a large circular room the size of a two-car garage with twenty-foot ceilings, filled with displays of antique weapons—swords, spears, shields and axes and other blunt, bone-crushing objects. A large collection of helmets and two armor-clad mannequins, probably 17th Century, stood behind the glass. But the thought of facing men with guns jolted a fresh idea to mind. He needed something more powerful than what he'd seen so far. He frantically scanned the hundreds of weapons exhibited on the walls, until he spotted something familiar, something he'd used a million times before in his youth: a crossbow.

Jonathan again heard noise behind him. He had only seconds to decide. The crossbow rested on two hooks flat against the display's far wall. Jonathan darted to the other end of the room, picked up a chair and threw it at the glass. The alarm sounded instantly from multiple sirens, both in the large room and in the adjacent galleries. He lunged forward, his feet trampling over the glass remnants that littered the floor, and grabbed the crossbow and three arrows that lay below it. His heart quickened, and adrenaline gushed through his veins. He placed an arrow in the slot and checked the tension of the cord. He feared that there would be another dead man soon, within seconds, and he hoped it would not be him.

Jonathan ducked, peeked around the corner and focused on the shadowy figure pulling himself out of the ventilation duct in the floor. Once the man had exited the shaft, he raised his arm, and Jonathan saw the silhouette of the gun in his hand. A shot rang out just as Jonathan aimed his crossbow, trained instincts from his sporting days reawakening, and pulled the trigger. The man had missed, but Jonathan hadn't. The killer at the other end of the hall slumped forward on his knees, cried out briefly and collapsed face first.

Jonathan then heard the killer's partner shouting from the depths of the shaft, followed by what sounded like the man climbing his way to the top. Jonathan dove to where the killer lay dead or dying. He grabbed the man's gun, aimed it down the shaft and fired twice. A loud tumbling sound reverberated up the shaft.

He had outfoxed both his attackers, but he had no time to celebrate. The wailing sirens ensured he had only seconds before a brigade of presidential guards arrived. Jonathan raced up the marble steps, to the next floor. There, he found a room with no windows and another stairwell at the far end leading up.

He picked a direction at random and ran, not knowing where he was headed. He raced through two more galleries before finding what looked like an emergency exit, which he barged through. Ahead of him were more stairs leading up to a narrow corridor. As he reached the top, the faint sound of voices filtered through the blaring sirens. At the end of the corridor, he turned and immediately realized he was once more in a confined space, but now there was no turning back. He spotted a tight stairwell and hastily headed up. When he reached the next floor, Jonathan found a window, glanced out and quickly discerned his location. He was in one of the Kremlin towers, near the top of the walls' steep facade—an ominous sight, as it offered little chance of escape. The voices and footsteps of a dozen humans sounded more like a herd of rhinos. The guards were getting closer. In desperation, Jonathan yanked the window latch open, placed his right knee on the window sill and crawled out, quickly taking hold of the outside ledge with both hands. He carefully maneuvered laterally, taking only a glimpse of the precipice. The lower half of the wall appeared to have a slight incline. *It might soften the fall*, he thought, though he didn't want to try. *So will the snow on the ground below*. Jonathan now remembered his days at the Milneburg lighthouse, when he and Matt fearlessly jumped from its summit. *But that was twenty years ago*, he told himself. *And probably half the height of this tower.*

He slid farther along the wall, his feet clinging to a narrow indentation between the bricks. He lost his footing, but managed to clutch a drainage pipe as he slid. He held on tightly, now trying to make his way down.

A man shouted from the window Jonathan had just escaped out of. It was a guard, with a green army uniform and large hat, leaning over the ledge with a handgun pointed in Jonathan's direction.

Jonathan jumped. The thirty-foot freefall lasted two whole seconds, and the impact was hard, knocking the breath out of him, even though he did his best to roll his body to minimize the shock. He hadn't landed too well. In addition to the bullet wound in his shoulder, his feet and legs ached as if they had been ripped off of him.

"*Stoi!*" the guard yelled, but he didn't fire a shot.

Jonathan took a deep breath and quickly hobbled across the snow-covered grounds of the Alexandrovski Gardens, toward the busy avenue directly ahead. He did his best to straighten his back and walk normally, as he didn't want to attract any more attention than he already had. He scanned the traffic. There were plenty of taxis, and by the time he'd reached the curb, one had pulled up.

He jumped in, took a deep breath, and with a superhuman effort to sound calm, he said, "Hotel Metropol, *pozhaluysta.*"

Despite his aching shoulder, he harnessed a strange feeling of satisfaction. With extraordinary luck, he had managed to extricate himself from the bowels of the impenetrable Kremlin, kill the assassins who wanted him dead and obtain valuable leads. His pride seemed to anesthetize his gunshot wound, albeit for only a few more seconds. He glanced through the rear windshield at the fortress walls that gradually diminished in size and danger as the cab headed east to his hotel.

*I made it!*

# 19

THE LOBBY OF THE METROPOL WAS BUSTLING WITH GUESTS checking in and departing, with an army of staff who moved about like drones. This was no place to wander around after being shot, without being spotted. But Jonathan had no choice. He kept his hands in his pockets, hiding the stream running down his right arm. He could feel the warm, blood-soaked lining of his coat below his shoulder. He walked briskly, hoping he wasn't leaving a trail along the marble floor, but he was too nervous to look down.

He strolled through the lobby and toward the elevators, ignoring the pain and keeping his head down the whole way. He waited, his impatience rocketing out of control. The elevators were slowly making their way down. Suddenly, Alexandre appeared out of nowhere.

"Where the hell have you been?" Alexandre asked in an aggressive whisper. "I waited for you until the library closed."

Jonathan was in so much pain he simply looked at Alexandre and ground his teeth.

"Well, tell me wha—" Alexandre said, interrupting himself the moment his eyes glanced down.

They both looked at Jonathan's feet. Blood had dripped onto his black dress shoes, blending poorly with the dirt and asphalt caked on during his frantic dash across Alexandrovski Gardens.

"Where are you hurt?"

"My shoulder," Jonathan said, toning down his voice as he spotted several hotel guests approaching the elevators. "I don't think it's too bad."

"I can take you to a hospital right now."

"No," he whispered forcefully. "It's too risky."

The elevator doors opened, and they all went in. As soon as the other guests exited on the second floor, Alexandre threw question after question at him and Jonathan explained everything from the point Nikolai had finished showing him confidential files, culminating in the cab ride back to the hotel. Alexandre's shock was evident from his blank stare. Jonathan couldn't quite tell if he was angry, sad or both. His friend, Nikolai, was dead for sure. *No one could have survived that shot to the head*, Jonathan thought. *No way*.

"Get the key from my back pocket," Jonathan said, the sharp pain preventing him from doing it himself.

Alexandre retrieved the key card, slid it into the reader and opened the door for his wounded companion.

"*Pridurok!* You may have been followed." Alexandre spread his hands. "You realize this, right? The *Militsa* may find you. And I can't help you if you get caught."

Jonathan watched as melancholy gripped Alexandre, who was paler than the white of the Russian flag, his silence possibly coming from the realization that Nikolai was dead. Eliminated. Gone. Jonathan felt a strange sadness at the absence of Alexandre's usual boisterousness.

"I feel terrible about what happened to Nikolai," Jonathan said quietly.

"It's too late to worry about that. We have to make sure the police don't find you."

Jonathan mentally retraced his escape from the Kremlin. "I don't think I was followed."

Alexandre paced the room as Jonathan slowly began removing his jacket. "Ah, *dammit*. It hurts real bad."

"Let me look at it," said Alexandre as he held Jonathan's jacket.

Jonathan then removed his blood-soaked shirt and undershirt. "I think the bullet grazed my shoulder."

Alexandre leaned his head over the wound without touching Jonathan. "You're right, but there's a lot of open tissue and bleeding. It must hurt." He then went into the bathroom and brought back a wet washcloth and a roll of toilet paper. "Let's stop the bleeding first."

Jonathan again twisted his head to see the wound. The bullet had exited right above the collar bone. "A lucky shot," he said, shaking his head. "A little higher, and the round would have missed me completely."

Alexandre huffed. "A little bit lower and you would be in a Moscow morgue."

Jonathan sat on the edge of the bed, careful not to make any movements that would worsen the pain or the bleeding.

As Alexandre sat down next to his wounded pal, he accidentally pushed Jonathan's jacket off the comforter, causing a loud thud that shook the floor. Alexandre looked into Jonathan's eyes as if he knew damn well what made the heavy sound, but he asked anyway. "What was that?"

"I took the man's gun."

"As a trophy?" Alexandre asked with a semblance of a smile peering through his angry expression.

"I know I'd never get one from you."

Alexandre shook his head and stood up. "I'll call a doctor. Don't worry, he's a good friend. I trust he can keep a secret—he owes me a favor, anyhow."

As Alexandre moved to the telephone, Jonathan, now that his adrenaline rush was dissipating, began to come to grips with the possibility that Moscow police would somehow track him down. There was no telling if he'd passed in front of a security camera or if the cab driver or the hotel staff might have found him suspicious. The pain in his shoulder diminished as his anxiety over being caught grew.

After Alexandre dialed his friend, he returned to Jonathan's side. "Okay, he'll be here in about twelve hours."

Jonathan was flabbergasted. "What?"

Alexandre kept a serious face, but said, "I'm just pulling your goat."

Jonathan laughed aloud, ignoring the pain for a few seconds.

"What?"

"That's not exactly what you say in English,"

Jonathan said, enjoying the humorous distraction. "You either say pull your leg or get your goat."

"Oh." Alexandre got up and helped himself to a small bottle of vodka in the minibar. Straight up, no ice.

"I guess I'm not the ideal American tourist," Jonathan said with a smile.

Alexandre's brief moment of humor seemed long gone. He looked at Jonathan sternly. "Keep pressure on the wound and relax; my doctor will be here in about thirty minutes."

\*       \*       \*

RUSSIAN medicine has often been called the rudest of names, and judging from how the doctor clumsily prodded the wound and then haphazardly placed a hefty amount of gauze and bandages over it, Jonathan couldn't help but add a few more insults to the lexicon, like shoddy, unlicensed and medieval. He wondered if this man claiming to have a medical degree had perhaps practiced only on cadavers.

As archaic as his treatment may have been, the doctor had stopped the bleeding and handed Jonathan a welcome treat: a shot of morphine and oral painkillers, powerful enough, he'd said, to knock out a horse. He'd also offered his American patient a sling, but Jonathan refused to wear it.

Jonathan got up, thanked the doctor and walked to the armoire as Alexandre escorted the doctor out of the room.

Seconds later, Alexandre returned, and he wasn't happy about what he saw: Jonathan checking his wallet and putting his watch back on. "Where do you think you're going?"

"To find Mariya."

Alexandre walked briskly to face Jonathan as if he were on fire, spitting out a few angry words in Russian.

"I must," Jonathan insisted as he sifted through the hangers looking for another shirt to wear.

"No, you're staying right here. You've done enough damage for one day. You also need to rest; your injury is not a minor cut."

"I must find her." Jonathan turned to Alexandre, his soul begging his Russian friend to understand. "She knows the truth. Everything about the flight my brother was on. About Yakovlev. The farm. The reasons behind the operation. Everything."

Alexandre was livid. He grabbed the armoire door and slammed it shut. "They will kill you. If the police have your description, they will find you and kill you. Don't you realize at this very moment you are less than five hundred meters from the Kremlin? Don't be a fool!"

Jonathan stood silently, his mind made up. Only a round of bullets would stop him from tracking down Mariya.

Alexandre turned abruptly and slammed the back of his fist against the wall, cursing in Russian. After a long pause, he looked at Jonathan and said, "Very well, but I'm no longer responsible for you. Don't count on my help any more."

"I appreciate everything you've done, but this woman is probably my best and last chance to know what happened to my brother."

Alexandre shook his head and left the room, slamming the door behind him.

Jonathan finished getting dressed and, with the photo of Mariya that Nikolai had shown him engraved in his mind, he left by cab for the Baltschug Kempinski Hotel.

*I just want the truth*, he thought just as he sensed the initial effects of the painkillers. His arms and chest began tingling, and his head felt lighter. The pains in his shoulder and leg were slowly subsiding.

                    *          *          *

THE sun had set just over the line of buildings directly ahead. Jonathan's cab ride to the Baltschug Kempinski was short, barely enough time for Jonathan to think things through. The cab drove past the massive Russiya Hotel on the banks of the Moskva River, in the shadows of the Kremlin. Right across the bridge, the Baltschug Kempinski's pearl facade glowed from the floodlights at its base.

Jonathan had heard it was a German-managed luxury hotel, and this was evident the minute he walked in. Everything seemed elegant, orderly and spotless. The staff, their faces serious and their strides long, moved around like finely tuned robots, fully programmed to deliver opulent service in a land unaccustomed to it.

He didn't know quite where to start. *Should I ask for her by name at the reception desk?* he asked himself, before dismissing the idea outright. *Or stalk her in the lobby?* That's when he glanced up at the mezzanine, at what looked like a bar and lounge area at the top of the spiral marble stairs. *Or try to spot her coming or going while having a drink?* The bar it was. And it was perfectly situated, his large cushioned leather chair offering a bird's eye view of the entrance and lobby.

A scantily clad waitress quickly appeared, her slender Russian features offering a welcome air of exoticism in an otherwise cool, reserved Aryan palace. She quickly brought him his gin and tonic. *It will work wonders with my meds*, he thought. He sipped his drink and every few seconds glanced down at the lobby, scanning the hotel guests for Mariya. He was confident he would recognize her from the photograph.

He waited.

At eleven-ten, on his second round, he hadn't yet seen her. He gave himself another twenty minutes. If by then she hadn't come, he would simply ask for her at the reception desk, no matter what risks would come with doing that.

He paid his tab and lifted his glass but then suddenly froze in mid-sip. There she was, thirty feet away, strolling through the revolving doors. Unaccompanied, it seemed. He recognized her straight, dark hair and her stunning angular features. She carried her coat over her arm as she headed through the lobby, but then she stopped and looked back, toward the glass entryway.

That's when Jonathan realized that he had a problem. She wasn't alone, and the person who quickly joined her was no lesbian lover escorting her for a night of frolicking. The man was a two-hundred-something-pound lug, built like a Brink's safe. Perhaps a bodyguard, judging from the nonchalant way she seemed to treat him. Regardless, it didn't look good.

"*Dammit*," Jonathan whispered to himself, thinking that his gunshot wound would pale in comparison to what this guy could do to him. The fact that Jonathan had a pistol in his coat pocket didn't even cross his mind. And when it did, seconds later, he thought the bullets might simply bounce off the man. *Think, think*, he told himself as he headed down the stairs. He had little time to decide his approach. Should he just walk up to her and introduce himself, with the likelihood of being swatted away by her Neanderthal? *No way*. That's when a more insane idea came to mind, one that could land him in a Siberian Gulag where Alexandre would have better luck finding the Dead Sea Scrolls than bailing his ass out.

Jonathan strolled to the far end of the lobby and casually observed them. Her escort was certainly the problem. His long trench coat most likely hid an arsenal of weaponry. Jonathan wasn't so worried about her; she was dressed in a thin blouse, short skirt and carried a wallet-sized purse, all of which offered little place to hide a weapon, except, of course, if Russian agents had mastered the unconventional use of orifices.

Seconds passed and finally the beauty and the beast headed to the elevator. Mariya walked in first, the man second, Jonathan next and a hotel employee last. Mariya pressed the button for the sixth floor, just as Jonathan pretended to reach for the same one. The employee was headed to the third floor. When the elevator stopped, the employee said something in Russian, nodded politely and stepped out. Jonathan felt the increasingly pacifying effects of the painkillers, perhaps because of his drinks.

The confined space was ideal, Jonathan thought,

since their floor might be too open to keep the two in check. His heart began beating out of his chest and excited warmth filtered through his veins. He felt the pistol pressing against his hip. He'd have to be quick. Damn quick. And there was no room for error. The fourth floor passed. And the fifth. Then the light to the sixth floor lit up, the elevator decelerating.

Jonathan took in a deep breath to clear his head and then lunged at the man from behind. With his left hand he grabbed the man's head, his fingers digging deep into his hair. With his other hand he whipped his gun out and rammed the tip of the barrel into the man's neck. "Don't move!" he shouted. "Or I'll blow your head off."

Mariya jumped back and let out a restrained cry. Her accompanying piece of furniture yelled a series of words—profanity, for sure, Jonathan guessed, even if he didn't know the language.

"I'm not going to hurt anyone, but you must cooperate," Jonathan said coldly, pushing the barrel deeper into the man's neck. "I only want to speak with you, Mariya. That's all I want."

"You are a madman," Mariya said in perfect English. She seemed to be more curious about Jonathan than frightened.

"Put your hands on your head," Jonathan said, pulling the man's head back even farther, so that his face was now aimed at the ceiling. But gauging that he didn't understand his instructions, Jonathan quickly turned to Mariya. "Tell him!"

She did and her escort complied, grudgingly.

The elevator came to a stop, and the door opened.

"Move, move," Jonathan said in a more normal tone. "But you first," he added, glancing at Mariya.

"You're not going to get anything," she said stubbornly with a blank gaze. She stepped out. "You're not frightening me."

"Shut up and walk." Jonathan didn't like her attitude; she had recovered her confidence too quickly. He began to fear that she—a career spy—would easily discover that he was no professional.

Mariya walked ahead of Jonathan and his captive. As she got to the door of her suite, she turned and crossed her arms. "You are completely crazy," she said. "This is unacceptable behavior."

Jonathan was stunned by her brazenness and in no mood to play games. "I've been drinking, I've been shot, and I'm holding a gun," Jonathan said testily. "Are you sure you want to irritate me further?" Indeed, he felt both woozy from the medicines and booze and also weak, perhaps from the sleepless nights or the fact that he had barely eaten since arriving in Moscow.

"What exactly do you want?"

"Answers," Jonathan replied, pushing her bodyguard up against the adjacent wall.

"Answers to what?"

"Operation Tranquility."

The color suddenly drained out of Mariya's face. Her shoulders drooped. "I'm not your villain," she replied. "For that, you should go to your own embassy."

Holding on to the man's neck with one hand, Jonathan quickly patted him down. The thug was armed, as he'd expected. Jonathan removed a large pistol from the man's belt holster and tucked it behind his own belt. "Open the damn door."

Mariya hesitantly turned and slid her card into the reader. The three headed inside.

"Sit in that chair," Jonathan said to her as he prodded her bodyguard to move forward.

Mariya was now seated where she'd been told, but her eyes told Jonathan she was still unpredictable and dangerous.

With his pistol lodged against the man's ear, Jonathan pushed him face-first onto the bed, quickly removed the man's belt and began tying his hands with it. He then slipped the man's shoes off, pulled each sock off and bundled them into a ball. Jonathan reached his hand around her bodyguard's jaw, forced open his mouth and stuffed the pair of socks deep inside. "Hopefully for you, you wore clean socks today."

"That's a little mean, isn't it?" Mariya said.

"What's your thug's name?"

"Yuri."

"Okay, Yuri, do you understand English?"

Yuri murmured incoherently, sockmouthed and no doubt fuming.

"Get up slowly and sit in the corner of the room, behind the television. Now!"

The man crawled out of his position, stood up and did as he was told.

If Jonathan wasn't hallucinating, he thought he caught Mariya with a smile, albeit a momentary one.

"You're making him awfully mad," she said to Jonathan.

"Good, that makes two of us who feel that way."

Mariya crossed her legs and seemed at ease, which made Jonathan more nervous than he already was. She lit a cigarette. "Pour me a drink, will you?"

Jonathan glanced at the dresser. Two bottles of vodka lay next to four glasses. He also poured himself one. "Here," Jonathan said, handing her a full glass, "if it will make you talk." She took the glass in such a way as to caress his hand. It was comfortably inappropriate and reinforced his uneasiness. *She is a bizarre chick, all right*, he thought gazing at her from top to bottom. He tried to guess her age. *Forty, forty-five, maybe*. She had an air about her—part movie star, part serial killer.

"What do you want to know?"

"Your mission to disrupt Operation Tranquility."

"Oh?"

"Don't play dumb. I'm not playing games."

Mariya chuckled. "You're a rather good looking man; you can't possibly be with the CIA. All they have sent here lately are computer geeks and ugly, overweight paper shufflers. Tell me you are not one of them."

"I'm not telling you anything, lady. Not yet, anyway. You do the talking." He guzzled a mouthful of his drink and sat at the foot of the bed, his attention focused entirely on the Russian woman seated three feet from him.

"As you wish."

"I'm not here to cause any trouble," Jonathan said, finishing the last of his vodka. "I'm no spy; I'm not involved in your line of work, and I don't care about what you people do. This is a very personal thing for me.

I've gone through hell over the past ten days to find information about my missing brother. He was shot down over the Baltic seven years ago and I'm certain it had something to do with your plans, whatever they were."

Mariya lost the smirk. She tilted her head to one side and exhaled a long plume of smoke. "Shot down, huh?"

"Yes, sometime when—"

Suddenly, Jonathan heard the front door latch snap. The door opened, and a woman wearing a parka casually walked in saying something in Russian. As she strolled further into the room, Jonathan got up and pointed his gun at her, after which he saw only fear in her eyes.

"Move, move," he said loudly, motioning her with his gun to go around the bed to join Mariya on the other side of the room. But as Jonathan was about to say something else, he felt his fingers and hands tingling sharply, and his tongue too. He shook his head, but the numbness had spread to his cheeks and neck.

"Relax, will you?" Mariya said to Jonathan. She held her hand out to the woman next to her, who reached for hers. The two women smiled at each other. "You come at a perfect time," said Mariya.

The absence of feeling in his skin grew, and his mouth began to salivate profusely.

"Are you not feeling well?" Mariya asked, her arm now wrapped around the other woman's hips. She slid her hand up the woman's blouse.

"What are . . ." mumbled Jonathan before he couldn't utter anything more. His head was spinning.

He saw the women undressing one another, but his fuzzy vision gained such intensity that he could only focus on his hands. He heard Mariya and her companion laugh. He shook his head several times, fighting to regain his focus, but the weakness in his limbs made him fall backward onto the bed. The empty glass in his right hand fell somewhere near him; so did the gun from his other hand. He had no strength to speak, to get up, to do anything at all except breathe.

Mariya's half-dressed body rose up over the comforter, embracing her naked companion. The women rolled over Jonathan's legs as they kissed and fondled each other and continued to bump into him as if he were a stray pillow.

"You shouldn't drink from a stranger's bottle," Jonathan heard Mariya say as both women again erupted in laughter. He'd been drugged, and there was little he could do now.

Unable to move, he gazed helplessly at a slender, nude leg that rose above his head, the sound of passionate moaning filtering through his skull. The leg then descended and the heel slammed into his jaw, knocking him off the bed. The loud sounds of giggling, rustling bed sheets and mattress springs drowned the thud from his body hitting the floor. His surroundings melted into a kaleidoscope of fuzzy shapes and lights, and then suddenly, only darkness.

.

# 20

FREEZING PUNGENT AIR SEEPED INTO JONATHAN'S LUNGS. The rest of his body suddenly felt frozen. He opened his eyes as his grogginess slowly dissipated, but everything still seemed blurred. He blinked, but he couldn't move his limbs nor his head. A cobblestone surface lay in front of him at a strange angle. He coughed, a cloud of vapor exiting his mouth. He was on the ground, on a street. The smell of sewage grew stronger, as did the bitter cold, and then the pain in his shoulder. He saw small metal wheels. Two of them and then another two closer to him. And a large metallic object hovering above him. He blinked again. *A dumpster.* He lay partly under it. *Where the hell am I?*

He brought his hand to his face. His fingers were stiff and reddish-blue, and the skin felt numb. He slowly rolled over, his back crunching into a pile of snow. His body was now shaking uncontrollably from the cold, and the pain in his shoulder burned like the bullet was passing through it once more. He moved his legs, both of them as stiff as his arms. Dried blood covered his right hand. He heard the sound of an empty bottle tip over and roll along the stone pavement. Despite the pain and bitter cold, he managed to gather the strength to sit up and then, a minute later, to stand. He glanced down. His coat lay on the other side of the dumpster. It was soaked and looked as if a vehicle had driven over it.

The back alley was crammed between rows of mid-rise buildings—apartments, it seemed. There was no one around, but Jonathan could hear the sound of traffic not far away.

He rubbed his arms and chest to regain some warmth. When he turned the corner and passed a few shops, he realized from the looks of things that he had not left the city center. He then spotted, some fifty yards away, a large graded-arch structure with an "M" sign hanging over the entrance. Jonathan didn't know which Metro station it was, but it was an ideal place to get to safety. He crossed the street and headed into the Krasnye Vorota station. Fortunately for Jonathan, it was on the red line, just three stops from Teatralnaya, the closest station to his hotel.

After getting strange looks from the hotel bellman, no doubt because of his disheveled look, Jonathan headed to his room, showered, changed and came up with a plan. It was time to approach C.J. Raynes and see if he could strike a deal. Jonathan was convinced that C.J. was no ordinary diplomat, but he wasn't sure what role he may have played in the smuggling of the cargo, and ultimately in Matt's disappearance.

After looking through the hotel tourist guide, he picked out a place he thought would be well suited for a rendezvous with the American. Jonathan descended to the lobby. From a courtesy phone, he dialed the main U.S. Embassy number and, surprisingly, managed to be transferred to the guy himself.

"C.J. Raynes," the man answered after the fourth ring.

Jonathan nervously gathered his mental strength. "I have a deal to make."

"Who is this?"

"It doesn't matter," Jonathan said sternly. "Does Operation Tranquility mean something to you?"

Silence took over the phone line. Jonathan then heard on the other end what sounded like a door closing.

"I want to meet," said Jonathan, "and alone. None of your friends. Besides, Frank can tell you what happens when you don't play the game right."

"What the hell do want from me?" C.J. asked, his voice deep, his tone condescending.

"Maybe I should just go the Russians with the dirt I have on you. They would love what I have to say."

C.J. sighed. "Fine, meet me at—"

"No, no," Jonathan said, stopping him in mid-sentence. "This will be on my terms. Meet me at the Radisson on Berezhovskaya." Jonathan had passed the huge American-run hotel with Alexandre. "Be there, in the lobby, at two-thirty today, alone, unarmed—I only want to talk, so you won't need any guns or thugs. And carry a copy of the *New York Times* clearly visible in your left coat pocket."

"You're playing a dangerous game, Mr. Brooks," C.J. declared coldly.

Jonathan wasn't surprised C.J. knew his name, but it still brought a chill to his spine. It also helped Jonathan connect the dots. Vice-Admiral Scarborough and whoever else was involved must have given C.J. a heads-up. Jonathan realized that he'd have to play it smart—real smart—or else he'd be dead in no time.

"I have little to lose at this point," Jonathan replied, anger lacing his words. "A lot less than you." He hung up.

Before heading out, Jonathan went to the front desk and dispatched a telegram to Linda. "I am with you, my love," he wrote. "Don't worry." He gazed at it one more time before handing the form to the clerk. As trivial as the message seemed, it gave him strength to know that within hours Linda would read his words. He needed every ounce of courage he could muster.

*       *       *

*KIEVSKIY Vokzal*, the Kiev Train Station, was a happening place; two women in red stilettos, their bodies wrapped in giant fur coats, following a porter carrying their oversized luggage; a pair of leather-clad, spike-haired teens smoking by a pillar; a cluster of hyper Japanese tourists photographing each other in front of a food stand. Jonathan had arrived there by Metro a few minutes before two to survey the surroundings. The station was a large, bustling place, the perfect escape route should anything go sour during his rendezvous with C.J. It was the closest public venue to the Radisson.

Jonathan walked out, past the vast square facing the station. After a minute, he spotted the hotel a few hundred yards away. The Radisson's monolithic structure, some ten stories high, dominated the riverfront. Jonathan planned his next move. He'd go through the lobby and find a spot to observe the entrance, just as he'd done at the Baltschug Kempinski Hotel when he first tracked down Mariya. He was counting on the likelihood that C.J. would not dare do anything illegal in public, but he couldn't be sure.

Approaching the hotel, Jonathan methodically rehearsed his means of escape in his head, mentally etching the detailed images of each locale. He glanced at the row of cabs. He'd have to use one to quickly get to Kiev Station, if things got out of hand. *And then race past the ticket booths,* he thought, *down the corner stairs, through the passageway to the Kievskaya Metro station and on to the second platform on the left.*

Suddenly, the sound of squealing tires made Jonathan turn around. A white van had pulled up along the curb right next to him. Before he could even step back, the van's side door flung open and two men quickly disembarked and lunged at him. Jonathan tried to run, but one man grabbed him by the coat while the other took hold of his collar. Jonathan swung his elbow and felt it pound the guy behind him, but before he could land another hit, the second man had Jonathan in a choke hold. He was being dragged away.

Jonathan cried out as he felt a punch to his kidneys. Another punch followed, and he felt his body flying uncontrollably toward the vehicle. He landed face down onto the metal floorboard as the two thugs leapt on top of him and barked words in Russian. Jonathan looked up. The back of the van had no seats, nothing at all, just a couple unfriendly Russians, one of whom twisted Jonathan's arm behind his back. The pain ripped its way through his sore shoulder.

Jonathan heard the sound of duct tape being unwound. He had to get away, or he would surely die. The van accelerated violently, the sudden movement helping to loosen the assailant's choke hold. Jonathan whipped around and managed to pull himself half-up. The man behind him lost his grip, and Jonathan body-slammed him against the half-caged divider behind the driver's seat.

Jonathan saw the driver frantically dialing into his cell phone as he punched the second attacker in the back of the head. A revolver went flying across the floor, hit the side and bounced back to the center of the van. The Russian yelled something to his partner or to the driver. The other assailant lunged at the gun but Jonathan turned and kicked the guy in the groin from behind. Jonathan jumped on the other man, who was about to get back up off the floor, grabbed him by the coat and threw him toward the back of the speeding van, and the rear doors suddenly swung open from the force. The assailant was ejected, his head hitting the pavement first and his body rolling across the centerline, where a large sedan in the opposite lane drove over him and slammed into a stretch of parked cars.

Jonathan turned and attacked the other man. The speeding van suddenly turned sharply, throwing the men to one side. Jonathan again eyed the back of the vehicle, the doors swinging wide open with the swaying thrusts.

He punched the man's face and then dug his fingers into one and then both eyes.

"*Skotina!*" the man cried in pain and jolted back. Jonathan punched him again and again until the man collapsed onto his back. His adrenaline racing, Jonathan kicked him in the belly, pushing him until the man rolled off the speeding van to the street below, just like his cohort.

Jonathan turned to the driver, who whipped his head back at Jonathan and began to swing the van from side to side. Jonathan grabbed the ribbed metal wall in the van and crawled his way forward. He took hold of the caged divider with one hand and latched on to the driver's hair with the other. He pulled himself up and then dove partially over the divider.

Oncoming cars, their horns blaring, twisted away from the van's path as it crossed back and forth over the median.

"Stop right now!" Jonathan barked as he contorted the driver's neck to one side and pulled harder on his hair until the man's head was facing nearly straight up. The driver dropped his cell phone and gripped the steering wheel with both hands.

Jonathan stretched his body into the forward compartment, trying to take control of the steering. He headbutted the driver and then quickly repositioned his arm around the man's neck, squeezing it with all his might. The driver finally lost his grip on the wheel.

"Shit!" Jonathan barked, as he glanced out the windshield. The van jumped the curb and sped along the side-walk, downed a parking meter, and then another, the thumping sounds blending with more car horns and screams from pedestrians diving clear of the vehicle. Jonathan tried to grab the steering wheel, but the driver bit his arm.

Still traveling at a high rate of speed, the van scraped along the wall at the river bank. Jonathan again head-butted the driver, but the van swerved into a street lamp and mailbox, instantly peeling the hood up against the windshield and shattering it. The force catapulted the van back across the street. It then headed straight for a parked truck. Jonathan jumped back behind the driver's seat and braced for the impact. The smashing metal reverberated as Jonathan hit the van's roof and landed on his back.

Jonathan took a deep breath and got up. The driver's bloodied face was plastered across the mangled dash-board, the steering column jammed in his chest. Jonathan grabbed the driver's cell phone that had fallen on the floor below the front passenger seat. He then took off running, quickly escaping as onlookers gathered around. He caught sight of Kiev Station three blocks away and realized the van had traveled in a large circle before wrecking. He could still use his escape plan, but from a different direction.

Jonathan crossed the street, glancing over his shoul-der a few times to make sure he wasn't being followed. Sirens began blaring from a few blocks behind him. As he crossed the next street, a blue- and white-colored police car screeched past him, its lights on but no siren.

It sped away toward the river, most likely heading to the scene of the accident.

Jonathan darted through the train station, down the stairs at the far end, which led to the Metro. He stepped on the waiting subway car, breathing a sigh of relief. He leaned back against the side of the car and gazed at the doors as they closed. The platform edged away and all he could see out the windows was the darkness of the tunnel. He was safe. Safe for now.

When Jonathan approached his hotel, he pulled out the confiscated cell phone and dialed the last number the driver had called. The voice that picked up was exactly who he'd feared would be on the other end of the line. It was C.J.

Jonathan quickly hung up, realizing that not only would C.J. never agree to any deal, he was out to crush Jonathan, and he would do so with the surgical precision of a bulldozer.

From his room at the Metropol, Jonathan called Alexandre with a request. "I need a secure place to stay," Jonathan began.

"What's happened now?" asked Alexandre, as if he knew Jonathan had caused another disaster.

"I'll explain later. Please, pick me up here and take me where I can be safe. Things are out of control."

"I already knew that," the Russian lawyer retorted.

"Please!"

"I think these people won't stop until they kill you." Alexandre now sounded angry. "It's time to leave all this alone and go back to your country. And there's no evidence your brother didn't die seven years ago."

"I've come a long way for answers. My wife is on a hospital bed fighting to stay alive. Too many people have suffered to simply turn back now. I beg you, Alexandre. Please, do the right thing."

There was a long silence on the other end of the line. Jonathan stared out the window, at the gray sky the hung over the Bolshoi.

"Boris will pick you up in thirty minutes," Alexandre said, still sounding pissed off. But Jonathan couldn't blame him. He'd given Alexandre grief nearly every moment since he'd arrived in Moscow. "By the way, I have more news for you. And it's not good. I'll explain later."

\*        \*        \*

JONATHAN sagged back into his sofa and thought about what else he needed to do. He dug into his wallet and found the business card he'd carried with him since Stockholm. He began dialing, his mind calculating how he would approach Erland.

"I have news for you," Jonathan said excitedly upon hearing the Swedish intelligence officer answer the phone. "I'm in Russia and I got the information that—"

"Stop!" Erland protested. "Say no more. You should know there is no such thing as a private telephone call in Russia."

Jonathan sighed. "I also need another favor from you."

"We shouldn't talk so—"

"I don't care," Jonathan said. "Find out what you can about a man called C.J. Raynes, a diplomat at the U.S.

embassy in Moscow."

"Don't—"

"Please. He's tried to kill me, and I have no one to turn to right now, except you!"

Erland didn't reply right away.

Jonathan closed his eyes as he felt a momentary spike of pain in his shoulder. He'd taken another dose of painkillers minutes earlier. He thought of taking more, but it would surely send him into oblivion.

"I have an idea," Erland began. "Get a magnifying glass. Are you in a hotel?"

"Yes."

"Good. Get a magnifying glass and then look at the back of my business card. You will see three pairs of names. The three names on top are hotels, one for each city: St. Petersburg, Helsinki, Kiev and Moscow; the respective names below them are the contact persons. Go to the hotel in Moscow and ask the reception desk for that person. You will receive instructions on what you should do next. I will find out some information for you by the time you meet with your contact."

"When do I go?"

"Be there at four-thirty."

*     *     *

HOTEL Ukraina was a gigantic structure—part skyscraper, part palace. Its airport-sized lobby, paved in white marble, dwarfed any building he'd seen so far in Moscow.

As Erland had instructed, Jonathan went to the reception desk and asked for Sacha, the name printed next to the hotel identification on the back of Erland's card. The clerk disappeared into the back office for a moment and then returned with an envelope in hand. After showing his passport, Jonathan was given the envelope and quickly rejoined Boris outside.

Inside the envelope were a note and a tiny electronic device similar in size and shape to a cigarette lighter. He read the short, handwritten missive. It had instructions on how to use the device—how to record the information he had gotten about the Swedish Air Force DC-3 crash. Following the instructions, he pressed a small black button on the face of the device and spoke clearly. He mentioned the location of the crash site the way Nikolai had described it, and he also explained who Nikolai was and how he'd managed to get into the Kremlin.

Boris then drove Jonathan to an address on Gagarinskiy Pereulok, as was indicated in the note. There, Jonathan got out of the car, walked half a block to the large glass storefront of an art gallery named Genesis, noticing the spotlights illuminating several modern paintings and sculptures behind the glass. As instructed in the note, Jonathan held the device in his hand and approached the glass. He discreetly pointed it at a large painting with colorful, abstract cubes blending into autumn leaves. He squeezed a tiny button at the tip of the device, which somehow allowed the data to upload. The note said it would take only a few seconds. He sensed a bit of satisfaction at having made good on his debt to Erland, but mostly at having given the families of the DC-3 crewmen some peace. Their situation was not unlike his own. They all deserved answers to a haunting past.

The device vibrated briefly, signaling that the data had been properly uploaded. Jonathan returned to the car.

"I take you to Alexandre, *da*?" Boris asked.

"Yes," Jonathan replied, gazing at the bright store-front as the car whisked by. He was in awe of the efficiency with which Erland had organized this arms-length encounter. The Swedish sleuth had left an impressive mark.

# 21

THE SCENT OF PINE AND THE SOUNDS OF WINDBLOWN leaves magically transformed the dark forest around Alexandre's suburban dacha into a tranquil oasis. Jonathan stood on the porch, gazing at the snow-covered trees and the dusk sky, the array of stars slowly brightening.

Alexandre sat nearby, smoking a Marlboro Red and digesting everything Jonathan had told him, including the assault by the men in the van.

"How am I going to get out of this mess?" Jonathan asked him.

"Yes, you've stretched the use of your tourist visa to cause havoc in the streets of my city," said Alexandre, his tone half-joking. "But don't worry yourself to death. There has to be some solution, even if you don't see it yet." Alexandre had barely refilled his glass when he flushed the vodka down his throat. He exhaled deeply, the odor of booze wandering to Jonathan's side of the

porch. "It now just seems harder—and more dangerous—than before. All will be fine."

Jonathan sat on the wood railing and in an instant
decided to not dwell on the topic. He'd know soon
enough whether Alexandre had lost touch with reality.

"You must promise me to visit this place in summer,
and without all the problems you have today."

Jonathan almost laughed. "I'm not sure when all is
said and done, that your country will ever allow me to
come back."

"What did your military tell you about your brother's
death?"

"We were told it was a small transport plane—an
engine failure during a routine non-combat mission. And
then a few weeks later, we received what was said to be
his remains. And we believed them because we never
had reason not to."

Alexandre yawned and stretched his arms. "Well,
maybe America is not so different than the old Soviet
Union, with its lies, its half-truths."

"I can't judge my country that way. The only fact I
now know is that they lied about my brother and have
gone to great lengths to hide the truth. Whether it was a
few rogue officials or a much wider group is something
I hope to find out."

"Your wife should be very proud of you," Alexandre
said. "Your perseverance; your ability to escape catastrophe." Alexandre refilled his glass and seemed to
slowly slip into a state of liquid comfort.

"I'm the proud one. Linda is an extraordinary
woman, whose fabric of life is woven with threads of

Kevlar and velvet. She has New Orleans in her pulse, in her soul."

Alexandre smiled.

"But most importantly, she's my wonderful wife." Jonathan thought about how sappy that must have sounded to Alexandre, a bachelor genetically predisposed to a life of skirt-chasing. But it was true. Jonathan had no qualms professing his devotion, as cheesy as it might have seemed to others. As he thought more about it, he quickly became overcome with sadness. Her absence seemed to have a huge presence all its own, weighing his soul and silencing his rambling declaration of pride and loyalty.

"Are you okay?" Alexandre asked, seeming to sense Jonathan's mood.

Jonathan gazed at the stars and breathed from the bottom of his lungs.

For no clear reason, a precise set of images came to mind—images that Jonathan had carved twelve years earlier on the shores of Destin, Florida.

Only their footsteps marked the pristine sand, its color a pale rose from the setting sun. Their day had gone as one would have expected for day four of a honeymoon. The tactile feeling of the ring on his finger was still new, so satisfyingly fresh. The sounds of gently disturbed waves mixed with a Bob Marley tune that drifted their way from a nearby open bar. Life was finally good. The woman he'd known since grade school was now his wife, a title and word that had morphed into a strangely rich meaning. And everything seemed more potent than it had at any time before—whether it was her words or her gestures. And he remembered them all as if it were yesterday.

"Will you be there if nothing happens to me?" Linda had asked, her hands caressing Jonathan's shoulders. Her blond hair waved in the breeze, her inviting gaze luring him to kiss her. "Tell me, will you be there?"

He didn't quite understand what she had meant. "If nothing happens?"

"Yes, if for whatever reason, I don't attain what I'm reaching for. If I fail in my career; if I get laid off; if I burn out from the stress. Or if, God forbid, I just wanted to become a typical housewife."

Jonathan laughed. "There is nothing typical about you."

"And what if I become an invalid and you're still healthy, vibrant. Will you be—"

"Shh," Jonathan said, covering her lips with his hand. "You will never have to ask this again. What I have for you is much more than love. You have always been my destiny, as if we are reliving our lives—our wonderful lives—together."

The cool breeze numbed Jonathan's face. Moscow was not nearly as warm as that moment in Destin so many years earlier. But that moment of recollection had warmed him from inside. He was with her that very second, at her hospital bed side, in spirit, the thousands of miles of physical distance seeming so irrelevant. Jonathan smiled as he saw her peaceful face.

He turned to Alexandre, who had succumbed to a vodka-induced sleep.

Before falling asleep himself, Jonathan made two

important calls: one to Gary; the other to Linda. He told them everything he had learned since he'd last spoken to them. Jonathan felt it was even more critical now that they also know all he knew, in case his luck would run out in the hours or days ahead.

# 22

THE BEDROOM DOOR ABRUPTLY OPENED, AND ALEXANDRE charged in. "Wake up!" he said agitatedly. "There is a car outside. It's not good."

Jonathan sprang out of bed, forgetting his injury and a second later feeling horrendous pain rip through his shoulder. "Jesus!"

"Hurry," Alexandre said, his gestures frantic, his eyes spearing Jonathan with anxiety.

"What's going on?"

Alexandre didn't have time to answer. A loud knock at the door rumbled through the house, followed by an equally loud male voice shouting in Russian. The knocking became louder.

"What's he saying?" Jonathan asked as he slid into his pants.

Alexandre's gaze was serious. "Security services."

"How can you be sure?"

"I have to answer," Alexandre said as he quickly

turned around. "Stay in your room. Maybe even hide in the closet." He closed the door, and Jonathan heard him walk away.

Jonathan threw on a sweater and shoes and tied his shoelaces, his apprehension mounting rapidly. Despite what Alexandre had suggested, he slipped out to the foyer and spotted his Russian host opening the front door half way. There were at least two voices other than his host's, and all Jonathan saw was Alexandre's back, the rest of him hidden behind the open door. The men spoke politely, it seemed. Jonathan didn't know what to do, so he cautiously went to Alexandre's side.

Alexandre turned, a scornful expression contorting his face. "You . . . you should have stayed inside. I just told them that you were not here."

"Oh," Jonathan said, feeling rather stupid.

Alexandre shook his head and said a few words with the two husky men facing him, though judging from their demeanor, the tone was now quite different.

*Undercover cops?* Jonathan asked himself, wondering if they were armed under their winter parkas.

Alexandre leaned into Jonathan and said, "They want you to go with them."

"Who are they?"

"They say they are from the Interior Ministry."

"Why do they want me to go with them?"

Alexandre shrugged his shoulders. "They have questions to ask you."

"Tell them you are my lawyer, and that you will contact them to schedule an appointment."

"They want you to go alone, and right away."

"Are they arresting me?"

"I don't think so."

Jonathan glanced at a black BMW 7-Series idling in front of the house. At that moment the tinted rear window lowered, and a passenger's face came into view. It was Mariya. She leaned her head out and shouted in English, "Let's go." The window shut as quickly as it had opened.

Jonathan wasn't keen to obey her, but the two refrigerator-sized men facing him would likely not take no for an answer. He grabbed his coat on the rack and patted Alexandre on the back. "I hope this won't be as bad as it seems."

"Who is she?" Alexandre asked.

"It's *her*."

Alexandre's jaw just about dropped off his face. "You're right; this isn't good."

Jonathan replied by shrugging his shoulders. He brusquely pushed his way between her two goons and marched straight to the car. Mariya moved to the other side as Jonathan opened the car door.

"Where are we going?" Jonathan asked as he dropped into the hard leather seat, wondering if he wasn't making a huge mistake by going so willingly.

She didn't answer. Her eyes hinted at something mischievous. She signaled to her comrades to hurry.

Jonathan, nervously examining her every move, felt a sudden rush of air as one of her bodyguards slammed the door shut behind him. "Did Yuri not show up for work today?" he asked, hoping a little humor might help.

"It's his day off," she said, mockingly. "He's not very

happy, you know. Being tied up and having socks shoved in your mouth is the not kind of thing a former Spetsnaz would enjoy."

"Spetsnaz?"

"Russian special forces."

"Oh," Jonathan said, now feeling rather fortunate that Yuri hadn't fought back and dismembered him when he'd had the chance.

Mariya laughed. "Lucky for you, he's not here."

Jonathan could not agree with her more. But it was a small comfort in an otherwise bleak situation. He held on to a faint hope that Alexandre would pull something out of his ass and miraculously rescue him—with a magical legal proclamation, or better yet, a machine gun or rocket launcher. Anything with authority. A get-outta-jail card, Russian style. Anything to save him from this situation he'd gotten himself into. But it was a faint hope. The way Alexandre just stood there on his porch like a potted plant was an indication to Jonathan that he was now on his own.

Jonathan lowered his window and waved at Alexandre as if to say he'd be back by dinner, although he secretly feared that he'd be back in a coffin. He leaned back in his seat, as Alexandre returned a lazy wave of the hand. Evidently, camaraderie has its limits.

Jonathan's heart sank the moment Mariya's hired bulldogs crawled into the front seat. The motor growled as the vehicle edged out of the snow-covered driveway. There was nothing Jonathan could do now but go along for the ride and hope to gain a clue or two along the way and to return alive and unharmed.

They drove out onto the rural road that linked the dacha to the outside world. It was then that Jonathan remembered Alexandre's words. "No one will find you here," he'd assured him. "My place isn't even on the map."

*It is certainly on Mariya's map,* Jonathan now thought irritably. *It might as well have had a neon sign on the roof, blinking the words "Come get me—I'm a dumb-ass American who has confided in my Russian lawyer."* He began to wonder whether Alexandre had turned him in.

Mariya pulled her hair back over her ears and turned to Jonathan, but she said nothing. She checked her watch and crossed her long, slender legs, her right thigh emerging from the generous slit of her skirt.

"Where are we going?" Jonathan asked again.

"You'll see," she answered, reaching into her large purse by her feet. She wore a thin skirt and sparkly high-heeled black shoes—mind-boggling, given that there was about two inches of snow outside. As she leaned forward, her low-cut blouse revealed her small, shapely breasts. No bra. Her dark, pronounced nipples caught Jonathan's eye. She continued to rummage through her belongings and then pulled something out, her hand wrapped tightly around whatever it was.

The driver turned onto another road. They were traveling rather fast, well above what Jonathan imagined was the speed limit.

"You see this?" she asked, opening her hand flat to expose the object—a plastic test-tube containing a yellowish substance. "Guess what this is."

Jonathan wasn't in the mood to be quizzed. He was now persuaded that she had let him go yesterday to find out who had been helping him. The likelihood that this lunatic would let him go again was looking rather slim, and so he wasn't about to cooperate. "I don't know, and I don't care."

"You should care," she said, holding up the vial between her index finger and thumb.

Jonathan glanced at the vial again. The contents appeared to be a powder rather than a liquid.

"Give up?" Mariya asked with a raised brow. "*Francisella tularensis*—spores derived from the weaponized *Schu-4* strain developed in our labs at Biopreparat in the mid-'80s." She continued to hold the thing at eye-level, her slim, pale fingers and bright red fingernails offering a bizarre contrast to the yellow toxic contents of the tube.

*Sensuality and epidemic annihilation*, Jonathan thought. *Tantalizing, if it weren't so deadly serious.*

"What is Biopreparat?"

"You mean *was*. The Ministry of Health created a large number of facilities disguised as civilian biotechnology research centers, but they manufacturing some of the most advanced bioweapons ever conceived."

"But that was illegal, wasn't it?"

Mariya chuckled. "Of course. Just because our two countries signed the Biological Weapons Convention in the early '70s didn't mean we would actually abide by it. *You* were the dumb ones who stopped your bioweapons development."

Jonathan realized that he shouldn't have been surprised. With people like Mariya roaming the planet, there was no appetite for treaties and the rule of law.

"Don't act so shocked. Your military still found ways around the treaty. You still conducted research at places like Fort Detrick—so-called *defensive* programs. Let's not fool ourselves. Just because you call it defensive, doesn't mean you couldn't quickly turn to large scale manufacturing if you wanted to." Her eyes shifted again to the vial in her hand. "Aren't you amazed at the power of this object?"

"Your instruments of death don't impress me," Jonathan said. "I only want to find my brother and bring him home, even if only his remains."

Mariya frowned. "This is not a weapon of death, but rather one of surrender."

Jonathan's gaze swept over her with measured curiosity. "What do you mean?"

Mariya's eyes were fixed on the vial. "Isn't it incredible? There's enough here to infect five thousand people. "And not always kill them, mind you; just to incapacitate them for weeks and months. It's always been an optimal strategy to injure rather than to kill. An enemy is better destabilized if a large part of its army or population is diseased rather than dead." She then smiled.

Jonathan listened as if she had gone completely off the deep end. Only she hadn't. She was somewhat sane, clever, and, thus, dangerous as hell.

"I tell you, this is one of the most sophisticated weapons ever produced."

"That's despicable," Jonathan declared.

She blew out a breath. "It was the perfect weapon to

use for isolated attacks, because it would be difficult to trace it back to us. Tularemia is a naturally occurring disease, with several hundred cases in North America and Europe every year, usually from infected animals, like rabbits and squirrels."

"You mean isolated attacks as in . . . *assassinations*?" She tilted her head a bit and fielded a tortured smile. "Discreet targeting, yes, or group infections or even mass contamination, you name it."

A shudder of revulsion went through Jonathan. He was upset by her casual attitude even more than her information. He wondered if he'd live to tell anyone about this.

Mariya took a pack of cigarettes from the back pocket of the driver's seat. "Want one?"

Jonathan looked at her with growing suspicion. "No, thanks. They're probably laced with cyanide."

She shook her head, lowered her window and lit up. She then returned the vial to the depths of her purse. "We all played this game. Your side and mine. Your secret laboratories, just like ours, produced bacteria and viruses designed for the most ruthless of conflicts, while also endangering the entire human race."

Jonathan chuckled. "I suppose you were better at it, huh?"

"Perhaps," she replied with a hint of pride.

Jonathan shook his head in dismay. "What a wonderful contribution to humanity."

"The night comrade Yakovlev met with the Americans, he gave them nearly our entire stock of this strain. Someone at your embassy here offered to pay him nearly two-hundred thousand dollars for the inventory, and to fly him out of the country and help him settle in Canada under a new name."

"What a surprise," Jonathan murmured. The word "embassy" had a wholly different meaning after his run-ins with Frank Corrigan and the thugs near the Radisson. "Who was it?"

"I wish I knew. He worked through intermediaries—whom we promptly expelled."

Jonathan pulled in a deep breath and looked out the window. "What if I told you the man's name?"

She exhaled a plume of smoke and smiled as if he were being ridiculous. "Then you will earn my good graces."

"Does this mean you will kill me more mercifully than otherwise?" Jonathan asked jokingly, but hoping that it was within the realm of reality.

Her gaze at Jonathan was painted with skepticism. "Well, name him."

"He goes by C.J."

"C.J. Raynes?"

"Yep."

"Uh-huh," Mariya said, taking another drag of her cigarette. "But he's a legal attaché, I think. I've never heard of him going beyond the scope of his work. How do you know this?"

"He tried to kill me."

"So, explain what you said to me yesterday—that my plan was compromised. I want to know everything now. You have ten minutes left to tell me."

"Or else what?" Jonathan asked. "You will kill me?"

Mariya grinned.

Jonathan suspected that she extracted pleasure from the uncertainty over his fate and reluctantly accepted that he had no bargaining power whatsoever. It was time to tell her what he knew and hope for the best. He recounted what Dupree, the submariner cook, had said: the submarine surfacing; the orders to shoot down their own aircraft; the fireball in mid-air. And she listened, intently, without comment, until he was completely done.

"Someone obviously tipped them off," Mariya concurred, her look pensive. "What other reason could there be?"

"What do you mean?"

"We rigged the shipment to explode about twenty hours after the flight took off. It was our way of bringing the American operation into the open—by contaminating an area in your country."

Jonathan now understood. "To create a public outcry. Yes . . . that's clever, very clever indeed . . . and horrible for the innocent."

Mariya raised her chin. "There were no innocents, not in the Cold War," she hit back, sounding nearly angry. "Taxpayers and generals were equally supportive of our adversarial games."

An entire minute passed with only the noise of the car slicing through the air.

"You're not lying to me, are you?" she asked, extinguishing her cigarette in the door ashtray. "About C.J. and the rest of what you said, right?"

"I swear I've been truthful with you from the beginning," he replied, his hand patting his chest. "So you could have been a little nicer to me all along."

"I'm not *nice*," she whipped back. "I will be nice when I'm dead. Until then, I will remain a guardian of my country, a tough woman."

*You mean a cold-hearted bitch*, Jonathan thought, almost saying it out loud. But then again, there was something about her clever self-confidence that he admired.

The car was now traveling over a wide four lane highway, possibly the MKOD, the city's ring road.

"Could you please tell me where we are headed?" Jonathan asked.

"You will live through it, don't worry."

*How reassuring.*

She checked her watch.

The long stretch of blacktop road was lined on one side by a huge forest; on the other, by vast fields dotted with small wooden farmhouses.

"You too were there, at the airfield," Jonathan said coolly.

It was a surprise she didn't hide well. Her eyes widened, her stare an obvious sign she was deciphering how on earth Jonathan could have known this.

"I also know about the *farm*," Jonathan added, feeling a surging confidence that he now harbored something of value.

"Don't point the finger at me," she protested. She cocked her head back, her chin raised. "We all play our roles. I only did what was necessary to protect my country. Besides, who knows what you Americans would have done with our weapons?"

"Maybe we simply wanted them out of your hands," Jonathan suggested, "which would certainly make our planet a little safer, eh?"

"Ridiculous," she snapped back, waving her hand dismissively. "We were enemies then, and we are enemies now; it's just that we've now learned to make money together. And as enemies, we must always stay alert, remain divisive and plan for the worst. Without people like me, there would be no Russia left. You would have destroyed us long ago."

Jonathan had never followed the machinations of the Cold War, nor its aftermath. It never had a tangible impact on his life in New Orleans. The superpower clashes had all seemed so distant, so pedantic, with no apparent value to his existence *until* that very moment, when all Mariya had shared with him had collided with what he'd learned since his discovery in Gotland. The Cold War's ghosts had found him and changed his life and his family's. He gazed at Mariya with disgust. Hers was the kind of paranoia that probably perpetuated the conflict, when reasonable minds would have long put an end to it. "Have you ever thought that you, and people like you, may have been the problem all along? With your pathetic thirst for mischief—your games that ruin the lives of ordinary people, like my brother."

She jabbed her finger into Jonathan's chest. "Your brother was no ordinary person if he was on that plane. Have you asked yourself the real question? What was your brother doing there—sightseeing?"

She had a point, but Jonathan wasn't about to concede anything. "Without your despicable weapons of terror, he would never have been there in the first place. He was a translator, for God's sake. Only useful because he spoke your language. Nothing else. He was a gentle, young man who'd planned to work for the UN after leaving the military, and he never harmed anyone."

"Rubbish," she said, hastily pushing another cigarette out of her pack. "He was a spy, a thief for hire, except that he wore a uniform to justify his actions."

"No worse than you, my dear."

"You . . . you Americans," she whipped back, now sounding angry, "you think you are so above us, yet you've done the same things, sometimes with different methods, but nevertheless, equally vicious."

The man in the front passenger seat glanced over his shoulder to assess the growing war of words behind him.

"You simply can't admit it, can you?" Jonathan asked.

"Admit what?"

Jonathan felt that sliver of admiration for her evaporate as he realized that she lacked the courage to admit the obvious. "If the explosion had occurred as planned, thousands of innocent people would have been infected. All the—"

"Not true!" she barked, interrupting him. "It would have happened at an air base somewhere in Utah or Arizona. Only a few people in the vicinity would have been infected—just enough to cause an uproar."

"You can't be sure."

"We didn't want to harm anyone; we only tried to embarrass your government."

Jonathan shook his head. "This doesn't redeem your disregard for human life. You're evil, pure evil, Colonel Mariya Zhumavik."

She frowned. "Then so is everyone else involved, including your brother."

Jonathan was getting angry, and he quickly realized it wasn't a good idea to continue down that path. "Do you understand my frustration, Mariya? I only want to find my brother. I don't want to judge him, or you, or anyone else. I am . . ." He couldn't finish his thought. His sadness had suddenly choked his voice and filled his mind with images of young Matt at their home, at the levee, at the lighthouse and with their playful Dobermans.

"Are you sure the man Yakovlev rescued was your brother?"

"Yes," Jonathan murmured.

"When the mission failed, I asked Yakovlev to clean up the mess, but I didn't ask for details. I simply wanted him gone from my circle. My last dealings with him was to transfer his responsibilities at the Air Force Academy, partly to cover my tracks. I could not afford to be exposed. All I know is that a man was picked up in the Baltic and returned to a military clinic near Leningrad."

"And then what?"

"I don't know. For me, the dossier was no longer my concern. But knowing the way things worked back then, I don't believe your brother stood much of a chance."

"Someone, somewhere must know what happened to him."

She leaned forward and looked into Jonathan's eyes,

her hand briefly resting on his lap. And with psychotic smoothness, she transformed her facade into one of compassion. "I'm sorry. I just don't know. I purposely chose to know nothing more about that affair. And then, not long after, the world around me became insane, unimaginable, petrifying. The August Coup. The corruption. The collapse of our government institutions. A real disaster—the Soviet Union disintegrated, with most of our intelligence services left in disarray. And many people went missing, either defecting, joining the mafia or simply falling victim to revenge. Archives were mishandled or destroyed. Each ministry was in shambles. It was a prolonged agony, knocking my country to its knees. So to keep track of one sick foreign spy was obviously not my priority." She sat back in her seat and returned to nursing her cigarette.

"Then help me find him. I've helped you with my information. It's only fair. Or do you not understand fairness in your line of work?"

"There is no need to insult me further," she said. She looked out the window again and added, "Ah, we've arrived."

Jonathan glanced out. A cluster of pine trees and an open gate came into view as the car slowed to a crawl. They turned onto a snow-covered driveway and headed into the property. At the end of the path stood a small one-story house, its dark wood siding somewhat dilapidated. A brick chimney spewed smoke. The cottage was surrounded by trees and looked like the kind of cozy place where one would hibernate all winter and even into summer.

The car stopped right in front.

"Don't say anything," Mariya said coldly. "I'll do the talking. I haven't seen this person in years."

"Who is it?"

"You'll see."

They got out, Mariya's two bodyguards leading the way. The taller of the two knocked at the door with his bulky hand, which Jonathan imagined had broken a few jaws in the past.

The door opened, and a man in his sixties answered. He had short, silver hair, his eyes small and beady. He looked surprised to have visitors, even more so when he spotted Mariya. He said a few words to her in Russian.

Mariya responded coolly, though Jonathan had no clue what they'd exchanged. The man appeared to be uncomfortable with her presence, but he opened the door wide and waved them in. Mariya nodded for Jonathan to go in first. Her bodyguards stayed outside.

She introduced Jonathan to the man only by his first name, and then in English said, "This is Doctor Karmachov, one of Russia's finest scientists."

Jonathan shook his hand as his memory instantly replayed Vladin's words during the prison visit. Karmachov was one of the men waiting for Vladin at that strange farm that had only rabbits and squirrels.

Karmachov, who walked with a mild limp, ushered his guests into the home and pointed at the table that separated the living room from the rustic, open kitchen. Mariya sauntered ahead of Jonathan and seemed to scan the entire room with her eyes.

"He's offering us a drink, so sit down," Mariya

abruptly said to Jonathan as Karmachov took a full bottle of vodka from the cabinet and clumsily removed the top, his hands shaky, his glances nervous. Jonathan sensed that this was no joyous reunion for the two Cold War veterans.

"Doctor Karmachov and I go back a long while," she said, sitting down. "Since the late '70s."

"Does he speak English?"

"Hardly any, so you'll have to be patient."

Karmachov joined them at the table carrying the bottle and three glasses. He spoke with Mariya as he poured the booze, but she didn't translate his words. It wasn't until five minutes into the conversation that she turned to Jonathan with something to say. "I told him you're an American official with some important information to share."

"And what exactly do you want me to share?"

"It doesn't matter. Just say anything—a sentence or two. I'll decide what he hears."

"Okay." Jonathan nodded and sighed, wondering what this woman was up to this time. He thought it might help to be funny. If anything, it would throw her off a bit.

"My penis is so long, it has an elbow."

Mariya briefly cracked a smile but then returned to her stoic facade. "Good, you understand." She then spoke with Karmachov, no doubt saying something completely different. And judging from Karmachov's expression, her words were not pleasant.

"What did you tell him?"

"That you have an international arrest warrant for

him in connection with the air crash in March, 1989."

"You're joking."

"I am completely serious," she replied sternly, leaning back into her chair.

Karmachov protested, banging his fist on the table and raising his voice.

Mariya responded, her voice calm but her words surely cutting him to shreds. She was methodical. Calculating. Dangerous. "He's asking on what basis you are arresting him."

"He has exceeded the amount of nostril hairs permitted under international environmental treaties."

Mariya gazed vacantly at Jonathan, having gained the ability to repel the effects of his humor. She turned to the angry scientist and spoke some more, and again Jonathan asked what she'd said.

"I told him that we know that he betrayed his country. That he was the only person other than me who knew the cargo was wired with explosives. Not even his closest colleague, Doctor Vadenko, knew this."

"And," she continued, "he had a motive. He was enraged that he wouldn't be able to leave Russia, as he was promised."

"Vladin too was promised that," said Jonathan, "and he too wasn't happy about not going."

"That's different," she said, appearing shocked that Jonathan knew about that. "Vladin found out much later that he wouldn't be leaving. This bastard was told a few hours before the rendezvous with the aircraft."

"Why did you plan for them to go to Europe if you had rigged the plane to blow up in the U.S.?"

"That was the deal. The Americans paid good money for the cargo. They got visas for Karmachov, Yakovlev and four others of Yakovlev's choice to leave Russia, and I didn't want to make the Americans suspicious by not allowing them to leave. Remember, the Americans had already purchased other weapons systems and relocated seven scientists. But that was done before we caught on to Operation Tranquility."

Jonathan was trying to piece this all together. "Why did you change your mind?"

"That day, I had a strange feeling. I couldn't accept the risk that my top scientist would leave, even if it was for a few days. I wasn't sure he'd ever come back. It was bad enough to have Yakovlev—who was often just plain drunk and careless—roaming around Western Europe or Canada."

Karmachov blurted out something, after which she lobbed a response—from the sounds of it, an insult.

"*Nyet, nyet!*" Karmachov shouted. He now looked defiant rather than defensive.

"*Vresh!*" she shot back. "Fucking liar!"

It became clear to Jonathan that she wasn't seeking answers from this man. She was out for blood. He saw it in her incendiary eyes.

Karmachov shouted some more and again banged his fist on the table.

Mariya glanced at Jonathan, her rage climaxing. "He says he did what he thought was right," she said, finishing her words with a hiss. "He didn't want to kill any civilians."

Jonathan   considered   this   possible.   Perhaps

Karmachov wasn't vengeful at being denied travel to the West, but rather was repulsed by the fact that an unknown number of innocent Americans would be infected by the detonation. "He would be right to think that."

Mariya scoffed and Karmachov rambled. "He is lying. He just wanted us to fail; it was revenge."

Jonathan was about to say something when Mariya brought her purse up from her lap, dug into it and took out a chrome-plated revolver, pointing it at Karmachov, who immediately shut up. She spoke at length this time, raising her voice more with each sentence.

Jonathan bolted to his feet. "Mariya, calm down!"

"Quiet! I'm explaining to him why he's a coward, a traitor, an undeserving scum. I'm telling him what you told me—that the Americans were warned that the plane would explode."

Jonathan began feeling sorry for the scientist. Anything was possible with Mariya, and there wasn't a thing Jonathan could do. "Maybe someone else found out about the explosives?" Jonathan suggested, quickly constructing another possible explanation in hopes of averting bloodshed. "Perhaps they found out by tapping his phone or by some other means."

"I don't think so," Mariya said with the iciness of a madwoman.

"Put that gun away. Let's talk with him in a civilized manner, for God's sake!"

Mariya returned a burning stare and said, "He's a treasonous bastard who deserves to die."

"Don't!" Jonathan pleaded, wanting desperately to

lunge at her and stop the insanity.

Karmachov gripped the edge of the table, the rest of his body remaining frozen in his chair.

"After everything we've done for him," Mariya said. "Unlike his unpleasant colleague, Doctor Vadenko, he was one of the most decorated scientists at Biopreparat. He was given the most expensive Western instruments, the most talented staff and the cleanest laboratories. And all for what? To betray our country? To put our security in the hands of American spies?"

Karmachov's shoulders sank. His eyes shifted frantically between Mariya and Jonathan. He spoke a few words, but Mariya seemed oblivious to the scientist's desperation. Her grip on the gun seemed to tighten.

Jonathan became angrier. "What is he saying—and don't lie to me!"

Mariya also stood up, steadfastly holding her weapon straight out in front of her, the barrel pointed at Karmachov's face. "He says . . . he's admitting it. It's true, it's all true. He called Yakovlev's American contact to put an end to the—" She then interrupted herself and yelled at him in Russian.

Jonathan couldn't be sure that she was accurately translating what Karmachov had said. Her words now sounded too self-serving.

The scientist looked like a man trying to crawl out of his own skin. But there was no escaping. Mariya was the master of ceremonies, her eyes bright with fury, her veins bubbling with adrenaline.

Jonathan gripped the back of his chair with both hands, anticipating the worst. "Please, put the gun down." He quickly pondered knocking the weapon out of her grip, but what of the two men outside? The act would be futile, perhaps ending in two corpses instead of one. "Don't do this."

She glanced coldly at Jonathan. "You should want him dead, too. If it weren't for his actions, your brother would be safe today."

"If it's vengeance you want, Mariya, then settle the score without me. I want no part of—"

An earsplitting bang burst through the room. Karmachov's forehead ripped open from the high-caliber round, his body falling back with his chair and slamming on the floor.

"Holy shit!" Jonathan barked, eyeing Mariya in horror as she lowered her gun. A plume of smoke snaked out of the barrel. "You fucking nut job!" He stepped back, bumping up against the window sill behind him. "Jesus! Jesus Christ!"

"Calm down," she said, as if Jonathan was the one being unreasonable.

"You killed him, you freak!"

She slipped the gun back into her purse and glanced at Jonathan with a crooked smile. "I hope so."

Jonathan didn't want to move. From his vantage, he only saw the surface of the slightly bloodstained table, and not the body that lay on the floor behind it. He'd seen too much death since his Victory Lines case had taken him down this twisted path—more bodies and bloodshed in less than two weeks than most criminals witness in an entire lifetime.

Her bodyguards rushed into the house and quickly

grasped what had happened. Judging from their sterile expressions, perhaps they had already known her intentions for this visit. Her driver picked up both Mariya's and Jonathan's glasses, emptied the remnants into the sink and threw them in a clear plastic bag that he had pulled out of his pocket.

Mariya pushed a cigarette out of her pack and lit it with a surreal calmness.

"Are you shocked?" she asked, her voice devoid of emotion.

"Oh, no," Jonathan said, sarcastically. "I think it's perfectly normal to kill someone in cold blood and then relax with a smoke." His pulse continued to quicken.

She then shook her head as the fine, long hair fanned over her slender shoulders. She raised her chin and met Jonathan's gaze. "Have sex with me, and I will help you."

*Are you nuts?* Jonathan said silently and shook his head in disbelief. *Of course she is.* He crossed his arms. "You need to check into the nearest mental clinic. They have those here, don't they?"

Mariya moved toward the American and dipped her hand into her purse. "His bedroom is over there, behind the kitchen. Fuck me like you've never done before, and I will help you find your brother. Refuse, and I will kill you like I did Karmachov. If you think I'm so evil, then I want to live up to it."

Jonathan was both scared and livid. If he'd had a gun, he'd have shot her as one would a venomous snake. But it was she who was armed.

"Well?" she said, appearing impatient and perhaps

insulted that Jonathan had not already yielded. "Keep moving," she added as he slowly walked through the kitchen, toward to the bedroom.

*It would be just a fuck, a demented fuck in return for something of value, to end this nightmare once and for all*, Jonathan thought, before quickly feeling guilty about Linda and repulsed that he'd even considered such a thing. *Over my dead body, you crazy whore.* He grew angrier as he watched Mariya strut her body his way.

She waited for an answer, her hand still hidden in her purse, probably grasping her gun. She briefly turned and said something to the driver as he headed out with his colleague. She then gazed back at Jonathan. "Come on, let's have a little fun together."

Her twisted smile sickened him.

"And you'd better last more than thirty minutes."

Aside from the sole redeeming quality of her amazing physical features, everything about this woman was repulsive. Everything, including her very existence.

"Is this the only way you can get pleasure?" Jonathan said spitefully. "To torture someone into touching you? You have no dignity."

"I can be with anyone I want," she barked back, her hand emerging from her purse with the gun pointed at him, and he realized that if he didn't give in, death might come his way.

Jonathan glanced at Karmachov's metal-framed bed and turned his gaze back at the woman. He slowly stepped backward until he felt his legs butt up against the edge of the mattress. He stared at the armed woman approaching him, reckless mischief painted across her face. Raising the gun to aim at Jonathan's face, she dropped her purse and began unbuttoning her blouse with her other hand. She untucked it and flaunted her shapely breasts. Her hand slid down her leg. She gripped her skirt and raised it until her inner thighs were fully exposed. She wore no underwear. A thin glaze of perspiration coated her smooth, inviting flesh.

"Have me," she declared in a loud whisper.

He felt himself weakening, but as he watched a nearly nude Mariya swaying in front of him, images of Linda lying on a hospital bed suddenly flooded his mind. He saw Linda's helpless gaze, her struggle to survive.

He knew that what he would say next could get him killed. "Nothing is worth betraying my wife. You of all people should know what betrayal means. You just killed a man for that reason. So, respect my decision to say no. I can't. I won't. No matter how much I want your help to find what happened to my brother, I cannot sell my soul in return for that knowledge."

Mariya let go of her skirt and sighed. "I can make you."

"No, you can't," Jonathan said. "There must be something in you, somewhere deep inside, that makes you human and compassionate. There just has to be. And this is where I draw the line. You are an incredibly attractive woman, but I can't betray the one person who has held my world together for so long."

Mariya was angry, but probably not hurt. *Women like her don't get heartbroken, or they certainly wouldn't dare show it,* Jonathan thought. Instead, they inflict pain on others as if to soothe their own insecurities, their own dissatisfaction with life. But Jonathan wasn't about to get lured into feeling sorry for her. She was evil.

Suddenly the sound of a phone rang out from Mariya's handbag. She lowered her revolver and frowned at Jonathan before retrieving the phone.

Jonathan glanced at her uncovered chest. It looked tender, flawless.

She answered the call, sounding trite. "*Da, da*," she said repeatedly, giving the caller intense attention. She then tossed the gun back in her purse, which brought Jonathan a welcome sense of relief. She said a few more words and hung up, her merciless facade transforming into a rather dispassionate shell. "I have some new information. It's complicated. I will . . . I will know more very soon. We must leave right now." Seeming embarrassed, she quickly buttoned her blouse and tucked it back into her skirt.

Jonathan approached her. "Thank you for not—"

"Don't say it . . . just don't," she said, raising her hand. The fierceness in her eyes dissipated. "Let's forget this happened."

# 23

ALEXANDRE WAS AT HIS DACHA WHEN JONATHAN ARRIVED later that night, escorted by Mariya's henchmen. They had dropped her off first, at a tall glass office building in the Arbat area, close to the river.

"You're alive and you're not in jail," Alexandre said, opening the door with a stunned look about him.

"Is there any doubt now about my resourcefulness?" Jonathan said playfully. "Or my ability to cheat death and dismemberment?"

Alexandre laughed. "No, no more doubts. You are like a cat."

"Perhaps, but I think I'm now on my ninth life."

"Let me get you some *chai*. I want to hear what happened."

Jonathan huddled comfortably in the plush leather sofa of the quaint, rustic living room. Alexandre had fixed up the place with an eclectic assortment of collectibles, from American Indian ceramics, to Asian rugs, to Spanish and French porcelain figurines, to contemporary paintings, mostly acrylic.

"You like that one?" Alexandre asked, noticing Jonathan's curiosity over a large watercolor of a woman, her face painted pale yellow, her hair green and blue.

"Striking."

"It's by Anatoly Zverev, a Russian painter from the '50s and '60s. He was a controversial figure in Soviet days."

Alexandre's cell phone rang, startling them both.

"*Allo*," he answered, shrugging his shoulders. "*Da, da*." He handed to phone to Jonathan. "It's for you— your girlfriend."

Jonathan smirked, taking the phone and knowing exactly who Alexandre meant. "Mariya?"

"Get out of there," she exclaimed. "Right now."

"What?"

"The police are on their way with an arrest warrant. Apparently C.J. Raynes knows some powerful people in the Ministry of Justice that I do not. Get out now, or you will be arrested!"

A chill ran through Jonathan's body as he looked over at Alexandre, who had walked to the windows. "What is it?" Jonathan asked Alexandre.

"I see blue lights," Alexandre said rapidly. "Several cars heading through the trail."

"We need to leave," Jonathan told him. He then said to Mariya, "They're already close; I'm heading out the back, through the woods."

"Good," Mariya said. "I'll see what I can do. I'm a few kilometers from there, coming your way."

Jonathan hung up, darting to the back door of the country home, and shouted, "Are you coming? Hurry!"

Alexandre turned into the hallway. "No, you go. I'll stall them. They're not after me." He threw his cell phone at Jonathan. "Good luck, my friend."

Jonathan turned back to Alexandre, and the two men gave each other a strong hug.

"Thank you," Jonathan said. "Thanks for everything. I mean it. And don't forget to send me your bill—"

Alexandre chuckled. "Don't worry, I won't forget. It will be a big number. Now, hurry through those woods straight ahead, and you will find a trail. Follow it for a few hundred meters, until you see a stream. The best way is to cross the stream, pass through the next part of the forest until you find the main road, about one kilometer away. Call me from your phone when you reach the road, but realize that the police may still be here, and I may not be able to answer."

"I'll try to get Mariya," Jonathan said, holding the door open. "She's on her way."

Alexandre shook his head. "I'm not sure she's the first one I would trust, but if you have no other choice..."

Jonathan rushed through the snow-covered back yard and entered into the woods, his dress shoes quickly becoming soaked. He heard the sound of cars pulling up to the front of the house. The fear that bolted through him made him run even faster. And then he heard something even more disturbing, the sound of dogs barking, followed by loud voices of their masters. He realized the danger he was now in. It was one thing to outrun humans; quite another to escape from police canines.

The bright glow of the moon filtered through the tall trees above, lighting the path ahead. He scurried across the wet ground, stepping over branches, shrubbery and other obstacles that canvassed the forest.

He ran, weaving through the trees, glancing over his shoulder every few seconds, until he found the trail Alexandre had mentioned. The barking grew more intense. He guessed that there were at least two dogs, perhaps three, but he was confident that his lead was at least a couple hundred yards.

Jonathan squinted, trying desperately to find the stream nearby. He left the trail and ran into a denser part of the forest, the darkness hampering his search. He stopped and listened. Despite the nearing sounds of dogs barking, he heard the faint sloshing of water, and he ran toward it. It was only about a foot deep, with rocks at its bottom, but the water was painfully cold, nearly frozen. His shoes, socks and lower pant legs were soaked, his skin chilled and approaching complete numbness. He gripped a tree root to pull himself out of the rocky edge of the stream, on the other side.

"*Stoi, strelyat budu!*" Jonathan heard a cop shout.

Suddenly, out of nowhere, a heavily-built, dark figure in white and green fatigues jumped in his path, aiming a rifle from his hip at Jonathan, who skidded to a halt. Another man lurched from behind the tree next to him. Before Jonathan could backtrack, another three men popped up from the snowy ground, their combat uniforms blending perfectly with the surroundings. They all carried assault rifles, two of them pointed at Jonathan.

*Soldiers?* the thought flashed through Jonathan's mind. *They're not cops. No way.*

Jonathan heard a dog barking, and it sounded closer—much closer—than the others.

The man standing directly in front of Jonathan raised his rifle to eye level, aimed the long barrel and leaned his head into the large scope fastened to the top of the weapon. Desperate, Jonathan dove sideways into a bush, feeling someone grab his ankle.

Two muffled shots rang out, the sound no louder than a BB-gun. *A silencer*, Jonathan thought, now wondering why he was still alive. The barking behind him suddenly turned to loud moaning. He swung around. The dog was down, right in the middle of the stream. It twisted its injured body in a circle, water splashing everywhere. Another round from the silencer quieted the moaning for good.

The soldier lowered his weapon and motioned to his comrades, who instantly swarmed over Jonathan.

*I'm dead now.*

He swung at the men, but outnumbered and overpowered, he didn't stand a chance.

The troops grabbed him by his arms and lifted him off the ground. The pain from his old gunshot wound bolted through him again. The men whisked Jonathan forward, away from the stream he'd just crossed. His feet barely touched the ground, the strength of his captives surprising him.

The sound of other barking dogs diminished.

"Where are you taking me?" Jonathan asked, feeling the gauze and tape covering his wound tear open.

"Shh," replied the soldier controlling the right side of his body, motioning for Jonathan to stay quiet.

Through thick shrubs, Jonathan could see the momentary signaling of headlights. A car idled just ahead, perhaps at fifty yards' distance. Jonathan emerged from the forest with the men tightly clustered around him, his body shaking from the glacial air. They finally reached pavement and hurried across the road to the waiting car.

Mariya got out of the vehicle and greeted Jonathan with a half-lit cigarette dangling from her grinning mouth, her shoulders wrapped in a lacy, red shawl. She took the cigarette from her lips and exhaled a plume of smoke. "Looks like you could use some help."

Jonathan frowned. The soldiers set him on hisfeet and backed off and after Mariya's quick wave of the hand, they melted back into the forest.

"Get in," she demanded, and Jonathan did so quickly, silently.

The car tore away, descended the rural road at a high rate of speed. Jonathan was freezing, especially his feet and legs.

Mariya took her cell phone in hand. "I have something to ask you. It may be difficult."

Jonathan tilted his head and wondered what this woman could possibly throw his way next, but his aggression toward her had been softened by appreciation for saving him from the cops."

"Did your brother have a tattoo on his left arm?"

Jonathan's face sagged, and he needed a few seconds to grasp the intensity of the question. "Yes—a small dagger on his biceps." That's when images of Matt crossed his mind, especially the first time his brother had come home on leave from West Germany. He'd proudly shown Jonathan his tattoo, along with a picture of a well-endowed Bavarian girlfriend.

For the first time since Jonathan had met her, Mariya looked sad. She seemed to hesitate.

"A man in his mid-twenties was photographed at an airfield in Voronezh in early April, 1989," she said. That was his tattoo. I have not seen the photograph, but I am waiting for information from an old contact. He may call later today. In the meantime, you will stay with my driver. And don't try to put a sock in his mouth. Unlike Yuri, this man has no restraint. He'll break your neck before you can flinch."

Jonathan glanced at the back of the driver's big head and broad shoulders. He looked like a piece of Russian farm equipment.

Mariya refused to answer any of Jonathan's questions. She repeated that she would know more in the morning. The ride back into the city was uneventful, a perfect moment for Jonathan to unwind from the close call earlier at Alexandre's dacha. Before Mariya confiscated his cell phone, she had allowed him to call Alexandre's home, but there was no answer. He only hoped Alexandre had not been arrested, but Jonathan feared that was entirely possible.

The driver dropped Mariya off at the Kempinski and then headed back out of town. They parked in an industrial area, in front of a small warehouse, where the driver escorted Jonathan at gunpoint to a small storage room in the back of the building that reeked of paint and thinner. There, Jonathan stayed the night. He remained locked-in throughout the morning as well. The driver had led him out to the bathroom only once. The silence, the unanswered questions, the recurring worries over Matt and Linda were driving Jonathan berserk.

It wasn't until four-thirty in the afternoon that Mariya's driver opened the door of Jonathan's small room and signaled that it was time to go. Jonathan gazed out the car's window, at the buildings and monuments along the way that gave Moscow its striking beauty and grandeur. When the driver crossed the river near the White House, Jonathan realized he was headed back into the heart of the city, toward the Kremlin, toward trouble. His heart began to race.

# 24

THE FIVE-POINTED RED STAR RADIATED IN THE DUSKY SKY.
Its webbed, crystallized texture contrasted with its stunning fluorescence at the top of Spasskaya Tower.
Jonathan eyed its crimson facade, the large gold-leafed
clock and the elegant white stone accents, understanding
the power and history that lay below it in the Kremlin,
the seat of Russia's government and a place he'd seen
from the inside at nearly the cost of his life. The fact that
he'd roamed its cavernous underbelly, killed two men in
the Armory Museum, escaped from the Komendant-
skaya Tower and lived to come back and stand at its
gates gave him a huge boost of confidence. Two guards
in uniform roamed the entrance to the tower, each smoking a cigarette, ignoring Jonathan some thirty feet away.

He glanced through the cracked glass of his wristwatch. 6:30 P.M., Mariya had told him. He was on time;
she was not. Red Square was desolate. The strong, cold,
sustained breeze sweeping from the south was not the

kind of weather that would draw many tourists. Not in November.

The shadow cast by the Kremlin walls over the cobbled ground slowly merged with the base of St. Basil's Cathedral. Jonathan lowered his hat to cover more of his forehead, as the temperature continued to dip. It was nearly seven and Mariya had still not shown up. He feared that something had gone wrong, but he'd sensed that before, nearly every moment he'd been in the Russian capital. *If something were going right*, he thought, *that's when I should really worry*.

Suddenly he heard the screeching of tires behind him. A long, black limousine, a Russian-made ZIL like the ones Alexandre had pointed out when they had driven past the Russian Duma, whipped around the from the riverfront road and headed toward Jonathan. It flashed its lights and then slowed to a crawl and parked next to him. Jonathan leaned down, trying to take a look inside, when the back door opened and Mariya emerged with a thick fur coat over her shoulders, not quite hiding her trademark short leather skirt and high heels.

"I am late," she declared, stating the obvious without an ounce of remorse or apology.

Jonathan nodded. He'd given up trying to predict her moves. "So, what are we doing here?"

"Just wait," she said, lighting a cigarette and fanning her hair back. "Whatever happens, please don't say a word. I mean it. Not one word. That's the only way my plan will work."

*Oh, no, she has a plan*, Jonathan said silently, shaking his head. *Someone is bound to get shot*, *proving yet again that there is nothing mundane about life in Moscow.*

"There he is," Mariya said, raising her head in the direction of the Moskva River.

A black Chevy Suburban, followed by a dark gray Ford Explorer, all their windows tinted, snaked through traffic past the huge Russiya Hotel along the embankment.

"Who?" asked Jonathan, his eyes trained on the convoy that whipped left and headed toward the

"Your buddy, C.J. Raynes. And if you say anything that might cause him to guess who I am, I'll have to kill you on the spot. I don't want to have to do that, as I've grown rather fond of you. So keep you mouth shut."

The SUVs pulled up beside Mariya's limo. A tall, hawk-nosed man stepped out, callousness glazing his face. Another man stepped out behind him, his jacket distended by what was surely a handgun. He marched to Mariya. "What's he doing here?"

Jonathan said nothing, just as he was told. He stood close to Mariya met the American diplomat's stern gaze. "I wanted to make sure we were talking about the same guy," she answered with a sneer.

C.J.'s face sagged. "It's not what we agreed. You told me he would be on the next plane out of Russia. This is completely unacceptable. I will inform my ambassador about this."

"Save your bravado for someone who cares. This man has done nothing to you. And you are welcome to tell you ambassador, because I'm sure he is unaware of Operation Tranquility, of the extraordinary measures you went to weaken my country, of all your manipulations—which, mind you, are not compatible with your diplomatic status."

C.J. turned to the armed man behind him. "Get back in the car." C.J. tilted his head and glanced at Jonathan.

"Yep, I told her everything," Jonathan couldn't resist saying.

Mariya scowled at Jonathan and then returned to her duel with C.J. "Mr. Brooks will be escorted to the airport in a few minutes, as we agreed. But I'm offering you the chance right now to do two things: apologize to this man and tell him why his brother was sacrificed."

C.J. scoffed, his long arms crossing over his chest. "I've already spoken to this jerk." He then laughed. Not a light laugh, but a throaty, mocking bark.

Jonathan fantasized slashing the man's jugular with one of the swords from the Armory Museum.

"Apparently," Mariya said, "your *conversation* was rather . . . violent, shall we say?"

C.J. looked away for a moment. Jonathan knew that C.J. was in a difficult situation, even more so if his superiors hadn't authorized his actions with Scarborough. Jonathan understood his predicament, but he felt no pity.

C.J. stepped forward and drew his pointy face to within inches of Jonathan's. "Your brother was killed in an accident far, far away from this hellhole," he whispered harshly, his hands nearly touching Jonathan. He was a patriot, like everyone else who died on that plane. That's all there is to it."

Jonathan gazed at C.J. in disgust. "With what I've learned, you and your cohorts are going down."

C.J.'s face turned red, his eyes filled with fury. "All you're doing is fucking with people who've dedicated their lives to making your little world *safe* back home—so you can walk the streets of New Orleans not thinking about nuclear, chemical or biological weapons detonating in your backyard; so cocksucking lawyers like you can continue to whine about the pettiest of disputes, while the real war rages on this end of the globe, where the true heroes battle for victories you couldn't even fathom."

Mariya grabbed Jonathan's arm. "You, get in the car," she said, pulling the door open. "Now!"

Jonathan wanted to hit C.J. across the face—one good punch to crack his jaw. But he didn't. He had already won. He knew his brother had at least survived the plane crash. He had uncovered the plot. And as a litigator, he preferred to define victory without bloodshed, without violence, even if in these egregious circumstances, a physical revenge would have been very satisfying. He got in the car, glancing into his enemy's eyes one last time.

Mariya remained outside, and all Jonathan witnessed were the gestures and the facial expressions until finally, she joined him in the backseat.

"Are you really kicking me out?" Jonathan demanded.

"Yes," Mariya said contritely. "But in 72 hours. Until then, you will go through the motions."

"You promised me that—"

"I have some constraints, my friend," Mariya said. "I brought you and C.J. here to see if perhaps he would confess, but also to see his demeanor. It's always nice to see your victim before he dies."

"Dies?"

Mariya gazed in the direction of C.J., who was getting back into his Suburban. "Isn't it prodigious? Even exhilarating? To look at a dead man walking. This evening, as he walks through the lobby of his apartment building on Zubovskiy Bulvar. As he presses the elevator button and thinks about his warm supper and satellite television show. Before the elevator door opens, his life will terminate violently—a terrible, sudden thrombosis, not completely unusual for a man with rather high cholesterol in his late forties."

"Just like the old days, huh," Jonathan grinned. "Trademark moves of the old KGB."

C.J.'s convoy drove away.

Mariya shook her head and smiled. "It's not quite like the old days. Today, every day, in every way, there are the same dirty tricks. Vengeance. Gamesmanship. Power. Gambling. All sides still draw the line and take care of loose ends. What has changed is that it has become more polished, at times more restrained."

Jonathan was chilled by her icy matter-of-factness, but he knew the result of her predatory hunt would make justice reign in one small corner of the tragedy that had overtaken his life. One wrong that could, in a strange way, be right. While he didn't agree with that, he had to admit that he admired her stamina and her ability to shut off emotions to make what she believed to be rational decisions.

Mariya took out a pen and wrote a few words down

on a napkin, and then handed it to Jonathan, looking into his eyes. "You will go to this address, in a town called Bobrov, though you will not be happy with what you find there," Mariya said. "But you will have your answer; you will find your brother. I am sorry I didn't know about this sooner."

Goose bumps crawled up Jonathan's spine. His heart skipped a beat. "What do you mean?"

Mariya didn't answer.

Jonathan took a deep breath. "He's not alive, is he?"

She dug deep into a leather duffel bag by her feet, next to her purse. "Here, take this with you," she said, pulling out a compact video camera to show Jonathan, who was puzzled. She put the camera back in the bag.

"What that's for? What am I going to find?"

She shook her head and then caressed Jonathan's face with her hand. "*Beregi sebya.*"

He rested his hand on hers for a second and then let go, leaning back into his seat.

"Now, go. You don't have much time." She opened her door and stepped out. "My driver will take you to the airport. Do as you are told." She shut the door and tapped the top of the car twice, signaling the driver to get going.

The limo pulled away, and Jonathan gazed at Mariya as she strolled toward the twenty-foot-high wood doors at the bottom of Spasskaya Tower. Two red gyro lights flared on each side of the doors, which the guards opened for her as she walked inside.

The driver never said a word during the entire drive to Sheremetyevo airport. When Jonathan arrived, two husky men in suits yanked him out of the limo by his arms and rapidly ushered him through the terminal. All Jonathan had was the duffel bag Mariya had given him. The two suitcases of clothes he'd brought to Russia were still at Alexandre's.

The men waved ID cards at security clerks manning the checkpoint to the departure lounge, still holding Jonathan tightly. The trio bypassed security, prompting strange looks from other passengers.

"Look there," said one man holding onto Jonathan, his accent thick. "Security agent from American embassy."

Jonathan glanced at a man in a trench coat, his paper folded under this arm. They locked gazes.

"He here for make certain you go on plane for America."

Jonathan was getting angry. "But Mariya said I had 72 hours."

"*Da*, you do."

The men escorted Jonathan past the crowded waiting area and led him through the gangway to the aircraft. But prior to reaching the plane's hatch, Jonathan felt a tug at his arm. One of the men pulled him toward the side exit door.

"Quick, go down," the lead man said. "You not take this plane. Only for show to American."

Jonathan now understood. He ran down the metal stairs to a waiting van that quickly took off the second the men were seated. The vehicle sped under the aircraft's wing and headed across the apron. Jonathan looked back at the terminal building behind him. The van hurried down the taxiway as if it were an aircraft preparing for takeoff. They crossed the two parallel runways and approached a set of buildings on the other side of the airfield.

"Your plane is that one," Jonathan heard the man next to him say. "You take to Voronezh, where you go to city and take bus to Pavlovsk—it make stop in Bobrov." The man then jotted down some notes on the back of what looked like his plane ticket. "If problem, this is instructions."

The van drove right up to the plane, and the two men waved for Jonathan to head up the stairs. The smell of jet fuel filled his lungs. With his ticket and duffel bag in hand he walked up and entered the plane, where he waited nearly an hour before the other passengers began boarding.

# 25

"YOU WILL FIND YOUR ANSWERS THERE." JONATHAN recycled the words he had heard from that demented woman some nine hours ago. Mariya's frosty, elusive expression—the gaze of a seasoned killer—gave no hint about what he would face. It was all he had to go on, along with an address scribbled on a napkin.

The bus slowed down, jolting passengers as it navigated over deep potholes in the muddy, rural road. Jonathan sat alone in his row, gripping the handle above the seat in front of him. He glanced at the people around him. Some were young, some old. They all wore rugged faces. Mostly women. Had he not known better, he would have guessed they were refugees of a distant war, the vestiges of which lay in their gloomy stares and leathery, fatigued faces. The floor creaked as the bus maneuvered its aged chassis across a land none of them would by choice call home.

He wiped his sleeve over the fogged glass and peered

out. The sky was a patchwork of charcoal clouds ready to unleash more snow. Tall, powder-covered trees were everywhere, as far as the eye could see. Aside from the dirt road and utility poles, there was no other imprint of civilization. Jonathan had seen miles of virgin land in his home state of Louisiana, but never as much as here. He hadn't spotted a single house or farm in over an hour. Nothing at all except fields and forests.

The ride had been filled with recollections, an uncomfortable, silent journey with people who spoke a strange language and ignored his foreign face. Strangers with no clue who he was, no idea of the pain holding his psyche hostage. All they saw were his stylish clothes, steel blue eyes and clean-shaven face.

He thought about what waited for him, what Mariya had said—that he would find his brother. And from her hesitation and apologies, all he could imagine was a tombstone in some godforsaken place. The sadness again drowned his thoughts, just as it had on the evening flight to Voronezh and at the city's bus terminal, where he waited nearly six hours through the night for the next bus to Bobrov. While at the station, he had written four postcards to Linda, spilling his fears, his tribulations and his hope that the truth was no longer so distant. And he had reread them dozens of times as he lay for hours on an uncomfortable bench, but he decided to send only one postcard—the one about hope. He didn't want to stress her out.

He replayed all that had happened. Every detail. Every word. Every face, friend and foe alike. He looked up at his backpack on the overhead bin, crammed among the many rudimentary red- and blue-striped vinyl bags common to travelers in this nation.

*What will I film?* Jonathan asked himself, thinking of the video camera Mariya had given him. *A fucking grave?* He inhaled the stale air.

The bus' fatigued engine rattled and its gears ground loudly. The bulbs on the ceiling flickered. But the wreck, like its passengers, slaved forward unfazed.

Despite the emotional agony that had plagued his days in Russia, Jonathan's two-hour bus journey was a physical respite from a terrifying course of events. His shoulder ached, but not as much. His legs were finally at rest. He was safe, for now.

"Matt," Jonathan whispered. "Oh, Matt." His eyes moistened, but he wiped away the tears before they reached his cheeks.

He pulled out an envelope from his coat pocket and removed the letter inside. The note was fragile, its edges torn and the ink smeared at the top. He needed to read it again, even though he had long ago committed every phrase to memory. His fingers trembled, perhaps from the sweet, heavily caffeinated teas and sodas he had consumed over the past few days to stay awake.

"Dear Jonathan,

"I heard you're kicking butt in court these days. I guess a lawyer in the family can be a good thing. It's just as well that you, and not I, take on those astronomical student loans, spend a fortune on fancy suits and write those incredibly dull briefs! On a more serious note, though,

I'll be coming home soon. I'm scheduled for
tests at Walter Reed—that same problem again,
my blood condition. And the uncertainty makes
me homesick. I'm having those strange dreams
again—our bike rides along the lake and at the
old lighthouse. I'm afraid, but I don't know
why.

"Love, Matt."


It was the last letter he received from his younger
brother. He tried to contain his sorrow, and make sense
of his unanswered questions, and everything else that
troubled him. But how could he? It had only been a couple weeks since everything he had been told to believe
had taken a sudden, cataclysmic turn.

Another pale, frail face had boarded the bus at the
small town of Peskovamka. She sat across the aisle, her
crescent shaped back uncomfortably leaning on the
barely padded seat. Jonathan gazed at her for a moment.

A light drizzle began tapping on the bus' fatigued
metal skin as it bounced over the dirt road. The lush
forests had passed, giving way to immense, barren
fields. Miles and miles of deep green, left for nature
alone to rule.

He looked at his watch again, perhaps for the tenth
time. It was nearly seven in the morning. A deep nervousness swept again through his body. Three weeks
ago, it would never have occurred to Jonathan that a lie
under oath would have led to all the death and mayhem
he'd experienced in New Orleans and Moscow.

But now, certainty could no longer escape his reach,

and it shouldn't—not after all that had been plundered, lost and stolen. Fairness, justice, divine certitude had to, in his eyes, have its place somewhere, somehow, or how could anyone think there was anything more to our mortal, molecular existence? Had the world aspired to such a shallow slavery to mere coincidence, man-made events and eventualities? Had it all been exclusively directed by the hands of the Tranquility madmen, in their positions of power, separating national security from conscience, and choosing more often than not the former, undeterred by history's punishing powers or by a higher being able and willing to dispense vengeance from one hand, equity from the other? The cold warriors had cast their spell on one and then two unsuspecting men, and they had won long ago, hadn't they?

Jonathan knew not what to think, only what to sense. Like an animal relying only on what was apparent, not what was promised or owed, he held on, waiting for the endless journey to conclude at the village. A final stop, which he hoped would be just that.

*        *        *

THIRTY minutes later, Jonathan stood up, grabbed his duffel bag from the overhead bin and followed two elderly women towards the front of the bus.

"*Do svidaniya*," he said to the bus driver, who returned a curious stare.

He was at an intersection of dirt and pavement, two paths that led nowhere familiar. A dozen drab concrete buildings lined the adjacent square. Bobrov was at best Russia's armpit. And from a quick scan of the surroundings, he knew there would be few redeeming qualities to this place. There was no sign of the magnificent architecture and vibrancy he'd seen in Moscow. This was not entirely unexpected. When he had told a fellow passenger on the plane he was headed to Bobrov, the woman's tilt of the head and raised eyebrows were enough to signal that there was no apparent reason for anyone to travel to this destination.

Jonathan walked over the dirt-covered sidewalk, observing the eeriness of this near-vacant town. The passenger in the plane had also told him of the factories that lay dormant, but which still saturated the soil with noxious pools of sulfides, dioxin, and other chemical carcinogens, courtesy of Mother Russia's state-controlled industrialists. She'd also told him about the uranium reprocessing plant that contaminated countless residents until it closed in 1993. Yet, more than two thousand people, among them the few on the bus, still called this wasteland home. The people who'd stepped off the bus quickly dispersed to their final destinations, mostly in a cluster of six-story prefabricated dwellings a half-mile down the widest street. They appeared to have been erected haphazardly, as if the only purpose was to provide concrete in three dimensions void of any aesthetic qualities. There were few sidewalks or traffic lights.

Jonathan glanced at the note Mariya had given him. He couldn't read her cursive Cyrillic, but he understood that it was some sort of address. He crossed the street to what appeared to be a bar or restaurant. There were few cars around, but in the distance he noticed a horse-drawn cart lugging a pile of large logs.

Jonathan pushed open the door and walked inside. The bar was a smoke den, with three obvious regulars lounged over the shabby wooden chairs and tables.

"*Dobriy den*," Jonathan cordially greeted, unsure at the reaction to his presence. His accent seemed to convince everyone within earshot that the Americans had finally arrived, though it seemed not as invaders, just curious anomalies of an otherwise gray, monotonous existence in the middle of an all-too-Russian nowhere. Jonathan smiled as he grasped their surprise.

The aging, large-breasted bartender smiled, pointed at Jonathan and shouted, "*Piva?*" Fortunately, it was a Russian word Jonathan had picked up during his short stay. It meant beer, and after all he'd gone through, he was happy to have one.

Holding the note that Mariya had given him, Jonathan asked—putting together a collage of poorly pronounced Russian words—the bartender for directions.

She read the handwriting, grinned and shrugged her shoulders. The words rolled so fast off her tongue that he couldn't grasp a single thing. She then repeated her words louder, as if that would help him understand Russian any better.

Then, as the bartender handed Jonathan a beer, a rough-looking man with matted hair and mismatched clothes seated at a table in the corner of the stale, smoky room got up and made his way toward Jonathan. The man tapped his knuckles on the bar. His body reeked of booze, but, to Jonathan's amazement, he began uttering words that resembled English.

"Fack, facking good dahy," he said at first with a deep laugh. "Mikhail Jackson compatriot?" He laughed again, stumbling forward toward Jonathan and then babbled some more. "*Angliyski, Americanski?*"

Jonathan responded with a simple, somewhat desperate nod.

The bartender rolled her eyes as the man stumbled onto the stool next to Jonathan and grabbed the note with his oil-stained hand.

"Me Igor," the man said, reaching his hand out to Jonathan's. "You?"

"Jonathan Brooks." He reluctantly shook the man's filthy hand.

After reading the note, Igor scratched his bristly cheeks and nodded.

Jonathan guessed that Igor knew the address. "Can you tell me where it is?"

Igor said something in Russian to the bartender, who peered over Jonathan's note, her pair of gold teeth sparkling from the two oil lamps on the bar's weathered Formica surface.

The disheveled man patted Jonathan's shoulder—his wounded shoulder—making Jonathan cringe from the pain. Igor held out his hands, gesturing the international sign for steering wheel. "*Poshli k mashyne*. Drive. Yes?" he said, smiling and pointing to his chest. "Me have caar."

Jonathan understood and got up. For lack of any other apparent means of getting to the address, he reluctantly agreed to follow the drunk outside. Igor waved for Jonathan to take a seat in his tiny four-door Lada, a vehicle that appeared stripped to its core—even the springs in the seats stuck out like flowers.

*       *       *

IT was a short drive out of the village, about four or five miles. They turned onto a wide paved road, with no buildings in sight. Woods approached on the left, and a thicker forest appeared on the right. After a about a half-mile, the pavement ended and they continued over a dirt road. Finally, after another five minutes, a small five-story cement block building came into view. Igor leaned into Jonathan and again glanced at the note. He seemed uncertain and pulled off the side of the road. He grabbed the note again, his drunken eyes focusing on Mariya's rough penmanship.

"*Da, da, tam*," Igor said, nodding in the direction of the small wooded area across the road to their left.

Jonathan stepped out as Igor pointed into the woods at what appeared to be a metal gate between two cement pillars. On it was a sign, barely legible, its paint weathered. Crossing the road, Jonathan recognized the number—it was the same as on his note. Boris waved and drove off.

Approaching it, Jonathan realized to where he had been led. He noticed behind the wrought iron fence at the edge of the woods one, then two, three and then dozens of headstones. He stopped in his tracks a stared ahead, his eyes quickly filling with tears. A few thoughts came to mind, but they no longer mattered.

"This is it," he whispered to himself.

The dew had lifted, but the air was still dense, and the smell of pine filled his lungs. He breathed in deep, two long breaths, and then walked through the gated entrance. His shoes quietly stepped over the broken pavement, cushioned with withered, wet leaves and powdery snow.

He entered the cemetery, scanning the first group of graves with the scrutiny of a scribe. He pored over the Cyrillic words on each headstone, hoping to find something familiar. His feet trod lightly over the weeds near each burial spot as he leaned forward to read each name aloud.

Some had photographs wrapped in cellophane and nailed or pasted above the men's names. Some pictures had faded so much they were unrecognizable. All, it seemed, were of military men, many so young, posing in their pressed Soviet uniforms, never realizing that these portraits would so soon decorate their graves. Those poor young men, their faces reminding Jonathan how far he was from where he should otherwise be. It surely was a place no Westerner had ever set foot.

Most of the headstones were unostentatious cement blocks, with only the minimal information engraved, though he strolled by a couple that were marble. A dozen more were simple wood planks sticking out of the earth, weathered and cracked in places.

Many of the soldiers had died in the 1950s and 1960s, but the wooden stumps had no visible markings to indicate when those servicemen perished. Jonathan walked to another set of gravestones; these had small wrought iron fences surrounding each plot. They too were of men, many dying in their twenties and thirties, most of them in the 1960s and 1970s. But it appeared that a long time had passed since a visitor had laid flowers on any of them. They were forgotten, condemned to become a meaningless speck of history. This spot of remembrance, not worthy of even a respectful dot on the map hadn't preserved anything sacred, but instead gave the vibe of a place that was cursed, hated, discarded by those who may somehow have known of its existence.

What had happened here, in this small wooded area, thousands of miles from acceptable civilization? What hatred lay at the root of this abyss that caused those brave faces laminated in wilted plastic, to be left abandoned, seemingly forever? There were also some more graves covered by bushes that had grown over them in time, obscuring even the most minimal symbol of a life once lived.

*       *       *

AFTER examining the writing on every grave—some eighty in all—as best he could, Jonathan realized that whatever he was meant to see was not there. He had expected to find Matt's name inscribed on one of the stones. Not so. He looked around, making certain he had not missed anything.

Jonathan headed back to the entrance and examined the sign that marked the name and address of the cemetery. With his hand he wiped the dirt off the steel plate to make sure. The number on the sign was 17, and that's when he realized he was at the wrong place. The note said 117.

Suddenly, he heard a woman yell something. He turned around and spotted her. She was a chubby woman, dressed in a thin trench coat. "Mister Brooks," she yelled, now walking faster and waving at Jonathan, who returned the gesture. "Mister Brooks."

As she drew nearer, he saw her nurse's uniform behind her open coat. But it didn't seem to be a normal nurse's uniform, but rather that of a military nurse, he guessed.

She reached Jonathan and was out of breath. "Sorry, sorry," she said, breathing deeply through her reserved smile. "I'm Ivaniya. I've been expecting you. You come with me, okay?" Her English was quite good, which gave Jonathan a welcome sense of relief.

"Yes," Jonathan said, guessing her age to be in the mid-thirties. "Where are you taking me?"

"To that building over there."

The two walked a couple hundred yards around a cluster of trees to the five-story building Jonathan had spotted earlier when Igor had dropped him off.

As he walked through the gravel parking lot, Jonathan noticed the desolation of the place.

"It is our old clinic. Still in use today for a few patients."

Jonathan suddenly felt lifted by those words. *Can he be alive? Is it possible?* He stopped on the stairs at the entrance of the building and gazed into Ivaniya's eyes. "Is my brother here?"

"Yes," she said somberly. "He is here, and he is dying."

Jonathan's heart sank. "Take me to him." She led the way through the quiet, vacant lobby. Only one other person was in sight, manning the reception desk.

"Why has he been here so long?"

"I ask myself that same question," she replied, walking fast ahead of Jonathan. "He's been here since when this part of the clinic was a research area. Patients here were not expected to leave. And he was very sick, too. He didn't speak for nearly three years."

Jonathan had a hard time understanding how this could happen.

They took an elevator to the third floor, and he followed her down a long hallway, lined by empty, dilapidated rooms. "Why did no one contact the American embassy or the nearest consulate?"

"We didn't know who he was. Just before his caretaker—Doctor Vadenko—died, he destroyed most of the files on his research, including files about his patients. We only knew your brother as patient number twelve." She then raised her hand. "Shh. Let's be quiet now. Please, things are very bad now."

She slowly walked to a large metal door. She pushed on it hard and then nodded for Jonathan to follow her.

They passed two empty rooms before she turned into the next one. And there was Matt, sitting in a wheelchair in the corner of the room, his eyes closed and his body covered by a thick wool blanket. Jonathan took a deep breath. He couldn't speak for a second. He slowly moved closer, and closer yet, as the nurse stepped back outside the room. "Can he hear?" Jonathan whispered to Ivaniya.

She nodded.

"Matt," Jonathan said softly, taking his brother's hand in his. Matt's face and arms were emaciated, his skin pale. "It's me."

Matt turned his head and began to awaken, but barely. His sunken eyes opened just a bit, and then a bit more. They stared at each other. Matt's eyes began to water and a surprised smile emerged. Jonathan heard Matt whisper his name, but his voice was weak and scratchy.

Jonathan glanced at the nurse. "Thank you," he whispered. He had a million questions, but for now, he just wanted to gaze into the eyes of his brother and hold him. The outside world no longer existed. Nothing else mattered at that moment.

# 26

***Three weeks later, Washington, D.C.***

THE BAILIFF WALKED BRISKLY BEHIND THE LAST ROW OF chairs and approached the heavy double doors.

"Please lock'em," a voice echoed through the speakers above the audience.

"Yes, Mr. Chairman," the man answered as he opened the doors and quickly closed them behind him as he stepped out. A buzzing sound followed and a small green light above the door flashed twice and then turned red.

"Are all attendees registered and verified?"

"Yes, sir," a man near the panelists responded, his voice muted since he didn't have a microphone.

"Very well, let's proceed," said the chairman, Senator Harris, nodding at his fellow panelists, who flanked him on both sides.

Jonathan gazed at the eight men in front of him. He

had center stage, a unique opportunity to be heard. But despite his outward lawyerly composure and his firm grasp of the facts he'd gathered through his ordeal, Jonathan was nervous.

Gary covered the microphone with his hand and leaned toward Jonathan. "Now, be kind to Senator Labenne," he whispered. "He's your only ally up there."

Jonathan turned his eyes onto the senator from Louisiana. Gary's fine work over the past two weeks had won Jonathan the privilege of addressing the distinguished group that made up the U.S. Senate Select Committee on Intelligence. Jonathan was also impressed that Gary had obtained all the senator's questions ahead of time.

Half of the thirty or so seats behind Jonathan were filled with faces he didn't know. Most wore suits, some wore uniforms. But one man was no stranger to Jonathan. He glanced over his shoulder for one more look at the man he recognized: Vice-Admiral Scarborough, who sat with his hawkish stare aimed at Jonathan. This was the man who'd tried to kill Linda. A man whose authority remained intact, his rogue powers still unchecked. And Jonathan hoped to change that this morning.

"Ladies and gentleman, I call this session into order," the chairman announced. "This is, of course, a closed-door session, and I need not remind the audience that all discussions held in this hearing are strictly confidential."

"Mr. Chairman, if I may," Senator Fischer from North Carolina interrupted. He was the committee's vice-chairman, and, from what Gary had uncovered, a former Navy Seal. "For the record, I believe that some of the information that will be discussed this morning is considered compartmentalized, and may require secret or top secret clearances. I believe all here, with the exception of the witnesses, have such clearance, but just to be absolutely clear, if anyone here does not have such a clearance, you are kindly asked to leave this session.

"As for our principal witnesses, Gary Green and Jonathan Brooks, neither have the appropriate security clearances. However, I understand they have signed—I believe last week—the standard non-disclosure agreement provided by this committee." Senator Fischer turned to his colleagues. "But just to reiterate, the witnesses do not have the proper clearances to hear *all* the information in the folders in front of you, so I urge caution with your statements and questions during this session. I'd feel more comfortable if you'd allow me, Mr. Chairman, to interrupt the proceedings if and when the information discussed here today strays into restricted territory."

"Very well, thank you for clarifying this for us." Chairman Harris opened the folder in front of him and jotted down notes.

Another senator at the far end of the panel leaned into his microphone and said, "Mr. Chairman, I'd like to reserve some time after the witnesses leave to discuss the issues among ourselves, and with the subpoenaed military officers that are here today.

"Your statement is noted, Senator Derringer. I'll save thirty minutes at the end of the proceedings for this purpose."

"So, for the record, I'm Senator Harris, Chairman of the Select Committee on Intelligence. Other Committee members present are the Honorable Senators Paxton, Calderman, Derringer, Fischer, Bradford and Labenne. Senator Ravenberg will join us in a few minutes, I've been told." After his staffer whispered into his ear, Senator Bradford added, "Our Committee has issued three subpoenas for this hearing, and let the record show that all the witnesses are in attendance, with the exception of Mr. Tillerman."

"Our committee has reviewed your initial written statement, as well as your follow-up correspondence. I understand that you have a written statement prepared for this hearing?"

"Yes, Mr. Chairman," Jonathan said solemnly. "And one exhibit as well. I'll also be happy to answer questions upon concluding my statement."

"Yes, Mr. Brooks, you may start momentarily." A clerk then approached Jonathan and administered the oath.

Jonathan went to the first line of his typed notes. "Mr. Chairman, and members of this distinguished panel, I am testifying here today because there has been a terrible injustice committed to an American family. Lives have been lost, lies have been told and our nation's honorable adherence to the rule of law has been stained."

Jonathan gazed at the senators, and then continued to read. "My brother, Lieutenant Matthew Henry Brooks, wasn't a player in this game of lies and treason. He was only twenty-four and a mere speck of dust in the grand, vile scheme of things that, in the end, caused him to lose everything in life, all hope, until his last breath. Yes, such an insignificant loss to a superpower, to the men who control these decisions in the name of us all, for God and country, for liberty or death, for freedom, for principles—whatever they may be—but this insignificant member of your arsenal was a most significant part of my life, of my family's life. This nation has dealt a devastating loss to us, to him, to all who were blessed by his presence and moved by his words.

"Someone once said, 'when the taking of a life is claimed to be blessed with royal assent, it is more likely than not that it was done when God blinked.' In the case before us, fairness and justice were blinded, but this is your chance to scrutinize the events that have scarred so many innocent people. An array of lies stretched into the deepest dungeons of our government, for right or for wrong. Its name was, or is still, 'Operation Tranquility'. Its result was catastrophe.

"Its masterminds were cursed with delusions of divine invincibility in their plan to covertly obtain the Soviet Union's most secretive weapons in exchange for spiriting out select military officers and resettling them in Canada or elsewhere under new names. And all this with a complete disregard of the hazards of transporting deadly materials through allied and our own airspace. They never thought their sinister plan would go wrong. Well, it did. One of their prized bribed officers, Major-General Yakovlev, was a double-agent. As part of the Soviet scheme, the aircraft was rigged to explode over U.S. territory. It is only by sheer luck that it did not. An informant alerted his American handlers in Moscow about the intended sabotage. Consequently, our own military was forced to shoot down the aircraft. Sadly, my brother, who was merely a translator, was on that flight."

Jonathan took a sip of his water. He was momentarily overcome with grief.

"You are the last guardians of decency and righteousness," he continued. "You are wise men that understand the limits of fair play in the traitorous vocation of Cold War gamesmanship. My brother, after all, you did not meet. You did not experience the laughs of this genius' humor, the wisdom of his young, powerful mind, or the straightforwardness of his loyalty. His will to live, even under the cacophony of a Soviet empire that banished his very existence to an abandoned corner of our planet, even with a Pentagon machinery working to silence this truth; even with the drugs that rendered him a mere shadow of the vibrant soul he once was.

"All this would have been remained hidden if I had continued to believe the words of the letter I received from our Navy, which disguised a tragedy of global proportions. Its name was Tranquility, but there was nothing tranquil about it. It wreaked havoc in the lives of ordinary people, none of whom ever suspected that some in our government would deceive them with such ruthlessness and in such a way that endangered the lives of thousands of civilians both here and abroad. These words I leave for your consciences to weigh.

"Mr. Chairman, I'm not bitter, no longer enraged. Those simple, volatile feelings faded quickly, replaced by a far more valuable sentiment—that I am finally at peace knowing that my efforts led to this room, to this prestigious audience with the power to undo this calamity. I pass the baton of judgment to your table, and what you do with it is entirely in your discretion. But before I conclude, I have a short video to show you."

Jonathan nodded at the clerk standing beside the oversized monitor. The screen lit up, at first with static and then beige wallpaper came into view. The image panned right, focusing on Matt, who lay in his chair, his back propped somewhat upright. Jonathan eyes closed as he began hearing the faint echoes of his brother's voice.

"I am . . . Lieutenant Matt Brooks," Jonathan's brother had said into the camera, his voice barely audible. "I was in plane crash, . . . somewhere, . . . somewhere over Russian airspace." He had tried to say more, but only air existed his lips. Jonathan had zoomed in closer. Matt was worn, his eyes barely open. He was only in his early thirties, but he looked fifty. He breathed hard and seemed to fight to speak some more. "We were . . . supposed to . . ." His words ended with a mumble. The video panned left, exposing the dreary room Matt had lived in, like a prisoner, for so many years. The tape ended.

"Mr. Chairman," Jonathan said, reopening his eyes. "My brother died at Army Clinic Number 241 at nine-twenty in the morning, two days after this video. He never returned to his country alive. Instead, for over three years his body was used for scientific experimentation by a small group of researchers. Their goal: to study how Matt's physiology had resisted their mutant strain of tularemia. They continued their research, using Matt as their test bed. And then, when the Soviet system collapsed, they disappeared along with their documents, and Matt was left abandoned—a patient without a name, without any hope."

The senators were visibly moved by what they had just witnessed, and nearly all of them glanced at the chairman, as if waiting for him to say something."

The room was silent.

"Thank you, Mr. Brooks, for sharing this with us. As you can imagine, my distinguished colleagues and I have a number of questions."

For next half-hour, Jonathan testified about all he had learned, beginning with the lies and secrecy in the Victory Lines litigation, to his confrontation with Scarborough in Washington, D.C. and of his discovery on Gotland. The destruction of his house and Linda's condition. He explained his journey in Moscow, the many attempts on his life, the horrific scenes of carnage in the bowels of the Kremlin. He told them everything he knew. And through all if it, he was happy to have Gary by his side, whispering advice but more important-ly, standing by as his ally in a roomful of men he wasn't sure he could trust.

When he finished answering the last question for the senators, Jonathan stood up and walked along the center aisle of the room, with Gary walking a few steps behind him. Nearing the door, Jonathan glanced at Scarborough, who was seated next to a man in a suit, probably an attorney. The vice-admiral did not meet his gaze. Jonathan knew that this villainous military officer was caught in the most difficult predicament of his life.

"Justice applies to all of us," Jonathan calmly said to Scarborough on his way out the door.

\*       \*       \*

### New Orleans, Louisiana

MOZART'S Concerto Number 21, second movement, filled the air from the CD player on Linda's nightstand. She was crying, but she smiled at Jonathan as he squeezed her hand. He had just told her everything: what had transpired at the Senate hearing.

"I am happy that you went," she said, her voice still weak, "and that you found out all this, and mostly, that you saw Matt, even for such a short time. I wish I could have been there with him, too."

She was not yet out of danger. Jonathan had spoken to her doctors. They had outlined the challenges that lay ahead. The burnt tissue on her right leg was infected and had not yet adequately responded to treatment. She also had ligament damage in one arm and tissue damage in her nose and upper trachea.

"How is your shoulder?" Linda asked.

Jonathan smiled. Even with all her injuries, she was thinking about his health. He gazed at her and felt a rush of love.

Gary arrived. He'd come to pick up Jonathan for a court hearing on a new case. Gary gave Linda kiss on the cheek and handed her some flowers, which she took with her right arm.

"I see you're getting back to normal."

"Not yet," Linda whispered with a smile. "But parts of my body seem to be cooperating now."

As Jonathan and Gary headed out, Gary leaned into him. "I have some great news."

"Oh, what is it?"

"I hear additional criminal charges have been filed against both counselor Tillerman and Vice-Admiral Scarborough, and for the first time three other officials at the Defense Intelligence Agency and one rather senior fella at the CIA have been charged with conspiracy. Looks like you've brought some accountability to government, huh?"

Jonathan shook his head. "Only at a very high price."

They headed out of the hospital, down the front steps, when Jonathan spotted a black Lincoln Town Car idling by the curb. As Jonathan reached the bottom stair, the driver opened the rear door and a passenger got out. It was Vice-Admiral Scarborough, dressed in his dark navy uniform, his unfriendly stare pointed at Jonathan.

Gary grabbed Jonathan's arm. "Isn't that . . ."

"Yes," Jonathan answered as he stopped to gauge whether he was in danger or not.

"Can we have a word?" Scarborough asked, looking rather haggard, like a man who hadn't slept in a week or a man who'd suddenly found his power to be hollow.

Jonathan turned to Gary. "It's okay. I'll talk to him for a minute."

Jonathan approached Scarborough, who leaned up against his car as his driver returned to the front seat. "What do you want?"

"There are a lot of other things that you do not know

about what we did in Russia," said Scarborough, avoiding looking directly into Jonathan's eyes. "I could fill you in on these details; anything you want to know about what happened. I'd like to help you . . . in return for you not testifying against me again and for helping to drop the charges against me."

"No, I already know more than I ever wanted to about your reckless campaign," Jonathan replied, his anger returning.

"I too have a family," Scarborough pleaded. "They don't need to go through this—to see their breadwinner go to jail. I am a patriot. Always have been. What you're doing is unjust. All I ever wanted to do was to defend this country of ours. And instead, you want to put me behind bars."

"That's where you belong." Jonathan had half expected to hear only fighting words from Scarborough, not this kind of defeatist tone.

Scarborough paused and raised his head. "Fine, then. Have it your way. But then you will never know from where it will come. Maybe as you drive under an overpass, or while you take a shower, to when you sit by your corner office window, or when you or your wife go shopping for groceries. It will happen. You will die. You have pissed off too many powerful people."

Jonathan's voice hardened. "Your threats mean nothing to me."

"They should," Scarborough said, glancing up at the hospital's facade.

Jonathan knew exactly what he meant. "You better hope she recovers fully," he said coldly. "If she doesn't, one morning in your jail cell, you won't wake up. I promise you."

Scarborough returned a disgusted glare and slipped back into his car. Jonathan stepped back as the Lincoln drove off. But when he glanced at the other side of the street, he spotted a woman at the wheel of a car—a woman who he immediately recognized, even though she wore a strawberry blond wig and large sunglasses. It was Mariya. She briefly met his gaze, but then her sight was drawn to Scarborough's car.

Jonathan stood riveted to the pavement. He wasn't sure if he was in danger.

She waited, a hunter in repose.

Then, once Scarborough's Town Car had turned the corner, her car came to life, the engine roaring. She turned and smiled—that calm, psychotic smile Jonathan had come to know and fear while in Moscow. She was there for blood. And she would find it. She glanced one last time at Jonathan and winked as her car slowly sliced through the sultry N'awlins afternoon and disappeared in the distant traffic.

*- The End -*

# Mystery novels by
# A.C. FRIEDEN

*Other novels available today:*

## CANVAS SUNSETS NEVER FADE

*Coming to a bookstore near you . . .*

**2008**

## SIN: A DEADLY ANTHOLOGY

**2009/2010**

## THE SERPENT'S GAME

## WHERE SPIES GO TO DIE

For other titles and author news, visit:

**www.acfrieden.com**

# Notice to book clubs, bookstores and libraries:

A. C. Frieden conducts book signings and readings throughout North America and Europe. If your book club, bookstore or library is interested in featuring A. C. Frieden, Avendia Publishing would be happy to consider the request. For more information, please send an e-mail to:

**editor@avendiapublishing.com**